PRAISE FOR *THE HANDLER*

"*The Handler* is top-notch storytelling, blending nanny spies and ripped-from-the-headlines international intrigue with a cast of brilliant, colorful characters. Monica McGurk has crafted yet another propulsive adventure story that is also a moving elegy to family and loss. Superb."

—DAVID MCCLOSKEY, former CIA analyst and author of *Moscow X*

"A gripping tale of espionage, self-discovery, and survival . . . McGurk masterfully blends the action, mystery, and character-driven moments together, delivering a worthy sequel that will leave readers anticipating the next installment."

—*PUBLISHERS WEEKLY* BOOKLIFE, Editor's Pick

"Involving dual plotlines, complex historical and political contexts, and intricate spy missions, *The Handler* is a suspenseful young adult thriller."

—*FOREWORD* CLARION REVIEWS

". . . [T]he author balances the action with amusing banter. As the characters navigate a world of divided loyalties, surprising revelations will keep readers guessing. A consistently suspenseful espionage tale that deftly handles its multiple timelines."

—*KIRKUS INDIE*

MONICA McGURK

THE NORWOOD NANNY CHRONICLES:
Book Two

THE HANDLER

RIVER GROVE
BOOKS

Published by River Grove Books
Austin, TX
www.rivergrovebooks.com

Distributed by River Grove Books

Design and composition by Greenleaf Book Group and Mimi Bark
Cover design by Greenleaf Book Group and Mimi Bark
Cover images used under license from ©Shutterstock.com/Anabela88;
©Shutterstock.com/Martial Red

Publisher's Cataloging-in-Publication data is available.

Print ISBN: 978-1-63299-735-7

eBook ISBN: 978-1-63299-736-4

First Edition

To Melissa,
and the many manifestations
of her mother love.

CONTENTS

"Heaven has no rage
Like love to hatred turned,
Nor hell a fury
Like a woman scorned."

—William Congreve

———

"And thus the whirligig of
time brings in his revenges."

—William Shakespeare

———

"Her absence is like the sky,
spread over everything."

—C. S. Lewis

PROLOGUE

Northern Ireland, 1971

Even a week later, the rubble was warm to the touch in spots.

The young woman scrambled over it, the broken beams and shards of glass splintering her skin and scorching her fingertips where she touched them.

That she even had access to the site was not lost on her; nobody in power really cared to keep it secure as a scene of a crime. The narrative—that the IRA mishandled a bomb meant for others, inadvertently killing its own—had taken over before the victims had even been dragged from the destruction. The Protestant Ulstermen spread the story as swiftly as they could, their lies doing as much to impede any real investigation as the scores of little children who had taken to playing in the wreckage, drawn by the novelty of it all.

The blast had been indiscriminate. It tore apart bodies while the same force ejected and preserved the things that had been right there on them, next to them: a set of dentures, sooty but unchipped; a doll, stripped naked of its clothes, but its pull-string voice box still intact; random detritus of the lives that had been taken by the bomb.

She had watched them pull out the bodies, had choked back a sob as her friend Peggy's corpse had been drawn from the pile, Peggy's younger sister's coming after. They had been in the corner near the phone box, she supposed, trying to get their da to come home for supper, and it was from underneath the mangled steel of it that both their bodies had come.

They had not identified Peggy's body at first. The little purse she always carried with her identity card had been wrested away by the explosion, rendering her officially unknown, even though those who had known her knew it was her. It took her mam coming to the morgue to identify the body, even though the rest of her family had already been accounted for and it was a foregone conclusion that this, too, was Peggy's end. She had heard that Mrs. Kelly had suffered the knowledge in silence, nodding once, stiffly, as they pulled the sheet from Peggy's face.

It was only after the crowd had dispersed, clumps of people trailing Peggy's mam back to the house, that she had realized it: Peggy's identification papers could still be there, in the smoldering wreckage, waiting to be claimed. That is, if they had not already succumbed to the fire.

All she had to do was find them. If she could, then she could have a new life, in America, far away from the violence that was slowly engulfing her. Find them and she could slip through the closing noose of discovery that threatened her very existence. Find them and she'd be free—free as she could be, until the day she gained another chance to help her Irish brethren walk in independence too.

She thrust her hand underneath pieces of twisted metal and crumbled plaster, rummaging around until her nails were torn and her cuticles bloody. Still, she persisted, ignoring the pain of burnt fingertips and lungs filled with rancid smoke. Finally, as the rising morning light threatened to betray her and force her away from the heap, her fingers brushed against something soft, smooth. She pulled out the purse, brushing the soot away and ignoring the thoughts of Peggy that came to mind, unbidden.

She had found her prize.

Chapter One

BREE

Present Day, Alabama

Late summer in The Shoals was just like its music. Sweaty, throbbing with an overabundance that at first blush seemed to make no sense. Teeming with life and threatening to burst up like kudzu and overtake everything in a chokehold so tight you might not ever hack your way through it, might even lose yourself if you didn't pay enough attention to the rhythm and the order and the rules that, despite everything, did exist.

To her astonishment, Bree found that in the face of this summertime abundance, words failed Dashiell. Or maybe, not words, but imagination.

"It's rather hot," he muttered, wiping his patrician brow with a monogrammed handkerchief. His normally well-kept hair was plastered in ringlets at his temples. It was perhaps not how he had envisioned their respite before plunging back into their "academic" life at Norwood.

Bree laughed. "You told me London was built on a swamp. You should feel right at home."

Dash shook his head, fanning himself with a sheaf of papers. "It's not a proper swamp. More of a floodplain. And it never feels as oppressive as this."

"Be careful!" Bree snatched the papers from his hand and added them to the pile next to her on the seat of the porch swing. She smoothed them out carefully, setting the swing in motion with an absentminded push of her toe. "We want to keep them in order."

Dash sighed, staring at the pile with pained boredom.

"You've read them over and over, Bree," he said gently. "You've memorized them by now. Even I've memorized them by now."

"There's got to be more to it than is here," she insisted. "Something we're not seeing."

"Well, let's sum up, shall we? Maybe go for a walk while we think?"

Bree dragged a toe and let the swing skitter to a stop. It was hard to gain the motivation to move in this humidity, but Dash was right. A change of scenery might help her see what she was missing.

They had been in The Shoals for over a week now, Bree installed in her old room at the orphanage and Dash, a member of the British aristocracy, squeezed unceremoniously into the little kids' bunkroom, the only place with beds to spare. Her favorite member of the youngest cohort of orphans, Ollie, had taken a shine to Dash, insisting he get the top bunk over Ollie's—a position of privilege, Bree knew, even if Dash's feet did dangle over the edge of the bed. The little boy had been their shadow for the first few days, clinging to Bree and rapt with fascination at Dash's English accent and formal manners, until Rodney, the administrator of Thornton Children's Home and the one person whom Bree considered practically a parent, had discreetly come up with some "summer school" work for Ollie, giving Bree and Dash some privacy.

"So you can recover," Rodney had said solemnly, scanning her once more as if he was afraid she would fall apart right in front of his eyes.

Even now, as she limped along the hard-packed dirt path around the orphanage grounds, she could number her injuries: the pin in her wrist, the broken ribs, the contusions and sprains that left her feeling as fragile as a tattered piece of lace. That Rodney believed the story the administration of their college, Norwood, had shared with him—that she had had a car accident while nannying her summer charges—was something for which she was grateful, because she did not know if she could lie to his face. Moreover, she did not want to have to tell him the truth.

The truth being that Norwood, the prestigious British college for nannies to which she had won a scholarship, was a cover for an international ring of spies. That the patron of the orphanage in which she'd been raised—the woman, Judy, who'd helped win Bree's admittance to the school—was one of them, a spy through and through, and had manipulated Bree's path to Norwood literally from the day Bree had shown up at Thornton's doorstep. That Bree and her Norwood friends—Dash among them—were now being trained to join this deadly cadre of spies. That her injuries were not from a simple car accident but were inflicted upon her when she'd been placed in her first field assignment, during which she'd uncovered an international arms-smuggling plot. The young Turkish children left in her care—the Askers—had been snatched away, held as collateral by the unknown people smuggling the arms. It was in trying to unravel their disappearance that she and Dash had ultimately uncovered the fact that their own classmate and roommate—and romantic interest for Dash—a young woman named Susmita, was a mole working for the Chinese.

It had been a disastrous operation. The four Asker children remained missing and, according to Norwood, their mother, slain. Bree had almost lost her own life. In addition, two agents were dead—one of them Susmita, at Judy's hand, as Bree had watched. Judy claimed she'd pulled the trigger to save Bree's life, but Bree thought it just as likely she was trying to stop Susmita from divulging more secrets about Judy's role in the arms smuggling at the heart of the Asker case. Judy's involvement was a secret Bree didn't dare disclose to the others. Not until she learned the truth.

Bree knew they couldn't trust Judy. The problem was she did not know whom they could trust. Meanwhile, Judy had presented Bree with the one thing she wanted more than anything else: a file of information about her dead birth mother—one Margaret McCarthy, Norwood graduate and spy—an agent who'd been run by Judy herself. Deep down, Bree knew the gifted file might be a bribe to keep her quiet, perhaps even a false one. How was she to know if the information was legit or complete? But her hunger to unravel her past made her push her suspicion down, preferring to think of Judy's dangled carrot as a reward for hard work.

Once left to themselves, Dash and she had pored over the papers from the file folder Judy had given Bree, trying to piece together the story of what had happened to Bree's mother and what, in turn, had led to Bree becoming an orphan. They had run into dead ends.

"Let's try again," Dash began in a hopeful tone, taking her by the elbow to steer her to a shady part of the path. "What have we learned about Margaret?"

Bree began counting things off on her fingers. "Basics first. She was Irish American, from Chicago. Her father a McCarthy, a salesman. Her mother, Mary Margaret Kelly, an immigrant from Ireland proper—Bogside, in Derry, Northern Ireland—listed as homemaker. She never took US citizenship. Hence, Margaret's British citizenship and qualification for Norwood."

"And there is our first odd little clue. Why would someone descended from Irish refugees—for surely, Mary Margaret was a refugee from the Troubles—want to go back to the UK? Back to enemy ground?"

"You're assuming she sided with the Irish."

Dashiell shrugged. "It fits. The census records show her mother came over in 1971, right after a pub bombing that was one of the worst incidents of violence against the Irish up until that point. A young Catholic girl, coming over on her own from the hotbed of the IRA? She must have hated the British."

Bree turned to him as they continued walking. "Maybe it wasn't that at all. Maybe her mother came over because she wanted to put that all behind her. Margaret's application to Norwood says she wanted to take advantage of an opportunity she couldn't get anywhere else. That she wanted to work with children. Could it be as simple as that?"

"You know it's not. Because we know, at least from her records, that she never went back home to Chicago. She stayed away on purpose. She even got special dispensation to stay on campus during holidays."

"You're right." Bree sighed. "And we know her father died after falling down the stairs of their flat, intoxicated, freezing to death in the middle of winter." She grimaced. That her grandfather had been a drunk raised all sorts of possibilities she didn't want to imagine. "So," she added briskly, "possibly sympathetic to the IRA. Possibly just trying to get away from a difficult situation. In any case, no reason to go home again."

"What else?" Dash prompted, pulling a prolific vine of kudzu out of the path so they could pass.

"She was a goody two-shoes," Bree noted, pulling a face.

Dash snorted. "Whatever do you mean?"

"The recommendations that came with her application to Norwood were from the parish priest and a bunch of nuns. Oh, and from the person in charge of administering her high school's honor code. She was valedictorian of her high school. She was top of the class at Norwood, too. Perfect grades—you saw the report cards."

"Yes," Dash acknowledged. "Perfect marks, even while taking Mandarin."

"She was Head Girl, like Montoya-Craig." Bree grimaced at the thought of the upperclassman who'd had charge of her cohort at Norwood the previous year and who had taken particular delight in torturing Bree.

Bree continued, her voice tinged with disapproval, "And she sat on the Norwood Honor Committee. She was in the choral society, leading that treacly school song at every assembly. So a suck-up and possibly a snitch, with all that honor-code business."

"Hmm. You don't sound very sympathetic to her."

"She sounds just too . . . perfect."

"And yet, don't you wonder? Was she bullied, perhaps, for being Irish? And American? Was all that perfection so that nobody could find a chink in her proverbial armor? I doubt it was easy, coming to Norwood at the height of the Troubles. I'm sure everyone regarded her with suspicion."

"Why are you defending her?"

"Why are you attacking her? You seem intent on disliking her. Perhaps you blame her for getting herself killed?"

Bree stopped in a spot of shadow on the path. "I don't know what I'm supposed to feel. I just know that I don't feel any closer to her now than I did before. I only have more questions."

Dash steered her on, tactfully shifting the conversation.

"The Mandarin bit. It's intriguing, isn't it? Especially given her trial placement after first term was with a visiting consul from Hong Kong, who was trying to negotiate an increase of visas and residency permits for people trying to flee before the handover of the island to the PRC. That China connection, again. It keeps popping up."

"It could be a coincidence."

"As I've said before, coincidences are just the universe's way of birthing forth the truth."

Bree looked up. They'd wound their way back toward the orphanage's main buildings and now stood in the shadow of the abandoned barn.

She gulped and squared her shoulders. "Let's go in," she insisted, rushing ahead before Dashiell could stop her.

She heaved the heavy door to the side, wincing as the rusty wheels whined against the track. As she crossed the threshold, she was instantly plunged into darkness. She waited for her eyes to adjust, her nostrils picking out the ancient smell of dusty hay and faded, oily cotton bolls. Eventually, the dust motes floating in the shaft of light from the upper window, the decrepit ladder leaning against the loft, and the forgotten handcart all came into view. She swung her head around and saw it then—the lusterless metal ring in the wall, the frayed length of rope hanging from it dragging on the ground.

She walked over and stared at it. Then, she grabbed an old plastic bucket, turning it upside down, and took a seat. Dash trailed in behind her.

"Is this it, then?" he asked softly.

She nodded, unable to speak.

"You don't have to do this, you know."

"I think I do," she whispered. "I haven't been in here since."

The dust motes floated down around their heads.

"Here's what I think," she continued. "The whole time that Rodney was away, caring for his sick wife in the hospital, I think Judy knew what the temporary caretaker was doing to me. She let it go on because, to her, it was a test—a test to see if I was strong enough to be a spy, like my mom. She only intervened and put a stop to it once she had her answer."

"Oh, Bree, I don't know, maybe . . ."

She reached out to take the rope in her hand. Absentmindedly, she stroked its frayed strands.

She turned suddenly to face Dash. "Who does that, Dash? Who lets someone tie up a scared little kid in an empty barn? Who lets a child suffer until their wrists are raw and bloody, just out of curiosity?"

Dash squatted next to her and pushed the sleeve of her cotton shirt up, trailing his thumb over the shiny scars that encircled her delicate skin.

"Someone like Judy," he said. "Which is why you know, as well as I do, that she did not give you this information about your mother out of mercy or goodwill. She has a reason, Bree. Was it an incentive to keep you from divulging her existence to the Norwood leadership? A pat on the head to keep you in line while she readies you for her next mission? What does she want from you?"

Bree slumped on the bucket and threw the rope down to the ground in frustration. "I don't know. I feel like I'm further from the truth than ever. All I know is what she told me, that she feels this is her opportunity to fix whatever went wrong on that mission in which my parents were killed."

"Very well. Let's go with that, then. There's a very good chance your mother was IRA."

Bree drew herself up to protest, but Dashiell silenced her with a shake of his head.

"Look, the signs are all there. Catholic Irish émigré mother, father also of Irish descent. From Chicago, a hotbed of support for the old country's rebellion. If you were the brass at Norwood, would you take a gamble on bringing in a possible IRA plant in hopes of turning her and using her for your own purposes?"

"But to what end?"

"The Irish threat was one of the greatest facing Britain in that period. And what was her first assignment, Bree?"

She was so stupid, she thought to herself. "My father."

"And . . .?"

"And he was MI5. British Intelligence. Which means he was probably focused on domestic terrorism. She was spying on him," she exclaimed, jumping up from the bucket and knocking it over in her enthusiasm. "Of course she was! Judy as much as told me. But for whom? The IRA or Norwood?"

"Maybe both. One thing's for certain. We need to see if we can establish a definitive IRA link."

"How? We've already searched the online emigration and family records. Mary Margaret Kelly must have been the most popular name in all of Ireland. We don't even know who we're looking for, really. We're just spinning our wheels."

"Come now, it hasn't been all a waste. You did find out your grandfather was a close cousin to that paragon of anti-Communist virtue, Senator Joseph McCarthy."

Bree grimaced and wondered if that, in and of itself, was a clue.

"Maybe it's time to take a different tack," Dash suggested.

"What do you have in mind?"

"DNA."

Bree scoffed. "You're grasping at straws. No self-respecting member of the IRA is going to spit in a cup and help the authorities track him down. We'd be wasting our time."

"But don't you think it is odd for an Irish family to ship off a lone, young daughter for no reason? Maybe they were trying to protect her from the Troubles. But maybe, just maybe, she—or they—were in the thick of them. And it will take no time at all to take a swab from you and submit it to the genealogical sites. We can do it under a fake name and an anonymized account so nobody will be the wiser."

He looked at her expectantly. "No harm in trying," he nudged. "Besides, don't you want to do it before Norwood starts requiring it? In your shoes, I'd want to know as much as I could about my background before the Agency does. Right now they are hobbled by the government's strictures on genetic testing. You and I both know that won't last forever. They'll find a loophole to exploit. They always do." He tapped the tracking device at the base of his neck—the one implanted into every Norwood agent—as a reminder of exactly how brutal Norwood could be.

"Oh, fine," she said, throwing up her arms. "I suppose you're right. Again. I don't suppose you already have a swab kit back in the house?"

He beamed. "You know me so well, my dear."

"Fine. Let's go get this out of the way. As for this place . . ." She looked around the shadowy barn, pushing back the encroaching memories that threatened to consume her. "I'll speak to Rodney about tearing it down."

"How will you do that?" Dash asked. "Won't you have to explain why?"

"I'll say it's a safety hazard. Or an eyesore. It doesn't matter, so long—"

Just then Ollie bounded in, running up to throw his arms around her, effectively ending the conversation. "Bree! Bree! Did you look up in the loft?"

"No, buddy," she said, ruffling his shaggy hair. She worried about him—he hadn't seemed to grow much since she'd left for school in England. "What's up in the loft that's got you so excited?"

"It's going to be a construction zone now," Ollie pronounced. "I'm not allowed to go up. But if *you* gave me permission, I'm sure that Rodney wouldn't mind. Can we? Huh, can we, Bree?"

Bree looked warily at Dash, who simply shrugged.

"Construction zone, is that right?" Bree answered. "Well, I'd better talk to Rodney about that before we go poking around. Come on back with us—I bet you there's some lemonade in the kitchen."

Rodney had aged significantly since the time he'd visited her in Bath, during the Christmas holiday. His slack skin had taken on an ashy tone. His tightly coiled hair was now completely white. His eyes seemed permanently tinted pink with weariness. She didn't know what was going on, just that it couldn't be good.

"You're working too hard, Rodney," she scolded, plucking a fresh peach from the basket that graced the countertop in the industrial kitchen. She tossed it to Dash, and another one to Ollie, before picking out one for herself. She probed, trying to keep it light while she sought out the truth. "Are these kids giving you trouble, now that I'm not here anymore to keep them in line?"

Rodney peered over his reading glasses at her, amusement flickering across his face. "Long arm of the law, you were not, Bree, and you know it. More like the instigator."

Bree grinned and took a bite of her peach. Slurping through the juices, she continued to pester him. "You haven't answered my question. What's going on? You seem stressed. It's not money, is it?"

Rodney busied himself in the cabinets, opening doors and counting, ticking things off on his shopping list. "I'm just feeling my age these days, Bree. There's a lot going on. But nothing for you to be worrying yourself about."

"If it's my school expenses, I can take a break," she stated boldly, testing his reaction. In her heart she wanted him to say, *yes, Bree, how about staying back here and helping out*, protecting her from all the trouble waiting for her back on campus—trouble he knew nothing about.

Instead, he turned and put his notepad and pencil down on the gleaming steel counter. "Like I said, for once, money is not a problem. I've got some new children coming in, this time with funding."

"Ollie was telling me something about construction in the barn. Would that have anything to do with that money you've got coming in?"

Rodney shrugged. "You know as well as I do that we need some modernization around here. And that barn has been sitting empty for years.

We could put it to better use as extra housing or even a learning lab. One of the sponsors was here while you were out." He gestured at a half-empty glass of lemonade, abandoned next to a pitcher and a smattering of cookie crumbs on a plate left on the counter. "A refugee program. There are so many children coming through Atlanta now—really, everywhere—with nowhere to go. We're on a tight timetable."

Ollie interrupted. "Is a learning lab like a school, Rodney? I don't want more school. Could we build a computer room instead?"

"See?" Rodney smiled. "We have no shortage of ideas of what to do with that space. And for once, no shortage of funds."

Bree tried to act nonchalant. "Why not bulldoze it? Might be better to start all over. Cheaper."

Rodney snorted. "Now what would we do that for? A perfectly good building like that?"

"It might be stinky," Bree asserted, grabbing at straws. "From all the animals?"

Rodney scoffed. "Nah. It's been empty for over a decade, and it's been even longer since there was any livestock in it. There's nothing wrong that some good lumber, insulation, wiring, and paint can't fix."

Bree looked imploringly at Dash, who was watching the exchange between her and Rodney like a tennis match. Seeing her look of desperation, he cleared his throat. "Why don't you two take a walk to discuss it?" he suggested. "Ollie and I can tidy up the kitchen a bit while you're out."

"There's not much to discuss . . ." Rodney said, his voice trailing off in confusion.

"Please," Bree said simply. "Let's at least go sit on the porch."

Dash pretended to busy himself, focusing inordinately on the dirty dishes. As she and Rodney stepped out onto the shady porch, Bree could hear Dash chatting away, asking questions, having latched on to the hand-drawn storybook pages she and Ollie had left strewn about the kitchen. She could hear Ollie's bright young voice answering him, interjecting the details of their traditional storytelling topic—the adventures of an imaginary Wonder Dog, as they had come to nickname him—and how they were creating a book together so that Ollie could pretend she was still there to tell him bedtime stories after she went back to England. His enthusiasm made her feel a little less guilty about leaving him behind.

Rodney didn't wait to take a seat before he started questioning her.

"What's gotten into you, Bree? I never noticed you caring that much about the outbuildings. Why this one? Why now?"

She looked at his dark eyes, now deep with worry, and knew she couldn't tell him. She tried to find another way, by changing the subject.

"Do you miss Beatrice, Rodney?"

The question took him by surprise. "My wife? Yes. Yes, I do. It's been over a decade, of course, but I miss her every day."

He let out a loud exhale. After a pause, he eased himself onto a rocking chair.

"That's what this is about?"

She nodded, going with the unexpected opening.

He rubbed his hand over his face.

"Beatrice wasn't from here. I think you know that. She'd been places, seen things. How she ended up with me will remain one of God's great mysteries. But if you remembered her better, you'd know she wouldn't want us to freeze her memory like that. She was vibrant and full of life. Changeable. She loved to try new things and was always encouraging me to do the same. For you kids. For myself."

"You said she'd been in Bath?" Bree prompted, suddenly intrigued by the way Rodney was describing his wife. She was, to Bree, a cipher, like so many other people and things in Bree's past—a shrunken form in a hospital bed in the middle of the living room, a feeble voice calling for ice chips . . . a grave they visited on holidays. Bree didn't remember the time before the illness. The cancer had blotted out everything else, like a cloud in front of the sun.

"You told me that, before I left for Norwood." Bree nudged him again.

He nodded, remembering. "She'd been a PhD candidate there," he said. "At the University of Bath."

"Wait—what?"

Rodney nodded. "She was a neuroscientist, if you can believe it. A woman working in that field back then was quite unusual. Her research area was memory loss. The university had a lot of pharmaceutical and technology expertise. She was leading a program for them, something to do with aging—pretty unusual for someone who hadn't even earned her stripes yet. I met her after I stumbled across a paper she'd had accepted in a journal."

"You were reading psychology journals? And you went all the way over to England after reading her research paper?" Bree gaped.

"Bree," he sighed, looking at her with disappointment. "I know it's a lot to have you kids imagine we had lives before you existed, but have you really never noticed the shelves in my office? I majored in psychology, myself. It was a professional interest I've kept up for a very long time. So, as it happened, I didn't have to go to England to speak to her. I tracked her down at a conference I attended at which she was speaking."

His gentle rebuke left her to stare at the ground. It was, she admitted to herself, hard to imagine Rodney anywhere else but here—the center of his universe, she'd assumed, and, for a very long time, her own.

"Anyway," he continued, "she'd done the research with someone in the developmental psychology department at Harvard on a whim. Can you imagine? Being so brilliant you can pick up research on things like the long-term psychological impact of being in foster care, for *fun*?" He shook his head. "But that was Bea. When I read the paper, it raised so many questions for me. I had to know more. I had to know *her*. The rest was history, as they say. She fell in love with you kids, just as much as I had. This place became her home. I was surprised she was willing to come back to the States, but she actually insisted."

Bree thought about all that Beatrice and Rodney had sacrificed, not just for her, but for the countless children who'd come through the doors of the orphanage, and she felt guilty all over again.

"We don't honor Bea's memory by keeping things the same," Rodney added with finality. "And tearing down that barn wouldn't accomplish that anyway, would it?" he added, pointing out her muddled thinking. "No, it's better to put it to some useful purpose. Now," he segued, the topic of the barn closed, "where is that young man of yours? He seemed awfully eager to help you out."

Bree blushed. "He's not *mine*. He's just a friend."

"A friend who accompanied you all the way to a teeny tiny bit of nowhere, Alabama, hmm?"

Bree shrugged. "British aristocracy slumming it, I guess."

Rodney chuckled. "Um hmm. I see. Even doing the dishes and cleaning up after the children for me? I wonder who he's trying to impress?"

Bree smiled. "I see he's weaseled into your good graces with housework."

Rodney waved her comment away. "That's an equal opportunity for anyone willing to pick up a dishrag. Listen, I've seen how attentive he is to you. And I appreciate how he's cared for you after your accident. He's been your shadow ever since you got home. You can't have him come all this way and just mope around this dusty old farm. That would not be up to the standard of Southern hospitality I'm sure he's expecting."

"I don't think he had any expectations," Bree countered.

"Still," Rodney nudged. "I've been treating you like glass, but it's obvious to me you're made of tougher stuff. You should go out, both of you. It'll be good for you."

"I guess I could take him out to the Rattlesnake or FloBama, let him hear the sound?"

Rodney pushed his glasses on top of his head, staring at her in disbelief. "You know better than to take him to one of those touristy places. If you're going to take him anywhere, you need to take him to John's place."

Bree paused. She felt oddly vulnerable at the thought of leaving the farm. John was an old friend of Rodney's, one of the best guitarists she'd ever heard, and had been like an uncle to her. But she'd never been out in the woods, to his makeshift bar, on her own at night. It tended to attract an unusual clientele.

"You think?"

Rodney looked over his readers. "You want me to go out there with you? I might spoil the mood for you and your date." A mischievous look stole over his face as he settled into a rhythm with the rocker.

"It's not . . . he's not . . . I mean, no. I'm perfectly able to go on my own." She pushed her hesitation aside. "It's just been a while. And I'm not sure if the English can stand that many mosquitos."

"What's a little discomfort in exchange for a glimpse of the face of God when John starts playing?" Rodney gestured grandly at the thought of the music, his grin broadening. "John has known you since you were a little girl. He's practically family. He'll take good care of you both."

Rodney paused for a moment, taking in Bree.

"You've lost your accent already, Bree—probably didn't even realize it. All the roundness, the softness, has slipped away. It'll be good for you to get a dose of that music, reconnect with your roots."

He looked her over with what Bree thought was a touch of wistfulness, before rising to head back into the kitchen.

Dash and Bree were hunkered down at a gray, weather-beaten picnic table under the inky night sky. The dense pines obscured the stars. The soft glow from the pole shed and several sagging strings of lights marked a tiny perimeter. In the shadows, a smattering of other guests lingered, talking low, nursing icy beers and Mason jars of something stronger as they waited for John—or whatever act he'd conjured up—to appear. They were a few hardscrabble locals punctuated by bikers and truckers, obvious strangers, passing through. More were streaming in, emerging from the makeshift parking lots in the woods and canyon: a mostly rough, anonymous crowd.

Dash swatted at his face. "Are you sure these are insects? They seem large enough to be an avian species."

Bree laughed. "They like you. Drink your beer—maybe the hops will make your blood less sweet to them."

"Who am I to challenge a prompt to imbibe more alcohol? To blood-sucking miniature birds, vestiges of the time of the dinosaurs and everlasting nuisances to us all," he declared, raising the bottle in salute before taking a great swig. "Now, Bree, explain your connection to this place again?"

"John is an old friend of Rodney's. I guess they used to play together, back in the day, before Rodney got too tied down by the orphanage."

Bree frowned. She ran her finger over the splintered wood of the table, trying to remember, reflecting on their conversation earlier that day. "I can't say for sure how they met. Maybe they were at school together? I never really asked Rodney, and he doesn't talk much about the past."

"Hmm. Seems to be the theme with you people." Before Bree could protest, he pressed on. "Aren't you going to go see this John before the show starts?"

She shook her head. "He'll be busy. We can say hello later."

"Well, you've been promising me you'd explain this music ever since you shocked our little monster of a Head Girl, Montoya-Craig, with your delightfully inappropriate song at orientation. And I must say, your intriguing dancing on the tables at the bar in Bath only heightened my interest. What exactly is this music to which you are so devoted?"

"I can't explain it. It is just, well, soulful. People from around here used to say there was a ghost or a spirit in the river who sang songs to protect her tribe. Some people think the songs come out of the mud. You'll have to listen for yourself and see." She nodded at the pole shed. Musicians were setting up, adjusting their chairs for the meager light, though in reality, Bree knew, they didn't need it. They knew everything by heart. It was in their bones.

There was no announcement. The band simply started playing.

Bree closed her eyes and let the music envelop her. A funky, dirty mix of horns, saxophone, and guitar jumped out into the night, laced by the throaty, soaring voice of the woman gripping the mic. The words, heady and plaintive, pierced through her, and the steady beat commanded the very beat of her heart, the blood in her veins whooshing to the swooping rhythms of the band. Then the music shifted, the bass throbbing, intense and insistent, danger spilling out with every note.

She was swaying, letting song after song wash over her.

She felt Dash squeezing her fingers. "Look," he shouted at her over the music. She looked around. The crowd was on its feet, couples draped over one another, hips moving in unison, others swinging and rolling, loose limbed and oblivious to anyone around them.

"Let's go." He grinned, pulling her to her feet.

Before she could steady herself, he expertly twirled her about, then pulled her in, breathless, tight against his chest. She closed her eyes. She could feel his heart pounding in his chest, could smell his expensive cologne mixed with sweat and mosquito repellent.

He laughed out loud, the vibrations traveling through his chest and tingling her fingertips like little electric shocks.

"Look at me, Bree," he insisted.

She opened her eyes. His eyes locked with hers as he pulled her tighter.

"I think I like this Shoals sound," he whispered into her ear, his mouth up against her loose hair. "And I think I like what it does to you even more."

The music stopped, then whooping appreciation and applause punctuated the sudden silence.

Dash let his hands run from Bree's shoulders down the length of her back. He wrapped his hands around her waist and then frowned as they came to rest on the gun she'd tucked under the back of her shirt.

"What's this?"

He arched his eyebrow, waiting for her to speak, his arms locking like steel bands around her.

"Bree! I thought that was you!" A heavy Southern drawl interrupted them.

Dash hesitated, then dropped his hands to let Bree turn.

"John." She smiled at the man who was approaching them. "Great show. You were incredible, as always. Rodney will be disappointed when I tell him what he missed."

John ran his hand through his wild mane of silver hair and laughed, his sweaty, tan face crinkling into a mess of smile lines.

"I wish I could say I believed you, but I don't know anymore. He won't come out—it's almost as if he can't feel the call of the music anymore, Bree." He shrugged, the words spilling out of him. "I don't think I've heard him play in over ten years. But that second song in the set? You remember it? That was his, you know. He wrote that back in '79. Always had a talent for the groovy stuff. But come here, you. Let me give you a proper welcome home."

She folded herself into his great bear hug. He stepped back to inspect her. "Definitely older. Maybe wiser. Probably not, if you brought this one with you," he said, winking as he tilted his head toward Dash.

Bree rolled her eyes. "Dashiell, let me introduce you to John Hardy, proprietor and, as you've just witnessed, musician extraordinaire."

John grasped Dashiell's hand between his two. "Dashiell, is it?" He looked him up and down, noting the pressed linen shirt and pants. "Definitely not from around here, are you?"

"I'm afraid not," Dash answered, laughing. "But I hope to be invited back again. Tonight was spectacular. I think I'm beginning to understand a bit about what makes Bree's home so special."

"If you come back, I'll expect a proper introduction, over a meal. Bree, you hear? Listen, you two, I've got to run—I need to be sure everyone is watered and fed before the second set starts—but stick around. Enjoy it. Just mind yourselves. There's a group that has had a few too many over there," he added, shooting a worried look at a particularly loud corner of the audience, "and I wouldn't want you to get into any trouble. Rodney would never forgive me." He squeezed Bree's shoulder. "You kids have fun. I'll see you later."

He bounced off, slapping shoulders and shaking hands as he made his way through the crowd, back to the hum of the makeshift stage.

Bree and Dash stood awkwardly, and Bree was unsure where to pick up. The space between them seemed too close now, the moment lost.

"He seemed nice," Dash began, giving Bree the feeling he was rapidly retreating to neutral, more distant ground. "You're a much better dancer than I remembered from the pub," he continued.

"Um. So are you. I mean, better than I expected," Bree stammered, grateful that the black night would cover the embarrassed stain spreading across her hot cheeks. She hesitated.

"You know, maybe we should go. It's getting late," she added lamely.

"Of course," Dash said, retreating to formality. "It was entertaining, but it has been a long day. And we've a bit of a drive back to the farm." He picked up their empty beer bottles from the table and gestured ahead. "After you, my dear."

They picked their way through the crowd, winding their way through the press of bodies and into the cover of the woods. The small light of the makeshift music hall in the clearing gave way to darkness. "Stay close to me, Bree," Dash urged, trying to make out the path back to Rodney's ancient pickup.

"I'm not scared of the dark, Dash," Bree retorted, her words coming out a little more sharply than she had intended, her ego stinging from what felt suspiciously like a rebuke and maybe even a rejection.

"Of course not. What have you to be afraid of? Especially when, for some inexplicable reason, you're packing a gun in the waistband of your pants."

They walked in silence, Bree trailing Dash, feeling a unique blend of confusion, regret, and frustration.

"Hey! You there!"

A dark figure stepped out onto the trail in front of them, emerging from a clutch of parked trucks.

"You think you can get away with insulting me that way?"

The man loomed before Dash, sneering into his face.

"I'm sorry, chap, I don't know to what you are referring. But I'm certain I did not deliberately insult you. I don't even recognize you. Though I admit it is hard to see your visage through this obscuring darkness."

"You think big words can get you out of this?" The man shoved Dash, sending him stumbling back. He was hard to understand, his words slurred and strange. "You sure don't spill my beer and get away with it. Your fancy talk's just gonna make it worse for you."

Dash laughed uneasily as he steadied himself, positioning himself between the drunken man and Bree. "I see. I must have bumped you as we were leaving. Now that you mention it, I can smell the beer coming off you. I do apologize. Can I give you some money for your troubles, buy you another beer? Call it even between us?"

"Dash," Bree said it quietly.

"Not now, Bree. I've got it under control."

"Dash," she said more urgently. "He's not alone."

Another figure quietly stepped from the shadows.

"You just give us what we want and nobody has to get hurt," the second man began. His accent was honed sharp, with none of the soft curves of a Southerner. A stranger here too.

"What do you want?" Bree demanded, stepping up to Dash's side. "You already got your apology."

"We want information." The second man continued talking, taking the lead.

"About what?"

"Not what. Who. We want to know about Roberta."

"Roberta? I don't know any Roberta. Dash, do you know a Roberta?"

"Not a one."

The first man chuckled. He let the fake drunkenness and his bad imitation of an Alabaman accent fall away. "We think you do. And until you tell us everything you know about her, we can't let you go." There was a burst of applause from the clearing. "They play three sets tonight. Nobody's coming this way for a long time. It'd be better if you talked. For your own good."

"How do you know about the sets?" Bree asked sharply. "You're not from around here—I can tell by your accents. And John doesn't publish a set list, or a plan. His shows are spontaneous. Always have been."

The first man shrugged. "It's not so hard to spread a little cash to the band and get them to 'spontaneously' keep things going. Musicians love to accommodate their fans, especially the musicians that fancy themselves artists. You know the type—living the hand-to-mouth lifestyle and wearing it like a hair shirt while secretly longing for a night spent in a hotel instead of a beat-up bus. Wrap up a bribe as appreciation and it goes down easy." Bree noticed him smirk at his own cleverness. "So, like I said—start answering our questions."

Dash shrugged. "We can't help you. And even if we could, we wouldn't be inclined to do so, after such a display of atrocious manners. Just who did you say you are, again? Who are you working with? We'll be sure to file a complaint."

"You think you're funny, do you?" the first man sneered. "You won't think so when that old man at the orphanage pays for your smart mouth. Or those kids."

Dash squared off on the path and seemed to grow even larger with indignation. "That's not very sporting of you, is it? He has nothing to do with this, I'd wager. Though what *this* is, we have no idea. As I've said, we don't know your Roberta and have no idea what you're talking about. Now if you'll excuse us, we'll be on our way. Bree?"

In the darkness, Bree had stolen over and climbed into the bed of the closest pickup truck to get a better angle. She'd pulled her pistol out and now, with a satisfying click, placed one of the men within her sights.

"Like you said, the band will be playing long and loud into the night. Nobody will hear a thing if I need to use this. And since you threatened my family, I *will* use it, if I'm forced to. I'll hunt you all the way across the state line if I have to. Your choice."

"This isn't a game, little girl."

"Oh, you shouldn't have called her that." Dash shook his head. "You'll only make her angry."

Before the man could answer, Dash swept his legs out from under him, bringing him down to the ground. With his knee on the man's neck, he patted him down and stripped his pistol.

"Silencer, Bree. We are apparently dealing with professionals." Dash held the gun against the man's temple, keeping a close eye on the one who seemed to be in charge. "We seem to have arrived at a stalemate, my friends. Perhaps if you throw down the rest of your weapons and disarm yourself like your partner, here, we can discuss this in a civilized manner."

"As you wish," the second man murmured. "Just step away so I know I can trust you."

"I've got him, Dash," Bree stated flatly. "You can get up. You—" she said, nodding toward the second man. "Slowly. Take your weapon out and throw it into the woods. We can't have you armed on the way to the police station."

Her voice was firm. She was glad that in the dark nobody could see her hand shaking.

Dash released the man's neck, stood up, and backed away, still training the confiscated gun on the man's head. Coughing and gasping for breath, the man pulled himself up to his knees. His partner moved his hands slowly, reaching behind him for his own weapon.

Through the woods, the distant music crescendoed, the crowd screaming for more.

The second man pulled his gun and dangled it in front of his body, as if he were going to throw it. Instead, in one swift, terrible move, he aimed it at his partner and shot him in the back.

"No police," he stated. Then, with a grim smile, he put the gun to his own head and pulled the trigger. His head snapped with a burst of gore before his lifeless body collapsed to the ground.

The music stopped. The hooting and hollering of the crowd, chanting for more, echoed through the trees.

Bree and Dash stood, horrified, staring at the crumpled bodies, until the cheering petered out. The silence jolted them.

"Well, that was extreme," Dash finally choked out. "It didn't really seem necessary, did it?"

"Whoever they were working for," Bree said, ignoring the nausea that threatened to overwhelm her, "they were willing to die for them rather than be captured."

"What do we do now?" Dash asked.

"Wipe down that gun. You have to remove your prints. Wipe it down now and throw it away. We don't have much time."

Dash stood in a daze.

"Wait. Why?"

"We can't be linked to them, Dash. Not by the police, not by anyone. They threatened Rodney and the kids. We can't let whoever is running them find them. We can't take that risk."

"How did you know?" Dash asked. "What made you bring your gun tonight, Bree?"

"Dash," Bree commanded sharply. "Focus. I mean it. We don't have time. Do it now."

Bree re-engaged her safety and shoved the pistol back inside her waistband, her movements automatic as she kept reasoning her way through the mess in which they found themselves. She kept talking, her nervous chatter settling into a steadier pace.

"We'll just leave them. Hide them off the path a bit so it will take a while to find them. Nobody from here will be looking for them, so that should help. Hopefully, by the time anyone else realizes they've gone missing, we'll be long gone. Dash." Her voice softened. "I didn't know. I was just nervous, but I'm glad I decided to have it on me. Now, we've got to finish the job."

Dash acknowledged her comment with a nod and wound up to hurl the gun.

"No! Wait!" Bree shouted.

Dash froze, confused.

"That won't make sense. They were fighting each other." Bree jumped down from the pickup truck, reasoning out the story in her head. "They drew guns on each other. He needs it in his hand."

Dash hesitated.

"Do it, Dash! We'll drag him over there, and then you'll wipe your prints off and put it in his hand. And let's hurry. Before anyone else comes along."

When they'd dragged the bodies a dozen or so yards away, down the hillside and behind a heavy clump of vines, Bree patted down their pockets.

"Nothing," she spat with frustration. "No ID. Like you said, professionals. At least when they're found—"

"*If* they're found," Dash interjected. "Let's hope they're not."

"If they're found, it will be that much harder for the police to identify them."

From the path, they heard the chatter of loud voices and drunken laughter. They crouched lower, waiting for the concertgoers to pass by.

"We need to get out of here," Dash whispered urgently. "And I don't mean these woods." He grabbed Bree's wrist. "We need to get out of Muscle Shoals, Bree. We're putting Rodney and the kids in danger if we stay any longer. Whoever these people were, they're part of something much bigger than we understand. So big they would rather die than be captured. There will be more of them. Which means this"—he gestured to the lifeless bodies—"doesn't stop with them."

Guilt surged through Bree. "But how can we leave the orphanage unprotected?"

"They are only at risk as long as we're here. Whoever is after us will use them to get to us. But that's the only reason. That much is clear. It's time.

We need to get back to Norwood and put the safety of distance between us and them."

"You're right," she murmured.

He clutched her wrist even tighter. "And you can't tell Judy. Not a word, Bree. We can't trust her. Not even with this."

The tight knot of worry in Bree's throat got bigger. "She could help protect them, Dash . . ."

"But what if she's somehow connected to this? After all, wasn't it her idea for you to even come here?"

"Yes," Bree acknowledged. "And she didn't really seem all that excited to have you join me."

"See? It could be nothing, but we can't take that risk. The best thing you can do to protect them is to leave. We leave now. And we don't look back."

Chapter Two

MEG

1990, Chicago

They huddled against the wind, bracing their umbrellas against the lashing of the rain.

"Requiem aeternam dona ei, Domine, et lux perpetua luceit ei. Requiescat in pace. Amen."

"Amen," the scattered crowd intoned.

Meg's mother pinched her elbow.

"Amen," Meg mumbled, pulling her arm away and stepping out of her mother's reach.

Why did her mother insist on being so extreme? she wondered, rubbing the sore spot on her elbow. Meg sighed. She knew, after all, that her mother's piety was disingenuous—but why put on such a show?

She went to Catholic school, like many of the girls in her neighborhood, but as far as she knew, she was the only person in her class who still attended Latin Mass—an incredible feat in this day and age. They had to cross the city to find one, joining a mostly Polish congregation to do so. It was an inconvenience on an early Sunday morning—especially if one was suffering from a hangover.

It had been just another reason for her parents to fight, her mother's exaggerated Catholicism another filament in the cloak of martyrdom with which she enrobed herself.

"Anima eius et animae omnium fidelium defunctorum, per misericordiam Dei requiescant in pace. Amen." The priest made the sign of the cross over her father's coffin. More muttered amens floated into the sharp spring air as the mourners, mostly fellow parishioners, hung their heads in respect.

Stone-faced, Meg's mother picked up a clod of dirt and dropped it into the hole. She turned without bothering to see where it landed, not even bothering to pretend that she was grieving.

"Come on, then, Meg," she ordered. "We'll want to be there to greet everyone at the luncheon." She dragged Meg behind her, not waiting for an answer.

Meg's veil whipped in the wind, its long tulle twisting in her unruly red hair. Annoyed, she batted at it.

She endured the reception line, full of people—mostly men—she did not know. They were cops from the neighborhood, and salesmen like her dad, people from the church, and a smattering of distant McCarthy cousins who had come from as far as Milwaukee and even Baltimore. She tuned out their talk of perestroika, their excited discussions of the Soviet Union's promised withdrawal from Hungary and Czechoslovakia, their enthusiasm for the Solidarity movement and Lech Walesa's ascension to Poland's presidency, and their whispered hopes for the collapse of the Evil Empire.

It was only to indulge in this kind of eager speculation that her father had even tolerated his mother's attendance at the Polish church. Her father had loved politics, she thought wistfully as she pushed the cold mashed potatoes around on her plate.

No, she reminded herself. He didn't love politics. He hated Communists. Almost to the point of obsession. Deep in his cups, he'd expound upon how the IRA had almost been ripped asunder by the emergence of a so-called Red Wing more interested in a united workers' front than freeing the Catholics; how, split in two, the cause of Irish freedom had almost been lost in the seventies. His embrace of American politics only extended as far as it intersected this passion. It rendered him an unending Reagan booster and an unapologetic supporter of George Bush, whose photos he hung on the wall next to those of his heroes, Pope John Paul II and Michael Collins.

"Any man who can keep the pressure on those Commie bastards gets my vote," he would say, taking a swig of his beer, his eyes shining at the abstract thought of freedom being offered up to whole countries of people he didn't know, couldn't even imagine.

But always, before all else, he'd dreamt of a free Ireland.

Her father had lived his whole life in the same neighborhood of Chicago. His sales territory had never expanded beyond the city limits. His was a small life. He had worked the same sales route, peddling the same machine parts for the same company for decades. He had sat at the same booth in the same bar with the same cronies, night after night, for even longer. He circled from apartment to sales office to bar, a tight orbit punctuated weekly by church—if he was not too hung over—and the occasional neighborhood festival.

No matter where he was, after he got past ranting at the daily newspaper, his conversation always turned to the same themes: the defeat of communism, the hope of a free Ireland, and the corruption of those who got in the way.

And now, he would never see his dreams realized.

At home, after the luncheon, Meg folded away her veil and stripped out of her modest Sunday dress, hanging it neatly in the closet in exchange for a pair of baggy jeans and a long, neon sweatshirt. She pulled her hair into a scrunchy and scrubbed her face. She tallied up the homework that had gone undone since her father's accident, the hours and days of missed classes. The Sisters would be lenient, but only so far. She would need to start digging herself out of the hole, this very afternoon and well into the evening.

The next day, sleepy-eyed from the late night spent poring over her schoolbooks, Meg awoke to a sharp knock at her door.

"Margaret, come out here," her mother was saying. "I wish to speak with you."

Her mother's tone set her on edge, and she sat bolt upright in her bed, all grogginess gone. She braced herself for a lecture as she walked the short hall from her room to the kitchen of their apartment.

Her mother sat at the table, her hands gripping a tumbler of brown liquid. She worried the glass, as if unsure what to do with its contents.

"Sit down," she began. Meg did as she was told.

"Your future will have to be different now. With your father's income gone, it will be impossible for us to send you to that fancy college you've your heart set on."

Meg did not respond. Her mother had never wanted her to go there to begin with. It didn't surprise her that she'd seized on her father's death as a new excuse to prevent her from going.

"But I've a proposition for you. A deal, if you will. Well, your Uncle Brian and I."

Meg watched with astonishment as a man she'd never seen—never even heard of—emerged from the shadows.

"Hello, Margaret. It's good to meet you after all this time." He spoke with a pronounced brogue, greater than her mother's, the edges of which had softened over the years. Indeed, it was a heavier accent than she'd ever heard, other than the way some of the brand-new Polish émigrés at their church spoke.

She reeled in her chair. "Who's he?"

Meg's mother snorted. "Sure, you wouldn't have heard me speak of him. Not until now. Your father and I didn't agree on many things, and to be fair to him, he gave me free rein in most matters, but that was one thing he made me promise. And I kept my promise."

Brian sat down. "There's a great deal you don't know about your mam, Margaret."

"Apparently," Meg retorted. Brian ignored her rudeness and patted her hand.

"I know it's a shock, losing your da and all. This may be shocking to you, as well. But it's time you knew the truth."

"The truth about what?"

He looked searchingly at her mother, who nodded, reluctantly.

"You're a McCarthy, all right. But you're not a Kelly, not really," Brian continued. "You're a true Donnelly."

Meg stared at Brian, then her mother, who fidgeted in her seat. "I don't understand. Am I adopted?"

Brian laughed. Meg's mom fiddled with a pack of Marlboros, pulling a cigarette out with shaking fingers.

"You're not adopted," she muttered as she lit the cigarette. After a long drag, she pinned Meg under a hard stare. "The good Lord knows that the eighteen hours of labor I suffered through with you were real enough. No—you're my own daughter. So it's time you know your own name, my name—which is Fiona Donnelly. Brian, here, is my brother, one of many I left behind back in Ireland. Mary Margaret Kelly—Peggy—was my friend," she added, her tongue stumbling over the admission. "I stole her name and papers to emigrate. I had to get out. I had no choice."

"You had a choice, dear. But you made the right one," Brian said gently. "It was getting too dangerous for you."

"Wait. What?" Meg stared at them both, confused. "You've been living with a secret identity this whole time? And Dad knew this?"

Fiona nodded. "We met in the early seventies after I'd come over. I met him at some cultural function. You know how prideful he was about his Irish roots, like he was fresh off the boat, himself. I told him the truth when he asked for my hand. I didn't want the risk hanging over his head without him knowing."

"Risk? What risk?"

"The Donnellys were IRA, Meg," Fiona stated quietly.

"Are. We still are," Brian added proudly. "Until the Troubles are over and the Irish are free of the English, the Donnellys will fight."

Meg's mind raced. "You? IRA?"

She looked at her mother. Her hair, severe, was skewered with pins and her face looked sick under the kitchen's fluorescent light.

Brian chuckled. "Your mam was one of the best. She was a courier for us, Meg. A fierce one, good in a fight, too, if you got in a pinch."

Meg jumped to her feet and laughed. "There's no way. You? No. I don't believe it."

Fiona shrugged. "All you ever saw was mild little me, clutching my rosary beads, haranguing your da. But that's because it's what you wanted to see. You worshipped him—even though he was a drunken fool by the end—so you chose sides and only saw the caricature. But it was useful. Those stupid men with their old-fashioned ways, they'd never suspect a thing. I was there, under their nose the whole time, and they have never seen me for what I am."

"What are you, then?" Meg asked, as intrigued as she was horrified.

"Your mam works the Irish circuit here in the States to raise funds for us, Meg. And, next to Boston, Chicago is at the center of it. She's damn good at it too. Built it up to be bigger even than New York for us. Church socials and Irish dancing clubs, cultural exchanges and all those sentimental fools trying to track their ancestry—all of it makes for a good cover. You spend enough time and you can pick out the people who will be sympathetic . . . who want to fight for the underdog. They just need some guidance on how to help. Your mam helps them find the path, as it were. Sometimes it's cash. Sometimes she arranges more important things, like arms. Either way, she's done as much, maybe even more for the Cause from here than she could have ever done if she'd stayed behind in Derry."

"And Dad?"

Fiona shrugged. "He had his anti-communism. I had this. As long as I didn't endanger you or him, he didn't care. For a while, we even worked together, until the new blokes in the IRA started seeming a bit pink to him, if you will. He wanted Ireland to be free as much as I did, you know? That's what drew me to him in the beginning. He wanted to make a difference. He wanted to be so Irish, you know—he was proud of his blood." She smiled, a thin, pressed thing. "Sometimes I thought he liked it. Maybe was a wee bit proud of me, even. At least, he used to be, before he was drunk all the time and could no longer think for himself."

"Why are you telling me this? And why now?" Meg asked.

"Like your mam said—we have a proposition for you," Brian began. He watched her carefully, gauging her reaction. "You have but a year left before you graduate from high school. You'll be thinking about your future. Your da's untimely death has left your family in a bit of a financial lurch, if you will. Your mam could take a bit out of the funds she raises, but she won't. Even though it would be justified if she chose to. So as I said, you're in a pinch."

Meg saw her mother's jaw lift an inch, stubborn and proud.

"Go on."

"You see, Meg, you're a smart enough girl. And your mam here has never let her British citizenship—or rather, Mary Margaret's—lapse. Which means you are a British citizen too. Your mam made sure to register you, to win you that right."

"I don't see why that's relevant."

Fiona took a deep drag on her cigarette, her eyes boring holes into Meg. Meg knew that look. She was being sized up, the same way her mother had sized up Tommy Murphy when he came to take her to the prom. Seeing if she was worthy. If she could be trusted.

Fiona stubbed out her Marlboro in the ashtray, having made up her mind.

"Listen carefully. We have reason to believe that a school for nannies—you know, a training program for women who live in with wealthy families as babysitters—that is based in the countryside of England is actually a cover for a ring of British spies. If we can get you in there, with the right connections, you can spy for us. For the IRA."

Meg gaped. "You're joking."

Meg's mother's eyes narrowed. "About what part?" she asked, cocking her head.

"What part? All of it! Babysitters who are spies? Me, being a spy? For the IRA? Have you both lost your minds?"

Brian shook his head. "I'm afraid not. Our sources are absolutely convinced this school's the thing. We need someone on the inside. You're a good candidate, if we can indeed get them to accept you into the program. That could be difficult, of course, with you being Irish, the rampant discrimination and whatnot. But it is worth a try."

Meg didn't know what to think.

"You don't have to decide now," Brian said kindly.

He pushed his chair back from the kitchen table and readied himself to go, reaching his big arms into the sleeves of his coat and fumbling about for his gloves. Meg could see, now, the resemblance in the face to her mother, the way their chins jutted proudly out, even if they were quiet. His hands were large, and powerful. She could imagine them doing violence.

Fiona rose, as well, suddenly seeming exhausted. For the first time in days, Meg noticed, her eyes glistened with tears. When she spoke, it was so softly that Meg had to strain to hear her words.

"I know you didn't see it, Meg, but I did love your da. The best of him, the part of him you barely got to see—the dreamer I met all those years ago. The man who loved his wee baby daughter so much he wept the first time he held her in his hands. Wasn't his fault he didn't have the imagination or skill to do more than dream. Maybe the work will be a continuance of those good memories, and an honor to him—if you pick it up and join us. But that's enough for one day. As your uncle said, you don't have to decide now. See him out, like a good girl, Meg," she said as she retreated wearily down the hall. "I've a headache. You'll have to fend for yourself for supper later. There should be a hot dish or two in there for you to warm," she added, gesturing vaguely at the refrigerator. "The ladies from the church have been so generous."

Her mother closed her bedroom door firmly behind her, leaving Meg with Brian. Meg stood in the doorway, looking warily at her uncle, who seemed to be taking pleasure in her befuddlement.

"Why should I do what you ask?" she prompted him.

He shrugged. "You'll have to think on that for yourself, now, little Margaret. But remember, your family back in Ireland has been watching you grow, loving you from afar. This is part of your birthright, if you accept it."

He buttoned his coat against the evening chill, preparing to leave.

"It is a way out of this flat, I suppose—a way out you might find through no other path. And you may want to reflect on the manner of your father's death. Him falling down the stairs here, all the way to the landing in that manner."

Brian left the landing and began descending the staircase that unfurled down the center of their building.

"What do you mean?" she called after him.

He didn't look back as he answered. "Did you never stop to consider how he wound up outside, on the front stoop, to freeze, after falling down that flight of interior stairs? Nor wonder how the police report failed to notice such a curious matter? Your da may have been a drinker, but I reckon he didn't break his neck in a stupor and then walk his dead self out the front door. No, your mam did right calling me for help . 'Twas a message to her, I reckon. A warning, like. Whether from the unionists or someone else, we don't know. We'll be watching you both now, protecting you real close, but it may be good for you to learn how to protect yourself at that school. Learn to protect yourself and fight back."

He let the implications of his words sink in, his footsteps echoing in the stairwell.

Chapter Three

BREE

Present Day, Bath

The hard benches were familiar, but that was about all Bree could think of that was even remotely good about being back at Norwood's convocation opening up a new academic term. The enormous wood-paneled auditorium that had been so daunting to her as a new student had, after hours of sitting through lectures and exams, become almost commonplace, its quasi-Gothic tracings and dramatic, soaring ceiling comfortably in the background. Last year she'd been uncertain, trying to disappear into the crowds in the rows of seats and shrinking as far away from the stage as she could. Now, she knew she belonged, and unfortunately knew what lay ahead of her.

"Can you believe it's been a year?" Dash whispered to her.

She cast a sideways glance at him. His face looked harder, almost grim, in comparison to the joking young man she'd met on the first day of school. Somehow, even the ridiculous formal uniform he wore did nothing to lighten his aspect.

Bree nodded, then pointed to the podium. "Look, there she is."

Their roommate, Ruby, was mounting the steps to the stage. Having won honors with the highest grade point average in their class, she'd been named Head Girl.

Bree waved. Ruby pursed her lips, shaking her head slightly. She stared ahead resolutely, ignoring them along with the rise and fall of the chattering crowd.

"Look—already she's becoming self-important," Dash complained. "I can't believe she's going to follow in Montoya-Craig's tyrannical footsteps," he muttered. "Who would even want such a horrible honor? Not to mention the paperwork."

"Shh," Bree scolded. "She's just trying to focus. This is her first outing as Head Girl. You know how ambitious she is. It's good for her. Be supportive."

"What if she turns all nasty, like Mon—"

"Mr. Heyward!" Dean Albourn peered at him over her glasses from the podium. The hall had fallen into silence without Bree or Dash noticing. "I have called the convocation to order," Albourn continued. "Can I direct your attention to Fripp, who will be leading us in our sacred school song? Unless you would like to do so yourself? I did hear that your young summer charges, in addition to requiring you to wear lederhosen, also trained you up in the entire cycle from *The Sound of Music*?"

The second-years all twittered behind their white gloves.

"No, ma'am," Dash answered, his polite tone just barely hiding his annoyance. "I am duly chastened. My apologies to all assembled and most of all to Miss Fripp. Please, carry on."

"Thank you for your permission to proceed, Heyward," Ruby said, dripping with sarcasm. "Whatever would we do without our manny?"

"See," Dash whispered vehemently to Bree, as Ruby swept to the podium and hit a note on her tuning fork. "See what I mean? She's already acting different."

"She always went after you, Dash. The only thing that's different now is she has an official platform from which to do it. You'd better get used to it."

"She's just angry that we left her behind to visit your home."

"Shh," Bree insisted. "Just sing, will you?"

Bree was relieved that this convocation promised to be short. They were second-years now and expected to know the ropes. She mentally noted all the things that were already sorted that would make second term so much easier for her. She, like the rest of her classmates, had her rooming groups and was pursuing electives in her own individual course of study, so would not be forced to listen to an overview of classes. She knew the rigors that lay before them, a knowledge felt most keenly by those— like Dash, Ruby, and Bree herself—who'd found themselves forced into the shadowy secret training program for spies, for which the vaunted Norwood Certificate Program for Nannies was a mere cover. She knew the dangers, as well. What had seemed abstract and almost laughable at this time last year—that their lives could be forfeited in the course of duty—was now something she lived with every minute of her life.

As if reading her mind, Albourn took the podium to close.

"Many of you may be unaware of the terrible tragedy which has befallen one of our own, indeed, one of your very classmates. In the course of her summer placement, Susmita Duncombe sadly perished. You may remember her as Susie," Albourn added.

Bree couldn't help but wince at the mention of her former roommate's name. Dash reached over and took her hand in his as a murmur swept the hall and their classmates turned to gape.

Albourn lifted a hand to quiet the assembled nannies. Ruby stood behind her shoulder, her eyes steely.

"Yes. Quite sad, really. Her family is one of England's oldest. It is out of respect for their privacy I will say no more than that she died bravely, as a Norwood nanny should do, so that her likeness will join that of the others fallen in the line of duty whom we honor in Memorial Chapel. As we always do here at Norwood, we strive to respect the privacy of our employer families by keeping such unseemly news from the media and work assiduously to gain the full cooperation of our nannies' surviving family members in this endeavor. So again, out of respect for Susmita's memory and out of discretion for her employer, we ask that you adhere to our policy on press relations and not speak to any member of the media. Should you be sought out for comment, please refer any journalist to the administration's Communication Office. A service in her memory will be held next week in the chapel."

A deadly hush had settled among the students. Nobody said a word. Dash pressed Bree's hand in his as curious eyes turned to stare at them.

"That is all. Your confirmed course lists are available in the hall outside. Proctors, please join Fripp on the stage to prepare for the welcoming of the first-years."

Ruby bellowed, "Dismissed!"

The throng parted for Bree and Dash, making space around them as if they were contagious—as if by getting too close, they, too, would experience the snuffing out of the life of a roommate. They made their way to the tables outside the hall, trying to ignore the bits of conversation that came to them in snatches.

"She probably did it to herself in an accident, she was such a bimbo. Remember that stapler?"

"What are the odds it was a lovers' quarrel, do you think? Would Heyward have known . . .?"

"Maybe he was involved!"

"I heard her uncle was covering it up, just like her father's disgraces . . ."

"Come on, then," Dash urged. He grabbed Bree by the shoulder and steered her through the spreading brushfire of speculation. "Grab your packet so we can be off."

They each swiped a manila envelope emblazoned with their names and burst out of the dark hall into the sunshine. Bree took a deep breath.

"They have no idea, do they?"

"I'd like to keep it that way," Dash muttered, steering them to the street, toward their apartments at Jaguar House. "The less anyone knows, the better."

"Still, it's a shame. Their memories of her will be of a stupid, shallow girl. She was many things but she was not that."

Dash looked at her curiously as they walked. "Better they think of her that way than get themselves—or us—in trouble with the truth. Nobody needs to know she was a saboteur working against her own country. Nobody need know the truth about any of us. You realize that, don't you, Bree?"

"I know. But it does make me feel guilty to hear them speak about her that way."

He stopped on the sidewalk. "You can't possibly feel sorry for her. Not after what she did to you? And the Asker children?"

Bree shook her head. "She made her choices. But she had a hard life, Dash. I wish it hadn't ended the way it did. If someone had shown her love in her life, maybe she'd have turned out differently."

Dash scoffed. "She didn't really blossom into a flower of virtue under my attentions, now, did she?"

"You didn't really love her and you know it."

They resumed walking, Bree lost in thought. A familiar guilt ate away at her. Dash believed Susmita had been cold and calculating enough to kill Bree first, if she'd had the chance; hence, he believed Bree was justified in supposedly killing Susmita and didn't give it further thought. It still bothered her that this was the way Susmita would be remembered, even if it was true. Even though she hadn't technically pulled the trigger, she felt responsible. While Susmita had been crowing about her activities as a mole working for the Chinese and the way she'd undermined the mission on which they'd all been assigned—directly causing Bree to lose the children in her care—Bree's mentor, Judy, had been listening in the shadows. Bree had frozen in the sights of Susmita's gun, but Judy had stepped in to kill Susmita before she could hurt Bree—and before Bree could delve any further into the wild claims Susmita was making about Judy's past.

"If she hadn't died, we might know where the Asker children are," Bree began again, her brow knotted in concentration. "We have to find them, Dash."

"This is not the place, Briana," he warned quietly, looking about the busy street for classmates. "Wait 'til we are back at Jaguar House." Picking up his voice, he changed the subject. "What classes did you land, then?"

Bree shrugged and ripped open her envelope, rattling off the course nicknames she'd memorized, before reciting her classes' official titles. "*House Divided*—more formally known as *Divorce, Remarriage, and the Modern Blended Family; Spots and 'Staches—An Introduction to Navigating Puberty; Smile, It's Sawdust!—Introductory Sugar- and Gluten-Free Baking;* and *Hippie Dippy—Self Care of the Nanny: Stress Management and Exercise in the Face of Sleep Deprivation.* Of course, we will get our other courses for the certificate program assigned in this evening's meeting. What about you?"

"*House Divided* and *Spots*, as well. And then I've landed *Whips and Chains—Advanced Disciplinary Methods,* along with *Medea to Mommie Dearest—A Survey Course of the Psychology of Mothers.*"

"We won't have anything with Ruby, I bet."

"Probably not." Dash shrugged. "I heard her say earlier she was taking *Accounting* and *Marketing*." He gave an exaggerated shudder. They'd arrived at the leafy courtyard of Jaguar House. He pulled out his keys as they continued talking. "But it suits her plans. All the better to embed herself into the good graces of the administration and become the spymaster of her dreams."

"You're starting to sound like you don't trust her," Bree pressed, as they walked into her apartment.

Bree tried not to look at the place where their roommate Susmita's body had bled out on the linoleum floor. A few shiny tiles, newly laid, stood in stark relief against the faded, grimy field of the old. She tried not to remember the blood seeping over the linoleum—it had followed the grooved impressions like rivulets as Susmita's glassy eyes stared at nothing. Bree blinked hard, trying to ignore the memory of her own mentor, Judy, standing with a gun over Susmita's body.

"Bree—I said, do *you*?" Dash parried, cutting through her distraction. He folded his long, lean body into the futon. "You know as well as I do how ambitious she is. What if they try to use her to get to you?"

"Don't you mean us?" Bree asked.

"You're the one who was under suspicion for throwing the Turkey operation, for losing the Asker children, and for Susmita's murder."

Bree's temper flared. "So it's me against the world, then?"

Dash sighed. "You know that's not what I meant. I don't want them pitting *any* of us against one another. Look—we've not even been here five minutes and already we're quarreling. Come on now, Bree. I'm on your side. Sit down."

Bree did, perching herself on the edge of the futon as far away from Dashiell as she could be. He halfheartedly hid an amused smile.

"I only meant, in commenting on Ruby, that she knows a lot. Not everything, but a lot. And they have a strong hand on her now."

"We don't even know who 'they' are," Bree pointed out, relenting as she sank back into the sofa. "It's possible that the Norwood administration doesn't know what happened either. That's what they claim, anyway. In which case, maybe we'd be better off telling them everything we know."

"What good would come of that?"

"If they saw the tape of Gul and knew about the arms diversion, maybe it would help them find the children."

One of the only proofs Bree had that their failed operation had been deliberately thrown was a video she'd found inside a hidden nanny cam. The video had contained a secret message from her coworker, Gul—another dead girl in the wreckage of the Turkish fiasco.

"Maybe. Or maybe it would lead them to Judy. How would you feel if it did?"

Bree said nothing.

"We all know Susmita was a liar, Bree. But what if she was telling the truth? What if Judy is the one who was diverting the arms to the Uyghurs in China, disrupting a major NATO operation? What if Norwood discovers Judy was involved, and that you've known it and deliberately hid it from them? They would expel you. Or worse."

Bree couldn't help but touch the bump on the back of her neck—the bump over the implant that made it impossible for her to disappear. She'd seen for herself what Norwood did to people it couldn't trust to keep its secrets—they'd obliterate her memory, not caring if she turned into a vegetable in the process. She didn't want to end up like that.

"Judy wouldn't betray me," she insisted.

"You—we—will have to take *Jeopardy!* this semester for our spy qualifications under the certificate program," he said brusquely. "We'll all learn then what people are apt to do under aggressive interrogation. And don't forget—Susmita all but said that Judy is the one who betrayed your parents. Why would Judy protect you?"

"She's protected me this long. Why stop?"

Dash pushed to his feet, exasperated. "You're incorrigible. I suppose that is part of your charm."

"You find me charming?" Bree grinned.

"You're such a child sometimes, Bree." Dash stormed off to his own bedroom, closing the door that connected their suites.

Bree gazed after him and wondered—had they removed Susmita's bed? The designer clothes she used to slip into as soon as she could peel off the abhorred synthetics of her Norwood uniform? Had they whisked away every sign of Bree's former roommate, just as they'd removed the stains on the linoleum floor?

With a sigh, she realized that in her spat with Dash, she'd forgotten all about trying to devise a way to find the Asker children. And she had wanted to mention the odd fact that the administration had not mentioned the death of her partner in Turkey—Gul—during convocation at all.

None of it was sitting well with her.

Bree had gotten used to the late-night meetings that were required for the secret spy portion of her Norwood training. As she walked under the harsh lights of the gymnasium, she could feel the electricity in the air, the buzz of gossip. Some of it, she figured, was just the normal chit-chat of friends reconnecting after a summer away. But some of it would be about her dead roommate and their mysterious mission gone wrong. She knew she couldn't avoid it. She could only minimize it, taking tactical steps such as separating from Dashiell and Ruby to make the three of them less of an obvious target for gossip.

She braced herself for the onslaught of curiosity and strode toward the back of the crowd. She locked eyes with Ruby, who simply shook her head slightly, as if in warning.

A crowd of young women congregated around Bree, all speaking at once.

"I heard she did something stupid again, Bree—is it true?"

"Is it true her family's covering it up?"

"What happened, Bree? You must have been there, right?"

Bree just shook her head. "We were separated. I don't know anything more than you do."

She felt the flush spreading up from her neck and hoped her class-mates chalked it up to her discomfort being in the spotlight—and didn't suspect her of a blatant lie.

"Ladies, compose yourselves." Dean Albourn pounded her walk-ing stick on the shiny pine floor of the gym, calling them to attention. "This sort of gossipmongering is ill becoming. Leave Fripp, Heyward, and Parrish alone and stop picking over their grief like vultures. You were called here this evening to receive your certificate program class assignments and an overview of year two. Let's not waste any more time. Shadduck? Keep it brief, if you please."

Their physical education professor stepped to the front and took over the briefing.

"Three mandatory courses this term—*Gadgets and Weaponry*; *Introduction to Interrogation*; and *Seduction and the Spy*—plus the second sequence in your physical training. *Bling, Jeopardy!* and *Pooh Bear*, you call them, isn't that right? Clever, that last one: a literary reference to honey pots; very clever. And *Wonder Woman 2* for physical training? Pity you students couldn't be more creative with that one. You each drew an elective, as well. You are receiving a text with your placement as I speak."

There was a quiet murmuring of buzzing phones. They all resisted the temptation to look, attentive to Shadduck.

"The course load is heavy, as usual. But you will find you now have the opportunity to explore your own interests and develop a specialty or two as the year unfolds. And remember, this is your last year of formal training. Year three is total field placement. Your assignment will be directly correlated to your performance in this year's coursework."

Albourn picked up from there. "We will dismiss you for the evening. But I remind you—if you are proctoring first-years, you are expected to join Fripp at 2200 hours for a briefing in the faculty lounge. Fripp, Parrish, and Heyward: Shadduck and I must meet with you briefly. Everyone else, dismissed!"

The dean and Shadduck strode off, leaving Dashiell, Ruby, and Bree to trail them back to the administrative offices, feeling the curious stares of their training mates burning holes in their backs.

The dean wasted no time once they reached the quiet of her office, turning to face them where they stood across her desk. Bree could sense her efficient impatience.

"Tell me your course choices, please."

They looked at one another, confused.

"Go on, then. I find them curious. Heyward—your elective?"

Dashiell cleared his throat. "*Next-Level Malware*, Dean Albourn."

"They, the student body, call it '*Hal*,' do they not? Hmph," she pondered, pursing her lips in mock concentration. "And what will you learn in this class, Heyward?"

"Techniques for penetrating private information technology networks to gain information, ma'am."

"Information such as passwords and the like, I imagine," she mused. "And methods of rerouting and intercepting private communications, no doubt. Planting fake communications, even. Communication irregularities like those of which we know were implicated in this terrible Turkish affair. Interesting."

Dashiell blanched, and Bree imagined his sudden paleness brought the dean no small measure of glee and delight. Albourn continued pacing.

"And you, Parrish? You have registered for what the students call *Boom!*, have you not?" She read from the registrar's manual: "'*An Introduction to Bombs—Their Construction and Armament.*' So it is to be more chaos, death, and destruction from you, is it?"

Bree stuck her chin out defiantly. She had done nothing wrong on the Turkey operation. She wasn't going to be bullied into feeling guilty.

Albourn threw the heavy course guide down on her desk with a thump.

"And then there is you, Fripp. You have not only signed on for *Accounting* and *Marketing* in your normal course of study, you have embraced the path of the desk jockey by raising your hand for '*Bookworm*.' You know why the students have saddled the *Managerial Administration* course with such a name?" She waited for a response, brow arched.

"No, ma'am," Ruby muttered.

"Tell them, Shadduck."

Shadduck grinned. "'Book' for keeping the books, obviously. And 'worm' because the active field operatives scoff at those who willingly embrace the safety of a desk job as their path of choice."

Bree bit her lip and stared at her feet. That one would hurt Ruby's pride, she knew.

Albourn cut into her thoughts. "A review of your interesting elective choices is not why I asked you here. As amusing as this discussion has been, I must ask your cooperation on another important matter. When we have a death in the family, it is important the Norwood community have an opportunity to heal. I am asking for your help to make that happen."

Bree stared at her, sneaking a furtive glance at Ruby and Dash, who looked just as confounded.

"By which I mean," she continued impatiently, "I must ask you to avail yourself of opportunities to interact with the non-certificate program students. Mingle. That sort of thing. We must squash any rumors or sense of secretiveness."

"But didn't you deliberately pull us apart last year, so that the truth about the program would not get discovered?" Bree challenged.

"Yes, of course. But circumstances have changed. We must change with them. Integration. Sociability. Those are important at times like these. We need you to socialize and put on happy faces."

"How, pray tell, are we to find time to socialize with our classmates when we are carrying a double course load, Dean Albourn?" Dashiell asked with arch politeness.

Shadduck answered for the dean. "We are offering to guarantee your grades if you can go out of your way to accommodate the dean in this manner."

Bree saw Ruby's eyes grow wide, her stoicism seemingly out the window at the idea of such an affront to merit. But before Ruby could say anything, Dashiell broke in.

"Why, of course. We would be delighted to help in this manner. Er, just to confirm—the other professors are informed of this arrangement?"

Shadduck rolled her eyes. "Give it up, Heyward. Of course not. We will fix your grades discreetly, behind the scenes. As I am directly responsible for your instruction in *Wonder Woman 2*, I shall handle that myself. We are not inviting slacking, mind you. Just recognizing the extra burden we require you to carry at this time. And note—your electives will not fall under the jurisdiction of this arrangement. In those, you are on your own."

Ruby pressed further. "How are we to do this, practically speaking? In what manner do you expect us to socialize?"

Albourn threw up her hands. "You're a clever girl, Fripp. You'll think of something. Sit at a different table in the dining hall. Hold a study break party. I don't care. Just make sure the three of you are seen as happy, well adjusted, and normal. You'll have to make a show of attending grief counseling, of course—and you, Parrish, will need to clear your psychological screening. Should have had that taken care of before reissuing your weapon, but never mind. We'll tidy up that loose string now—standard procedure after an agent injures or kills in the line of duty. Anyway, you are all to use your conversations to squelch any rumors. Soon this business about Miss Duncombe's demise will be forgotten."

"What about Gul?" Bree blurted, referring to the fallen agent who'd been with her in Turkey.

Albourn's eyes narrowed. "What about her?"

"Why did you not announce her death, as well? I thought all Norwood nannies who fell in the line of duty are honored in the chapel. Why not her?"

Albourn shrugged. "We can't have too many deaths all at once now, can we? That would no doubt rattle the fragile among us, those who have weaker constitutions. We will wait and announce Gul Avci's passing at the right moment. As she was an alumna from several years ahead of you, her death—and the timing of the memorial—will have no practical bearing on your class."

Shadduck leaned up against the radiator and crossed her legs. "Do we have an understanding, then?"

"Yes. We'll do our bit," Ruby sullenly answered for them all.

"Very well. You may leave now," Albourn said with a vague wave of her hand, dismissing them from her office.

They shuffled back the uphill walk to Jaguar House, muttering among themselves.

"They can't possibly still suspect us, can they?" demanded Dashiell.

Ruby shook her head. "No. I gather they were trying to get us off balance before making their demands."

"Or just being cruel," Bree added.

"They must really be worried about the rumors, to go to these lengths," Ruby mused. "Something must have leaked."

"Don't you already know, Miss Bookworm?" Dashiell teased.

"What? You want to mock me?" Ruby's prim British tones gave way as her Trinidadian accent came to the forefront, as it always did when she was angry. "Go right ahead. Yes, I want to be management track. I don't want to get killed. If I'm stuck in this godforsaken spy business against my will, I'm going to damn well be the one giving orders, not taking them," Ruby spat back in a heated whisper.

"Let's not fight, y'all," Bree admonished. "We need to stick together. Dash does make one good point, though, Ruby. We're lucky to have you on the inside. You can help."

"Help with what?"

"To know what's going on with the investigation into the operation. To find out if they have any leads on the Asker children."

Ruby bristled. "You should just leave that alone, Bree. There's nothing good that will come of continuing to dig. They shut us out for a reason. The sooner you accept it, the better."

Bree's retort was already on her lips when she saw Dashiell shake his head, almost imperceptibly. She swallowed it down, wondering if he was warning her off due to his own suspicions of Ruby.

They walked in silence the remainder of the way to Jaguar House. Dashiell kept trying to shoot meaningful looks at Bree; Bree kept steadfastly ignoring them. Ruby left them at the stoop of their apartment door, swooping through the common room and making a show of slamming the door to the bedroom she shared with Bree.

Dashiell sighed. "And so second year begins."

Chapter Four

MEG

1993, Bath

She still found it odd how they convened at the long tables for their meals to be waited upon by the servants who were supposed to be invisible. It was an indication of class, the administration had said, underscoring that as nannies to society's elite families, they were supposed to blend in and be used to the ways of the rich.

Meg thought it was more likely a way to assert control—when you ate, what you ate, all under watchful eyes, the other students as hawklike as the professors—another part of their daily routine as ordered and regimented as a Mass.

The thought gave her a start as she realized that, even after two years, she actually missed Mass. But being Catholic at Norwood was not really possible. It wasn't that it was frowned upon or forbidden. It just did not exist. So Meg trudged across the yard to Memorial Chapel along with her classmates and kept her rosaries to herself, alone in bed at night.

Alone. She was alone a lot. Even in the midst of a crowded campus, she was acutely aware of her singularity. Being plucked from the crowd as

Head Girl had not made her isolation any better. If anything, it had set her further apart, an object of curiosity, but also of derision and resentment.

She had attempted to mingle, trying to avoid being seen as the administration's pet, but her efforts had earned her very little.

She picked at her plate. It was a Friday, and they had served a *côte de boeuf* for dinner, leaving Meg to push her beef aside to eat her bread, potatoes, and soggy vegetables, longing for the Friday fish fries of St. Stanislaus. Her stomach rumbled. With no server in sight, she folded her napkin and extracted herself gracefully from the bench, suffering the stares of those seated around her, to search out another roll.

The stray foot that tripped her as she walked across the dining room, sending her sprawling on the gleaming linoleum floor, was just another of the indignities she'd trained herself to endure.

The hall fell into a hush.

Slowly, she pushed herself up from the floor, noting the skinned knee, bloody, underneath her torn stockings. A year ago, she would have been blinking back tears. Now, it was the rage bubbling over that she fought to control.

As Head Girl, she had many weapons in her arsenal, and they all knew it. The two classes of young women held their collective breath as she turned to face them.

Not worth it, her brain calculated, hissing at her through her anger. *Not worth it at all. Don't stoop to their level.*

Her face burned red, and she choked back the bitter words that had been on her lips. Forcing a smile to her face, she announced, "Silly me. So clumsy. I clearly need extra time with the athletic trainers."

A soft murmur went around the dining room. She looked hard at the women seated at the tables near her, searching their faces, memorizing them, knowing one of them was the culprit. She noted which ones stared at their plates; which ones held their hands to their mouths, attempting to cover their indiscreet snickering; which ones boldly stared back, daring her to do anything.

Another, deeper part of her brain whispered to her. *You'll punish them in your own time. They'll see.*

She turned on her heel, feeling Dean Simpson's eyes burning a hole in her back, and went to wait, her hunger forgotten.

The dean made her wait another hour before she joined her in her office in the administration building.

"You are getting a better handle on your temper," Simpson noted approvingly as she peeled off her gloves, sitting in the giant leather wing-back chair behind her desk and picking up the pack of cigarettes that rested on a gigantic crystal ashtray. "That will serve you well undercover."

"I don't like taking this abuse, ma'am," Meg responded. "I still don't understand why you insist upon it."

"You know why," Simpson sighed, sucking in the nicotine and smoke that signaled the end of her day. "I cannot show favorites. It is better for you in the long run if people think you are a misfit, not the center of some grand plan on whom we've pinned our hopes."

She waited for Meg's acknowledgment. When it wasn't forthcoming, she continued.

"And now we begin. At long last, the assignment for which you've—we've—been waiting." She slapped a file on her desk, in front of Meg. "Go on, take a look."

Meg took up the file and began scanning its contents.

"A bachelor?" She looked up, an eyebrow raised in skepticism.

"Divorced," Simpson clarified. "As you see, one child, of whom he has custody."

"How unusual. Circumstances?"

Simpson took a deep drag on her cigarette. "Working wife. Unfit mother. Very unseemly. She's out of the picture now, anyway. Hence the need for a nanny."

"The ex-wife is totally out?" Meg clarified, wanting to know what she was getting into.

"As far as we know. Anyhow, that's the least important detail. You saw who he is?"

His name was meaningless to Meg, who still struggled to understand the intricacies of the peerage and British social strata—but not his job.

"Domestic intelligence," she responded, stunned by their luck. "Undercover, infiltrating the IRA. And you think this is the perfect situation for us. You suspect he is a double agent?"

"There has been some speculation. He was sent in to manage a series of Irish shell companies sympathetic to the cause. We believe they are a front for money laundering, a way to fund arms acquisition and terrorism. Either that or an intelligence operation. He's been at it for some time now, but his efforts have yielded very little by way of information or arrests. His superiors insist it is a case of mere mediocrity. Norwood wants to know what he's truly up to."

"And take him down if your intuitions are correct."

"Take the entire operation down, my dear. If we are correct, this man is a cog in a bigger wheel. We need to know who is behind him. He comes from very good stock, so it is surprising to see him implicated in this manner. That said, he does have some Irish on his mother's side, so him flipping is not inconceivable. Something bigger must be going on, and we need to find out exactly what it is."

Simpson's eyes gleamed at the notion of finally bagging her enemies.

"And so, you will be his nanny. We have concocted an adequate paper trail for you— there is no way with that accent," she said with a disparaging flick of her eyes, "that we can hide your American-ness. But that will work to our advantage in this case. He will be curious—we have heard he has an inquisitive nature. He'll find your dual citizenship strange, your choice to come to a British school an oddity. We will plant enough seeds to let him dig his way to the discovery that you have hidden your true identity, raising the possibility in his mind that you have Irish sympathies. That will be important if he is, indeed, a turncoat. You, meanwhile, will make yourself as charming and intriguing as possible. You must make him trust you, if not love you, and get him to bring you into his confidence."

Meg took this all in, her mind's edges glittering with questions and objections. "His family business is a good cover," she noted.

Simpson shrugged. "Import businesses can cover a plethora of shady activities. At least it gives him a plausible reason for being interested in trade. If he is a double agent, you'll find out. One way or another. You must make him confident that you are on his side—whatever that is."

"It seems a stretch. What motive would he have? What if we're wrong?"

Simpson's gaze was steely. "Then you must find out the truth, so we can root it out."

Meg closed the file and placed it back on the desk. "The child sounds like a brat," she said.

Simpson waved her hand about, the cigarette smoke wreathing about her. "Indeed. You will be the fourth nanny they've brought into the home, though the first from here. In her defense, wouldn't you be difficult, with a mother like that, who abandoned you? I daresay that child may be the key to it all. Tame the child, bring her around, and you'll earn his respect. And respect is what, Miss McCarthy?"

"Respect is the first step toward love." Meg recited rotely one of the foundational truisms of her *Seduction and the Spy* class.

"Indeed. If this weren't such a tangled mess, we could attempt to exploit his baser animal instincts, go with simple seduction . . . but in this case, I believe this route will be better. You will of course need to avoid any hint of women's liberation or such nonsense. It will not work with this setup, not given his social status and messy divorce. I am sure that has left him stinging, and he longs for nothing more than a good mother for his daughter."

It was all Meg could do to stop herself from rolling her eyes.

"You've had a good two years here, McCarthy," Simpson concluded, stubbing out her cigarette for emphasis. "This placement as your third-year assignment will be the culmination of everything you and we have worked for. It may take longer than twelve months, but it's a start. I know I don't have to tell you that if you do well on this, your loyalty as a British subject will never be questioned again. And your future with Norwood will be bright."

"Are we working with MI5 on this, ma'am?"

"Don't be ridiculous. They are as secretive and protective of their own as they come. That's why such a step is necessary. Our NATO colleagues agree. We cannot afford to let this IRA threat linger. An unstable Britain makes for an unstable alliance."

Meg gulped hard. "Next steps, ma'am?"

"Ready yourself for your interview. Learn your new legend—this fictitious background—cold." She shoved another file across the desk. "You have one week."

Meg took the file and rose. "I won't let you down, ma'am."

Excused, she left the office, closing the door softly behind her.

Alone in her bedsit, Meg clutched the file to her chest.

Everything she had gone through was worth it, just to get this chance.

She laid the file open on her desk and fanned the papers out in front of her, her eyes dancing over the pages, unsure where to start.

"Hello, lovely," she breathed when she spotted her new identity. She trailed her fingers over the name, struck by its solidity, there in print. "Margaret Shield. Welcome to the world."

She grinned, thinking of her Uncle Brian.

"Those loyalists in Ulster won't know what hit them."

Chapter Five

BREE

Present Day, Bath

Bree was lingering about the nursery play yard. The kindergarten class was lining up, preparing to walk to the park where they could watch the rowers cutting their graceful swath through the river and feed the ducks at the fountain.

"Lurking again, are we?" Dashiell interrupted her thoughts.

"Just thinking about the Askers," she admitted. "It's been months, Dash, but there's still no word of the children. Or their mother, Handan."

He placed a kindly hand on her shoulder. "I know how much it weighs on you. It weighs on all of us, you know."

"Does it?" she asked, her eyes lingering over the chattering children. "It doesn't seem to bother Ruby much. She won't even let us talk about it."

"She has her own way of dealing with things," he asserted. "Come, walk with me."

She turned her back on the nursery class and joined him as he steered her back toward their apartment.

"I have news for you. Your DNA results have returned. And they are quite irregular, I must say."

Bree's heart skipped a beat. "Irregular? In what way?"

"I took the liberty of exploring the linkages in the online database before discussing them with you. There is some evidence of what we initially understood from your mother, Margaret's, student file. You demonstrate clear McCarthy lineage, including significant shared DNA with that horrible demagogue, Senator Joseph McCarthy."

"The anti-Communist? You were able to confirm it, then?" Bree could feel her breath catch with excitement as she spoke.

"Yes, the very one. That is interesting, of course, but that's not the irregularity to which I refer. The curious thing is that you exhibit no DNA matches whatsoever with anybody named Kelly. Maybe a few very distant matches, well in the past, but nothing remotely close to a grandmother or even great-grandmother."

"What? What does that mean?"

"It is hard to say, definitively." Dash continued cautiously. "But it would appear that neither your mother, nor her mother, were members of the Kelly family. Which means your grandmother was living under an assumed identity." He pulled her down to sit on a bench alongside the sidewalk and began showing her documents captured on his phone. "You see . . . her immigration papers, the ship manifest for her voyage to America, and her marriage license are clearly in the name of Kelly. So it would seem deliberate on her part."

Bree's heart sank. "So we've hit a dead end."

"No! Quite the contrary. That is the exciting part. By chance, I have found a large number of relatively high-degree DNA matches of a clutch of people living in and around Londonderry. They seem to be a part of a family called Donnelly. Does that name mean anything to you?"

She shook her head. She had no memories of her parents, and nothing in her mother's student file had mentioned the Donnellys.

"You're sure?" Dash pressed her again.

"You know I don't remember anything, Dash."

"It's strange," he said, acknowledging her point. "You exhibit no close matches to anybody in the United States, but this grouping in Londonderry suggests that they are your closest connection on your maternal side."

"What do we do now?"

"Well. Let's assume that your grandmother hid her identity purposefully. That would mean these people may not want to be found. There's one other thing, Bree, that suggests this may be the case. I found an extremely close match with an elderly man living somewhat remotely in the outer area of Londonderry. The match is close enough that there is no doubt he is your great-uncle."

Bree's heart raced. "Go on."

"The match came through the UK's National DNA Database, the NDNAD."

"And?"

"In 1994, the government established this as a criminal database," he gingerly explained. "After the Birmingham Six were acquitted of the charges of planting an IRA bomb, confidence in the criminal justice system waned. The NDNAD was formed in response."

She winced. "He's a convicted criminal?"

"No," he clarified gently. "I found he was not. He was suspected and arrested—held for quite some time, it seems, on suspicion of IRA activity. More than once, apparently. However, they were never able to make a conviction stick. Which brings me to the DNA sample. The laws waxed and waned, but there was a lot of abuse in how these samples were used. Various acts redefined what was considered a 'non-intimate' DNA sample so that anyone even remotely suspected of a crime, no matter how small, could find themselves subject to police seizure of a saliva sample from a used glass, for example, or, as some would have it, by pulling out hair by the roots in a scuffle. For a while, these samples could be kept on file indefinitely. In 2010, the European Court of Human Rights ruled it a violation to retain the samples of people found innocent and commanded them to be destroyed within six years, to protect their privacy and allow them to move on. His sample shouldn't even exist. But here we are. And because of it, we've found your family."

Bree found it hard to speak. "What's his name?"

"Brian Donnelly. Take a look." He offered another sheaf of papers to her.

Bree's eyes raced over the pages, her finger tracing the records and connections.

"Dash!" Her hands were shaking. "He had a sister. A sister named Fiona."

Dash smiled. "I haven't looked for her in the databases, but I suspect when you do, you will find the paper trail for her mysteriously ends sometime in the seventies. And if you search online, you'll be able to learn more about Mr. Donnelly's arrest and the allegations against him in the nineties."

Bree jumped to her feet, shoving the papers in her bag, her mind already moving on to the implications. "If this is true—"

"DNA doesn't lie, Bree."

She pulled a face at him for interrupting her. "As I was saying, if this is true, then we need to go see him this weekend. We'll go and see if we can convince him to tell us what he knows."

———

"Parrish—kindly advise us of what could possibly be more interesting than the extension of this study's landmark findings on parental alienation to cases of sibling rivalry and sabotage?"

Bree's attention snapped back to her lecture.

"Nothing, Professor. While alienation theory has been used primarily to explain disputes between adult siblings in the financial settlement of parental estates, the underlying concepts, rooted in parental neglect, could naturally explain early displays of aggressive sibling rivalry, as well. I think. The research paper was a little hard to read. It seems that academics, in their efforts to outdo one another, often take very extreme stances and cover up their illogic in tangles of obtuse prose."

Professor Clifford coughed, trying to hide her amusement at Bree's assessment.

"Mmm, well said, Parrish," she grudgingly allowed. "Let's give the author the benefit of the doubt and assume that sibling rivalry is just a cover for deep psychological issues—not an exaggerated platform for the author's efforts to receive tenure. I don't suppose you can enlighten us as to the character pathologies that may be present?"

"Narcissism, borderline personality disorder, and mythomania," Bree rattled off.

Clifford harrumphed behind her lectern, obviously grumpy that she couldn't catch Bree out as unprepared. "Fine. Well then, you should all read up on this scientist's additional work related to biomarkers of stress and family violence related to parental alienation. The extra chapters will be posted to the portal this evening."

A collective groan went up.

"Dismissed!" Clifford shouted over the noise, and the students began to pack up their books.

"So, hypothetical children Anna and Dickon fight over the board game and now they have psychopathic tendencies?" Bree's classmate Anya muttered under her breath as she shoved her things into a rucksack. "That's mighty rich, don't you think, Bree?"

Bree turned in her seat to smile at Anya. "I suppose we live in a society that seeks complicated excuses for behaviors we don't want to deal with."

"You mean that kids are bratty and it's the parents' fault?" Anya snorted. "Yes, that sounds about right. Seems a pity we must take an entire term of *House Divided* to come to that lofty philosophical conclusion. Will you be joining us at dinner, then, tonight?" she asked as she struggled out of the tiny desk. Anya was a tall, muscular woman— one of the consistent leaders in their *Wonder Woman* physical education courses—and the schoolroom's seating, designed in an earlier era of tinier, supposedly more feminine frames, was extremely uncomfortable for her.

Bree shook her head. "No. Dash and I are taking a weekend trip to one of his family's estates in Ireland. We won't be back until late Sunday." She blushed a little as she shared the excuse she and Dash had concocted for their outing to Derry.

Anya arched a brow and grinned. "You've been spending a lot of time together. Fraternizing, some might say. Against the rules. Naughty."

Bree's cheeks burned. They'd known their story would get the rumor mill going, but they couldn't think of anything better. "It's really not like that, Anya."

Anya chortled. "Well, if you'd asked me last year, I'd have thought he was gay, so you could have knocked me over when he started seeing Susie—I mean, Susmita. And now, you. Sly fellow. You two should just make sure you don't leave poor Ruby to her own defenses. She's having a hard time of it, you know, and you two haven't been around to back her up."

"What do you mean?"

"She had words with someone in the dining hall last night when they made a joke about Susmita's death. It's hard enough being Head Girl, without having to deal with all the rumors. You two seem all squirreled away together. You're leaving her exposed."

Bree felt chastised.

"I didn't know."

"Well, now you do. Make sure you and lover boy do better by her when you get back." Anya hoisted her rucksack onto her shoulder. "Have a jolly time."

Someone had defaced the road sign, black spray paint crossing out the "London," leaving "derry" standing alone.

"Some things never change," Dashiell stated flatly as they drove by in their rental car. They were skirting the medieval city walls, going around the town in their quest to reach the tiny village where Brian Donnelly supposedly lived.

Bree clutched her hands in her lap, trying to imagine what she could possibly say to this man who was her uncle—a man whom she was about to meet for the first time.

Dash tried to fill the silence. "We'll have to take a detour, of course, to visit Ullabreagh. You might like it, really. The grounds are beautiful."

"What?"

Dash smiled. "Ullabreagh. My family's estate. You didn't think it was a complete fabrication, did you? It is open to the public and used as an event venue now. We'll have to go and linger a bit. You know, for this." He tapped the back of his neck where the tracking device that monitored their every move had been implanted. "Keep up our alibi in case they are watching, all that. We could probably stay overnight if need be."

"That would be nice," Bree responded automatically, staring out the window. The landscape alternated between patches of technicolor green pastures and the flaming oranges and reds of the trees' autumn leaves. Here and there, the belching smoke of industry marred the rolling hills. But nothing seemed to register.

Dashiell left her alone with her thoughts until they reached the last roundabout.

"Ready now, Bree?" he said cheerfully. "We're almost there. The app says we've only a few kilometers to go."

They rolled through a main street that scarcely deserved the name of village—a pub, a post office, an ancient Catholic chapel—before turning off onto a narrow, rutted road. The stone walls on either side leaned ever so slightly, crowding the car. Dashiell slowed.

"This should be it."

He pulled the rental to a stop on the patch of gravel that stood in for a lawn in front of the cottage. The house itself was trim—stark white, punctuated by vibrant green shutters that picked up the colors of the meadow behind. Bree could just pick out the fluffy shapes of the sheep grazing in the back. Everything was quiet.

She turned in her seat to face him. "Dash—I think it might be better for me to go by myself, first. Less threatening."

Dash frowned. "Are you certain?"

She nodded once. "You'll hold this for me?" She drew her pistol out and offered it to Dash, who took it and tucked it into the pocket of the driver's-side door. With that, she let herself out of the car.

Her throat felt tight as she knocked on the black wooden door—once, twice—and waited. She had memorized his face from the news coverage of his arrest in the nineties, but a lot of time had passed since then. What would he look like now? Would she be able to discern traces of herself when she finally saw him, face to face?

She heard a shuffling on the other side. Slowly, the door opened a crack, the chain on the other side barely allowing room for the elderly man behind it to peek through. His face had an unhealthy, bloated pallor to it, a web of broken blue capillaries spreading across his nose and cheeks. Annoyance rolled off him in waves.

"This cottage isn't for let," the man growled. "You've no doubt made a wrong turn." He made to slam the door on Bree.

"Wait!" Bree snaked her hand into the open gap in the door. "I'm not looking for a place to stay. I'm looking for a person. A Mr. Brian Donnelly."

"Remove your hand, missy, before you lose your fingers."

Bree ignored him. "Is he here?" she persisted.

His eyes narrowed. "What of him?"

"I need to talk to him."

"You'll be needing to get off my property, is what you'll be needing," he growled again, making to slam the door. "I've never heard of the man. Now, move your hand like a nice girl and be gone with you, before you get hurt."

He disappeared behind the door, which closed with a heavy thud. She banged on it until her hand grew sore and then turned, dejected, back to the car.

"No luck, then?"

"I guess I can understand, after all he's been through, why he wouldn't trust a stranger."

"Perhaps there's another way."

"What do you mean?"

"His property conveniently backs up to Ullabreagh. We could cut through the grounds and fields and come up to his backyard. It won't make him any friendlier," Dashiell cautioned, "but at least we might be able to draw him out, or catch him out with the sheep."

Dashiell motioned for her to buckle up, and he backed the car into the lane, steering them toward the estate.

"It's awfully convenient that your family's property is right here, next to my uncle," Bree mused. "Another one of your infamous coincidences-slash-universal-truths, do you think?"

Dash shrugged. "I suppose. Ullabreagh is one of my father's only successes, though he can hardly take credit for it. He won it in a card game. We've no real connection to the place. A real moneymaker. No thanks to him."

Bree's curiosity was piqued.

"Who'd he win it from?"

"A school friend."

"Isn't your family English? How'd your dad come to have a presumably Irish school friend? I thought the English and the Irish didn't mix."

"You've got to consider the Anglo-Irish—a lot of old blood that gained estates during the Plantation resettlements and so forth, in exchange for their loyalty to the Crown. Even with intermarriage, those families are more English than not. Everyone all chummy at boarding school and university. Even the Catholics. The ones in England often kept their holdings here. Not so surprising, after all."

"It's very confusing," Bree murmured.

"Ireland? Or the peerage?"

"Both."

"Yes, I suppose you're right. Here we are."

They pulled through an immense, granite Georgian gate and crept up the gravel lane through an expanse of emerald-green lawn. Around a curve, the house itself came into view—a big, square pile, shimmering in the afternoon sun. A forest of blazing oranges and yellows spread out behind it.

"It's gorgeous," Bree whispered.

"It is," Dash acknowledged. "Takes a lot of effort to keep it up, mind you. But I think it's worth it. And the gardens! You'll see."

After Dashiell had twisted the arm of the concierge to secure them rooms, well away from the wedding crowd, he suggested they take a few minutes to freshen up before setting out through the grounds. At the prearranged time, Bree found him waiting for her in a sturdy pair of shoes in the grand lobby.

"I had a chance to look a few things over in the office while you were upstairs," he mentioned in a low voice as he led her outside. He waited until they were out of earshot of any of the groundskeepers before sharing what he had found. "Technically, Brian Donnelly's cottage is a dependency of Ullabreagh," Dash began, guiding Bree along the gravel paths through broken brick walls festooned with vines.

"What does that mean?"

"Donnelly doesn't own it. It's part of Ullabreagh."

"So?"

He smiled. "Another coincidence. I must be honest with you, Bree. I'm not sure if our location at Ullabreagh is sufficient to disguise our intentions. Technically, given the dependency, we will not leave Ullabreagh's grounds, even if we gain entry into Donnelly's home. But you know as well as I do that today's GPS technology can pinpoint our location within yards. So anybody keen to track us will know exactly where on Ullabreagh we have wandered. If they care to find out."

Bree frowned as she picked her way over some broken flagstones. They'd approached a terrace with a view over a dry ravine. She leaned against the balustrade, thinking through the implications of what he'd said.

"How did you find Donnelly's address, Dash?"

"I had to do some digging," he admitted. "It's not as if a former IRA fugitive would list himself in the phone book."

"Alleged," Bree insisted.

Dashiell patted her hand. "If it makes you feel better, my dear. Alleged." He wrapped his fingers around hers. She did not pull away.

"You had to look hard, then?"

"Yes, quite. If someone knew to look for Donnelly and has access to the same systems, of course they could find him. But they'd have to know to look for him. Which they won't, unless they are tracking everything we are doing, or already know everything about your past."

"In which case it won't matter."

"In which case it won't matter," he assented.

"And if they look up the address of Donnelly's cottage after we've been there?"

"Public records won't show anything but Ullabreagh. There is no record of his lease. His is apparently a private arrangement."

Bree turned from the terrace and began walking again. "Let's go, then. We don't have much time."

By the time they had made their way across the pastures, the sun was hanging low in the sky. The sheep parted for them, their lowing drifting across the grass in snatches carried away by the wind. The cottage glowed from across the field as the sun struck its whitewash.

"No doors on this side," Dashiell noted.

"It doesn't matter. A window will do just fine. This isn't a social call. I just need to get his attention, and get him to come out to talk."

"Looks like you won't need to," Dashiell muttered, nodding toward the cottage. The old man she'd met earlier was now stalking around the corner of the house, a rifle trailing from his hand. Dashiell and Bree instinctively raised their hands to show they meant no harm.

The man stood at the edge of the field, where the clover turned into a graveled yard, and squared off.

"I told ye once, you've no business here," he shouted, his voice carrying to them on the wind. "The man ye seek isn't here. Turn around and go back to the big house. Or wherever it is you came from."

Bree could get a good look at him now. He had a shock of white hair atop a weathered face. He was a big man, powerfully built, but the flesh under his eyes was puffy, his rugged face, once probably handsome, now jowly.

"We just want to talk to you," Bree protested.

"I've no interest in talking." He raised the gun to his shoulder in one swift move. This close, Bree could see it was no ordinary rifle.

"That's an Armalite," Dash whispered. "They were all supposed to be buried in concrete when the IRA gave up its arms."

"I mean no harm to you," the man shouted. "But I ask you to respect my privacy. Turn around like I told you and you can forget about me."

"But I . . ."

"I'm not asking ye again." They heard the click of the safety being released.

"Fiona would want you to talk with me!" Bree blurted out.

The man's head jerked as if he'd been slapped. He hesitated, lowering his gun with narrowed eyes.

"Fiona's dead," he growled. He raised the gun again. "Who are you to be speaking of my sister?"

"I'm Fiona's granddaughter. Meg's girl," Bree yelled. "Your great-niece."

The color drained from his face. "It cannot be."

She nodded, taking a step closer.

"Stay there," he commanded gruffly, holding out his hand as if to stop her as he shuffled backward. "Say your name. Tell me something true so I can know it's really you."

"My name is Briana," she choked out. She had only this one chance, she knew. Whether she was certain or not, she had to try, so the words started tumbling out of her mouth. "Your sister, Fiona, took a false identity to emigrate to the United States in the early seventies. She sent my mother, Margaret, over to the Norwood School in Bath. I was orphaned in a car crash that killed my parents in 1998. I had a half-sister who was in the same crash. I've spent my whole life wondering about my family. And now I've found you."

He stared at her, mouth agape. His body sagged, all the spirit knocked out of him. The gun dropped to his side. A lone tear trailed down his craggy face.

"Please," she said softly. Remembering, she fished the chain out of her shirt and pulled it over her head. "This was with me when I survived the car crash." She tossed the chain, with the battered tag from her diaper bag, across the expanse between them. The man caught it neatly with one hand and brought it up close to his eyes. Bree held her breath as he read, mouthing the words as he went.

He rubbed the name tag under his thumb, stunned. "They told me you were dead," he said, his voice breaking.

Silently, he turned on his heel and disappeared around the cottage walls.

Bree didn't wait for an invitation. She ran after him. She found him unlocking the front lock. He turned away from her and leaned his forehead heavily against the door.

He straightened, wiping his eyes on a handkerchief he pulled out of an oversize pocket in his waxed raincoat. With a great sigh he finally spoke. "I suppose that boy belongs to you. You might as well bring him in too."

The cottage was cozy, everything centered on a primary room that served as both kitchen and living room. Papers and books were piled haphazardly on nearly every flat surface. An iron woodstove tucked into an old fireplace served as the focal point. Dashiell had ducked through the doorway and looked like an overgrown Great Dane in such snugness.

Brian had stripped out of his jacket as soon as he'd walked in and now stood over a side table, pouring some whiskey into a teacup. His hand shook, spilling some of the liquor.

"Would you like some?" he waved the bottle in their general direction.

They shook their heads.

"Suit yourself. As for me, after such a shock, I believe a little nip is warranted. Sit down and tell me, Briana, how did you find me? And how did you come to know these things you've shared? This could be a ruse, after all. You could be one of those nasty Norwood spies, for all I know."

"You know about that?" Bree countered, surprised.

"Of course I do," Brian stated emphatically. He swallowed deeply of the whiskey before continuing. "We sent your mother there deliberately to try to infiltrate them and give us an upper hand against their double agents. As I said—you could be a spy and simply have read her files."

Bree flushed deeply, feeling the need to defend herself, but unsure if he would open up if he knew that they really were from Norwood.

"Then why are you talking to me, if that's what you think?"

Brian shrugged. When he spoke, his voice was ragged. "You look like her—even more like your da, from what I remember."

"You knew him?"

He looked at her quizzically. "Of course. We spent many an hour together. They used to visit me. I used to dandle you and your older sister on my knee, I did."

Bree let that sink in.

"At my age, I suppose, I wish to think the best and hope that something good has survived out of that mess. So, tell me, how did you find me, and perhaps more important, why? Where did you get that American accent?" He looked pointedly at them both. "While you're at it, explain to me who your young man is, here. I don't trust the silent types."

For once, Bree realized, Dash was being discreet, waiting to follow her lead.

"It's hard to explain, but you're right, in one way. Dashiell and I are from Norwood." Bree gauged her uncle's reaction. He cocked his brow.

"The boy, too?"

When she nodded, he whistled low. "Now, isn't that something? A man at Norwood." He gripped his tiny teacup even more tightly in his massive hand and took a swig. "Things must be desperate for the Kingdom, then."

Bree ignored the barb and continued. "It's a long story of how we got there. Perhaps easiest to say we were coerced into it and did not know what Norwood really was—is—until it was too late. The advantage is that it gave me unexpected access to my mother's files. That's how I even came to know who she was. From there, it was a DNA test. That was Dash's idea. We found you in one of the government databases."

Her uncle snorted. "I always knew those bastards would hang on to that kit. Go on."

"When my parents were killed, I somehow ended up in an American orphanage. I still haven't pieced that part together. But that's why I have this accent."

"They let you into Norwood even though you're American?"

"The administration knew of her British ancestry," Dash interjected. "We aren't sure how much they know of her real identity."

Brian frowned. "If they are manipulating you, it means you cannot trust them. They are likely watching you even now. Just like your mother. You play a dangerous game. You've put me in danger by coming here."

Bree tried to ignore the wave of guilt that swept over her. "Can you tell me about her? And about my sister and father? I know almost nothing." She tried to keep the pleading sound out of her voice.

Brian poured himself more whiskey and settled into his rocking chair. "Where shall I begin?" he murmured, taking a small sip. He seemed to rummage around in his brain, determining exactly where to start his tale. With a sigh, he set aside his cup and leaned forward. "I guess with a bit of history.

"Our entire family, the Donnellys, were staunch republicans. I don't mean Republicans like you mean in the States—not like a political party. I mean it in the Irish sense—we believed in our own freedom, in independence from Britain and the unity of the island. We lived in Bogside—that's in Derry—along with most of our lot. When the Troubles began, my sister, Fiona, was just a teenage girl, but she was fierce. She wouldn't join the women's council—she insisted on joining up in the army. 'I'm as good as any man,' she said. And she was right. She was tougher than most."

He smiled ruefully, his eyes glistening for a moment.

"She started off as a courier, removing hot weapons—knives and guns and the like—or carrying bombs to the cells that would later deploy them. Then she did some bank robbing for us, so we'd get funds to upgrade our rifles. We'd let them dwindle, you see; and besides needing more weapons, we needed modern guns to fight the unionist paramilitaries. By the end, she was helping us ferry people across the border when we needed. She was a good driver, see. And one of her boyfriends had access to a car."

He dragged his thumb over a crack in the teacup.

"When you say ferry people, what do you mean?" Bree prompted.

"When we found touts—traitors—she helped us make them disappear." Brian's voice was gruff. He did not look Bree nor Dashiell in the eye. He went on, staring into his lap.

"It was a different time then. There were weeks when a dozen lads would die, when the only social life we had was the attending of wakes. The city was choked with rubble and concertina wire. The young folk had no prospects—fighting back seemed to make sense. We did what we had to do to survive. Things were getting hot. When Fiona's friend Peggy was killed in a pub bombing, she decided to get out. That's when she took Peg's name, and her papers. She disappeared into the Chicago Irish community, where she met your grandfather and raised your mam—Meg. Back then you could do that, still—just disappear. The government didn't have all the bells and whistles to track you and check your identity and the like. So that's what she did. All the while she was helping us on the other side, raising funds and helping us to rearm. Now, Meg knew nothing of this, knew nothing of her family back in Ireland, until her da died. It was then that we told her everything, and she decided to go back to the UK and try to fight for the cause of Irish freedom."

"Why would she do that?" Dashiell interjected. "Someone who was raised as an American and knew nothing of her ancestry?"

Brian lifted his head and smiled. He drained the cup of whiskey before he answered. When he spoke again, his eyes twinkled wryly. "I came to her myself to suggest it. Believe it or not, I can be very charming when I try. And remember, she'd been surrounded by a sort of Irish nationalism her whole life, whether she was aware of it or not. No doubt the memory of her father motivated her.

"Our plan was for her to infiltrate Norwood as a nanny candidate and get placed inside the UK Ministry of Defence to see if she could detect their plans against the IRA. It was a long shot—she'd need to succeed in the program, and get placed in the right spot. But we knew that it happened to fit Norwood's needs too—we'd heard chatter they thought they had a double agent problem and needed to figure it out. We banked on them being desperate, if you like, and it turns out, it worked. They were willing to gamble, placing an Irish American girl to spy on an MI5 leader who was fronting an operation inside the north of Ireland. None of us figured on her falling in love with him, and finding her loyalties torn, but she did."

When she finally spoke, Bree was breathless. "She really loved my father?"

Brian nodded. "She was defiant about it. But she was so honest—which is a strange trait in a spy, let me tell you—she had to tell me the truth. Would have been easier for her to say it was all make-believe, but she wouldn't have it any other way. She needed me to know. It infuriated us, it did—especially at first. But she loved him, and that made her actions both doubly effective and doubly risky."

Brian got up to stoke the fire. Before he took his seat in the rocking chair, he topped off his empty cup.

"Can you tell us who her father was?" Dash prompted.

Brian took a long sip before he answered.

"I'm surprised you haven't already found him. He was posing as a gems and precious metals importer out of Hong Kong. Apparently his family had been in the diplomatic service and had spent a good part of their time there, back in the day. He has some Irish in him, he did, so he was able to convince the leadership that he was truly on their side. His cover as a tradesman enabled him to launder money for the IRA. What he was trying to do from there, Meg never told me. David Hutton was his name."

Dash gasped. "Hutton. Of course."

Brian raised a brow. "You recognize him, then?"

"The Huttons owned Ullabreagh."

"They did, and then, they didn't. I never did learn the whole story of how the property passed hands—it happened while I was underground. But now you know how I ended up here. It was your father's doing to arrange me a safe house here, Briana, holding aside a place right here on the property, in perpetuity, in case I ever needed it. The new owners honored the contract—never gave me any bother when I washed up on their doorstep one day. Didn't ask too many questions, either, for which I was grateful."

"I think I'll have a glass of that whiskey now," Dash choked out. Bree imagined his mind was now racing with questions. Brian obliged him, pouring Dash a cup while the words kept tumbling out.

"Of course, your parents tried to keep their marriage a secret. It was against the Norwood rules, for one thing. So, they had a parish priest marry them, right over in the next village, using false names. You can find it in the registry—you're smart enough, you'll find them in a flash. It was a little hard on him, with the whole Church of England thing, but he bore it well. The priest was discreet. He knew a thing or two about what was going on and wanted to help Fiona's daughter out. Priests were like that, then. Part of the cause, themselves.

"David had a little girl already—Rowena. Meg loved her, too. In fact, she bore a look of your mother. If you didn't know it, you would have thought she was Meg's own. A right spitfire, that one, but much too small for her age. You were closing in on her by leaps and bounds, you were. But size didn't hold her back. No, sir. Saw her knock a little bully out cold one day, when she was only but four or five. And climb! Oh, she could shimmy up a tree or a wall like she was a wild beast. Daring, she was. Brave. Rowena was one after my own heart. And you, Briana—well, you were named for me." He said it with quiet pride.

Bree was overwhelmed. Dash took her hand and patted it, picking up the questioning.

"Did Hutton know his wife was a spy?"

Brian looked reflective.

"Now, that is a fine question. I don't rightly know. I never could tell if they knew about what each other was up to. I suspect it was understood, but unspoken between them. Meg was very clear with me—she was convinced he was harmless to the IRA. Maybe even a bit of a bumbler. Made me promise to call off the dogs, as it were."

Bree exchanged a glance with Dash. From the look on his face, she could tell that the idea that Brian had the clout to direct IRA operations was not lost on either one of them. Before they could ask a follow-up question, however, Brian turned to Bree in earnest.

"Your mam and da had the wind knocked out of them when the Good Friday Agreement was signed. It was like they didn't know what to do with themselves anymore. That was the beginning of the end for them, I always thought. Like many of us."

"Why is that? I would think they would support peace, in the end. Didn't the IRA negotiate the terms directly?" Bree asked.

"No!" Brian cried, angry spittle underscoring his emotion. The veins in his forehead pulsed. He stabbed the air with his finger, punctuating the word. Then he took a deep breath. "You'll forgive me, Briana. I forget you don't really know what happened back then. The newspapers, not to mention the history books, were all co-opted. The Brits wanted it to seem fair, but they got their way, didn't they? And the American politicians, they just wanted a diplomatic win so they could pat themselves on the back. Everything reported was twisted and false, propping the Agreement up so's to rush it through and get the people to swallow their doubts.

"But know, both of you, that the Agreement was no work of the IRA. The IRA was betrayed by Sinn Fein and that Gerry Adams. For years and years we fought, vowing that we'd not give up until the island was united and the British were gone. All those deaths. All those murders. Adams made us do unspeakable things. And for what? So he could sit in Parliament and write books? Bah. None of us wanted it. We were tired, but we didn't want to give up! It was Adams who wanted the politics. He did it for himself. The rest of us were left to pick up our broken lives, while he claimed he'd never even been a part of it, washing his hands clean of us. Gerry Adams, not a member of the IRA? He was our leader, don't you know! A travesty, it was. A lie.

"Your parents, now, I know they felt the same. They didn't have to say so—I could see it in their eyes. Your mam would have felt the smart of the injustice. And your father? Well, maybe he'd come round to some different views, maybe not. But just think on it: What does a spy do when their reason for spying goes away? What does an old soldier like myself do, for that matter, when everything you've fought for is ripped away, a meaningless piece of paper put in its place? I tell you, they were both lost."

Brian paused. He looked at them and Bree could see he realized how rattled he'd made them with his deluge of history and venom, by his litany of accusations that had been officially denied, over and over again, by Sinn Fein and Adams himself. He sagged into his chair, embarrassed.

"Briana, my girl. I'm sorry. You do need a bit of whiskey in you. I know this must all be a shock." He busied himself at the table, exaggerating the fuss over the pour while he calmed himself, before turning to press a glass upon her.

She gulped it down, the fire in her throat causing her to splutter.

"I forget myself, Briana," Brian continued, his voice now steady. "You didn't live all this. It is a lot for you to take in, I'm sure."

"Thanks," Bree choked out, sheepishly.

The old man patted her hand awkwardly. "Don't thank me. You're family. You will learn to keep your whiskey with time. Donellys always do. Now—where was I? Ah, the Agreement. Yes, your parents were at loose ends there for a while. That psychologist at the clinic I go to, if she had known them then, she might have even called it depression, like. And then, just as sudden, they were not. They were skittish, maybe, but their spirits seemed to lift. They were up to something, at the end—I just couldn't tell what it was. They seemed to travel quite a bit, even left you girls with me a few times. Can you imagine that? They thought being in Derry with me was safer than wherever they were going. Seemed to be off to the Orient somewhere."

Bree noticed that the more Brian drank, the steadier his hand became. His eyes flashed brightly now as he remembered.

"And then, they took you on a trip. They said not to worry, they'd be back in a dash. I believed them—after all, they left behind that little dog of yours. Next thing I knew, some lady, very English, all dressed up in a tweedy suit, was at my doorstep asking me to confirm identities and informing me that you all had perished. There was nothing left of you. The flames, she'd said . . ."

His voice broke.

"I'd buried a good many in my time, but that . . ." His voice trailed off. "It was the hardest to think of you babes. But now you're here." He reached out and patted Bree's knee while he cleared his throat. "I don't suppose we'll ever know if Rowena made it out alive too?"

Bree gripped his hand. "Someone has told me she did. We just don't know where she is. Or under what identity we might find her."

Brian shook his head gravely. "Know this: It was no accident. The English never can be trusted, Bree. Why they killed your parents, well, that could be simply in retaliation for what they did during the Troubles. Fair enough. But to break up sisters like that? And take you away from your family? And I thought . . . well, I never knew, did I? I never knew if it was your parents' work that brought that tragedy upon your heads, or if it was mine. I never knew for sure."

His eyes watered over. He dashed the tears away with his handkerchief, dabbing at his purply cheek before brusquely shoving it back in his pocket.

Bree reached out and touched Brian's other hand, its gnarled knuckles still wrapped around the delicate china cup. Her fingers trailed across them, misshapen and scarred. She noticed most of his fingers were missing their nails.

The fire crackled. Bree saw that the sun was almost below the horizon.

Brian cleared his throat and withdrew his hand, abandoning the cup.

"You'll stay for tea and spend the night," he insisted gruffly, the moment lost. "Fiona would have had my head if I didn't show you proper hospitality."

He hoisted himself out of the chair and busied himself at the cookstove.

Dash and Bree looked at one another, not daring to say a word. Bree suspected their thoughts were the same. Was it possible that this kindly old man, a little too fond of his drink, had committed the atrocities to which his arrest record pointed? The casual way in which he referenced Fiona's own terrorism made Bree uncomfortably certain that he had. What's more, did Brian's story point to more China connections as they unraveled the mystery of her parents' last mission? And why was he so certain that the English were responsible for her parents' deaths?

The rattling of pans interrupted her thoughts.

"I hope you like a good fry. I didn't plan on having guests."

As they ate, Bree peppered her uncle with questions about the family. He counted off the losses they'd endured in their quest for independence as if he were fingering the beads of his rosary. Generation after generation, the Donnellys had given up the best of their youth to the fight for freedom. His grandfather had been hung for treason. His father had left him half-orphaned as a child when he'd been shot down in a street brawl. His own brother had died mishandling a car bomb in London. Another had nearly wasted away in a floating prison maintained by the British. They'd had so many cousins in prison at the same time that they had formed a singing group and tried to raise money releasing bootleg concert recordings to the radio.

It was a recitation of grief. And of pride.

And then there was Brian himself—always on the run, from safe house to safe house, never sure whom he could trust, except for his sister, Fiona, who burned bright as a star in the dark night of the occupied North.

He'd made it for two decades, mostly fine, until the retroactive arrests—the witch hunts—began in the nineties.

He stared, eyes burning, at Bree, as if he was afraid she was a mirage, or an image conjured up by his drunken brain.

"You know the meaning of your full name, do you?" Brian prompted her.

Bree smiled. "Dash told me."

"A warrior! It's no accident. But I always found it peculiar that Rowena was named in that same manner, with a nod to history and myth."

"Not quite the same," Dash added, quietly.

Bree looked at them both, puzzled. "What do you mean?"

"Rowena was a spy, she was. A princess and a spy. 'The Mother of England,' they called her. Won Kent with a kiss." Brian was slurring his words.

"She was a mythological figure, blamed for betraying the Britons to the Saxons with a bit of seduction. A femme fatale, you would say," Dashiell explained. "Rumored poisoner. Definitely powerful. Later conflated with a witch. Some historians believe she was the model for Morgan le Fay."

"She was real, and powerful!" Brian protested. "Just as powerful as Bellona. She just used her power in a different way. Don't let anyone tell you any different. Besides—anybody who dupes the Brits gets my vote." Brian sloshed the whiskey over the sides of the cup as he raised it in a mocking toast.

"The Saxons became the British," Dash muttered tersely.

Bree shot Dashiell a worried look. He sighed.

"All right, man," Dash said. Bree could tell he was making an effort, brushing aside his irritation as he rose to stand. "Maybe it's time we got you to bed."

Brian didn't protest. He simply drained his cup.

With some effort, Dash managed to get the old man up from the table and bustle him into the tiny, sterile bedroom, tucking the covers in around him. By the time he emerged, Bree had already cleaned up the sparse dishes and was busying herself washing the pots and pans.

"Is it safe to stay here, do you think?" she asked.

"If you're talking about Norwood—it won't matter. We're still on the estate. If you're asking about him . . ." He shot a worried glance at the closed bedroom door. "I'm rather worried what might happen if we don't stay. Though, I would bet this isn't the first night he's drunk himself into a stupor."

He dropped an absent-minded kiss on the top of Bree's head. Bree froze, unsure how to process this bit of affection, but Dash didn't seem to notice, simply giving her shoulder a squeeze as he walked past, still talking.

"I'll dry the dishes. You'd better disarm that rifle and hide it away. Just in case he wakes up and doesn't remember who we are."

It took a while for the shouting and thrashing to break through Bree's consciousness. The day's high emotions had taken their toll, and she'd fallen into a heavy sleep, the discomfort of sleeping upright in a chair no challenge to her exhaustion.

A crash, the sound of something breaking into shards, finally jolted her awake.

She jumped to her feet. A thud drew her attention toward Brian's room. In just a few seconds, she crossed the tiny sitting room and pushed her way through the bedroom door.

The moon illuminated the spare room—the curtain rod and curtains having been torn off the wall, pockmarked plaster giving evidence to the violent power that had wrung them away, leaving the window bare.

Brian was writhing wildly in his bedclothes.

Bree moved to rush to him and gasped—she'd stepped on something sharp. She bent down and checked her foot; when she did, she noticed the shards of porcelain flung across the floor as if there'd been an explosion. He'd knocked over—or maybe thrown—a bedside lamp, shattering it and sending sharp fragments all over the room.

"No!" Brian was swinging at ghosts, his eyes open and terrified.

She kicked what porcelain she could aside and lunged for the bed. Brian shrieked and lashed out, landing his meaty fist on her chin. Bree was stunned, gasping for breath.

"Get away from me, you!" he shouted. He tried to climb away from her, scrambling from the covers to crouch on the bed, pressed against the Crucifix that hung on the wall as the room's only decoration.

He doesn't know it's me, she realized.

She fingered her jaw and quickly checked her teeth. One loose. She edged herself off the bed, watching her uncle.

"Brian," she soothed. "It's me, Briana. Come down. Let me help you."

"I can't breathe. For the love of God, let me breathe," he begged, his hands now held awkwardly in front of him as if somehow he was bound, the hulking man now weeping.

"Shh," she whispered. "I'm coming to help you now."

"My hands," he cried. "My hands." He held them, outstretched. A wet spot spread down the front of his pajama bottoms.

"Help me," he moaned.

She eased closer.

"Briana, be careful," Dash said sharply from behind her. "He seems to be in some sort of waking nightmare."

"I've got it," she said, brushing away Dashiell's concern.

"Brian," she began, now at the bed's edge.

Before she could continue, her uncle kicked crazily, losing his balance as he tried to fight her off. He bounced crazily on the bed, the old springs protesting with a metallic squeal. She flung her body on top of his, wrapping him up.

"Shh, I've got you now. Let me help," she breathed into his ear. "Let me help you."

Dash came around the other side to help. Together they held Brian until he stopped resisting, his body finally giving up its anger, now wracked with sobs.

"My hands," he wept, holding them out and sobbing harder. She looked at Dashiell, confused. He shrugged, just as bewildered.

"Shall I loosen them for you?" she asked, guessing.

"Oh, would you?" Brian moaned. "And the hood. Take off the hood so I can breathe. I promise not to look upon your face. I won't, I swear on the Virgin Mary." He held his hands out higher and closed his eyes tight.

Pity stabbed her heart.

She touched his hands and wrists all around, wanting him to feel the reality of her skin, her warmth, hoping it would break through his fear.

"There, all done now. Your hands are free." She held her hand against his cheek. "And your face, too. You can breathe now, Brian. You can breathe."

He took a deep, tremulous breath. "You're an angel. Thank you."

She sat back on her heels and mouthed to Dashiell, *Let him go*.

Dash released him and stepped away, watchful lest Brian panic and lash out again against his imaginary tormentors. But the fight had left him. The old man wept like a little child, his arms—now free of the bindings generated by his terrors—wrapped around his knees. He rocked back and forth, unable to come to the surface of reality.

"Why don't you step outside. I'll try to clean him up, and I'll take care of the floor. He must have a change of clothes in here somewhere," Dash offered, running his hand through his hair, perplexed.

"Thank you," Bree stated quietly. She picked her way through the pieces of broken lamp and closed the door softly behind her.

She put a kettle on the stove to make some tea. While she waited for the water to boil, she washed and bound the puncture on her sole with strips from a ripped dishtowel and wiped up the bloody footprints she'd made. Soft murmurs were the only sounds coming from Brian's room. By the time she'd poured the tea, Dash was emerging, weary.

"Ah. Perfect," he said with real gratitude, sinking into a chair at the kitchen table. He took a deep draught of the tea, not waiting for it to cool. He winced slightly, but barely blew over the cup before he took another, more careful, sip.

"What was that, Dash? It seemed he was reliving some sort of torture or interrogation from when he was in prison." Bree shuddered. "You noticed his hands, didn't you?"

"Yes." Dash nodded.

"I wanted to ask, but . . ." She paused. "It makes sense. The drinking. The nightmares. Something bad happened to him."

"Or . . ."

"Or what?" Bree asked, confused.

"Or, he may have *done* something bad. He was no angel, Bree. Surely you can see that now? Your family was deeply compromised during the Troubles, and before, it sounds like. He could be wracked by guilt."

"Guilt didn't smash his knuckles and pull out his fingernails!" Her voice rose sharply.

"Bree. I am not blaming anybody. I'm not taking sides. I'm just saying that there were plenty of nightmarish things all around him, probably his entire life. More than enough to cause trauma and stress after the fact. Us showing up here today may have dragged things to the surface."

"They took everything from him!"

Dash put down his teacup and rubbed a hand across his weary face. "Briana, please. Picking a fight with me is not going to make things better."

"I'm not picking a fight!"

He laughed grimly. "You forget—I've taken the same psychology classes as you. I am not going to argue with you over this. You heard him talk about his doctor earlier. The man clearly has post-traumatic stress disorder. It doesn't matter why. Let it go. In fact," he said, checking his watch, "you might as well begin dressing. We'll need to leave for the airport early if we're to make our flight.

Bree gaped. "We can't just leave him!"

"We must," Dash insisted. He began shoving his few things into the backpack he'd carried over for the night. "For his good, and ours, it's time to go. If we hurry, we might be able to stop off at that chapel Brian mentioned to look for your parents' marriage record."

"We can't disappear before he wakes up, Dashiell. Just think what that could do to him."

Dash didn't look at her. "You won't keep him any safer by lingering here."

Bree's voice rose. "I won't have him ripped away—"

"He's right, my girl." Brian had emerged from his bedroom. He was rumpled, but fully dressed, his face gray with exhaustion. When he spoke again, his voice was firm. "It's not wise for you to stay here. We don't know who might be monitoring your movements. Your priority must be your own safety."

Bree blinked back tears. "But I just met you. I can't—"

"You can. I'll still be here, later. When it's a wee bit safer. You've done me a great service by coming here. You've given an old man a bit of peace of mind, knowing that you—and your sister—survived that crash. That is a gift, Briana. But with that knowledge comes a responsibility—my responsibility to see you safe. Your young man is right, it is time for you to go. I'll be fine here, I promise."

"But, you're not well."

He grunted. "Like many of my generation. But I get by. I've gotten by before you, and I will get by now. Perhaps better, even, knowing I've something to which I can look forward. Here," he said, reaching into his pocket. He drew out a small square and held it out to Bree, the tremors in his hand making the paper quiver slightly. "Maybe this will make the parting easier."

Bree took it from him and looked. It was a faded photograph, mostly sepias, golds, and soft greens. A family of four—the children, two young girls, still in arms.

"I destroyed almost all the records I had of my family when I went underground, but I saved this. I took it the last time I saw you. Thought you might like to have it, now. In exchange, I might ask to keep the tag from your nappy bag. So I'll know I wasn't dreaming."

Bree pored over their faces, searching their likenesses, hoping for recognition. The girls, with their shocks of red hair, looked so similar, and so close in size, they could have been twins. A sharp longing overtook her. Had her sister ever seen this photo, ever wondered at their resemblance? And then there was the woman who she now knew as her mother. The look of grim determination in the woman's eyes was one she'd seen staring back at her in the mirror too many times to count.

"You've a home now, Briana. If you ever need a safe place, you come here," Brian insisted, his voice cracking.

Bree threw herself into his arms, her eyes pricking with tears.

They crept into the ancient chapel, alone, just before dawn.

Small and hewn from rough stone, it squatted in a patch of green, the yard around it sinking from the pull of the generations of dead buried in the churchyard. They'd expected the door to be locked but the heavy wood gave way to their push with scarcely a groan.

There was not much to it. There were no pews, just simple chairs set up in orderly rows before the stark altar that stood atop a few steps at the end of the aisle. The stone floor was worn in ruts where, for hundreds of years, worshippers had trod to receive Communion and absolution.

"What are we looking for?" Bree whispered, her breath giving off a puff in the cold air.

"Some sort of records, from the sound of it. There's a door at the back of the vestry—perhaps they're in there?"

Their footsteps echoed on the stone as they strode to the door to investigate.

The door yielded to a narrow passageway lined with shelves, like a library. Bree trailed a finger across the spines of the books. It came away covered in dust.

"Look at that—from four hundred years ago, those are. Lucky for us, they are labeled. Let's find the ones from the 1990s," she prompted. They squeezed through the hall, pausing periodically to check their progress through the centuries and decades, until they found the right shelf.

"Right. We still don't know for what we're looking," Dash paused, thinking.

"Brian said we'd recognize it when we saw it," Bree recalled, puzzling it over. "Did they use their own names, do you think?"

"Only one way to know," Dash said with a shrug. "Let's start looking. You take the first volume, I'll take the second."

They squatted on the cold floor, poring over the books, the script the priest had used to record every birth, death, baptism, and marriage sometimes swimming in front of their eyes in the dim light.

"I can't believe someone was doing this by hand as late as the nineties," Dash grumbled. "This would be so much easier to search if it was a digitized archive."

"Here," Bree breathed, ignoring him, her finger tapping an entry. "I think this is it." She presented the open book to Dash. "Look here. Brian was right—easy to find, if you know what to look for."

"You're right!" Dash enthused. "Tricky, weren't they? I wonder if that was a common thing for spies, then, the way they handled their identities?"

Bree took back the book and pored over the entry. In neat cursive, the village priest had written out David McCarthy and Margaret Hutton, married before God, June 12, 1996. There they were, hidden in plain sight by a simple swap of surnames.

She traced her fingers over their names and, across the chasm of time, she felt a spark.

It was late when they returned to Jaguar House. As they crossed the threshold to the apartment, they turned on the light. Ruby was sitting in the common room, waiting.

She stood up and crossed the floor to close the space between them.

"It would be easier for me to cover your tracks if you tell me what you're doing next time," she spat.

Eyes flashing, she threw a manila folder at them. Bree, scrambling, watched as a sheaf of papers fell to the ground around them.

"You're lucky I was on the desk these last days. Next time, you might not be so lucky."

Bree knelt down and picked up one of the pages. It was a tracking report. She peered at the fine print at the top of the sheet—alphanumeric coding she did not recognize. Heart falling, she pulled another page, and another.

"They were watching us, Dash," she whispered.

"We always knew they would." Bree heard his words and took a deep breath, calming herself. "There's nothing wrong with us taking a romantic holiday, you know."

Ruby scoffed at him. "Don't be stupid. You weren't on holiday."

Dash grabbed a page from her, scanning it quickly. Blanching, he picked up another, then another. "Dear God. There were photos? How?" He looked at Ruby, bewildered. "Where did you get these?"

"I volunteered for extra hours this weekend. After all, you two were gone." Ruby looked pointedly at them. "I didn't believe you. So I asked for the intel desk. This is what came in."

"How were they able to get this?" Bree echoed Dash's question.

"How do you think?" she spat, disgust dripping from her voice. "Norwood has a trace on your credit cards. It looks like they planted cameras on the car you rented. They also bugged it. You'll find the transcript somewhere in there, too."

"Damn," Dashiell swore. "I thought I was so careful."

Ruby snorted. "You don't get it, do you? There is nothing you can do that they won't know about. The only question, really, is if they can interpret what they see. In this case, I swapped some of your old records out and doctored your personal tracker feed, as well. But the question remains . . . what were you two doing?"

"We told you, Ruby—we went to Ireland," Bree persisted. "To stay at one of Dashiell's family estates."

"Don't. Don't even try." Ruby crossed her arms. She stood over Bree, where she still squatted on the floor, surrounded by a mess of paper. "I listened to the tapes. I watched the film. I saw your coordinates. You were barely at Ullabreagh proper. You were looking for someone—who? What was the cottage? And that church you stopped at? What were you doing?"

Dash opened up his mouth, but Bree shook her head, sticking to her story. "It's what we said, Ruby. We just wanted to be together. The cottage is on the Ullabreagh property. We did some sightseeing on the way back to the airport. That's all."

Ruby twisted her lips together. "Fine," she spat. "Have it your way."

She turned on her heel and stomped her way back to the bedroom she shared with Bree. They flinched as the sound of the slamming door reverberated through the apartment.

Bree sighed and plopped down on the floor, defeated. "I hope . . ." She cut off, struggling with words.

Dash took her hand in his and finished her thought. "Let's hope Ruby really is on our side."

Chapter Six

MEG

1993, Outer London

It was too much house for a man and child alone.

The sprawling Victorian unfolded on a double lot that backed into the garden Trust, the branches of weeping willows catching the breezes that danced across the lush green grass of the grounds. Tucked here and there about the lawns were the vestiges of a different age, when gardens meant more than leisure. A quaint bridge crossing a burbling brook led to a faux-Chinese pagoda plopped down on the middle of the manufactured island on the other side. Elsewhere: a fake temple to a false goddess, the marbled pediments and columns modeled after stolen artifacts that could be found in the archives of the British Museum; a miniature Sphinx, surrounded by a pebbled square; urns on pedestals. All of it laid out in perfect geometry, the symmetry and precision of the design as if to say that this was, of course, the natural order. Paths were marked by rows of snapdragons, and pansies, roses, and boxwood marched inexorably across the garden with the discipline of the invading armies that had long ago unleashed the will of the British Empire upon the world.

Gardens like these had been monuments to colonial conquest and power. But now this one was being ruled—nay, terrorized—by the whims of a headstrong two-year-old girl.

"Rowena! We must be gentle with the flowers!" Meg repeated for what felt like the millionth time, swooping in to take the toy shovel from her charge's hand before she lopped the heads off more lilies. She guided the little girl back to her sandbox—so incongruous in the midst of such order and splendor—and plopped her down in the sand. The brindle hound poked his head out of the shrubbery and wagged his tail, bounding over to lick Rowena's face.

Meg watched, bemused, as the toddler scowled and raised a fist.

"And with the puppy, too, Rowena," Meg warned.

Rowena cocked her head and looked at Meg. Deliberately, she raised her arm again, threatening the dog. When Meg arched a brow and crossed her arms, she pulled her arm back again, as if to wind up for the punch. Then, she chortled with delight. Making a great show of it, she leaned over the puppy, wrapping her arms around his neck and planting a kiss on his nose. Pleased with herself, she held out her hand for the shovel. "Please?" she asked, smiling sweetly, her rosebud lips turning the "l" into "w."

Meg sighed.

"Little stinker," Meg muttered. It was hard to resist such cuteness. That's where the trouble all started.

"You know exactly what you're doing, don't you? You've got us all wrapped around your finger." The fact that Rowena was underdeveloped physically made her seem vulnerable and even more appealing, a fact Meg suspected her young charge knew subconsciously and used to her advantage.

Meg knelt down and placed the shovel in Rowena's pudgy fingers. "You've a rake over there too. We've only a few minutes before I need to take you in for dinner. Make the most of it."

Rowena began digging with earnest. Meg stood up, brushing the dirt and leaves off her khaki uniform, and collected her thoughts.

She was a few months into her posting. She'd expected to be in central London, closer to Thames House, where she knew MI5 was headquartered and where she suspected her employer, David Hutton, spent a great number of days. She had envisioned herself tailing him, snapping photographs that showed he was not who he said he was, proving beyond a doubt he was betraying the British. She had some vague notion of using that information against him, to advance her own causes, but she hadn't gotten that far in her planning.

That was because, in good fashion, he was keeping up the image of being a "simple tradesman," as he put it, and had installed her with Rowena in an old family home in the suburb of St. Margaret, telling her the commute was a small price to pay for Rowena's happiness.

"It's so peaceful," he had said with a smile. "I spent so many happy days there myself. The child needs stability. And since I travel so much, no sense in being in the city. It will be perfect."

Perfectly boring is more like it, Meg had thought.

"Won't she be lonely? Won't she need more stimulation and distraction to get over the absence of her mother?" Meg had prompted.

He had flashed a brilliant smile at her. "Her mother was never here much to begin with. A businesswoman, you know. Plus, Rennie will have you for that. This will be better. Trust me."

So, she had moved to St. Margaret and into Kinross House, joining Rowena; Ralph, the gardener; Edith, the cook; Christopher, the butler who waited upon them in the dining room; and a small army of housekeepers that seemed to melt into the woodwork whenever Meg walked into a room. There were nine bedrooms, as well as a warren of chambers referred to as "studies" and "parlors" or by names such as "the India Room" and "the Great Room"—most of which nobody but Meg ever went into. They ate mostly in a formal dining room, the food and china whisked in and out as if by magic.

She was living in an anachronism.

It had kept her busy, scouring the house for evidence during those first weeks, and she had loved exploring. The rooms were decorated whimsically, a riot of bright colors and what looked like several hundred years' worth of collections from travels all around the world. It was easy to get lost in wonder, picking through the bibs and bobs of it all, but now she had to face reality.

Her investigations had yielded nothing so far. She had searched every room except three: Mr. Hutton's bedroom, his ex-wife's attached dressing room, and Mr. Hutton's personal office, which he kept locked at all times.

She had to get access to those rooms, for if there was anything incriminating in Kinross House, that was where she would find it. And now was the time. She'd been warned by HQ that her handler was being switched sometime in the coming month, a change HQ hoped would stimulate "new thinking" on her, Meg's, part. Their impatience with her lack of progress was clear. And Mr. Hutton was due home this evening, after a stint of what he vaguely referred to as "foreign travel."

Meg looked up at the sky. The late summer sun was hanging low.

"Rowena," she called, stretching her hand out to the child. "Let's get cleaned up for your father."

———

They ate late, at least late for a child. Rowena was crabby, worked up by the hubbub and the promise of seeing her father.

"Here, child, have some apple slices," the cook soothed, trying to buy Rowena's cooperation while she hustled to finish her preparations for the adult dinner Meg would share with David later in the evening. Rowena thrust the apples away, knocking them off the table and onto the floor. Her deteriorating manners as the evening wore on were the reason she, more often than not, had to be fed separately and put to bed before a true dinner could be served.

"Want juice," she insisted, pouting.

Meg tutted at the two-year-old, stooping to pick up the mess while she tried to reason with her. "No, dearie, you mustn't have juice. That will spoil your dinner. And you'll spill it on your pretty dress. You don't want to ruin your dress before your father can see you, do you?"

Rowena stuck out her tongue. "Want *juice,*" she insisted, louder.

"You should know by now there's no reasoning with a toddler," a booming voice, full of amusement, called out.

David Hutton strode into the kitchen, filling up the already crowded space, where the cook was busy preparing dinner. He was in a sharp suit, only slightly rumpled from his travels. A shadow of fatigue threatened to emerge beneath his dancing blue eyes. He shoved his briefcase onto a cluttered countertop, not caring what he knocked over. He did not bother to acknowledge Meg, all of his attention focused on Rowena. She might have been wallpaper, Meg mused. Or the dog.

"What little girl could possibly want juice when her daddy has brought her something much, much better?"

"Daddy!" the girl shrieked with joy, wriggling in her booster chair, her outstretched arms demanding to be picked up.

He laughed. "Of course you can have juice," he told her as he held her in his arms and she clasped the sides of his face, holding his head in place and grinning broadly. Meg could see he was as delighted with his daughter as she was with him and gave not a whit about disrupting any semblance of the order and discipline Meg tried so hard to put in place at dinnertime. "My girl," he said, lifting her from the chair and sweeping her effortlessly into his arms. "Look at these red curls." He twirled a ringlet around his finger. "More spice than sugar, I'd wager." He planted a kiss on her sticky cheek. "Just like your old dad. Have you been naughty for Miss S?"

"No, Daddy," she promised solemnly, basking in his attention.

"And what sayeth the vaunted Miss S, herself?" he queried, finally acknowledging Meg. "You haven't been driven away by Rennie's escapades?"

Meg knew it wasn't a real question. "She's really no trouble, sir."

"Rennie's been good for Miss Shield," Rowena stated with a grin. "So, so good."

David chortled at that. "I'm sure you were, little bear. And so, here you go." He pulled some trinket from his suit pocket and plopped it in Rowena's hands. "Now, let Daddy get settled." He handed her off to Meg. "No rush on dinner. I need to unwind a bit and will help myself to a Scotch. Thanks for keeping her."

He did not bother to wait for either the cook nor Meg, to answer before he walked off to his rooms.

The kitchen seemed to shrink, pale, without him in it.

Rowena began to cry.

———

Meg took a calculated risk and was late for dinner. She couldn't stay in the background any longer. She needed to make him notice her.

She swept into the room, conscious of the way the silk of her slip dress hugged her body. It made her look delicate, she knew, the way it highlighted her neck, the deep navy setting off the pale luster of her skin. She'd let her hair down, the auburn tresses bouncing on her shoulders as if celebrating their freedom from the mandatory restrictions of her Norwood protocol.

David Hutton froze, his fork held midway between his plate and mouth, and stared.

"I'm so sorry to be late, Mr. Hutton," she murmured, casting down her eyes to watch his reaction through lowered lashes.

"It's quite all right," he said, fumbling a bit with his napkin as he recovered his composure and rose to greet her. He gestured to the place setting beside him. "Join me. I had cook put Rennie to bed for you—she was getting fussy. I don't suppose you mind."

She blushed. "I'm sorry you had to ask her, sir. I know Rowena is my responsibility."

"That wasn't a reprimand, Miss Shield. You were occupied, and cook was more than happy to do the job. Sit down before dinner gets cold."

Meg sat beside him, draping the napkin across her lap. The cook appeared from nowhere, artfully arranging the food upon her plate before discreetly removing herself. The flames of the candles in the stately cande-labra swayed in an unseen draft.

"Bon appetit," Mr. Hutton encouraged her. She nodded her head and sampled her food. Her employer quizzed her while she ate.

"So, it seems to me that, despite being overtired this evening, Rennie's overall temperament has improved under your care. She seems less clingy, and the housekeeper tells me the girl has become more obedient, less inclined to tantrums. Do you concur?"

Meg looked him directly in the eyes. Eyes, she noted, in whose blue depths one could get lost. "It's not for me to say, sir."

"Of course, it is for you to say, Miss Shield. You are her nanny. And an expert in child rearing, educated at the finest establishment dedicated to the art of child development in this nation—nay, the world. I expect you to have an opinion. So, what say you?"

An impish grin curled the corner of her lips as she tried to fight a smile. "I'd say that Rennie's temperament is destined to be like her father's, no matter what I do."

"Well, what's that supposed to mean!" he blustered, halfway between amusement and dismay, setting down his glass so emphatically that the wine sloshed over the side, dotting the damask tablecloth.

"It means she is the spitting image of you. Her looks and mannerisms are yours—the way her cheek dimples when she giggles, or the way she furrows her brow and bites her lip when contemplating a challenge. She has your stubborn, insistent charm. Even the tendency she has to abuse physical objects—knocking the heads off flowers with her toy shovel, for example, or knocking over her blocks—to express her displeasure is yours." She gestured to the burgundy stain, seeping across the tablecloth, to prove her point. "She takes after you."

Now it was his turn to blush.

"More important," she continued, "she is a whirlwind of energy. Her mind is bright. She needs constant occupation lest she create a disaster simply out of boredom. She applies herself, her energy, so thoroughly to whatever is in front of her that she simply exhausts herself. Those tantrums? They are normal for a toddler, but hers are particularly acute. It's heartbreaking, really—her poor brain can't take the intensity of her curiosity and her emotions for the amount of time she demands it to sustain her. She hates to be alone, and she refuses to nap—if I try to force her, I find she's unmanned her entire wardrobe and turned every little outfit inside out, leaving them in a wrinkled heap on the floor by the time I go to wake her. Or she will do worse—shoving all the towels in the toilet, one day, rubbing lotion all over that poor hound dog another. So, we let her have her way. No naps. But by the end of the day she has simply wrung herself out."

She took a deep breath, squaring her shoulders before continuing.

"I see the shadows under your eyes when you come back from your business trips, Mr. Hutton. I see how spent you are. Like this evening. And I wonder if she gets that impulse, that restlessness, from you."

She hesitated. If she had overstepped her bounds, she could be ejected from the house and sent packing back to Norwood immediately.

Her employer leaned back in his chair, hands folded under his chin, eyeing her thoughtfully.

"You've been paying attention."

"I often find, sir, that one's role as a nanny extends to caring for the entire family, not just the immediate charge in question."

"Stop with this 'sir' nonsense. Please, call me David."

"If you'll call me Meg."

"Fair enough. Meg," he said deliberately, trying out her name. He stalled by refilling her wineglass. "Tell me what you mean. Speak plainly."

"I worry about you," she whispered, staring hard at her plate.

With a start, she realized it was true. She forced the idea to the back of her brain, to deal with later. She looked up and kept speaking, her voice stronger now, assertive. "And she needs you. She has lost her mother. You cannot let her fear to lose her father, too. It is too much for a child to bear."

He tilted his head, considering her. Frustrated and tired, he rubbed his eyes.

"Did you lose your parents, Meg? Is that why you care so much?"

Meg shrugged noncommittally. She knew her employment file had been doctored to make her appear a sympathetic orphan, hoping to arouse his protective instincts.

He threw his napkin down on the table, less a sign of anger than of exasperation.

"I have a business to run. Responsibilities. What do you propose I do?"

"Hire others to help you, so you can spend more time here. With us," she said, faking herself stumbling over the words. "I mean, Rennie."

He looked at her speculatively.

"Or," she said, acting as if the idea had just come to her, "you could take us with you. I am more than competent to travel with a child."

"I'm sure you are. But these travels . . . well, they are no place for a child."

"Are you so sure?"

He closed his eyes and slumped back into the chair. The candlelight flickered, exaggerating the lines in his face and making his five o'clock shadow look that much darker. She felt a pang of protectiveness for him and wondered what was carving such deep worry into his skin.

He chuckled, shaking his head ruefully and opening up his eyes. He took a deep draught of his wine and pushed away from the table.

"You are full of surprises, Miss Shield."

"Meg."

He laughed, again, a tad uneasy. "You always give me something to think about. Even in our first interview. Tonight is no exception. Indeed, your presence this evening—this conversation, your insights—proved definitely worth the wait." He looked at her appreciatively, before tearing his eyes away. "I will give your proposal consideration. In the meantime, I beg you . . ."

He stood awkwardly behind his chair, staring at some indeterminate spot halfway down the long dining table.

"Yes?"

"Please do not worry for me. I will take care. I promise you."

Doing her best to keep her face blank, she watched his discomfort, her heart in her throat. This would be the decisive moment. He turned to her, locking her gaze as he continued, his voice rough.

"It does me good to know you notice. I will not take your concern lightly."

She beamed at him, bestowing him with her most brilliant smile, and knew that she had won.

She had accomplished a lot in a very few short months, Meg thought with satisfaction as she walked through the empty house.

David had given her the set of master keys so that she could oversee the packing of the estate. He had gone ahead to Ireland to ready his house for their arrival, taking the hound with him.

"It will be small," he had warned her. "No servants, I'm afraid. But I suspect you will manage."

"I always do," she'd assured him.

They were almost ready now. The furniture—too massive and too much for where they were headed—was covered in sheets to protect it from dust. The few pieces they'd designated to be taken with them were marked with tags for the movers to pick up. Rowena's toys had been boxed up and shipped ahead, a small selection of her favorites set aside in a tiny rucksack for her to take with her on the plane.

Meg's new handler had been pleased; at least that was what she'd written. Meg had yet to lay eyes upon the woman. This one, so far, seemed to prefer discreet messages in code, left at designated safe locations—"dead drops," in spy industry speak—with the strictest instructions to destroy upon reading, or the occasional phone call in an out-of-the-way public booth.

The change of handlers had been sudden, Norwood's warning notwithstanding. Her old handler had simply disappeared without a word, the replacement slipping into place without a beat nor even a mention of her predecessor. Meg was learning to read the subtleties of tone in the questions and instructions that her new handler left, feeling ridiculously like a young schoolgirl seeking a teacher's approval as she pored over the messages. Sometimes they seemed abrupt, even angry. No, that might not be fair. Cold might be better. But, then again, Meg reasoned, the woman must have other cases to attend to and wasn't there to coddle her. Meg had taken a quiet satisfaction in conveying her success when David had finally opened up to her and explained that he was working in Ireland, and that he wanted her and Rennie to join him there.

What he was doing in Ireland, he hadn't bothered to explain. But Meg didn't care. That was her job to discover. That he was bringing them there to join him was a massive win, Meg knew. It would put her right in the center of things, giving her the opportunity to really surface his clandestine activities.

When her handler had pressed her as to how she'd done it, she'd demurred. "He simply wants more time with his daughter," she'd explained. "Though it is strange that the ex-wife continues to remain out of the picture. I don't think she was even consulted about the move. She must have been a real terror—no one ever speaks of her. I haven't picked up a lick of gossip, not even in the kitchen."

Meg drew the handler's last message out of her pocket. There was something strange about it, but she'd been unable to pinpoint it and was loath to burn it until she had isolated what was niggling at her brain. She scanned it again, pressing the creases flat as she read the questions. *How is the child reacting to the move? Does the child ask about her mother? Is the child taking a liking to Meg, herself?* A few more questions about David Hutton's business affairs. Nothing about what she should look for upon arrival in Derry, just that the handler would resume contact once Meg had settled in.

Odd. But perhaps—given her cover and the fact that, as far as the handler knew, her presence in Northern Ireland was completely dependent upon the child's happiness—understandable.

Meg dropped the message into the fireplace and set it aflame. As she watched it turn to ash, she fiddled with the chain around her neck and drew out the ring that she wore close to her heart. She slipped it off the chain and on to her ring finger.

David had been so excited to present her with the diamond. He had cautioned that people would talk—that they would be better off waiting to be public after they were away from gossiping servants and nosy neighbors. Meg had her own reasons for keeping their engagement a secret: She knew the handler might have eyes on her and didn't want to risk being taken off the case for breaking Norwood's rules. She didn't know this handler well enough yet to know if she could sell a story about the cover demanding a wedding—a successful seduction leading to a sham marriage.

She held her fingers out to the window and admired the way the diamond sparkled in the late afternoon sunlight before putting it away.

She poked the ashes in the hearth, making sure there was nothing incriminating left behind. Then, she resumed her walk through the rooms, making sure everything was just so, until there was only one room left for her to inspect: David's study.

She turned the key in the lock and swung the door in.

He'd packed it up himself. It was sparse, now—but then again, she'd nothing to compare it to. She'd never been inside before.

She walked idly around the room, pulling drawers, opening cabinets, trailing her finger along ledges to seek disruption in the trail of dust— searching for signs of what had disappeared, anything that might give a clue as to what David Hutton was really doing in Ireland.

Empty. Everything empty. Drawer after drawer of file folders, picked clean.

He'd left some picture frames on a shelf, forgotten in a corner. She picked them up. An older couple, standing stiffly on the steps of a manse she'd never seen—his parents, whom she recognized from other photos but had yet to meet. Another snapshot of what looked like schoolmates, sweaty and disheveled, clearly fresh from the rugby fields. And a formal one of him in his robes at university. And then this last one.

She picked it up, curious.

They posed behind a baptismal font. David held an infant, pale with a halo of fine reddish hair, in his arms. The infant—a girl, by the look of the bows—was swathed in satin and lace, cascading like a waterfall from her body; her tiny fists outstretched and wavering as she protested her confinement.

Rennie.

In the photo, David beamed, proud.

On his other side stood the figure of a woman. She was dressed in heels and a tweed suit, her angular body stiff and awkward as he clamped her at his side, as if she didn't want to be there, a Chanel purse clutched in front of her body like a shield, her hands rigid like claws.

It didn't look like the body of a woman who had recently given birth, a body that had nurtured a life. It didn't even look like the body of someone who wanted to be a mother, the space between her and her infant daughter an aching gulf in the photograph as she turned her body slightly away.

The woman's head had been ripped out of the photo.

"Poor wife. Erased. Disappeared," Meg murmured.

She set the frame back on the shelf and turned away. David would be hers now—hers to crack open like a safe, for his secrets; hers to love. Meg left the emptiness of the study and locked the room behind her with a sense of finality.

Chapter Seven

BREE

Present Day, Bath

"A warning, class. While collaboration is encouraged in your problem sets and even during your virtual disarmament sessions, tests are another matter. I cannot prove that any of you spoke to one another about last week's sessions, sharing details of the test," the *Boom!* professor warned, cutting into their headsets, "but I can suspect."

She paced behind a pair of students. Bree became aware of her presence only because the instructor had abruptly paused the program they had been accessing. Like her classmates, Bree had been in virtual reality mode, her gear simulating the force of a fifty-pound protective bomb suit and the weight of a virtual water cannon, the percussive force of which she was training on a series of digital pipe, suitcase, gas can, and flare bombs. Her goal was not speed, but precision—deactivation without explosion, no matter how long it took. On evenings like this, she and her classmates were excused from *Wonder Woman* due to sheer physical exhaustion.

"You might not actually be cheating," the professor continued. "After all, you two are astonishingly similar in your stupidity. Perhaps I shouldn't be surprised." She slapped some papers down next to two of Bree's classmates. "You correctly identified liquids and piping in the backpack you assessed for improvised explosive device status, but what you managed to 'disarm' was nothing but a bag full of personal lubricants and sex toys." She sniffed her displeasure while the rest of the class tittered underneath their goggles. "See me after class. The rest of you may resume your simulations. But not you, Parrish."

Bree swung off her headset and popped her goggles to the top of her head. "Professor?"

"I have a note here from the psychologist. It seems you haven't attended the last of your counseling sessions. You're wanted. Now." The woman thrust a paper at Bree. "Leave your gear. Staff will clean it up for you. Go on, then. Better to deal with the death of your roommate than brood over it."

"Stiff upper lip and all that," Bree muttered.

"Quite," she agreed. "On with you. You'll be expected, so don't dawdle."

Bree did, in fact, dawdle as she trudged across the campus yard toward the administration's main building. She had found the psychologist to be a bit unnerving, the way she sat in silence, waiting for Bree to speak. Bree had wondered what she was thinking, what she must think of her. She was one of the only people on campus who actually knew the supposed truth about her roommate Susmita's death—that Bree, herself, had shot her. Bree had been told that it was this woman's job to assess whether Bree was stable—more specifically, whether she could be trusted with any number of the weapons with which her fellow spy classmates trained, including her own gun, which had been confiscated from her as soon as she'd returned to campus from Alabama. But, so far, the psychologist had been strangely passive, littering the silence with observations and odd questions that felt to Bree like mines in a field.

She climbed the steps to the office in the back of the building and knocked on the door, which was slightly ajar.

"Come in, Bree."

The office was tiny, filled up by the love seat pushed against the window and the easy chair in which Dr. Pressle sat, her legs tucked neatly underneath her flowing paisley skirt. A diffuse light from a Tiffany-style floor lamp chased the shadows to the corners.

The cozy room should have seemed welcoming, but it felt like a trap.

"Please, sit down, Miss Parrish."

Bree obeyed, taking up as little space in the corner of the love seat as she could.

"It's interesting how you physically distance yourself from me. The same way in which you make yourself emotionally remote."

Bree scowled. "I'm not remote. I'm just quiet."

"Your files didn't note you as exceptionally quiet. It wasn't in the observations from your professors. Nor the field notes from your assignment in Turkey. Are you avoiding our conversations?" When Bree didn't answer, she shifted in her seat and leaned closer. "Were you quiet as a child, do you think?"

Bree shrugged. "I don't remember. Probably."

Pressle let the silence envelop them, waiting.

Bree sighed. "I didn't need to be loud. There was noise all around me, all the time. It was an orphanage. The only privacy I had was in my head."

"Do you like that? Being in your head?"

"It's not like it is a conscious thing. I just think a lot. I focus deeply."

Pressle nodded. "The bomb class you are taking requires that kind of concentration. One mistake and . . ." She let the implication settle.

"I find it soothing," Bree responded, boldly staring at Pressle.

"I hear they encourage you to become almost intimate with the bomb—I find that fascinating, don't you? Intimacy with an inanimate but highly dangerous object, in lieu of the danger of a real human relationship? But I digress . . . Miss Parrish, it seems you have a bit of the daredevil in you . . . a flair for it. Danger does not faze you, nor does the death of your roommate, it would appear."

Pressle stood up and turned to her bookshelf, running her fingers along the spines of the books, her fingers skipping lightly over the knickknacks and collectibles that littered the shelves, evidence of the doctor's travels.

"I find it curious, how little you want to talk about her. How little emotion you seem to have over your role in her death. Perhaps I am misjudging you, and you are simply keeping it inside. But if you are, how am I to release you back into service? It's a very tricky thing."

Bree sensed she was on shaky ground. "It was her or me," she said quietly. "I didn't want to do it. I had no choice."

"As it says in the file. So you feel no guilt?"

I feel guilt all the time, Bree thought to herself. *But not for the reason you think.*

Pressle turned, a gleam in her eye. "Do you remember your mother?"

"What?"

"Do you remember her?" Pressle tilted her head.

"Doesn't it cover that in that file of yours?" Bree picked at the edge of the love seat. "I don't remember anything about either of my parents."

"Curious about them?"

Bree shrugged. "I suppose."

"That would be natural. Have you ever actively searched for them, tried to find them? Gone online and looked for them, even?"

Bree's head whipped up. "What does that have to do with anything? With Susmita?"

"Just answer the question, Miss Parrish." Pressle pinned Bree in a hard, calculating stare.

"Sure, who wouldn't? But there's nothing to go on," she said, hoping her voice sounded the right bitter tone. "There's nothing there. No leads. I gave up on it a long time ago." On the inside, though, she felt a little panicked. Did Norwood actually know what she and Dash had been doing in Northern Ireland? *Don't give her anything,* Bree told herself. *Not a thing.*

"You and Susmita. Two motherless children. You had so much in common," Pressle speculated. "I bet it was hard when she betrayed you, turning on you like that, maybe even putting those children at risk. Betrayal and abandonment. Some say they are two sides of the same coin. It wouldn't be surprising if the whole incident dragged up very strong feelings about the loss of your mother. A lost friend and a lost mother. Very weighty stuff."

Bree swallowed hard. Whatever Pressle was digging at, she would get no satisfaction from Bree. She let the silence grow between them, determined to outwait the psychologist.

"Well." Pressle clapped her hands and smiled, a false bright grin that seemed grotesque on lips that had just spoken of the dead. "Hypothetically, the biggest obstacle to your return to the equivalent of active Norwood duty would be feelings of guilt. A sense of guilt at having pulled the trigger and *killing your own friend* might prevent you from engaging your weapon in a time of need in the future." She emphasized the words, testing whether she could wound. Bree sat impassively. "If you feel no guilt, no shame . . . if you feel what you did was necessary and just, then you will not be a risk to others if we clear you for future work. You are sure— still no nightmares? No other physical symptoms of distress?"

"No, ma'am," Bree said through gritted teeth.

"Then I can see no reason to delay authorization."

Bree sagged with relief—not so much for the authorization, as she knew it would be months before they would be redeployed for field work, as for the end to her counseling sessions with the doctor. She didn't wait. She pulled her bag together and made for the door. She'd already swung it wide when Pressle interrupted her.

"Miss Parrish—mother abandonment can cause all sorts of issues. Our society holds myths about motherhood—very powerful myths— and when our mothers don't live up to our expectations, it can unleash a torrent of feeling. The emotions can be contradictory. They can be nested like these little Russian dolls." She'd picked up a set of *matryoshka* off the bookshelf and began pulling it apart. "Grief." She touched the next doll, then the next, naming each layer with an emotion. "Shame. Longing. Hurt. Anger. Each emotion like a little secret to which our soul clings."

Bree stood frozen in place.

"As adults, we can react to these emotions in ways that are dysfunctional. We can have problems forming lasting relationships. We can accept abusive relationships, thinking that's all we are good for. Some develop anxiety, or even violent personality disorders."

The ground had shifted again under Bree. Suddenly, she felt like she might cry.

"My mother didn't abandon me," Bree croaked. "She was killed."

Pressle smiled. "You know where to find me if you need me in the future. Good night, Miss Parrish."

Dismissed, Bree fled.

Chapter Eight

MEG

1996, Northern Ireland

She was working the counter of the shop, straining to hear whatever the men were discussing in David's back room.

They operated three different companies out of this location in the more industrial part of Catholic Derry: a metals business, an import-export outfit, and a pawn shop. With the exception of the pawn shop, business had been slow. It was not the sort of location to attract much foot traffic—it was one of the lone survivors of the bombing campaign that had wiped out shops and warehouses a little over a year ago. But that hadn't stopped the steady stream of visitors in and out of the office where David did whatever David claimed to be doing as he transferred cash between the companies, in and out of accounts.

The sun had gone down. She should close things up, she knew, and make the short walk back to their flat, where she had left Rennie to be babysat by the neighbor so she could get a break. She peered into the playpen in the corner, where Briana was napping peacefully.

She was loath to leave without knowing what the men were discussing. So she took out her rag and began polishing the glass counter, once more, to see what she could learn.

Their deep voices were rising now, a heated debate coming to a crescendo behind the locked door. She frowned and rubbed harder.

Frustrated, she threw down the rag and tiptoed to listen at the door.

The men had been coming more and more frequently into David's shop. They didn't bother to introduce themselves, and David only referred to them as "trading partners," but she knew they were all IRA. They had a look about them that you couldn't miss—not after spending time with Uncle Brian and his cronies.

She had picked up their collective frustration with the lack of progress on negotiations—you didn't need to be a spy to do that, she conceded; it was plastered all over the local newspapers. And as David had shuffled money around, imaginary customers with massive orders had suddenly appeared on the books, large sums of money—often in dollars—had appeared and then vanished, while great boxes had materialized on their loading dock, only to be whisked away in the night.

It hurt, but was helpful, she sniffed, that David believed she couldn't do math. He didn't even bother to hide the extra copy of the books he kept in his office, the key to which he'd conveniently hidden in the obvious potted palm in the corner. That he'd let her do work here, instead of his downtown storefront where she normally sat, was a sign of how overwhelmed he was as his operation ramped up. He needed to give his full attention to the people he was managing, so he was willing to be a little sloppy with her, whom he trusted. She was making the most of her newfound access.

She strained at the door as their voices rose.

"We can't wait any longer. They've had their chance. It's time for our way, now."

"We can't! Our people will turn against us if it starts again here. They're weary. We turned them against us with the car bombs and the incendiaries in the shops. We cannot push them too far. We can't get isolated from Sinn Fein."

"It's the only way! They've taken us astray, I tell you."

David's voice interrupted them coolly. "We don't need to make the attacks here. We can take it to them. To the British people. It's time they feel the pain and pressure themselves. The bosses want to do it in London. It's already been decided. They don't need you to know more than that. But they're asking if we can count on you to move some goods."

"Who are you to tell us what to do?"

David laughed smoothly. "I'm a nobody, you've got that right. I ferry things and people myself. I know my place. I wouldn't ask you if it weren't a request straight from him."

Him. The commanding officer of the Provisional IRA's Derry Brigade was never discussed by name. Just the mere mention of him put terror in the ground troops.

"Goods, or people?"

"What's the difference? You'll find out when you get there."

"Do Gerry and Martin know?" The outright reference to the leaders of Sinn Fein was surprising, she thought, but then again, they thought themselves in safe company.

"It doesn't matter, does it?" David reasoned. "If they know, they approve because they don't want further ruptures within the movement. Yes? Besides, Gerry and Martin don't run Derry. We do."

There was a mumbling of assent.

From the far corner, Briana made a mewling sound. She was awakening, and soon, Meg knew, the tiny mouselike sounds would turn into an angry, ravenous wail. She crept away from the door and swooped Briana up in her arms. Briana rooted at her chest, smacking her lips hungrily.

She'd missed her window to run home and would need to feed her here. Maybe that would work to her advantage.

By the time the men emerged from their conference, Meg was seated in a chair, the blinds of the storefront pulled closed, Briana at her breast with a shawl artfully draped over her shoulder for privacy.

The men awkwardly shuffled by, discomfited by this overt show of femininity, and fled the store.

"You're still here?" David exclaimed when he emerged from his office. "I thought you would have gone home hours ago."

"I needed to tidy up a few things here and the time got away from me. Then this one woke, so here I am."

"I'll wait with you, then."

"There's no need. We just started. I know I'm late for Rennie—you know how Siobhan gets testy when we aren't on time to pick her up. Why don't you run ahead, and I'll catch up with you soon. If you could pop a meal from the freezer into the oven, it would be helpful. I'm too exhausted to cook much tonight."

He kissed her on the top of her head. "You shouldn't have to. Sometimes I wonder if I asked too much of you, dragging you here with me. It's not what you signed up for, is it?"

You have no idea, she thought to herself.

She smiled sweetly at him and answered, "I'd follow you anywhere, David, and you know it. Though honestly, at the rate it's going, I struggle to see how any of this"—she used one free hand to gesture about the spare office—"is adding any luster to your family name, or its fortune."

She dangled the question in front of him, hoping he would bite.

He simply shrugged and laughed. "You leave that to me."

"Very well," she assented. "Now hurry home. I'll be there as fast as I can."

She closed her eyes, pretending to rest as she fed Briana, and heard the rustle as David tucked his office key into the pot. When she heard him at the door, she opened her eyes and watched him leave, saw the careful turn of the lock as he made sure she was safe, alone. She listened as his solid, confident footsteps echoed down the walk and slowly faded to nothingness as he left the industrial park.

She didn't rush Briana. She didn't need to. What she planned to do would not take long.

When Briana was burped and changed, Meg laid her on her tummy on the bold-colored playmat she kept in the office. Briana was not yet fully mobile, but out of caution Meg made sure there was nothing nearby that her daughter could inadvertently roll into. Satisfied that Briana was safe and entertained, she fished David's key out of the pot and went into his office, slipping into a pair of gloves before she went to work.

She began in his desk, rifling through his files. The folders only bore numbers, numbers that seemed to have no discernible pattern to her, though one in particular seemed to show up more frequently. She slipped a miniature camera out of her pocket and captured them, in order, not really sure what she was looking at but hopeful someone else would be able to make sense of it. She then began looking through their contents. Each file had what looked like a label for a part of some sort and what she recognized as latitude and longitude coordinates. Some of the coordinates were the same, some were different.

"It's the plans for the movement of goods they were talking about," she murmured to herself, snapping more photographs and carefully replacing the contents of the files.

She undid the receiver of David's phone and installed a bug so she could better monitor his plans. And then she had a thought—maybe a wild hair—but decided to indulge it. She carefully locked up his office, replaced the key, grabbed a flashlight, and walked down the corridor through a heavy plastic curtain and onto the loading dock.

She turned on the flashlight and scanned the dock. A random box had been forgotten in a corner. She strode across the dock and approached it. It bore only a single label, a bar code and series of numbers that Meg recognized as matching one of the files in David's desk.

It was too heavy a box, sealed too tightly, to be tampered with without it being obvious. She shoved it with her toe, testing its heft; it didn't budge. Frustrated, she took a picture and slipped the camera back into her pocket.

Within ten minutes, she was out of the office, walking down the street with Briana bundled in her arms.

———

She arrived home to a shrieking maelstrom, just in time to witness the wondrous transformation of Rennie from cranky to delighted that only David could accomplish. He was tossing her in the air, her compact body seemingly nothing as he threw her higher and higher.

"More! More! More!" Rennie demanded, laughing maniacally, her hair a reddish corona around her head in the early evening lamplight.

Her whoop of delight turned to her sister. "Breeeeeeeee!" she called out as they walked through the door. David caught her in his arms, grappling with her wriggling body as he struggled to set her down before she could fling herself into thin air.

"Go see your sister," he said, with a note of satisfaction in his voice.

"Let me put her in her swing, Rennie. You'll be able to see her better that way." Meg picked through the minefield of toys and baby equipment to place Briana in the swing. She wound it up with a few good cranks and set it in motion.

"Don't push her," she cautioned Rennie, whose eyes sparkled with mischief.

"I'll just watch," Rennie promised solemnly. Meg didn't believe her for an instant.

Meg sniffed the air. "Is something burning?"

David blanched. "It must be the oven." He ran into the other room. She heard a creak and a rattle as a billow of smoke puffed through the doorway.

She smiled to herself. This happened at least once a week.

David popped his head out the door. "I'll just run down to the pub and get some fish and chips. How's that?"

"What if your mummy gives you cereal for dinner, Miss Rennie?" Meg didn't think the girl could wait long enough for David to get back, not when she knew he would be making the rounds and collecting intel.

"Coco Pops, Coco Pops, Coco Pops, Mummy!" Rennie abandoned the swing to parade around Meg, triumphing in the thought of chocolate cereal for dinner. It was a small indulgence, Meg knew, one that would keep the peace this evening.

"Your mum sure must love you, Rennie, my girl," David said. "She doesn't let me have cereal for dinner."

"That's because you're a naughty daddy," Rennie asserted, wagging her finger at David.

"Who's been naughty, Rowena?" David countered, his face taking on a mask of faux sternness. "Shall we tell your mum what happened at Siobhan's house today?"

"Time to eat," Rennie declared, turning on her heel to go into the kitchen.

Meg couldn't help but laugh. "She certainly knows how to keep the upper hand. I wonder where she got that from?"

David rolled his eyes. "Certainly not from me. I'm nothing but charm and light." He pulled on his quilted jacket and headed toward the door. "I'll be back in a flash, love." As he disappeared into the stairwell, Meg began peeling out of her own coat, knowing she was in for a long evening alone with the girls.

The bribe of chocolate helped ease Rennie through dinner and seemed to make her amenable to her evening bath. It was the time of day when everything became difficult. David was still out. Briana was wailing, not even the gentle rhythm of the swing able to placate her.

"Rennie, talk to your sister while Mummy runs your bath," Meg directed, distracted, propping the older girl up on a stack of pillows in front of the swing. "Maybe you can get her to stop crying with some funny faces."

She hurried off to the bathroom to run the bath.

She was grateful for the tiny respite. As she opened the faucet, the rush of water drowned out the cries of the baby. She leaned back against the cool tile of the walls, letting her hand drag into the water, testing it—not too warm, not too cold—the bubbling bathwater strangely soothing.

After what seemed like five minutes, she cranked the faucet off. Through the drip, drip, drip of the last bits of water, she noticed something odd.

It was quiet. Too quiet.

She rushed through the door and into the living room.

"Wheeeeeeeee!" Rennie cried. "Look, Mummy, look how happy I made Bree!"

Rennie had abandoned her pillows and had somehow managed to disengage the automatic setting of the swing and was now pushing it herself. Briana was arcing through open space, nearly upside down, her fat baby jowls flapping in the wind as she swung back and forth, back and forth, the rickety legs of the borrowed swing pumping as they struggled to maintain contact with the floor.

Meg pushed Rennie aside and dove for the swing, wrapping it all in a bear hug, struggling it into submission. When Meg had dragged the entire contraption to a stop, Briana emitted a little giggle.

Her first laugh.

"I did good, Mum! Look, I made Briana stop crying!"

She wrapped Rennie in her arms and kissed her fiercely. "You did good, Rennie. Now tell me, what did you do at Miss Siobhan's that got you so in trouble?"

Rennie smiled brightly. "I'll show you. Come here." She took Meg's hand and pulled her to her feet, dragging her into the small nursery Rennie shared with Briana. "Watch," she said solemnly.

Meg watched in astonishment while Rennie scooted up the front of the changing table, then used the changing table to jump onto the face of the armoire, her toes and fingers gripping into the deeply carved niches. Meg gasped, watching the heavy piece of furniture strain against the anchors David had so carefully installed, tethering it to the wall, but they held. Before Meg could stop her, Rennie clambered up the face of the armoire and perched herself on the top, crouching just below the ceiling like a cat in wait.

"Meow," she said, as if that settled the matter.

"Oh, my," Meg intoned. She didn't think there was anything more to say.

"She was soooo mad at me."

"I can only imagine."

"I was bored. And then she yelled, so I wouldn't come down until Daddy came to take me home."

"I'm guessing we may need to find another babysitter," Meg mused. She was finding it hard not to laugh.

"Can I sleep up here, Mummy? Can I? I promise not to fall."

Meg chuckled. "You have no shortage of confidence, Rowena, I must give you that. We will not be sleeping on the armoire tonight. But maybe, if you are good, you can convince your Uncle Brian to build you a tree house in the country where you can climb all you want. As for tonight, if you come down now, I will let you hold your sister as we tell bedtime stories. How does that sound?"

⸺

The good thing about having an overactive child, Meg had to acknowledge, is that once the typical bedtime struggles were over, sleep came swiftly and was deep, leaving Meg precious time to unravel exactly what David was up to.

David had been gone for hours now.

With both girls down, she pulled the radio transmitter she had hidden inside her box of maxi pads out from under the bathroom sink and set it up. It was programmed to record calls if she wasn't actively listening, intercept calls for live listening, and even tap conversations that were happening in the room. She had a feeling, given he'd clearly abandoned any pretense of bringing her back dinner, that he'd gone back to the office—perhaps for a meeting, perhaps for other reasons.

She locked the bathroom door, turned on the device, and nestled the headphones onto her head.

She'd caught him mid-conversation.

What he was proposing was outrageous.

She put away her equipment and checked the girls. Throwing on a coat and boots, she went across the hall and knocked.

Siobhan answered the door. When she saw it was Meg, her face hardened.

"I need to run out just for a minute. Just keep an ear out for them, please? They're sound asleep."

Siobhan grumbled. Meg pressed some money into her hand. "I'll owe you one." She didn't wait for an answer, just started running down the stairwell.

She ran halfway to the office before remembering her training. She forced herself to slow, doubled back and around, counting the precious minutes.

The front lights were out when she got there. She let herself in with her own key and waited.

"What do you think you're doing, David Hutton?" she demanded softly when he finally emerged from his office an hour later.

He flicked on the light. "Meg?"

"You think I don't know what you're doing. But I see things. I see those men. I see the boxes and the money and I see it all. And now . . . now I hear you talking about bombings in London and taking out people inside the Derry Brigade, like you're playing both sides. You cannot put us at risk without me knowing what game it is that you're playing."

He looked at her, appraising. "You heard all that, just now? When you followed me here?"

She blushed. "I've been seeing things for a long time, David. I just waited 'til now, when it seems it may be coming to a head, to say something."

He sighed and rubbed his weary face. He squatted before her, his hands on her knees. "It's not what you think."

"So those are not Armalite parts you forgot on the loading dock?"

Her wild guess hit its mark; he flinched.

"You're laundering for the IRA; that much is clear with the sums of money going in and out of these sham businesses. You're moving arms for them. But you're up to more than that, aren't you?"

He dropped his head. "Do we have to do this here?"

"I'm not leaving until you tell me the truth," she insisted, crossing her arms. "I went through your files, David. I can tell some of the numbers match the Armalite box, but many of them do not. What are the numbers, David?"

He stared at her, shocked. "You went into my office?"

"Your hiding place barely qualified as one," she said dismissively. "You can't expect me to watch the parade of thugs going in and out of here and not know there is something wrong."

He looked around nervously, as if trapped.

"Let's go for a walk," David said, defeated.

They took the long way, looping back to their flat.

"You're not really IRA, are you?" she began, when he seemed reluctant to talk.

"No," he said tersely. "But I'm not Royal Ulster Constabulary, either. I'm MI5. British Intelligence," he explained, assuming she would have no clue. "Counterterrorism."

She held her breath, waiting for him to reveal more.

"I've been running these businesses to launder money and arms for the IRA for years, trying to earn my way into their good graces. Now I've finally infiltrated the Derry Brigade. I'm just a driver, but drivers hear everything. And they trust me. They are using me to set up something big now—something that requires every piece to be separate, so nobody can put it all together. The siloes keep everyone safe and the siloes mean any leak could be detected. That's how the Nutting Squad keeps control, you know. Divide and conquer, isolate, separate, so that any touts can be easily rooted out."

"The Nutting Squad?" she asked, continuing to play dumb.

"Internal IRA Security. Truly bad men. Brutal. But they do their job well, efficiently. When they capture a turncoat, it's a matter of days before that person turns up dead at the side of the road, if their body is ever found at all."

Meg gulped. She knew this, of course, from Brian, but it was different coming from David's lips.

"What does this have to do with you?"

"This big thing I told you about—there are only a few, maybe ten, who could piece it all together. Technically, I shouldn't be able to, but because I'm running other agents—double agents—I can piece it together too."

"You're a tout, then," she said, shooting him a sideways glance.

"Or a patriot, depending on whose side you're on," he said tersely.

She didn't look at him.

"Are you leaking information about Brian?" she asked him quietly.

"Never! Meg, I would never do that. You've got to believe me. I wouldn't have let him stand godfather to Briana—to name Briana after him, for God's sake—if that was my intent. He's off limits. I swear."

"So now you and your men are going to bomb London?"

He stopped on the sidewalk. "So that's what you heard?"

She nodded. "I heard the arguments earlier. And then tonight . . ." She let her voice trail off. The less he understood what she knew, the better.

"It won't really happen," he vowed. "I'm arranging all the movements—everything in isolation, just like I explained. But MI5 will be completely apprised and able to stop it before it happens. And nothing will be traced to me. I swear."

"How many?"

"How many what?"

"How many bombs. Attacks. Whatever you want to call it."

He paused. "A lot. More than there have been in a long time."

"You'll break the cease-fire, then."

"The Derry leadership don't like the direction of the negotiations, so yes, they intend to break the cease-fire."

She started walking. He kept pace with her. She could feel him staring at her, trying to read her face.

"If the bombings are thwarted, someone will get blamed, will they not? This Nutting Squad—they won't stop, will they?"

He grabbed her hand and pulled her in close, peering into her eyes. "They won't find me. I promise you, Meg. I've been careful. So very careful."

No you haven't! she wanted to scream at him. *If I could get into your office and read your files and bug your phone and find your arms, all in the space of a single afternoon, you have not been careful. Not nearly enough.*

But she didn't.

She simply squeezed his hand, hard, and smiled up into his concerned face. He thought she was so innocent, she knew. It was one of her biggest assets. As much as she loved him, it pained her to be able to play him so easily.

"Maybe you should teach me how to shoot a gun," she suggested gamely.

His jaw dropped. She smiled to herself, pleased that she had astounded him with her faux naivete. She dropped his hand and kept walking, already planning how to get everything she'd learned to her handler, Judy.

Chapter Nine

BREE

Present Day, Bath

There was nothing, absolutely nothing, like the pit that formed in Bree's stomach in the hours leading up to their *Jeopardy!* class.

The anxiety was something she woke with, an off-kilter feeling that a morning run, deep-breathing exercises, burning incense, or even a good cup of coffee would do nothing to disperse. None of these techniques from *Hippie Dippy* proved useful against the existential dread she experienced as her body prepared itself to watch interrogations.

The course had not started off with video, of course. It had worked its way up to that. First, they'd been expected to master the motivations of a spy, to learn how to pinpoint the exact way to develop—or resist—psychological control. Money. Ideology. Coercion. Ego. MICE, as the professor called it. One or more of these weapons could be used to convince, to cajole, to bend a target to one's will, to persuade them to become a turncoat or a martyr—whatever suited the needs of the Agency.

From there, they progressed to learning the rules of interrogation for the moment when they would need to pressure a subject. They approached the subject like legal scholars, parsing the difference between interrogation and torture, trying to ascertain where the lines were drawn by examining the international conventions prohibiting the use of torture. What constituted "severe" under the law? What was the difference between "persuasion" and "coercion"? It was dry stuff, but underneath the legalese and mountains of case law was the gnawing awareness that they were being taught this for a reason. They were expected to be able to withstand interrogation, as well as to administer it.

They learned all the approved techniques. The direct approach. Use of incentives. The use of emotions, like hate or love, pride, and of course, fear. How to assert the futility of their subject's resistance, laced with warnings that we "know all." The use of rapid-fire questioning, repetition, silence. The deployment of sympathy and fear in a "good cop, bad cop" manner. Destabilizing the subject through a sudden change of scenery. Through being left alone for endless stretches of time.

It had begun to stick in Bree's throat more when they began classifying degrees and types of torture, the counterpoint structure treated as if it were as benign as the taxonomy of species, genus, family, order, class, and phylum of the animal kingdom. There were the methods designed to destroy the subjects' self-image: forced nudity, head shaving, sleep deprivation, hooding, sensory deprivation. There was force-feeding, starvation, waterboarding, ice baths, hanging stress, beatings and maimings of all sorts. Sexual abuse. The unique terror of a mock execution. There was indirect torture—forcing the subject to watch or listen as (as far as they knew) a loved one or associate was tortured in their place.

The number of ways the human mind had invented to crush the spirit and life of another was dumbfounding.

We teach this so you know what you must not do, the instructors murmured, assuaging their fears. *But remember*, they whispered at other times, *Norwood is no party to these conventions. We exist outside the framework of these treaties. We predate them. And because of this, you can expect no quarter from your enemies if you are ever caught.*

So be prepared. Do what you must.

And watch. Now you must watch, so that you can be strong.

"I'm already drunk," Anya whispered from the seat next to Bree. "I reckon it will be easier to stomach it this way. Take the sharp edges off. If you want any . . .?" She offered the water bottle to Bree, shaking it as if to entice her. "It's vodka."

"No thanks," Bree shot back. Since meeting Brian, she had felt a strange sense of obligation to witness what was happening—to truly see.

"Class," began their professor, "tonight you will be watching a live interrogation being streamed from an undisclosed location. You will find the briefing on your secure device. Take a few minutes to scan it so you know our objectives this evening. You will see that a third of you are assigned to monitor the actions of the interrogator and her effectiveness in soliciting the desired intelligence. A third are assigned to monitor the actions and resistance of the subject. The final third are to monitor the legalities of what you witness in line with the UN Conventions. Upload your observations at the close of the class. We will synthesize and compare them to the actual commentary of the official observers, who will not be visible to you during this screening, in our next session."

Bree tapped her password in and opened the briefing.

The Norwood agent conducting the interrogation was unnamed. "Agent X" had brought in a subject who was suspected of having disrupted, under nonspecified conditions that were labeled "unusual," a field extraction of someone under Norwood's protection. Goals of the interrogation: determine with whom the subject was working and why the extraction had been disrupted.

"We're live in ten seconds, people," the professor intoned as the automated screen slid down from the ceiling. "Remember, there will be a slight broadcast delay to allow Intel to respond in the event anything of significant national security implication is surfaced during this interrogation."

Out of the corner of her eye, Bree saw Anya take a swig of her bottle and smush herself deeper into the seat, drawing out a bag of popcorn. Ruby was already studiously taking notes. Dash was watching Bree from his seat across the room.

He mouthed, *Are you okay?*

Bree nodded once, then focused her attention on the fuzzy shot of a nondescript cell that sprang to life on the screen before them.

The subject sat in the center of the cell. They could see him only from the waist up, as he rested his handcuffed hands on the top of a dented metal table. He seemed muscle-bound, his dirty tank top straining against his chest. There was nothing notable about his face, but blooming across his chest and winding its way up his neck was a massive tattoo.

Bree held her breath and stared. She knew that tattoo. It was the same design as the one she'd seen on the soldier she and Gul had found shot dead when they were trying to escape with the Asker children.

Bree leaned closer.

The man was breathing heavily. His fingers tapped impatiently on the desk, rattling the chains of the cuffs. It was impossible to know how long he'd been sitting there, waiting.

There were sounds of a door opening and footsteps, then the scrape of chair legs against the floor. The interrogator had arrived.

"Who are you working for?" she demanded from off-screen.

Bree drew in a breath. That voice—it was familiar.

The prisoner—for that was what he was, Bree reasoned; no sense in calling him anything else—clenched his jaw.

"You think you've been so strong, don't you?" the interrogator continued. "Refusing to break so far. Do you even know how long you've been here?"

Bree noticed what looked like a glimmer of doubt in the prisoner's eyes.

"It hasn't even been three days. We're only getting started. You'll tell us what we want to know. One way or another. So let's try again. Who are you working for?"

"You know I work for the Americans. On the air base."

"And you know that's a lie I can easily disprove. Your records, for one thing." The interrogator threw a file down on the table in front of him. "And your tattoo, for another. Air Force policy doesn't allow them on the face or neck."

Bree was rattled. So *that's* why Albourn and Shadduck had been so interested in her description of the shot courier—they knew something was off the instant she mentioned his tattoo. As soon as she told them that detail, they knew the mission had been compromised before it had even begun. The question was just by whom.

"Who said I was a member of the military?" The prisoner smirked. "I just work there. Like hundreds of other people."

Bree was holding her breath, on the edge of her seat.

Off camera, the interrogator swore. "*Ecdanini sikiyim.*"

Bree gasped as she registered that the cursing was in Turkish—recognizing it as one of Gul's more colorful favorites.

Without missing a beat, the questioner continued.

"Unlike the hundreds of other people, your friend—who bore the exact same tattoo as you—somehow managed to replace an agent on my operation."

The questions were now coming in rapid staccato like a hail of bullets.

"How did he trick the real courier? How did he know the hail? Who gave it to you? How did he know 'Roxelana'?"

A surge of joy jolted Bree. Aside from the courier himself, only three people on their busted mission had known the password "Roxelana"— the hail that was to be used by the Air Force–arranged guide helping them move the Asker children to safety. Susmita, who was dead. Bree. And Gul.

The interrogator's voice was an angry roar now, hoarse as she demanded answers. "*Kahretsin*! I need to know! He threw my op, and in the process wound up dead. I wound up with multiple missing assets and a dead one to boot—"

The video feed suddenly cut out.

"Transmission failure!" the professor shouted over the confusion. "Sorry about that, class. Even with all the high-tech gadgetry, sometimes we've got simple problems with the Internet to contend with."

One of her assistants whispered in the professor's ear; the professor nodded, once, and sent her off through the classroom door.

"I'll tell you what. We'll rummage around the video library and find a taped interrogation instead. Take five now—we'll start over the old-fashioned way as soon as we can run down the equipment."

Bree felt her chance slipping away.

"But I want to see the rest of *that* interrogation!" she blurted out, her hands clenched into fists. Her classmates' heads all swiveled as if one, staring, surprised at her uncharacteristic outburst.

The professor watched her keenly. "Why's that, Parrish? Something in particular caught your eye?"

Out of the corner of her eye, Bree could see Ruby staring at her hard. Her eyes seemed to flash a warning—*whatever it is, keep it to yourself.*

"No. No, ma'am." Bree swallowed hard. She forced herself to visibly relax, unclenching her fists to fold her hands neatly in her lap.

"I didn't think so," the professor stated, closing off any further discussion.

Bree fought back tears of frustration.

But in the back of her mind, a triumphant voice was shouting *Gul is alive!*

She had to force herself to pay attention through the rest of the class, conscious the entire time of the meaningful looks that both Ruby and Dash were sending her at every chance they found.

They ran to catch up to her once they'd emerged from class into the muggy night air.

"What was that all about?" Ruby demanded.

Bree looked nervously at Dash. He nodded slightly, encouraging her to speak. Bree stopped and pulled them to the side, into an alley.

"That was Gul," she whispered excitedly. "The interrogator on that stream. I know it."

Dash looked shocked.

Ruby sucked her teeth in disbelief. "How could it possibly be?"

"She was throwing in Turkish words—curse words that Gul always used."

"Everybody curses, Bree," Dash said gently, clearly trying not to crush her hopes. "It was probably just a coincidence."

"That's not all," Bree interrupted him impatiently. "She was talking about our operation. The removal of the Asker children. She talked about dead and missing assets—"

Ruby cut her off. "That was not specific. Those assets could have been anybody."

"No! The interrogation subject had the exact same tattoos as the dead courier we found at the transfer site in Istanbul. The exact same! You heard what she said—those are not allowed in the US military. I knew Albourn and Shadduck recognized something was off in my description that time they debriefed me in the hospital. That was it."

Dash looked at her doubtfully. "Still, that's circumstantial."

"And the interrogator knew the passcode. 'Roxelana' was our hail. Gul and I are the only ones left alive who knew it. It had to be her."

Her groupmates eyed her skeptically.

"I recognized her voice, y'all. You've got to believe me," she pleaded. "It was her. I just know it."

Dash took a deep breath. A few classmates, laggards, walked by on the sidewalk. He eyed them warily. "We probably shouldn't discuss this here. Let's go back to Jaguar House."

Bree hesitated. "When did you last sweep it?"

"Yesterday," Dash stated firmly. Dash had taken to using his new-found electronic surveillance skills to ensure their own apartment was not bugged. "Unless someone literally went in during the last two hours while we were in class, it should be clean."

Bree watched Ruby's face for any reaction, but she remained impassive.

"We can even check the video surveillance if you'd like," Dash added for good measure.

"All right, let's go," Bree assented.

"I know you think I'm paranoid . . ." Bree trailed off as she scanned the security footage.

"I actually don't," Ruby said tartly. "I actually think you underestimate the risks you are taking. All. The. Time."

Bree pulled a face. Satisfied their apartment had not been breached in the last two hours, she closed the lid on Dash's laptop.

"So," she began, jumping straight into the heart of the matter. "The thing is, if Gul is still alive, that means Handan and her children could be too."

"Back up, Bree," Dash objected. "That's not the biggest issue here."

"Of course it is," Bree stated. "What could be more important?"

"What's more important is why the brass at Norwood would lie to you—to us—about Gul's death," Dash stated bluntly.

"They probably just wanted to keep Bree from trying to interfere in their investigation," Ruby reasoned. "Not surprising, given how mucked up everything became."

"Are you saying I'm the one who mucked it up?" Bree bristled at the insinuation.

Ruby sighed with exaggerated patience. "No, Bree. I'm not blaming you. I'm just saying that, at this point, the administration likely views the interference of a bunch of students as a nuisance they'd rather not deal with."

Dash cut them off.

"This is serious, you two. Stop sniping at one another. Why would they keep the truth from us? From you?" he asked, pointedly looking at Bree. "Unless they're trying to get you to trip up, somehow. Tip your hand . . ."

"What hand does she have to tip, eh?" Ruby retorted. She tilted her head, speculating, the slight motion setting her beaded braids clicking. "Are you keeping something from them, Bree? From us?"

"You're giving them what they want," Bree spat back in frustration.

"Which is what, exactly?" Ruby challenged.

"You're letting them turn us against each other. We have to stick together. We have to trust one another."

"There's no 'they.' I keep telling you—you're either with Norwood, or you're against it. You made your choice. There's no going back." Ruby crossed her hands emphatically, letting them know in no uncertain terms that she, herself, had already come to terms with that choice.

"Stop bickering," Dash said, exasperated. "Let's focus on the real question. Let's assume, for the moment, that Bree is right and it was Gul on that livestream. Why would the administration lie about Gul's death?"

"If we go with Bree's hypothesis—for *now*," Ruby said begrudgingly, "—it's safe to assume, from context, that they know and did it deliberately."

"They would have already known the courier at the transfer was a plant when I mentioned his tattoo," Bree continued. "So they'd be trying to find out how far back the job was compromised."

"Which means they don't believe it was Susmita," Dash added.

"Or that she didn't act alone," Ruby assented. "So perhaps they are still investigating Gul and you, both," Ruby continued, looking at Bree. "Maybe keeping you in the dark enables them to better pursue both angles and prevent you from conspiring. That is, if you were in on it together."

Bree felt her cheeks burn with anger at the implied accusation, but she had to admit, in Norwood's shoes, it was a reasonable hypothesis and a neat way of dealing with them. "Divide and conquer," Albourn and Shadduck had said when they'd interviewed her in her hospital room, referring to Gul and her splitting up at the docks. They'd turned the tactic to their own advantage.

"What if they showed that interrogation on purpose?" Bree blurted out, suddenly seeing a new possibility. "What if they're trying to get me to come forward and say more?"

"What more do you have to say, Bree?" Ruby asked coolly.

Over Ruby's shoulder, Bree saw Dash give a slight shake of his head. *Give up nothing*, she read in the tense set of his jaw.

"Nothing," she sighed, following his lead. "But still—they don't know that. If they still suspect me, they might stop at nothing."

"Yes," Dash agreed. "If you're right, and you don't speak up now—whether you have anything to say or not—their suspicion will deepen." He frowned. "They're bloody brilliant at it, aren't they? The manipulation. I just wish we better understood the game they're playing."

"There's no *game*, Dash," Ruby said emphatically. "Standard protocol when an agent is compromised is to pursue the investigation to the end. To make sure there is no further rupture of security. Even you have to admit, Susmita's death happened under suspicious circumstances. All the evidence pointing to her as the one throwing the operation is circumstantial. Bree's story is what clinched her as the guilty party. And nobody else was there to back Bree up as a witness."

The words stung Bree, but she could tell Ruby didn't care. Ruby seemed intent on giving them a cold dose of reality.

"If you think they've moved on from suspecting Bree—or any of us—you're simply naive. I've seen the files they've kept," Ruby let slip. "They aren't done with us. Not by a stretch."

Bree was startled to hear Ruby drop such a juicy bit of news. Did her status as Head Girl—or her administrative leadership track—give her that much special access? Maybe she was on their side, after all?

Dash plopped down on the sofa, frustrated. "What'll it take, then?"

"Like I've been saying," Bree reminded him gently, sitting down next to him. "It will take us finding those children. Then the truth will come out."

"We don't even know if they're alive," Dash said.

"We thought Gul was dead until a few hours ago," Bree countered. "Anything is possible now. We just need to keep trying. We need to go to Albourn. I mean, *I* need to go. I need to tell her what I saw on that streaming interrogation and see how she reacts." She looked at her roommates. "We need to act as if you two have no clue. The more you are separated from this, the safer we will be."

"I don't know, Bree. What if they snatch you or something?" Dash took her hand in his. "It's not safe for you to go alone."

Bree studiously ignored Ruby, who was stonily staring at their clasped hands.

"Trust me, they won't do it. They can't afford to have more people associated with that bad op go missing. It'll look too suspicious. Besides," Bree reasoned, "if I do get taken, it'll be better to have the two of you here, on the outside, to come find me."

"She's right," Ruby broke in. "We need to stay on the outside if we are to help in a pinch."

"Ruby," Bree changed the subject, "do you have a way to find out about those tattoos? Whether they belong to a particular terror group or something?"

"I can dig around," Ruby agreed. "Not sure what I'll find, but I'll give it a go."

"Brilliant. Thanks." Bree gave Dash's hand a squeeze. "Any chance that you could figure out where the interrogation was taking place? See if we can figure out where Gul is and maybe find the interrogation record?"

He ran his hand through his hair in frustration as he considered her question.

"A hopeless, Sisyphean task, that. Presuming she is still working *with* Norwood, theoretically any NATO, MI6, or MI5 facility would be available to her. I could start in Turkey, if you think that's most likely. But I wouldn't hold your breath."

"Why would she not be with Norwood?" Ruby shot back.

"Fair question. I'm just grasping at straws. But what if she is the mole? We never thought about her because we always presumed she was dead."

"Y'all—Gul is not to blame. I know it. I know it in my bones," Bree emphasized. She dropped Dash's hand and rose to pace their tiny sitting room. "You can't spend that much time with someone and not know what they're made of. And it doesn't matter, anyway. Whether she's guilty or innocent, we only gain by finding her."

There was a long pause.

"We thought we knew Susie," Ruby said quietly, her eyes trailing over to the spot on the linoleum that had been scrubbed clean of blood.

"Stop it, Ruby," Dash growled. He paused a moment and took a deep breath. Bree felt a tiny bit of the tension dissipate. "I'll see what I can do, Bree. But no promises." He got up, slumped in defeat, and walked to the door that divided his living quarters from theirs. He paused with his hand on the doorknob. Bree could tell he was choosing his words carefully.

"Before you go in to Albourn, we need to go over everything, and I mean *everything*. Every word, anything you plan to dangle in front of her. We need to consider every angle she may take so that we know you're prepared. There can be no surprises."

His back straightened.

"We can't risk losing you. Not now."

It was the first chill day of autumn. Bree stood in front of the steps of the administration building, gathering her resolve. The wind gusted, threatening to carry off her Norwood-issue brown hat. She crushed it down hard and chuckled grimly at herself.

"Like a knight clamping down his visor before the charge," she muttered.

She shook her head ruefully at her ridiculous comparison—she'd been hanging around Dash too much. Not that that was such a bad thing—but what she wouldn't give now to be in Rodney's kitchen, to have never, ever set foot in this place.

But . . . a voice in her head countered. *Think of all the things, all the truths—and all the people—you wouldn't have ever known.*

You've got to do this. For them.

She mounted the stairs and made her way down the hall.

It was a Tuesday morning and Mrs. Framingham, the receptionist, was at her desk.

"Good morning, Parrish. What brings you in today? Disbursement? Grades? Consultation with the honor council?"

"What's behind door number one?" Bree countered, twittering anxiously.

Mrs. Framingham shot her a sharp look. "Everything hunky-dory there, dear?"

Bree willed her racing heart to slow. After a deep breath, she answered. "I'm sorry. I guess I'm just a little nervous. I need to see the dean."

"Appointment?" Mrs. Framingham's eyes were glittering brightly; she had a nose for trouble.

"No, ma'am. But I'm hoping she will see me, regardless. It's about a very important matter."

"What shall I say it is about?" Mrs. Framingham stopped, poised, with the phone in her hand.

"Tell her it's about the Asker case. If you wouldn't mind. Thank you."

Mrs. Framingham tilted her head. "All right, then. Take a seat over there. I'll see what I can do."

Bree didn't have long to wait.

"You're in luck. The dean unexpectedly had a space free up in her schedule. You can go right in." Mrs. Framingham eyed her curiously.

Bree gathered herself up, squared her shoulders, and walked down the long hallway to the dean's office. The door was ajar, awaiting her arrival. Bree lifted her hand to knock, but the barking voice of the dean cut her off.

"Come in, Parrish. I've been waiting."

It felt to Bree like she was moving through quicksand as she made her way over to stand in front of Albourn's desk.

"Sit."

Bree perched herself on the edge of the uncomfortable wooden chair that faced Albourn. The dean didn't even bother to look up from the sheaf of paperwork she was reviewing.

"I suppose you've come to inquire about the status of the search for the children. If so, you'll be sorely disappointed. I have nothing to tell you."

Bree clasped her hands. They were clammy. "No. I've come for something else."

The dean looked up in surprise. "Speak."

Bree took a deep breath. "I need to disclose something that I believe pertinent to the investigation into the operation. Something that might help it."

Albourn tossed the files onto her desk. "Well, spit it out, then. I haven't got all day."

Bree's mind raced. If this whole thing was set as bait to get Bree to come in, Albourn was certainly playing it cool.

"I have reason to believe that Agent Avci is alive. I think she was the off-camera interrogator in a livestream questioning of a suspect that we were watching in *Jeopardy!* I mean, *Introduction to Interrogation.*"

Albourn's eyes narrowed. "What could possibly have led you to believe such a thing?"

"Her voice. The curse words she used," Bree responded, not able to stop herself from smiling slightly at the memory of Gul's frustration. "And her line of questioning. The subject in the livestream sported the same markings as the dead courier I told you about—the one who'd been shot dead at the point we were to transfer the Asker children. The interrogator referenced the tattoo and a dead colleague. It couldn't be a coincidence. Could it?"

Albourn leaned back in her chair. She clasped her fingers lightly under her chin as she considered what Bree had said.

"No. No, it could not be."

"But you told me she was dead. That the Agency had found her body."

Albourn nodded.

"Why? Why would you tell me that?"

Albourn shrugged. She made a display of straightening the lacquer box on her desk, then the papers. She fiddled with the cup holding her pens and letter opener as if checking that her treasures were all in place. Taking her time, she tapped her manicured fingertips on the leather blotter, fixing Bree with a stare. A low sound, suspiciously like a growl, escaped from her lips. And still she watched.

Like a dragon in wait, Bree couldn't help thinking.

"We lied. You didn't need to know, and we needed to be sure you could be trusted," Albourn answered simply. "Now we know."

Bree bit back her anger.

"Yes, Agent Avci—Gul—is alive. At this point, she is under the mistaken belief that you, yourself, were killed on that container ship. It's really quite tidy, actually. Gives us a lot of room to consider all avenues in resolving this ugly matter. So, in that vein, if there were any further information you could give us about her . . ." Albourn shrugged, letting her words hang in the air like the cigarette smoke that was beginning to cloud the room.

"Tell me what you know about the children," Bree countered.

"Tell me about your mother."

Bree flushed, thrown off balance by such a direct and unexpected demand.

"I don't know what you mean. You know I grew up in an orphanage."

Albourn brushed away her objection. "Don't play games."

Bree pressed her lips together.

"This is quite tiresome, Parrish. I know you are keeping something from me, yet here you are, offering up information about Avci's interrogation. I really would like to believe that you have the best interests of Norwood at heart. But for that, you must tell me something I don't already know. Something about your mother."

"There's nothing."

Albourn's left eyebrow shot up skeptically. "You expect me to believe that? That you just happened to apply here, by accident? That you knew nothing of your British birth? That you didn't know your mother was one of our own? Really, your audacity astounds me."

"But it truly was coincidental. I don't understand what's going on. Why is Gul being allowed on missions while I'm still under suspicion? If we're both still alive, you must have concluded that Susmita was, indeed, at fault. So why are we still being investigated?"

Albourn clasped her hands, shaking her head.

"Stop trying to change the subject. We won't stop looking for your mother, whether you help us or not. Your cooperation could be quite beneficial to you. However, I see that you are not yet ready to assist us. When you are, come back and speak with me. In the meantime, I'll throw you a bone or two. A gesture of goodwill to help you understand that we are on the same side, you and I."

She swept her files up off the desk and walked to her office door. She didn't bother to turn around as she spoke.

"Asker has been in communication with the group who kidnapped the children. We have proof of life. He has been told that he must find a way to resume the arms transfer or his children will be murdered. This time, the terrorists are making no effort to hide their motive: diversion of the arms to Uyghur groups deep in China. We—NATO—are complying with the demand. It serves two purposes: one, to shut Asker up before he goes to the Turkish government, which would put us in a highly compromised position; two, it gives us a chance to track down these terrorists—terrorists we believe are somehow connected to your mother's history."

The dean paused.

"That should give you plenty to think over. Your move, Parrish."

Albourn squared her shoulders and marched out, leaving Bree to sit in silence. One question rose above the others rioting in Bree's brain.

Why was Albourn talking about her mother in the present tense?

Dash and Ruby accosted her on the sidewalk the minute she walked back out through the wrought iron gate.

"What happened? What did you tell her?" Dash demanded, guiding her away from the campus.

"From the time you took, you must have gotten in to see her," Ruby added. "What did she say?"

"Not until we're back at Jaguar House," Bree reminded them.

They walked swiftly, eyes down, as if they could avoid being watched.

The instant they crossed the threshold to their apartment, Dash and Ruby fell on her again.

"Did she admit it?" Dash asked. "Did she admit that it was Gul?"

"She did," Bree said, collapsing onto the sofa and tossing her brown hat aside. "She said they were testing me, to see if I could be trusted. Apparently they're doing the same to her—Gul thinks I'm dead, too."

Ruby let out a low whistle.

"What else?" Dash prompted.

"She told me the Asker kids are still alive. The kidnappers—or terrorists, she called them—are holding them hostage to renew the arms flow, all the way to China. Gul was right, Dash. She was telling the truth."

"Gul was right about what?" Bree could tell Ruby's suspicions were alerted. "What did she tell you?"

"It doesn't matter." Dash rushed in, brushing Ruby's question aside. He continued, "Bree, you should be ecstatic. Why do you look so troubled? What else did she say?"

Bree noticed the stubborn look on Ruby's face. She knew Ruby hated being interrupted, especially by Dash. Before she could round back to the question of what Gul had told her, Bree offered another diversion.

"She asked me about my mother," Bree answered flatly. "And . . ."

"And what?" Ruby insisted.

Bree looked at Dash, her eyes questioning him for guidance. He gave a slight nod. Bree shrugged. She would have to spill it all, then.

"It sounded to me like she was insinuating my mother is still alive."

Ruby and Dash gaped at her.

"What?" Dash sputtered. "Surely you misunderstood?"

Bree shook her head quietly and stared at her hands. "She said they would never stop looking for her. Not her body. *Her.* And she said they think the Asker operation is somehow connected to her history. Not her *death*—her *history.*"

She pivoted on the cushions to face Dash squarely.

"She doesn't believe me, Dash. She thinks that somehow I am in on it all and that I know where my mother is."

Ruby sat next to Bree and drew her hand in her own. "I'm happy for you, Bree. If she's telling the truth, that is."

Bree snatched her hand away. "You're *happy* for me? Why should I be happy? If my mother is alive, it means she abandoned me for nearly two decades. What am I to make of that?"

A lone tear squeezed out of the corner of Bree's eye. She dashed it away, angrily.

"I didn't think of it that way," Ruby conceded. "I'm sorry. I don't know what would be worse—for Albourn to be lying to you, or for her to be telling you the truth. But maybe, just maybe, we should focus on the idea that the children are alive. And Gul." Ruby shoved herself up from the sofa and walked out of the room. Bree heard the bedroom door click closed behind her and instantly felt ashamed.

"Would you like me to put a cup on for you?" Dash offered.

Bree shook her head and blew out a deep breath.

"You know, besides Rodney, there are only two people who have ever talked about my parents' death—Judy and Susmita. They talked about it concretely, as if it had really happened. What if it didn't? What if they were lying? Then that means you could have been right—that the man who knocked me out on the ship could have been my father." She shuddered, not wanting to follow the thread of her dark thoughts back to the very instant on the mission where, mid-flight to safety, she was rendered unconscious and the Asker children had been snatched.

"I'm sure your father would not have wanted to hurt you. It was just a silly thought, me grasping at straws. You should forget it."

"I want to go see your father," Bree declared abruptly.

"Whatever do you mean?"

She jumped to her feet and began pacing the linoleum.

"You said your father won Ullabreagh in a card game—presumably, from my father. If your father was a confidant of David Hutton, he may know the truth. We've got to ask him, Dash. I've no other option left."

"Ask him what?" Dash sputtered, aghast. "If he knew Hutton was a spy? And oh, by the way, does he happen to know where he's been hiding all this time? Or were you thinking of inquiring whether he knows about Norwood?" He grabbed Bree's shoulder to stop her in her tracks. "Bree, have you gone mad?"

She shook off his hand. "I'm not crazy. He's the only person I can think of, Dash. Please, you've got to help me."

He stared at her. "You're serious, then?"

She nodded, jutting her chin just a tad. "I need to do this. I need your help."

He sighed. "Let's say for a moment I am willing to do this for you. What do you hope to gain from your interrogation of my father?"

She grinned. "Not an interrogation. A friendly conversation. We could ask him if he knew Hutton's wife, for starters."

"And just how, pray tell, will you even steer the conversation to the topic of David Hutton?"

"We can tell him you took me, your girlfriend, on an overnight visit to Ullabreagh and I was intrigued by the story of how he won the place? That even gives us a reason for you to be paying the visit—you want to introduce me to your family."

She paused. She could feel the hopeful grin spreading over her face as fast as a red flush of embarrassment was spreading across Dash's.

"Surely you can pretend for an evening, Dash, especially after all the new skills you've picked up in *Seduction and the Spy* class."

Groaning, he ran his fingers through his hair. "Woman, you are the *only* person for whom I would do this. I hope you know that. I make it a general rule and a matter of pride to give my father no window into my private affairs. It gives him no opportunity to criticize and it allows me to keep up the rakish ne'er-do-well air I have cultivated so carefully. Though perhaps the shock of actually meeting an alleged girlfriend may drive him to his grave, which could prove quite useful . . ."

She flung her arms around his shoulders. "Thank you," she whispered in his ear.

He enfolded her in his arms. "The *only* one," he whispered back, squeezing her just a little more tightly.

———

It took a few weeks to make the arrangements. Dash had suddenly become quite nervous about the prospect of bringing home a girl—even if it was for entirely understandable undercover reasons. It took some doing to find a weekend when his father would be home without Dash's reviled stepmother, but finally, they settled upon a date. He then fretted over what Bree would wear, and what sort of backstory they would create for her.

"No backstory," she insisted. "No more lies. It is getting too hard to keep up with them. For now, let's just tell the truth—that I am an orphan from America."

"It may shock him so deeply that he'll take to Scotch straightaway and loosen himself up. Excellent plan, Briana."

She rolled her eyes. She always knew that Dash was nervous, or serious, if he started calling her by her full name. She would never understand these divisions of class and rank in England. She just hoped she could make her way through the evening without embarrassing Dash too much. She considered why, when his whole life had been carefully cultivated to tweak his father's ideas of propriety, that Dash suddenly seemed to care about what his father thought. Perhaps he was more sensitive to his father's criticisms than he let on. Perhaps he was trying to protect *her*.

His father sent a car out from London to fetch them. The driver texted them from the curb to alert them he was waiting.

Dash stopped in front of the mirror beside the front door of their apartment and fiddled with his collar. Bree wasn't used to seeing him in a jacket, other than his Sherlock Holmes-esque manny uniform.

"You look great, Dash."

He looked down on her and smiled. "As do you."

She'd known he would want her to impress his father, so she had borrowed a dress from one of their classmates and taken a month's worth of
spending money to splurge on a decent pair of heels.

"Ready?" he asked, squaring his shoulders. She nodded. He reached
for the doorknob. "Oh," he added, inclining his head to the small stand
by the door. "You got mail today. Looks like it is from home. Why don't
you take it with you? You can read it in the car, steady your nerves."

She smirked—she wasn't nervous at all. Still, she swiped the stack of
mail and shoved it into her purse, taking it and her rucksack with her as
they swept through the door. Dash waited for her at the step and took
her hand.

She was getting more comfortable with his affection, she thought to
herself as he opened the car door and helped her settle in. Even though
sometimes she couldn't tell what was real and what was for their cover, she
was getting used to the feel of his fingers entwined with hers, to the way
he touched the small of her back to guide her forward on the sidewalk or
when they crossed the street.

"Hello, Charles," he said cordially to the driver when he eased next to
her on the soft leather of the back seat.

"Sir," the driver responded with a nod, his inquisitive eyes watching
through the rearview mirror.

"This is Miss Parrish. I suppose you will see her now and again," Dash
explained casually.

"Miss," Charles addressed her, politely.

"Hello, Charles. Thank you for driving us this evening."

"Of course, Miss."

"It will be a little over two hours," Dash explained as they pulled away
from the curb. "I'm sorry tea will be so late. I should have brought a bit
of something for you to snack on."

"It's fine, Dash. Really. I'm not hungry. I'll just do homework. I have lots to do. That essay for—"

Dash cut her off with a sharp look of warning. He tapped his ears and tilted his head toward the front.

"I'll just listen to some music, myself," he stated, popping his earphones in and settling back into the bucket seat.

Bree sighed. She was tired of having to be so careful all the time. Resigned, she unzipped her bag and dug out her laptop to power it up. As the green countryside flashed by outside the darkened sedan windows, she powered through her checklist, working methodically through the readings and assignments of each class. After nearly two hours, she reluctantly turned to the last item on her list, rereading the essay topic from *Seduction and the Spy*.

"Stories of so-called 'honey traps' and 'Romeo spies' are abundant in popular culture. Yet the use of actual sexual liaisons to entrap or recruit an informant, or gain access to targeted information, is quite rare. Why do such images persist in the public's imagination? When might such recourse be justified? And what intellectual or emotional elements of seduction actually are present in the techniques of the modern-day spy? Cite specific examples. Present your answer in 2,000 words or less."

She groaned. She had been relieved when all the rumors about their class—that they'd be learning everything from how to dress to entice a man, to actual sex techniques—were false. But she didn't like the subject, nonetheless. She didn't like dwelling on what had become known as the "Dark Triad"—the narcissism, Machiavellianism, and psychopathy that supposedly was the common link between sexual seduction and the work of the spy.

She thought about the people in her class and in her study group. Were they all emotionally broken? Did spy craft somehow manage to attract people who were otherwise a danger to society . . . people who were so estranged and bereft of normal ties that disappearing into a role or an operation—ignoring the insistent beat of conscience—became second nature? Or did the experience of being surveilled and manipulated, the way the Agency treated them every day, turn them into the psychopaths the dry researchers warned against?

After all, look at Susmita.

She snuck a glance at Dash out of the corner of her eye. He was leaning back in his seat, eyes closed. Every shadow and sign of worry had disappeared from his face, and a slight smile tugged at the corners of his mouth as he hummed along.

She felt her own features soften as she watched his pleasure in the music.

She let her mind wander to their last *Seduction and the Spy* class session. They'd taken advantage of the assigned exercise to get ready for their roles, boyfriend and girlfriend, in preparation for tonight. It had been convenient, that lesson: a review of a famous psychological study that had established that intimacy between strangers could be artificially— nay, freakishly—accelerated by having them ask one another a specific series of thirty-six personal questions. The questions were sequenced to have each be more probing than the previous, the underlying idea being that mutual vulnerability and sustained, reciprocal self-disclosure would create an unbreakable bond.

"You'll find these questions very useful to hook yourself a compliant asset. Say, to recruit an unwitting ally as you attempt to gather information, or even to overtly recruit a complicit agent. Perhaps it is a fellow staff member at a home where you serve as nanny. Perhaps it will be the master of the house. Use these as a fast track to deep trust. They'll do anything you ask. Just be careful you don't fall in love, yourself. Very messy, that," the professor had added with a wink.

She and Dash had paired up for the homework—the actual practice of the questions.

"Would you like to be famous? In what way," Bree had read off the notecard.

"Aren't I already? I'm the manny, after all," Dash had demurred. "Move on to the next question."

Bree had shrugged. "Before making a telephone call, do you ever rehearse what you are going to say? Why?"

Dash then had snorted. "Who makes actual phone calls these days?"

"You called your father, to set up our dinner," Bree had reminded him.

He'd paused. "Yes, I did."

"Did you practice what you were going to say?"

He'd looked at his watch. "Thirty-six of these, you say? This will undoubtedly be tedious."

She'd rolled her eyes. "Just answer the question, will you?"

"Yes, Briana. I rehearsed what I was going to say to the duke."

"How many times?"

He'd sighed. "A few. Several." Bree had watched him silently count. "Perhaps ten times."

"Ten times? Why?"

He'd made a face. "I've never brought a girl home before. I wanted this phone call—this request—to be perfect. I have a tendency to, shall we say, tweak him with every opportunity. I needed to resist the temptation this time because I couldn't afford to make him angry. I needed him to agree to dinner. For you." He'd then looked at his hands. "It is important to you, so it was important to me. That's why I did it."

Bree hadn't known what to say.

"My turn," Dash had then insisted, snatching the note cards from her hands and reading aloud. "What would constitute a 'perfect' day for you?"

"I don't believe in perfect. I believe in good enough."

"Boring answer. On to the next. When did you last sing to yourself or to someone else?"

Her heart had lurched. "On the container ship. To the Asker children."

He'd put down the cards. "Oh, Bree. I'm sorry to dredge that up. Though I suppose it must constantly be on your mind, lurking in the back somewhere."

"You're right. It never goes away, really. But it's okay. It's the exercise, isn't it? Not you."

"Right you are. What did you sing?" he'd probed gently.

She'd given a soft, rueful laugh, embarrassed to admit the truth. "I trotted out 'Mustang Sally,' can you believe it? A whole year of nanny school under my belt and that was all I could muster."

He'd laughed then. "Just like the first day we met."

She'd smiled, genuine happiness flooding her at the memory. "Just like."

He'd reached across to her and held her hands between his. "I knew we would be friends the instant we met, you know. There is just something about you, Mistress Bellona. You are quite remarkable."

Even now, Bree flushed with the memory of their exchange. It wasn't just the compliment that had made her blush. It was the way he had made her feel and the course of electricity that had sparked through her when he had taken her hand.

Now, in the twilight of the evening as they sped along the highway, she stole another look at him where he leaned against the seat, lost in the music.

He was bruised, maybe, but not fundamentally damaged. No, no matter what the theorists said about spies and their motivations, she and her friends weren't that dark. None of them were that broken.

Chiding herself that she'd let her own train of thought go so astray, she tossed her laptop back in her bag and reached for her purse. Maybe that mail would be a good distraction after all, she thought.

She flicked through the pile. Most of it was junk—fliers for computer repair, a couple of catalogs, a local newspaper that was mostly filled with real estate advertisements. The letter addressed to her was near the bottom of the stack. She smiled, recognizing Ollie's childish scrawl, and ripped open the air mail envelope.

She scanned it quickly, eager for news from Alabama. He rattled through news of his school and new grade, the antics of a new kitten the orphanage had adopted, and the completion of the barn renovations. She noted with surprise that some of the new children Rodney had mentioned had already arrived, Ollie describing them as having funny accents. She chuckled at the irony, knowing how indecipherable an Alabama accent was to most of the world. They'd begun trading little vignettes for Rascal, their imaginary Wonder Dog, by mail, to keep their storytelling going, and this letter was no exception, with a whole paragraph dedicated to the latest plot twist Ollie had devised. She skipped over some of the details, her eye drawn to his questions about Dash and his final plea for her to come home and bring Dash with her.

She nudged Dash in the ribs, startling him. He pulled out one earphone.

"A letter to me . . . but from your fan club," she said, smiling and offering the paper to him to read.

Confused, Dash took the letter and began reading. He grinned. "Rascal? Who's that?"

"The Wonder Dog from our stories, remember?"

Dash cocked an eyebrow. "Really?"

"Yes, why?"

"No reason. It just didn't ring a bell." He briskly changed the topic. "I appreciate having Ollie in my corner and would love to accept his gracious invitation," he said. Feeling suddenly shy, she looked out the window. "We're about five minutes away," Dash added. "I'll have to finish this later—the little man is quite prolific."

She turned away from the view and began to collect her belongings, but Dash placed a gentle hand on her forearm to stop her. "No need to pack up—you can leave your things here. Charles will stay with the car until we're ready to return."

The five minutes turned into ten, and then fifteen, as they moved with fits and starts through the traffic of Mayfair. Bree was now paying attention. With every block, she felt her stomach turn over a bit. Perhaps she *was* a little bit nervous after all.

"Isn't this—" she started. Dash cut her off, anticipating her question.

"The street with the bar where we took our drinks after that scavenger hunt—yes. You have sharp eyes."

She pressed her face to the window and counted the fancy boutiques and stately red brick mansions as they went by.

"It's . . ." she searched for the right word.

"Posh? Yes, rather. Don't worry. You'll be right at home, I promise you." He gave her hand a squeeze.

"We've arrived at the town house, sir." Charles parked the car and got out to open the door for Bree.

She stepped out of the car, and instantly she was aware that they were in a more private enclave. The traffic's noise had melted away; the street was traversed by one or two pedestrians rather than cars.

She stood and gawked while Charles tactfully stepped aside. Dash came over to take her hand.

"When he said town house, he meant like an apartment or condo, right?" she clarified, staring up at the impressive structure before her. A few perfunctory steps led down from a massive, peacock-blue door framed by columns. The entire building—all three stories of it, nearly a block wide—seemed wrapped in a pristine stucco that flashed in the dying sun. Brilliant light gleamed from the tiers of bow-front windows, studded by wrought iron balconies that wrapped the entire building.

Dash smiled. "No. That's what everyone calls their old homes in London. This one has been in the family since the 1800s."

She took a deep breath.

He patted her hand. "No need for nerves, Mistress Bellona. The duke will be on his best behavior. Shall we?"

He drew her up the steps and rang the bell.

Instantly, the door swung open. They'd been expected.

"Sir," an older uniformed man Bree took to be a butler addressed them. "Welcome home. Miss," he added with a nod, sweeping his arm wide to invite her in, "welcome to Chesterfield House."

Dash guided her over the threshold with a gentle press in the small of her back.

She had to consciously try to keep her mouth closed. She was overwhelmed by the massive entry hall. An octagonal pattern of inlaid marble tiles spread across the floor like a carpet. Twin staircases decadently curved from the second story, a crystal chandelier flaming between them. Portraits of men and women she could only assume were Dash's ancestors loomed on the walls, staring down at them over stiff lace collars and under towering pompadours.

The butler faded into the corner like a ghost.

Dash loosened his tie. "This way. My father will be waiting in the library."

Bree followed, still holding his hand as she trailed along, trying not to twist her ankle as she teetered on her new heels. She surreptitiously tried to grasp the history of Dash's family from the paintings as they worked their way back through the rabbit warren of his home. Some of the art seemed out of place—garish neon graffiti, weird abstractions, and ugly, depressing landscapes. Some walls had glaring gaps where art had been removed, the discolored dark rectangles of wallpaper a giveaway. Dash seemed to take note, glaring at a couple of these as they passed.

They kept walking, passing or going through countless rooms as they cut through to a back staircase—this one less grand—and climbed up one flight. Soon they faced a set of well-polished marquetry double doors.

Dash twisted the brass doorknob.

"Father, we've arrived," he announced as the doors gave way and he strode into the room, pulling Bree behind him. As her eyes adjusted to the dim light of the study, the duke's richly accented voice called out in response.

"So I see. Come in, son. You were a little late—I imagine traffic was a horror—so I had them lay the table in here. I thought we'd dine by the fireplace. There's a bit of a chill tonight, don't you think?"

She spotted him then, his back to the low fire, sitting in a wheelchair. He'd been pushed close to a small table over which a cloth had been draped. Covered dishes crowded together. Three places had been set. A stand holding a bottle of wine was at his side.

"Well, what are you waiting for? Come in and introduce me to this girlfriend of yours."

Bree saw the muscle in Dash's jaw twitch. Whatever he was going to say, he bit it back and led Bree across the room.

"Father, I would like to present to you Briana Parrish, my classmate at Norwood." Dash's father's mouth tightened at his deliberate mention of the nanny school.

Bree remembered her social-graces class and bobbed a slight curtsy, wobbly on her heels.

"Briana, this is my father, James Heyward, his Grace, the Duke of—"

"I daresay she knows who I am, Dashiell. No need to stand on formality. Briana, is it? It is a pleasure to meet you. I cannot say that Dashiell has told us much about you, but that is probably to be expected. I am therefore quite looking forward to getting to know you this evening. Come sit by me." He gestured to the seat closest to the fireplace with his right hand.

"And please, call me James. If you call me Lord Heyward or 'Your Grace,' I shall have to send you home without your tea."

Dash and Bree stared, tongue-tied.

"Are you not hungry, the two of you? Come on then. Sit down."

They scrambled to their seats.

"We shan't have any waitstaff this evening. I sent them away. Thought it would be cozier without extra people loitering about. So, please," James indicated with a nod of his head, "help yourselves." He reached from the chair to remove the dishes' covers, awkwardly maneuvering in his seat to tuck them with a clang in a shelf that Bree realized was built into the table.

"Briana, please," he urged her with careful, if exaggerated, politeness. "Begin. Cook makes a lovely chicken pasty. Just the thing for an autumn night such as this. You shouldn't let it get cold."

Bree scanned the utensils laid out across the table and made her best guess as to which one she should use. She studiously dug into the crust and scooped out a steaming serving of the pot pie onto her plate. It was awkwardly quiet as she served Dash and his father, in turn, managing to serve the main and then the sides without spilling on the damask table-cloth. James splashed some wine in each of their glasses and set to his plate, eating rapidly as if afraid the food was going to disappear. The soft food yielded to his fork easily; Bree guessed the meal was designed to avoid the need for cutting out of deference to his left hand, which drooped in his lap.

Before Bree could say anything to break the silence, Dash cleared his throat. "There appears to be more art taken from the galleries downstairs."

"Yes, yes," Dash's father acknowledged with his mouth full, vaguely waving his fork around in the air as he explained. "Your stepmother had another one of her little projects to fund. You know how she gets."

"You promised," Dash said quietly.

James frowned. "We've made a lot of promises to one another, my boy—both of us—which we haven't exactly kept. Do you wish to air them right now in front of this young woman? Or shall we enjoy a civilized conversation with our dinner, instead?" He carefully placed his fork down and stared at Dash, waiting for an answer. There was a faint glimmer of anger—or maybe desperation—in his eyes, Bree noted, like a wounded animal preparing to strike.

Dash sat in stony silence.

"I thought so," James muttered. He quaffed down his wine and poured another glass. "Briana, tell me about your people," he demanded, brusquely changing the subject.

"She has no people," Dash spat through gritted teeth. He balled up his napkin in his hand. "I already told you that."

"I can speak for myself, Dashiell," Bree said softly, placing a hand on his fist.

Dash looked surprised, but relaxed his fingers at Bree's touch. She wrapped his hand in hers and turned to face James more fully. He was appraising her now. She could tell he was surprised she'd spoken up. From the slight droop at the left corner of his mouth, she guessed it had been a stroke that had put him in that chair. He narrowed his eyes, conscious of her gaze, and picked up his fork, hunching over his food to scoop another bite.

"I was raised in an orphanage," she began. "But I know who my family were," she averred, studiously ignoring the look of panic that came across Dash's face at her mention of her actual family. "I'll tell you all about them, if first you can tell me about that lovely estate of yours in Ireland."

"Which one?" James muttered, never looking up from his plate.

"Ullabreagh," Bree clarified. "Dashiell took me to visit it. He told me you won it in a poker game?"

"Ha! Yes, I did. My luck at cards was always better than my luck with business. Or women, for that matter. Ullabreagh fell into my lap in the most peculiar way. I don't believe even you know the full story, Dashiell."

"I doubt it," Dash said drily, pushing away his half-eaten dinner. "Please, enlighten us."

"I drew a royal flush." He paused, baiting them.

Dash tried not to show his exasperation.

"But from whom?" Bree asked, careful to keep her tone somewhat light and playful. "In what circumstances? It's not every day one puts an entire estate into the kitty in a poker game. Surely there is something more dramatic you can share with us?"

"Why should you care?"

"Because I find it interesting," Bree persisted. "Do tell us, James. I'd love to hear about it."

James tossed down his napkin and leaned back in the wheelchair. "I played a regular gentleman's game back then," he began. "There was a usual group of us, mostly men I'd gone to school with. One of our old mates had turned up—had asked to be invited, actually. I hadn't seen him since he'd married. An awful woman, she was. None of us liked her, to tell the truth, and our wives disliked her even more. She wasn't one of us, nobody really knew her, and she was simply . . . what would I call her? Cold. Off-putting. Unnatural. Anyway, we'd all let them drift out of our circle, if you'd like. Hadn't heard from him in a few years. Then, he just showed up out of thin air. He'd run into one of us in the city and had somehow talked his way into the next game."

"He'd known about the game, then?" Dash probed.

"I don't recall," James answered. He maneuvered the wheelchair a bit away from the table, as much as he could do with one hand. "Pour me a whiskey, would you, Briana? You'll find it over in the cabinet. No ice. There's a dear."

Bree fought the temptation to bristle and moved quickly, wanting nothing to interrupt his reminiscences. She fixed his drink, her back to him and Dash while she poured the honey-gold liquid from a cut-crystal decanter that seemed to weigh as much as a bowling ball. When she returned to place the drink in James's hand, the dinner table had been moved away. Dash was sitting on a stuffed chair a few paces away from his father.

"Thank you, Briana. Now, where was I? Ah, yes. The poker game. Our friend had arrived promptly for the game. He had an atrocious string of bad luck. He was dealt horrible cards all night, from what I could tell, and couldn't bluff to save his life; he was on tilt the entire evening—twitchy, it seemed to me. But something compelled him on. He refused to cut his losses. I, on the other hand, was having a spectacular evening. I wasn't quite gloating, but I was relishing the chance to step away from the table with some sizable winnings, for a change. Anyhow, our friend had already bumped up the limits we normally placed upon ourselves and we were preparing to call it a night, lest our wives take issue with our bad habit. But he insisted. He insisted, repeatedly, that he needed to win. He needed the money, desperately—he as much as said so—but he was down to the felt, as it were. So he made an astonishing offer—he offered to wager his family's estate in Ireland in return for the chance to win the evening's stakes."

"You weren't playing low stakes, then," Bree asserted.

James smiled a tight smile. "They were low to us, at the time, my dear. We were idiots to be throwing around that much money. It was a tidy sum, enough that he was willing to put up a nice piece of property for a chance to redeem himself. He wanted us to make a bet, all in. The rest of our chums thought he was insane and refused him. But I, feeling both sorry for him and a little invincible, decided to take him up on it."

"You drew a royal flush," Dash stated with a long, low whistle. "That's some luck."

"Yes, well. I didn't feel lucky once it had happened. All the color drained from his face. He only realized what he had done after the fact. I tried to laugh it off, give him a way to back out, but he was a gentleman, through and through, so he made good on the bet. I was sorry to see him do it, to tell you the truth."

James turned to his son. "That's part of the reason why I put Ullabreagh into commercial operation, Dashiell. I have no desire to spend time there myself. It just makes me feel guilty for having played a part in ruining someone so thoroughly."

"You think you ruined him?" Bree persisted.

James knocked back a slug of whiskey and nodded. "I'm sure he was on the brink when he came to the game. Why else gamble so recklessly? I'd heard he had gone through a nasty divorce—perhaps that had something to do with it. His family did not have that many landholdings, and as you saw, Ullabreagh is a gem. Losing it would have been a grievous financial blow, to be sure, not to mention the shame of it. I don't know that he ever showed his face again in London. He sort of just vanished. I never did hear what became of him."

Bree stifled a cry. What had been going on that drove her father to take such a drastic risk?

James looked at her sharply. "You judge me? You think I am a monster?"

She shook her head, unable to speak. She stepped away into the darkness away from the fire to compose herself, stumbling around the overstuffed furniture, blinking back hot tears. When she reached the end of the room, she gave in and let them flow down her cheeks.

All she'd wanted was a little glimpse of what her father had been like. She hadn't expected a reckless, desperate man, foolish enough to bet away his fortune. Was that what he'd really been like? Was it really something to do with his ex-wife? Or had something gone awry in his spying to provoke such desperation?

She could hear Dash and his father whispering softly, just out of earshot.

Then James raised his voice, angry, and a rapid volley of accusations—words she still couldn't make out—went back and forth between them.

Finally, from across the room, Dash called to her. "Bree, come here."

She wiped her face on her sleeve and reluctantly went back to join them beside the fire, standing awkwardly, unsure what to do.

"I told him," Dash said tersely from where he leaned against the mantel. She could see the muscles of his back strain through his jacket. "You can ask him anything you want. Anything at all. He will tell you what he can. He knows you're not here to demand your inheritance, though I wouldn't blame you if you did. He cheats at cards." He pushed away from the mantel and strode toward the door. "Take your time. I'll be waiting in the car." He slammed the door behind him.

James cleared his throat. "I never cheated at poker."

Bree gave a harsh laugh that died quickly in the stifling air of the library. "It doesn't matter. I didn't come here for that. I came to learn about my father. You said you knew him from school. What was he like back then?"

James sighed. "He was like all boys in our set, I suppose. Sporty. Confident. Smart. The Huttons were a good family, all right. He was an only child so a little spoiled, I suppose. His parents thought he could do no wrong and he knew it. Gave him a bit of arrogance, but if I'm honest, we all had it. He just had a bit more. He definitely wasn't that same David that I remembered when he turned up at the poker match. Maybe the divorce had done him in, though, good riddance, if you ask me. We all hoped he'd remarry but I didn't ever hear about that, either."

Bree bit her tongue. "The wife," she stated, jumping on his last comment. "You didn't like her. Did you know her well?"

He shook his head. "I told you, none of us did. He announced their engagement quite suddenly, and they married in what seemed like haste—though, in retrospect, they didn't have a child for a bit of time. So it wasn't forced, or anything like that—that would have been unlikely as she seemed rather without family, herself. With it being so fast, it wasn't much of an affair. Quite small, actually," he sniffed.

"You were there?" Bree pressed him.

"Of course. Our little Eton set always turned out for one of our own. The Huttons and some school chums, that was it."

"Do you have pictures?"

James threw up his one good hand. "Who knows? If I did, I would never be able to find them. My lovely bride has begun packing up all my things. I'm surprised you didn't notice the boxes in the corners. We've sold the place," he confided, with a bitter twist of his mouth, "to pay for her 'hobbies,' as she likes to call them. Hundreds of years in my family, and now it will pass to some Saudi Arabian's hands. I'm like the rest of my neighbors in that respect, I suppose." He reached over and pulled a cord near the mantel. A servant entered from a rear door and stood discreetly against the paneling, awaiting his signal.

"You can dig around in the boxes over there. Those will be old photo albums, school pictures and the like." He waved toward one of the darker corners of the library. "Help yourself to whatever you find. I will be amazed if you can surface anything in that heap of detritus, but I was amazed by this entire evening, so perhaps you shall prove me wrong. Barbara," he said wearily, waving the servant over. "Take me to my dressing room."

Barbara expertly gripped the handles on the back of the chair and wheeled him toward the door. "You can let yourself out when you've satisfied your curiosity," he told Bree, his dismissal of her serving as his goodbye.

Bree didn't wait for the door to close behind him before darting over to the stacks of boxes. She felt her way around the walls until she found a light switch. Flipping it on, she doused the entire library in blazing electric light. To her relief, she found each box was labeled clearly, the years of its contents written in black marker on the outside. Within ten minutes, she located the ones for which she was looking and began ripping open their duct-tape seals.

An hour had passed by the time Bree threw herself into the back of the waiting car. Dash had drifted off to sleep. She shoved at him, hard, startling him awake.

"We need to go." She leaned over the front seat to Charles. "Charles, we need to go. Now. Back to Bath."

"Sir?" Charles asked, confused.

Dash yawned, stretching, and gave her a cross look. "Well, hello to you too. Let me revisit the norms of polite society for you, Briana, as it seems you may have forgotten while under the scintillating influence of my dear father. 'Thank you, Dash, for sitting through a hellish evening with your father so that I could satisfy my curiosity. Thank you, Dash, for waiting for me in the car while I did God knows what for over an hour. Thank you, Dash—'"

"Dash!" She pounded the leather seat with her fist. "We don't have time for this. Can we get going? Please? I want to go home. Now."

Out of the corner of her eye, Bree saw Charles arch his eyebrows as he looked into the rearview mirror, waiting for a sign from Dash.

Dash sighed, rubbing the sleep away from his eyes. "Of course. Charles, please. Go on. And roll up the divider glass, will you? I believe Miss Parrish and I need to have a little chat."

He waited until the soundproof screen was fully in place, and they were on the road, before asking Bree, "Whatever has gotten into you?"

"This." She pulled something out of her pocket. "Your dad let me go through the boxes in the library and—"

"What boxes?" Dash interrupted.

"The ones being packed for the move."

"What? Did you just say they're *moving*?" Dash burst out in anger, working himself into a sudden but full rant. "Did he sell the house? Why hasn't he told me? It's for the money, isn't it? I knew my stepmother would stop at nothing—"

"Not now, Dash. He told me where to look to find photos of David Hutton at Eton with him, and pictures of David Hutton's wedding. Look." Hands shaking, she thrust a three-by-five-inch slip of paper at him. She watched his face as he peered at it in the dim light.

"It's very faded," he said doubtfully, stifling a yawn.

"Look at the bride, Dash. Look at her."

He peered closer, squinting, and gasped. "But—"

"You see it too."

"My God."

He held the photo out to her, his own hands shaking now, too. They tilted their heads over it, staring at the surprising face that looked out, unsmiling for the camera, from under a flimsy cascade of tulle.

Judy Roberts had been David Hutton's first wife.

They sat quietly, stunned. The sick feeling in Bree's stomach did not diminish as the miles of the M4 sped by.

"We need to pull over," Bree demanded.

"We can't just stop on the roadway, Bree," Dash explained, trying to rationalize with her. "It's not far now. Surely you can—"

"Now! I need to stop now!"

Dash banged on the glass and signaled Charles to pull off. Bree hurled herself out of the car and leaned over, vomiting into the ditch beside the car. She retched until there was nothing left but acid. When she'd stopped heaving, Dash pulled her wracked body up into his arms, brushing back her hair and patting her back in circular motions until she stopped shaking.

She pulled herself out of his embrace and dragged her sleeve across her mouth. Drawing a shaky breath, she looked up at Dash.

His face was contorted in the red flashing emergency lights of the sedan, but she could see that something more had shifted. His confident manner had vanished. His erect carriage had collapsed with weariness. His eyes looked frightened and confused.

"What is it, Dash?"

He worked his mouth wordlessly. Giving up, he pulled a piece of paper out of his jacket pocket. "Ollie drew a picture on the back of his letter," he said, his voice flat. He held the paper out to her. "I noticed it earlier, when we were pulling up to meet dear old Dad, but I didn't really pay attention to it. I went back to finish the letter while I waited for you, and I looked at it, *really* looked at it, and grew suspicious. And now, with what you just told me . . ."

She took the page and looked.

It was three little girls—she could tell they were girls despite their extremely short hair because of the dresses they wore—and a little boy. Ollie had carefully labeled his crayon masterpiece *The New Kids*, under-lining the careful letters in black. Below the title, he had written, "They aren't from here, but they know some songs."

He had drawn little speech bubbles coming out of the children's mouths.

"Itsy Bitsy Spider," said the first one.

"Little Miss Muffet," said the next.

"Fish? Fisk?" said the third, the first word crossed out, the second misspelling a dead giveaway. *It's fis*, she thought to herself, fiercely, the remaining words of the Turkish lullaby that had been so dear to her little charges bursting forth from where she'd repressed them in her brain.

Bree drew her hand to her mouth, unable to breathe. She didn't need to, but she forced herself to read the words Ollie had depicted being sung by the fourth child.

"Ride, Sally, ride."

Her lungs screamed out for air. Her ragged breathing chased the feelings of rage and hope and fear that competed for supremacy in the tightness of her chest.

She howled in frustration.

The missing Asker children, singing the songs they'd desperately sung in the hole of the shipping container—nursery rhymes and the old R&B tune that she had taught them—had surfaced at her childhood orphanage home in Alabama.

Back at Jaguar House, they huddled over the kitchen table. It reminded Bree of the night they'd learned the truth about the Agency—the night they'd learned they weren't to become just nannies, but spies.

Only this time, there were only three of them.

Dash and Bree, uneasy but seeing no other choice, had waited for Ruby to return from the library. Under the blinking fluorescent light, Ruby's face had taken on an ashen gray pallor, marked by heavy shadows, as she contemplated the implications of what they'd learned.

"We have to go get them," Bree asserted. "They're in danger."

"Bree, it looks like Judy is behind this all," Dash began, his manner seeming to Bree as if he was picking his way through the minefield of her emotions. "And if she is, you have to consider—"

"Rodney isn't involved. I know it." Bree pressed her lips together and crossed her arms, refusing to even contemplate the possibility.

"Bree," he continued gently. "Think about it. I'm not saying he's guilty. I'm just saying you have to consider it. You're sure you haven't heard anything from Judy? Nothing at all?"

"What are you accusing me of?" Bree spat at him. "None of that matters. We have to go get those children."

Ruby arched a brow and shot Dash a skeptical glance. What she said next surprised Bree. "You can't go anywhere, anyway, with those trackers in your neck. It's time they came out."

"How?" Bree shot back.

"The way I've said from the beginning. We dig them out."

Dash shuddered. "Isn't there another way? Can't we somehow disrupt the signal?"

Ruby curtly shook her head. "I've looked into it during my free time on the management desk. Discreetly, of course. They lied when they told us it was a GPS device. It actually uses wireless RFID technology, which makes sense: It doesn't need batteries because any wireless station within a mile can power it. As a failsafe, it has a chip that taps into our own bodies' electrical charges to keep going. It has virtually unlimited networking potential, as the grid it taps into is everywhere. So the only way to cut it off is to cut it out. Literally."

Bree gulped and ran her fingers over the bump in the back of her neck. "How big is it?"

"You think it's big, right? If you're like me, it feels huge underneath your fingers, a massive lump there where they shot it in. But it's tiny. Like a grain of rice. MIT technology, that—right clever. But I can get it. I know I can."

"It's a sensitive area, Ruby," Dash said, contemplating her proposal. "What are the risks?"

Ruby stared at him, chin jutting. "Theoretically, if I cut too deep, I injure your spinal cord. It's placed high enough up into the cervical area that I could paralyze the muscles used for breathing. It would be fatal, unless we had access to a ventilator, and it would be permanent. But I won't. The reason it feels so big to your touch is it wasn't embedded very deeply. It's not too far from the surface of your skin. It won't take much to extract it."

"How do you know?" Dash pressed.

"I've been practicing," she said quietly. "I knew this day would come."

"How?" Bree asked, bewildered.

Ruby shrugged, the beads on her braids clinking matter-of-factly. "I had my mum ask the doc she works for if I could use an old lab. Didn't tell them the reason why, of course, just that it would help me get extra credit for Norwood." She grinned. "So, I've been injecting objects into lab animals to see if I can extract them without killing or maiming the animals. And I'm pretty certain that if I can do it on a bunch of shaved-down guinea pigs and mice, I can do it on you."

Bree gaped. From the gloating look on Ruby's face, she knew Ruby was reveling in the satisfaction of having irrefutably proven, once again, her superiority. This time, though, Bree didn't mind. She was down-right grateful.

"A tad gruesome, Ruby, but effective. How will we keep Norwood from knowing we've removed the trackers?" Dash asked.

"Simple," Ruby reasoned. She ticked off the key points of her impromptu plan on her fingers. "We just leave the sensors here, on your pillows. We pretend you're unable to attend classes because of illness. I'll make sure to talk it up, how sick you are, how contagious you may be, so no one wants to come calling. I'll work the schedule to ensure I get extra office duty—that way, I can be in place to intercept and doctor the readouts of your vitals. That should give you a few days' lead before they know you've bolted."

"That will expose you, Ruby," Bree cautioned.

She shrugged. "Leave that to me. I'll find a way to handle it. Unless you have a better idea?"

A desperate thought came, unbidden, out of Bree's mouth. "Could we just go to Albourn and tell her the truth?"

"Are you mad?" Dash scoffed. He and Ruby both looked at her like she was crazy. "You said yourself, you don't know who's in on what. Sure, if Norwood is on the side of good, we'll be greeted as heroes when we return the children, and we'll receive no more than a slap on the wrist for violating their precious rules. But if the Agency is not . . ."

He left the statement hanging in the air.

"Remember," Ruby added, "any time a child is protected by an Agency nanny, it simply provides a cover for Norwood's true purpose. The mission will always come first. We know that now."

Bree knew what could happen if they were wrong. They were betting their lives.

Bree turned to face Ruby squarely in her seat. "How much time do you need?"

"Give me five days. That way I can arrange to pick up the extra office shifts to ensure I'm on duty when this all goes down. We should aim for Friday, directly after classes. No one will look for you over the weekend, which will give you a head start. I should be able to cover for you for at least three more days, maybe five. That will give you up to a full week to get to Alabama and get those kids out."

"I'll get working on transport. That will be tricky, but I have an idea," Dash said.

"That leaves me," Bree said slowly, bitter acceptance seeping through her like a poison, "to figure out exactly how to confront Rodney."

Dash reached out to wrap her hand in his. "Let's hope it doesn't come to that."

"Hope is not a strategy," Ruby retorted tartly. She sized them up before shoving away from the table. "If we're agreed, let's get moving. Bree, make sure you have a plan for weapons."

Bree swallowed down her panic, focusing on the logic of things. "Transportation will matter. If we go commercial, we'll only be able to take in the disassembled plastic pieces Norwood has issued us. They'll escape detection by security. That leaves us one gun each. I can always build some small bombs once we're on the ground," she added, chewing her lip.

Ruby nodded. "I knew that *Boom!* class would come in handy one day—I just didn't realize how soon." She continued, philosophically, "The good thing about America is you should be able to figure out how to get access to as many chemicals and guns as you need, if Loverboy here can find a way to get you in. If we're smart enough, you'll never have to use them."

Satisfied with their plan, Ruby walked down the hall to their bedroom.

"She seems almost made for this, doesn't she?" Dash mused, watching her close the door. "Do you trust her?"

Bree found the question complicated. On the one hand, though sometimes rude and overbearing, Ruby, in all her bluntness, possessed an air of transparency and authenticity—what you saw was what you got, no artifice. And Bree had experienced her brusque practicality as a cover for emotions that were, deep down, quite caring. On the other hand, Ruby's streak of self-promotion had been evident from the beginning. And Bree was unsure if Ruby still secretly blamed her for their roommate Susie's death. What trade-offs would Ruby be willing to make as she weighed the balance of friendship, justice, and ambition?

"Briana?" Dash whispered when Bree didn't answer, breaking into her tangled thoughts with a squeeze of her hand. "Briana? I said, do you trust her?"

Bree shrugged. "I don't know if we have a choice."

"I snuck some spyware onto her laptop, just in case. I'll be able to watch every keystroke she makes."

She sighed. How fragile the trust was between them. "When did you do that?"

"That night I gave you a backrub . . . after *Boom!* You were so stiff from bending over the bomb mechanisms, remember? You fell right asleep. It only took a minute. Her password was easy to guess."

"What was it?"

He paused, thumb rubbing the tops of her knuckles. "InMemory ofSusie."

She let her head fall to her chest, swallowing her sorrow and misgivings, harsher than whiskey.

"Are you alright? Do you want me to stay up with you for a while?"

Bree raised her eyes to meet Dash's look of concern and smiled weakly. She squeezed his hand, in turn, and shook her head. "No, Dash. I'll be fine. You go on to bed. I'll turn in soon. I promise."

He peered into her eyes, the worried crease of his forehead deepening. "You're sure?"

She nodded and forced herself to smile more brightly. "Go on, then. I'll see you in the morning. Turn the light off as you go, would you?"

He watched her for a moment and then nodded, releasing her hand. He flicked the light switch off as he passed through the door into his side of the suite. Bree sat in the dark, breathing deeply to battle back her mounting anxiety.

If we're smart enough, we'll never have to use the guns.

She repeated Ruby's words to herself, like a mantra.

But just as insistently, she heard Judy's voice, chiding her from over Susmita's fallen body. *"You have to be prepared to use your weapon, Bree. You could have died because you were too slow."*

In the woods of Alabama, behind John's makeshift stage and bar, she'd thought she was ready to do it, when the threat had come from a stranger.

But could she do it if the threat came from within?

Chapter Ten

MEG

1998, Northern Ireland

The ache in the small of her back was growing. Briana had stopped sleeping through the night, the disruption of household patterns throwing off her routine. Despite being undersized for a toddler, she was really too big to be carried around in the old baby sling, but it kept Meg's hands free for Rennie if the girl also woke in the middle of the night and gave her one less thing to worry about as she paced in the dark, trying to puzzle her way out of her dilemma.

In the heat of the negotiations with the British government, David had been made.

She knew she'd never get to the heart of who had done it, or exactly why. But the IRA was a sinking ship now, giving up on its principles to grasp at the flimsy excuse for peace that now presented itself. Infighting was tearing it apart. The British had been adamant that there must be a reckoning—that those who had committed atrocities be brought to account—a sticking point that for now was holding up the negotiations. There would be sacrifices to appease them. They would serve up the vulnerable:

bombers, smugglers, assassins, and chauffeurs who knew enough to seem significant but had burned out or run afoul of the commandants within the IRA power structure. They might throw in a few mid-level higher-ups in the commandant ranks to make a show. These individuals would all be offered up for punishment in hopes that it would be enough to stop the Brits from looking too deeply into the past as the IRA closed ranks and protected the truly big fish.

Meanwhile, accusations of treason flew as those still opposed to the negotiations desperately threw anything they could think of to sub-marine the talks. They were naming touts, going to the press to incite public opinion, and initiating purges from within—generally doing all that could be done to make the foundation of trust upon which the flimsy negotiations were built collapse under the weight of suspicion and horror.

David, her David, had been laid upon this altar.

He'd been fingered as a member of MI5.

He'd managed through the years to work his way into the inner sanctum of the IRA's Derry Brigade as a driver for the ones calling the shots—close enough to know everything that was taking place, but in the shadows, never the limelight where he might have detected suspicion. It gave him a ready excuse to go back and forth to Belfast, where he could pop unnoticed into the 220—the office deep inside Castlereagh Police Station that served as the headquarters of the government's anti-terrorism unit—running his own network of informants from within.

But someone had tipped off the Brigade. The raid on the house across the street from them and the pointed stares at the pub had made it clear—the Brigade expected David to turn himself in, to come in for a chat. She knew, more than most, that he would never come back from such an interrogation. If she was lucky, they would find his body, broken and burned, his eyes ghoulishly forced shut with masking tape, at the side of the road just over the border.

Her uncle Brian couldn't help. He had washed his hands of the IRA, joining a splinter group that vowed to never concede until the island was reunited under Irish rule. There was nothing he could do, now that he was an outsider—he'd be shot on sight.

In her room, Rennie cried in her sleep. She'd been rattled by her father's sudden disappearance. The years in Derry had kept David closer to home than when she was little, his trips to and from Belfast short enough that she barely missed him. They'd grown closer than ever. He'd been underground for a week now, and Rennie was distraught.

Meg had no choice but to ask for help. She didn't dare to signal anything in the window—she knew the house was being watched at all times. Same with a phone call—the boxes in her neighborhood were all destroyed and their own phone was tapped—a fact they'd used to their own advantage to place misinformation in the past.

She'd need to do a dead drop while walking the girls. After Mass would do.

She was restless, waiting for dawn and the low tolling of the bells to mark the early service. She managed to keep her patience when Rennie refused to eat her breakfast and Briana threw her own on the floor. She sat quietly in a pew toward the back, kneeling and praying and praying and praying, for she knew that it would take a miracle to get what she wanted.

She made sure she wasn't followed on her stroll, with the girls lolling in the double pram as she pushed resolutely through the neighborhood, past the murals, memorials, and walls that served as a constant reminder that this was no place for little children.

Meg made her drop and went back to the house to wait.

They'd pre-planned what to do in case of emergency. After the drop, she had to wait forty-eight hours. Then Judy, her handler, would set up a brush contact in the grocery store, passing Meg instructions during her weekly shop. They'd never had to use it before. She didn't know if David even had forty-eight hours. But that was protocol.

So she waited.

Tuesday evening, she begged her neighbor, Siobhan, to watch the girls so she could stock up on a few things, bribing her with a promised carton of cigarettes. She couldn't tell if Siobhan was one of the ones feeding information to the IRA, but it didn't matter. Meg's own desperation—her need to get away from the girls, her need for air to clear her head—made her pleas for help real.

The supermarket was crowded. She'd forgotten it was a payday. Not that there were jobs, she reminded herself bitterly. The surge was mostly those who'd received their dole.

The crowd would make it easier to proceed unnoticed.

She didn't even see the drop when it occurred; she found the note in her handbag once she was back in the house, unpacking her groceries. Her heart fell as she decoded and read the short response.

You must do your duty.

The postscript gave her one bit of hope to which she could cling: *Midnight tonight, usual location.*

———

The Protestant cemetery gates were unlocked and freshly oiled, allowing Meg to slip in. She didn't turn on her flashlight. She didn't need to—the moon was bright, hanging low in the sky, illuminating the path between headstones.

Judy was waiting for her, sitting on a tomb and smoking a cigarette. From the butts on the ground beneath her, it looked as if she'd been there for a while.

"You're late," she said gruffly.

"I needed to get the girls asleep. Even so, it's risky, leaving them alone like this. What if they wake up? What if something happens while I'm gone?"

"We'll have to make it fast, then, won't we?" Judy stubbed out her cigarette on the headstone and stood up. "Walk with me." She turned and began strolling through the graves, leaving Meg to scramble behind her.

"Why won't you help us escape?" Meg started in.

"You can't escape these people once they're on to you, Meg. Surely you know that."

A shudder went through Meg. "You don't know that."

"But I do. Without money and new identities, you'll be sitting ducks for the IRA. The British government won't help either one of you—you'd both be disavowed. There is too much at stake."

"We can get the money," Meg asserted, jutting her chin. "We could even forge new identities. But we need help getting out, because of the girls. It would be nothing to you to help us slip out of the country."

Judy laughed softly. "So you can get the money, can you? Do you know what your beloved husband has done in his desperate attempt to do just that?"

Meg's heart sank. "No."

"Oh, yes. You told him not to, I wager. At least I hope you did. But he did it anyway. He gambled it all and he lost. Not just your cash. He lost his family's estate."

"But how?" Meg cried in frustration.

Judy stopped and turned to face Meg, not bothering to hide the smug satisfaction on her face.

"Don't ever think the two of you can outsmart me, let alone the British government, Meg. Your fool of a husband telegraphed his intentions from the day he showed up in London. From there, it was easy—an easy thing to place an agent, to stack a deck, to spike a drink, to throw a game. Too easy. No, if you're going to get out of this mess, it will be my way. And you'll owe me. It is a debt on which I intend to collect payment."

Meg clenched her fists in fury. She was trapped.

"What do you want?" she spat.

"There will be time for that later. In the meantime, I have a way for you to get your entire family out of this mess you are in. It will require some work on your part, though."

She reached under her trench coat and pulled out a manila folder, holding it out toward Meg. Meg snatched it and began reading, straining under the moonlight.

"You can't be serious," Meg breathed as she took it in.

"Dead serious. The only way out of this is to distract the IRA leadership with a bigger piece of bait. You'll bring them this one and they won't have time to worry about Hutton."

"You want me to sneak into Castlereagh—by myself—and steal the file of the biggest double agent the British government has placed inside the IRA? Are you insane?"

"Do you have a better idea?"

"But why? Why this, when you could just let us go?"

Judy shrugged. "I told you. I'm not done with you yet."

"How can this possibly serve the British government? Or Norwood?"

"That's not for you to question," Judy said tersely. "You're a part of a bigger plan. You leave the Agency to me." Judy turned on her heel and began making her way toward the front of the churchyard. "You'll take some other files while you are in there, of course. One will have doctored surveillance on Hutton, exonerating him. Easy enough—he's turned out to be small potatoes, hasn't he?"

"You never liked him," Meg countered, rising to David's defense.

"What do you care? You should just be grateful I'm bothering to help you save him. He never managed to run a volume of arms to make anyone take notice, and his own agents have proved rather unreliable, wouldn't you say? Nobody would care if he disappeared. He'd just be a number. But at least you'll do something useful for me in exchange. Some of the other files will detail the personal details of other double agents. They'll be identified by code names, of course, but the files will make it easy to connect the dots so the IRA can determine their real names. They'll most likely lose their lives. The Brits will do their best to protect their prize double agent, so you probably won't have his blood on your hands, too, if that's any consolation. Of course," she pondered, "he *is* a psychopath and deserves to die, but that decision is above my pay grade. So, any questions?"

Judy stopped where they had started, standing in a scatter of cigarette butts.

"How do I—"

"Everything you need is in that file. Maps, weapons caches—everything. All you need to do is find a babysitter. Perhaps your underground uncle can do that for you. You can drop them off on the way to the Station." She smirked, apparently finding this complication funny. "That's all, agent. No need to contact me, even after it's done. I'll know from the chatter whether you've succeeded or not. And when you have, we'll work on getting you and your family out of this country to start a new life."

The handler sat down on a tombstone and drew another cigarette from her handbag, lighting it and taking a deep drag. Meg watched how Judy's hands trembled slightly as she waited for the nicotine to hit her system and wondered how a woman with such control could find herself so dependent.

The tension seemed to seep away from Judy's body with the ring of smoke she exhaled. Judy seemed thoughtful, pensive even, as she changed the subject. "The girls have been happy here, haven't they?"

Meg was startled by Judy's question. She cautiously answered.

"Yes. Well, Briana wouldn't know anything different. But Rennie has really come into her own. She has been happy."

"Adjusted to you, now?"

Meg couldn't help but smile. "It *has* been years, so it would be surprising if she hadn't. But, yes, we seem to have made another breakthrough.

She calls me Mummy now. I know it's ridiculous and sentimental, but it's left me absurdly pleased."

Judy grunted and took another drag of her cigarette.

"That's fine. Just fine. It's funny, isn't it, how resilient and flexible little children are? See how your stepdaughter has embraced you? It's as if you're the only mother she's ever known. And when you leave Ireland, they are both so young they'll forget all about it. It will be as if this place never even existed for them. Happy memories or sad, it will fade away into nothing, eclipsed by the here and now. Do you wonder if the same would be true if you didn't come back from your mission?"

Meg took in the horror of the thought before replying, her voice small but measured. "Why would you say such a thing?"

Judy didn't answer. She just smiled. "Now scurry home. You don't want those babies waking to find you're gone," she concluded, waving Meg away.

Meg hesitated, confused by the line of her handler's questioning and the abruptness of her dismissal, before letting herself out at the gate. As she walked home, her mind began turning over the near impossibility of the mission she'd been assigned. She turned back and noted the small red sparks of the tip of Judy's cigarette, floating in the darkness of the cemetery, until they were swallowed up by the night.

An American working undercover inside the facility had leaked a map marking a clear route to Room 220 through the maze-like corridors of the Castlereagh complex. Meg studied the path, memorizing it and a dozen byways in case of incident.

Her plan was bare bones, at best. She didn't want to take the time to think too deeply about it, for if she did, she knew she would be terrified.

She showed up at Brian's cottage doorstep, the girls and dog in tow. She didn't tell him where she was going, or what she was doing. She simply told him he needed to take the girls for forty-eight hours, maybe longer, and asked if she could use his loo. When she emerged, her hair was black and shorn like a man's.

"It'll be harder to get past the checkpoints as a man," Brian said gruffly.

She shrugged and handed him an envelope. "If I don't turn up within a week, read this, then burn it." With that, she kissed him on the cheek and left.

She pushed the stolen car Judy had arranged for her out of the woods near Brian's house. She felt a twinge driving past Ullabreagh's gates, wondering if what Judy had said was true. For Brian's sake, she hoped not.

It wasn't even two hours to Belfast. Her intel had indicated where the laxest points of entry could be found, but that didn't stop her heart from racing while she lined up behind the other cars to wait her turn at the checkpoint. She glanced into the mirror—with her sunglasses and cap, bundled in layers to bulk her up, she'd be fine if they didn't look too closely and if they didn't make her speak.

After all this time, her accent was still a dead giveaway.

She was getting to the checkpoint on a Saturday, late in the afternoon, when the soldiers were eager to go off duty and have a night on the town. She was counting on their distraction to get her through.

She felt suffocated by it all—the armored trucks, the soldiers sporting helmets and camouflage uniforms, their machine guns strapped across their chests. They were waving cars through ahead of her. She pulled up and parked next to the barricade. A soldier knocked on her window. She rolled it down.

"Papers?" he asked, bored.

She passed them through without saying a word.

"Turn off your car. Step out and open your trunk."

She did as she was told. Her mind was racing. In her haste, she had made a rookie mistake. She hadn't checked under the vehicle, nor in the trunk. She had no idea what they might find. Holding her breath, she turned the lock and popped it open.

There was a spare tire and a dozen empty cans of Guinness.

The soldier grinned, pointing to the cans and nudging Meg jovially in the ribs. "That's me in an hour. Go on, then, off with you," he said amiably, passing her back her papers. "Don't cause any trouble while you're here, mind you."

She nodded, grateful that he couldn't tell how weak her knees felt as she forced herself to amble back to the car. She gripped the wheel, white knuckled, as she drove on through the barricades.

She parked her car at Ormeau Park, abandoning it, and wandered the neighborhood like a tourist, making wide loops to the east to case the Station. The railway depot—her escape—lay to the north of the park, over the River Lagan. Her circles took her past the Orange Order headquarters to the south, in the very shadow of the enemy. She walked each block, noting hiding places and dead ends, plotting her escape. She made a few deposits along the route—explosive insurance to create a distraction and ensure a clean getaway. She confirmed that the police truck was in place where Judy had said it would be. At the end of her sweep, she darted into the park, casing the playground and the pavilion nearby.

She spent that Saturday night in her hotel room, quietly assembling her gear and waiting.

In the early hours of the morning, she reached into the ceiling vent over the vending machine outside the coin-operated laundry room on the first floor and pulled down the police uniform that had been placed for her. With the cap, her short hair, and a pair of sunglasses, she figured she would pass at the first security gate with little question, especially with her police identification, which looked as real as they came. She shoved the things into a collapsible lightweight rucksack and went up the back stairs, back to her room.

She swapped her clothes, belted on her guns, and tucked the ID into her back pocket. She folded the empty rucksack and shoved it into another pocket. In the hallway, she crept into the housekeeping closet and shoved her old clothes into the bottom of a laundry cart piled with used towels and sheets. She left the hotel by the side entrance, skipping out on the bill.

Castlereagh was one of the most fortified police bases in Northern Ireland. She would need to pass through multiple levels of security to get to her prize—Room 220, the heartbeat of the undercover operations run by the Special Branch, the department of the British police force that dealt with political crimes and terrorism. In Room 220, a handler operated a twenty-four-hour agent hotline, fielding tips and calls for help from the countless IRA informants and undercover agents the British had placed deep inside the independence movement. If the folder Judy had given her was correct, she would also find files with the code names and contact information for these informers, along with the identities of the Special Branch agents operating in Northern Ireland themselves.

She was to ignore the interrogation rooms. No matter how badly she longed to shut down the torture of IRA suspects—many of them innocent civilians—she knew was taking place within, she did not have time to take that on too. Not if she was to save David.

She recited her plan to herself as she strode through the quiet streets of Belfast, her chin tucked low. Nobody paid her any attention—British military officers carrying guns and normal beat cops were a commonplace sight these days, and she was in a relatively pro-Union part of the city. Still, she kept her guard up and kept moving. She knew in these violent times it was risky and unusual for even a soldier to be walking alone. Every now and then, she scanned the blocks of buildings and utility poles for security cameras. She didn't know how much closed-circuit television was in place throughout the city and didn't want to be caught on tape, even fleetingly.

She was on autopilot as she approached the truck.

"Truck" was a misnomer. "Tank" would have been more appropriate. Armored and fortified against Molotov cocktails and grenades, it was a hulking mass, mounted with searchlights, cameras, and speakers, all of which were encased in protective cages lest a carefully aimed rock render them useless. Splatters of paint and smoke damage attested to the fact that this beauty had seen action. Mesh protected the underbelly of the beast, preventing anyone from sneaking below to plant a bomb. From habit, she checked anyway. Satisfied there was no sabotage, Meg climbed into the front seat, appreciative of the truck's solidity.

It was a short drive to the Station. This was a relatively peaceful part of the city, with few barricades or checkpoints. She barely registered the occasional graffiti protest or sad memorial that cut into her peripheral vision.

Her first goal was to pass the guard station at Castlereagh.

She approached the low-slung complex with cautious confidence. It was sprawling, but only a few stories high, wrapped by a high wire fence that was covered in green metal across the bottom to shield the Station from prying eyes. The brown brick gatehouse was built like a bunker, with deep, narrow windows to allow for surveillance and inspection.

Without hesitating, she took a deep breath and pulled in.

A squat man in a standard police uniform emerged from the guardhouse, his belly bulging over his gun belt. He wore no armored vest and carried nothing more than a pistol and a set of cuffs. Meg shook her head. He looked better prepared for a cuppa than to stop someone from storming the Station.

"Arrogance," she whispered to herself.

He ambled over to her truck and rapped his knuckles on the window. She lowered it and flashed her ID, which he barely even gave a glance. Peering around her, he asked, "No partner today?"

She shrugged. "Sicked out," she responded as huskily as she could.

"Young guy, like you?"

She nodded.

"Fecker's probably with some tart, lolling about in bed." He chuckled to himself. "In you go," he concluded, pounding the hood of the truck and waving Meg through.

She let out a deep breath as she drove through the gate, surprised at how fast her heart was pounding.

She left the truck in the vehicle yard, carefully registering its return in the logbook as any good officer would, and went in through the employee entrance. She flashed her badge and weapons, moving seamlessly through the layers of security at every stage, chin down, holding her breath lest anyone look too closely.

No one did.

The place was teeming with hundreds of Special Branch personnel, scores of liaisons and would-be soldiers aligned to the pro-Union Protestant paramilitary forces, and countless police. Yet she slipped, almost invisibly, through the early Sunday morning hubbub to get to the back passageways that led to the most secretive part of the complex.

She paused in front of the badge scanner. Normally, a simple officer would not have access to this part of the building. She swiped her badge and held her breath.

The light flashed from red to green.

She pulled the door open and slipped through before she could be seen.

On the other side, she leaned against the wall and breathed. Her weapons were loaded. If all had gone to plan, two men on the inside had placed others for her, in the event she needed them.

Her next step was to disable the security cameras so she could do her work unseen.

She strode off to the right, having memorized the location of the on-site security office. This early on a Sunday morning, there should only be one officer on duty. The shift change would not happen for another hour, leaving her plenty of time to escape before being discovered.

They hadn't even bothered to disguise the office, she noted disdainfully, the words "Security Office" emblazoned on a tidy faux burlwood placard next to the door.

She scanned her badge and slipped inside. As predicted, the guard was alone.

"How about a cuppa?" she asked, not bothering to disguise her voice.

As the man turned around, smiling, she knocked him out with the butt of her pistol.

From inside a pocket in her utility pants, she drew out some zip ties and duct tape and, rendering him helpless, deposited him in a corner.

She scanned the controls to find what she needed. First, she uploaded a video loop that would provide a continuous feed of fake footage for a full sixty minutes. Then, with a few switches and some simple commands, she transitioned the live closed-circuit cameras to the new feed. With a few more feats of simple programming, she turned off the locks that protected the delivery loading docks in the back of the complex. She overrode the system between the main police station and the back hallways, rendering everyone's security clearances invalid. It would take them a full team of IT experts to get around what she'd done. For the next hour, then, she only had to worry about the people already on this side of the door, and those who could be waiting for her once she got out.

She checked the bonds of the man in the corner one last time, just to be safe.

Now, she needed to get to Room 220 and take the files.

She consulted the map she'd hastily scribbled on a scrap piece of paper. Satisfied, she tucked it away and slipped out the door, heading down the corridor to the left. Dull linoleum stretched ahead of her, the way dimly lit by a string of stuttering fluorescent lights dangling from the cheap ceiling tiles.

She didn't check her map again, turning left and right, climbing back stairways, until she stood before an unmarked door toward the back of the building. Another scanner was all that stood between her and the center of the spider's web.

She checked her watch. She had at most forty minutes left.

With a sense of time ticking away, she scanned her badge and waited. Nothing.

She tried again.

Nothing.

As a sense of panic threatened to engulf her, she kept scanning and scanning, holding back her frustration as she got no response but a dull click. Desperate, she tried the door.

It was unlocked.

She sagged with relief—apparently, her insiders had already disabled the security system for this room.

Cursing herself for having wasted a good three minutes, she unholstered again and strode through the door into a small vestibule.

There was a scramble and crash as she turned the corner, gun brandished.

She heard a soft thunk and looked over her shoulder. A bullet had lodged in the wall, sending a cascade of plaster crumbling to the floor. She threw herself to her knees as a flurry of shooting continued. Flinging herself flat, she rolled across the linoleum to a corner where she could protect herself, crouching behind a desk. Taking quick aim, she took out the overhead light, plunging the room into near darkness.

The shooting stopped.

She quickly took stock. She was flat against a bank of filing cabinets. The desk phone—the one outlet to the outside world—was plugged into the wall near her. She yanked the cord out, severing the connection.

Another bullet whizzed by her head.

She dove under the desk.

She tried to control her breath, ragged and heavy, as she evaluated her next move. From the footsteps, she could tell her target was alone. One person—a man, no doubt—was all that stood between her and the mission. The only thing that stood between her and bringing David safely home.

She listened to the footsteps as the man carefully made his way around the room.

When he hesitated, she took her chance.

With a groan, she shoved the desk overhead, sending it crashing into her enemy. Caught off guard, he fell backward and lost his weapon, which came skittering across the floor. She stood up and stopped its spinning with her foot, neatly kicking it up into the air, where she caught it in her left hand. He was pinned beneath the desk, and now she had two weapons aimed at his head.

She'd trapped him. She sat down on the desk for good measure. She grinned at him in the dark as he struggled. "Quite a desk job you have here, mate," she sneered. Anger flooded her veins.

"Whatever you want, you'll never get away with it," he threatened.

She laughed at him, riding the thrashing desk like a children's ride at the amusement park. She screwed on her silencer. "We'll see," she said, acknowledging him for the last time.

Without another thought, she shot him between the eyes.

He, and the desk, fell still.

She put her pistol back in the holster. She checked his—he'd been down to his last bullet. It would not be that useful to her now, not when she already had two of her own guns, so she wiped it clean and threw it in the corner. Then she stood up to inspect the files.

Everything was as Judy had said. Meg bundled up what she'd come for, unfolding her extra rucksack from her utility pocket and strapping it, with the files, onto her back. She tucked the papers that exonerated David into her bra.

She checked her watch. Time to go.

She ran, now, knowing that at any moment her cover could be blown and the entire population of Castlereagh would be at her heels. She plunged through the corridors to the back stairwell. She flung a rope with a carabiner around the rail. With a tug, she tested it before flinging herself over the side, rappelling to the bottom. In the back of her mind, she could almost hear David chiding her: *"Show-off."* Maybe it wasn't so necessary, she thought to herself, but every second mattered. Plus, she needed to keep her adrenaline going if she was going to make it out of here in one piece.

She abandoned the line and emerged from the stairwell into the warehouse. She ran through it. Everything was quiet, she noted with satisfaction as she sprinted to the loading dock. She pushed open the door, her override of the security system having held. She stepped outside and crouched down, hands on knees, to catch her breath.

The yard was still quiet; a few mechanics were conducting truck inspections while drivers loitered about or made their way toward the employee entrance. Word of the security breach hadn't gotten out, but it could at any minute, she acknowledged. In one of the garages, there was a back door that led directly to the street. All she had to do was make it across the yard and through the maintenance crew to get there.

This was the most dangerous moment of her mission.

She straightened her uniform and climbed down the steps from the dock.

She grunted as a few police colleagues nodded at her, holding up a hand, nonchalant, as she worked her way to the garage.

She ducked into the long maintenance garage. She didn't hesitate as she passed the phalanx of trucks and overweight mechanics in overalls. She strode past the tool bench, snatching the bolt cutter that had been left out, within reach.

At the back door she sheared off the deadbolt and let the chain rattle to the stained concrete floor.

"Hey. What are you . . .?"

She didn't wait for the end of the sentence. She pushed open the door and ran, knowing she would outpace any of the mechanics, if any deigned to follow her.

She crisscrossed the back alleys until she got to her first hiding place. There, she pulled out a remote sensor. With a touch of a few buttons, she set sirens off across the entire district. The police, fire, and emergency ambulance services would be occupied for hours responding to false alarms. She dropped the device in the bottom of a dumpster and moved on.

At her second stop, she fished an abandoned bag of civilian clothes, along with a long blonde wig, from a hole in a wall behind a pub. She ignored the drunks who stared as she changed her clothes, giving one the finger when he looked a little too much. She scattered the remains of her police disguise in various trash bins, throwing lit matches into the bins, as she continued walking, moving in a circuitous route to close in on the train station.

She would be searched at the train station, she had figured, no matter how innocent she looked and no matter how much she batted her eyelashes. She needed to stow her bag lest its contents be found. At Ormeau Park, she confirmed she was alone and then worked quickly to duct tape the rucksack to the underside of a loose plank in the pavilion near the playground, then she threw the roll of tape into a pond.

David's papers she kept on herself.

———

She'd gotten the attention of the IRA, and everything was going according to plan. Forty-eight hours later, having taken the train from Belfast to Dublin, she was escorted, hood over her head, into an office that was not supposed to exist, full of men who were not supposed to be there. Her hands were twisted behind her back, bound. From everything David had ever shared with her, she knew they had their guns trained on her head.

"Speak," one of the IRA men commanded.

"I stole the files of your bloody spies and touts," she spat. "I took them right out of Castlereagh. There are more than you realized. Enough to keep your Nutting Squad up in Belfast busy for months, if not years, seeking revenge. You'll find the files in a rucksack when you sweep the playground in Ormeau Park."

There were murmurs of consultation as the men considered what she'd said.

"That's not all. There's something in my pocket you need to see. Right front of my trousers."

There was a scraping of chairs and a shuffling.

"Easy, there," she cautioned as someone patted her down and yanked the papers from her pocket. She heard a soft rustle of pages being turned over. When it stopped, she cleared her throat.

"I found that in the files I stole. That there is proof of my husband's loyalty to the IRA. Read it yourselves. And when you're done, I expect you to call off your dogs and let him come home."

She heard what she took to be a slight cough of skepticism. There was more shuffling, and a murmur.

"Get her out of here," a man ordered tersely. "And you," he directed at Meg, "never speak of this to anyone."

Rough hands dragged her backward, through a door, turning her around to hustle her away down a corridor that seemed to go on forever. She kept her back straight, commanding herself to not give away her terror when they shoved her hastily up into the back of a box truck.

She was alone in the truck, the passing of time merely a concept in her head as she breathed through the isolation of the hood that still covered her head. She counted her blessings, repeating them over and over to herself like the decades of the Rosary: They hadn't broken her fingers. They hadn't taped her eyes shut. They hadn't sucker punched her. They hadn't knocked her out.

They hadn't spoken the words she most feared to hear: "David is dead."

That counted for something, didn't it?

She counted her blessings and tried a find a way out of the zip tie that still bound her wrists, for she knew when the truck stopped, she might have to fight her way free. After a twenty-minute struggle, she gave up, succumbing to her exhaustion.

She was jerked awake by the lurching halt of the vehicle, thrown off balance and landing face down on the splintery wood that lined the truck bed.

She cursed at herself for the weakness of having fallen asleep. Frantic, she kicked, trying to right herself, as she heard the rear door roll up. Before she could roll away, she was dragged across the truck bed. The night air was a slap, jolting her awake. She writhed and bucked.

"A wildcat, are you?" one of her captors joked. Another deep voice laughed at her futile attempts to get away.

She aimed for what she thought was a knee and felt a satisfying crunch as she connected. The man cursed and loosened his grip. Instantly, she was free, dropped to the ground. She could smell the dirt through the hood; she could feel the dampness of the earth through her thin clothes.

Over the incessant stream of cursing, another man laughed.

"Put your gun away, man," he cajoled his injured colleague. "She bested you, she did. You should be proud. Remember, she's one of us, or at least they say her man is. There's a mate." There was some muttered negotiation and soothing of hurt pride. The truck gate was rolled back down with a clang.

It grew quiet. From the occasional sounds of distant traffic, she could tell she had been dumped at the side of a road. It was somewhere lonely, she imagined, where a body could languish for days before being found, or a hasty gravesite covered over so that not even the sheep would notice it. The only other sounds were Meg's own heavy breathing and grunts as she struggled to free herself.

"Don't do anything rash, now. There's a gun pointed at your head if you do."

Someone crouched over her, knee in the small of her back, pinning her down as he cut through the zip tie and freed her arms.

"Don't remove that hood until the truck has been gone for at least five minutes. And don't move for an hour," she was warned. "Remember, if you weren't a Donnelly, you'd already be dead. So don't speak of this to anyone."

Then they left her, face down in the dirt, trying to rub the feeling back into her arms.

———

"Hello, Mrs. Hutton."

As if he'd only gone down to the pub for a pint, David turned up a week later at Brian's cottage at Ullabreagh.

She rose from the floor, where'd she'd been picking up Rennie's blocks. She didn't ask him where he'd gone, nor how he'd survived. Her eyes pored over him. He was lean and gray, with a hunted look about his eyes, but he was whole.

With a strangled cry, she threw herself into his arms.

"Alright then, alright," he soothed as she held on to him. "I'm alright." She traced every muscle and joint, making sure her eyes had not deceived her, not trusting his reassurances.

When she was satisfied he was not hurt, she stood back, holding his hands, and laughed.

"I didn't know if I would see you again."

David drew one of her hands to his lips. "Nor I."

"Brian took the girls to see the sheep."

"I know. I saw them as I was coming up the lane. Told him to take his time," he grinned.

She felt a flutter in her stomach as he drank her in.

"Come, sit down with me near the stove," she said, leading him to the warmest corner of the cottage and sitting him down. Before he could ask, she poured him a cup of tea.

"I could do with something stronger," he said sheepishly.

"Fair enough." She swapped out a tumbler of Brian's best whiskey. David shot back a gulp, wincing a little as it burned his throat. Meg settled on the floor, laying her head in his lap. All of the fear was seeping out of her.

"What's this?" David twirled a lock of her shorn, black hair around his finger.

She shrugged. "I decided I needed a change."

"Fairly drastic," he mused, twirling her hair absentmindedly. "Almost like a disguise. If I hadn't been expecting to find you at home, I might have mistaken you for someone else. From a distance, even a man."

Meg froze.

"I like it," he said, as if that was the end of the matter. He ran his fingers through her hair. "It frames your face well."

She tried to relax again under his touch. But her nerves were now on edge. "So glad you approve," she said drily, pushing away from his lap.

"Now, don't be that way, Meg," he scolded softly, catching her hand before she got too far. "You'd think a husband could comment on his wife's hair, wouldn't you? Is that so wrong? Especially when I've been away so long? It would be wrong of me not to notice, don't you think?"

She tried to shrug away her worry. "Yes. Of course you're right."

"Come sit back down."

She let him draw her close again and settled in next to his chair.

"You always were full of surprises." He took a long draught of the whiskey, draining the glass. "Is there anything else you'd like to tell me?"

"Whatever do you mean, David?" She popped to her feet, agitated. His face was hard, now, his jaw set. "What are you getting at?"

He rose to confront her. "You know what I'm about, Meg."

"I'm sure I don't. Why don't you come out with it?"

"Don't lie to me!" He swept the empty glass off the table and against the wall. Meg watched the crystal shatter into pieces, the shards reflecting the waning light. Her back stiffened.

"MI5 briefed me. I know what you did. You went right to the IRA. Don't deny it."

Her heart skipped a beat. What, exactly, had they told him?

"Surely, I can't be the only terrified wife to go beg for her husband's life," she parried.

"That wasn't all there was to it, was it?"

She decided to call his bluff. She grabbed his shoulders and looked him in the eyes.

"I was briefed too. I know you lost Ullabreagh, David. I know everything."

He froze. Carefully, he pulled away. She caught his hands before he could completely disentwine from her. His face was careful and composed. She peered into his eyes, trying to plumb the depths of his thoughts, but they were closed off to her.

"What is that supposed to mean?"

"You know what it means, David."

"I'm afraid I don't, sweetheart," he insisted, wearily rubbing his face. He pried her fingers off and stood up, walking over to the side table where he poured himself another drink. His hands were shaking as he gulped the tumbler of whiskey down. He turned away from her and poured another.

"You know what it means, David," she repeated softly. "I always assumed that you'd figured it out but were just too polite to say it out loud. I'm a spy. And I have a handler. A handler, just like you."

His back stiffened. "You admit it then?"

She didn't answer.

"You've been spying on me?"

She cleared her throat. "Not for a very long time now. But in the beginning, yes."

He hung his head, the sickening sound of soft laughter trickling out of him as he set the tumbler down. "So you were. So you were. Did you find it worthwhile, that? Tell me," he demanded as he wheeled upon her, his eyes bright with anger, "did you decide to stop spying on me before or after we were married? Before or after you bore my child? Before or after I turned a blind eye to every goddamn act of terrorism committed by your uncle so that he could stand godfather for our daughter?"

"David, don't."

"Don't? How dare you tell me what to do when you have been working against me this whole time . . . when you have literally just informed me that everything about us is a lie!"

"No, David, it's not like that. It was never like that. I loved you! I love you now!"

"Who are you with? What agency?"

She pressed her lips together.

"Spit it out. CIA? That would make sense, wouldn't it," he told himself as he began to pace. "The Americans would want to monitor the talks, see if they could do anything to influence them. But perhaps I've got it wrong. Are you IRA, Meg? Are Brian and his goons running you?"

"Brian has nothing to do with this. He never has. All he's ever done is help you, when I asked."

"Then tell me who!" He gripped her shoulders and shook her.

Like lightning, her hand snaked out, her fingers closing around his throat.

"Please, stop," she insisted, her voice steel. "I won't ask again."

David froze.

"I'm going to back away now, David. Once I do, I'll tell you what I can. When I do, I want you to listen to me. Can you do that?"

His eyes narrowed, but he nodded. Meg let go of his throat and stepped back a few paces.

"I can't tell you my agency. What I will tell you is it works with MI5, as well as MI6. So you have nothing to fear. My work here is done. I negotiated an exit—an exit for all of us—in exchange for your life. I found a way out for you, thanks to my handler. We can go to America. We can go anywhere. All we have to do, now, is wait. Wait for our instructions and my handler will help us get out. That was the deal."

"We can't leave now! I need to be on the inside while these peace negotiations are going on. I need to know what the IRA are planning."

She shook her head. "I don't think they'll ever let you back that close. You were cleared, but there were so many others in those files . . ."

"What do you mean? You can't mean you actually saw them . . .?"

She nodded. "I did more than see them. I took them. The Castlereagh job was me."

A look of horror crept across his face. "You burned scores of agents, Meg!"

"I did it for you."

"I would have rather died than had the blood of that many men and women on my hands!"

"Not your hands. Mine. And I'd do it again."

He shuddered. "What have you done? Whose side are you on?"

Her chin jutted, defiant. "After all these years, that one's easy. *Ours.* I'm through with politics. I'm through with this bloody, unending war. All I want is for us to be far, far away from here. For our girls to be safe. For this to all be behind us."

There was a soft knocking on the door.

"Come in," Meg said. The door swung open. Brian poked his head through, eyeing them carefully.

"I don't want to interrupt," he said sheepishly. "I left the girls playing in the dirt. Gave Rennie a task to draw out her letters that should keep her busy for a minute. I wanted to see if I could have a wee word with you."

"It's all right, Brian," David said, turning away to compose himself.

Brian came in, standing awkwardly and pretending not to notice the shards of glass on the floor. "I haven't tried to hide myself and my doings from you before, and I reckon it's best I not start now. I believe you'll both have your reasons for wanting to hear what I'm about to say. My sources are telling me that the leadership in Belfast's saying there are too many touts and double agents—the entire movement is riddled with them, turns out. The files from Castlereagh were a blow, shining the sun on what amounts to rot at the very core of the IRA. The Nutting Squad would take years to get their retribution, and it would just unleash a new cycle of violence, a cycle that everyone seems too weary to face. So they are signing the peace deal. They're giving up."

David and Meg froze.

"So that's what it was all about," Meg whispered to herself, finally understanding the gamble Judy and the Agency had taken by sending her into Castlereagh.

Brian held his hands quietly in front of him. "I cannot let them trade away our dream for a piece of paper. I'll be going underground for a bit, trying to sort out a new resistance. I don't know when I'll be clearing out, but I wanted you to know. No surprises, and all that."

"Oh, Brian," Meg breathed. "I'm sorry."

"How can you say that?" David snapped.

"Regardless of what you or I think, this was—is—Brian's life. I can acknowledge his loss without being disloyal, or taking sides."

Brian was gracious. "I understand your point of view, David, I do. And I thank you, dear, for your sentiment. It's a setback, that's all, Margaret. A setback. Another decade won't matter in the scheme of things." Brian picked his head up and looked at them both, steadily. "You and the children are welcome to stay as long as you want. Just lock the cottage up when you leave."

"You may not be able to return," Meg warned.

Brian looked alarmed, but David cut her off. "The terms of the property transfer protected the cottage. It's his for life. No matter what happens to me."

"To us, don't you mean?" Meg took his arm. He shrugged it off.

Brian raised a brow and was about to say something, but Meg warned him off with a shake of her head. He shrugged and changed the topic. "I'll be taking the girls into town for some ice cream, if it's alright with you. I don't know how much more time I'll get with them," Brian continued, his voice trailing off. "We'll give you more time to catch up, the two of you.

Besides, if I don't get back out there, there's no telling what that Rennie will do. She'll likely be up another tree and on the roof."

"Of course," Meg said, emphatically. "Go ahead, Brian. Enjoy your time with them."

Brian closed the door softly behind him. Silence permeated the room.

"It's everything you've worked for, David," Meg said softly.

He grunted his assent. "Maybe. We'll see."

He crossed his arms. It was what he always did right before he gave up an argument. She tried to hide the smile that was tugging at the corner of her mouth.

"Will the government bring you back to London to work behind the scenes for the final talks, do you think?"

He shook his head. "I doubt it. I'd be a liability if anybody on the other side found me out. I imagine I'll have some work to do to protect those I can. I should be grateful, and relieved, I suppose, by what Brian just shared—it will mean less work for me. Instead . . . I'm just exhausted."

He sat back down in the easy chair and rubbed his face. He almost seemed relaxed enough to be able to talk about his work in the open, now that he was certain Meg knew.

"I would take the burden from you," she said. He held out his hand to her. She went to him, squeezing his hand hard.

"I know you would, sweetheart. Better you work on that plan to get us out of here. I'm not sure how long and far the grace of the IRA will extend. Whatever magic you did to make me appear innocent to them, I don't want to push my luck. Not with our family at stake. This handler of yours, is he good?"

"She."

He laughed. "Of course. She. You trust her?"

She paused. "It's hard to trust a spy, isn't it? But as far as spies go, yes. I do. It was her plan that got me into Castlereagh and helped me clear your name."

"Very well, then. We'll double down on our bet with her. Find out what favor she needs so that we can get to work. I don't want moss to grow under our feet here. The sooner we're gone, the better."

———

A month stretched out while they waited. Judy did not respond to the various dead drops Meg left for her. The silence all around—from Judy, the IRA, and MI5—made David and Meg both act like nervous cats. For the first time in years, they had nothing to do. The tiny cottage was stifling and close, too small for the five of them to be cooped up together, on edge. Every tick of the grandfather clock in the corner seemed loud with portent as they waited, watchful.

Being cut out of the loop was not a good place for either one of them to be.

Finally, Meg got a drop.

A contact would come to Brian's cottage. Meg would know him from a bit of poetry he would quote.

That was all.

After reading the message out loud to David, Meg crumpled the piece of paper and dropped it into the woodstove.

"Odd," David noted. "Your handler is very vague."

"Yes, she tends to be that way sometimes."

It was several days later, after the sun had gone down, that a knock at the door alerted them to their visitor. The girls were spread out on the floor, Rennie with a coloring book and Briana with some beads.

David and Meg looked at one another, then at Brian. They nodded at Brian, who took his rifle and scurried the girls into his bedroom, closing the door firmly behind him. They listened to the sound of the bureau being dragged to block entry to the tiny room. When the scraping noise stopped, they nodded at one another and moved to the front door.

"There's not even a damn peephole," David muttered. "We should have made this safer."

"Too late now," Meg said with a shrug. "Check the window."

He did. "Single man. No vehicle. As best as I can tell, he's alone. Can't get a good look at him, though—his face is in the shadows."

"Watch me." She slid the door open a crack. "Yes?"

The man cleared his throat and began speaking in a foreign language.

"'I'd rather betray the world than have the world betray me,'" Meg translated the Mandarin effortlessly. "Cao Cao. Technically not a poem, although spoken by a poet."

She swung the door open.

"I prefer to think of him as a warlord. But regardless, I am glad you recognize his work," the man replied as he stepped over the threshold. "I am impressed."

"Don't be." She continued speaking in Mandarin.

> "... the crows fly to the south,
> circling the tree three times;
> on what branch can they find rest?"

The stranger chuckled. "Ah, straight to the point, I see. There will be time enough to discuss your escape. First, we must talk of the task before you. The job. Mr. Hutton?" He extended his hand to greet David.

David took it, bemused. "You find me at a disadvantage, for I'm afraid I don't know your name. You haven't introduced yourself."

"And I won't," the man said with a tiny smile. His English was slightly British in intonation, his native tongue coloring his pronunciation enough that you could tell he was not from Hong Kong but perhaps somewhere on the continent. "You don't really need it, do you? You know I am the one who was to be sent to you. That is all that matters. Shall we?"

He gestured to the small kitchen table. Meg and David paused.

"If it makes you feel better, I will give you my weapon." The man reached behind his back and drew out a snub-nosed pistol, extending it out to Meg. "Go on. This is all I have. If you wish to search me, Mr. Hutton, I am at your service."

Meg grabbed the gun and nodded to David. The Chinese man spread his arms and legs and stood patiently while David patted him down.

"Clean," David declared.

The man nodded and gestured at a kitchen chair. "May I?"

They scrambled to offer him a seat and joined him under the halo of the dim kitchen light that hung over the scratched table. The agent folded his hands together. Meg inspected his neat manicure, his perfectly tailored suit, and waited.

"Your handler believes you are the perfect pair to help with the mission we are about to undertake. You, Mr. Hutton, due to your prior work in Hong Kong, which gives you a perfect cover to be in the East. You, Mrs. Hutton, for your language skills, which are impressive, I concur. You will need to adapt a bit to Guoyu, but that should come easily to such a quick study as yourself."

"Why would I need to learn a Taiwanese dialect?" Meg shot back sharply.

He smiled. "Because maybe you are going to be working in Taiwan. Or at least with Taiwanese, to protect their interests."

"Say more," David prompted.

"Do you have an ashtray?" the man asked, looking absentmindedly about the room for one.

David grabbed an empty jelly jar from the dish drain and slid it over to the man, who took his time shaking a Gauloises out of a pack and lighting it. After taking a drag on the cigarette, the man continued.

"You believe in Britain? In America? In capitalism?"

They nodded.

"Well, so do I. And I believe in China. One China, united. But not the vision of the People's Republic of China. The vision of a true China, not shackled by Communism. There are many, many others like me. And many in your agency, Mrs. Hutton, who share this view."

"Fights for reunification rarely succeed. We know, from experience," Meg said, unable to keep a twinge of bitterness from her voice. "Just look around you. It's been decades of bloodshed here. Nothing has changed."

"Perhaps. I do not come to ask you to fight all the way until the end. I just need your help long enough to make sure there is a chance for the battle to continue."

"Stop talking in riddles, if you would," David interjected. "We've been waiting for weeks. I'd like to cut to the chase."

"I was trying to appeal to your principles, Mr. Hutton, which I have been assured are quite strong. Your lovely wife's, too." He turned in his seat to face Meg. "I understand your father was an ardent anti-Communist. Isn't that right, Mrs. Hutton?"

She was startled. "Yes. I suppose he was."

"He came by it honestly, given his family. There is much to admire in his conviction."

Meg felt her color rising. "How do you know about my family?"

"Do you think you are the only one who can find a file and read it? Don't be alarmed. I only share this understanding with you because I believe you share his point of view. I want you to know there is a higher purpose in what I am asking of you. It will serve mankind, not just keep you both from going—what is the term in English—'stir crazy'?" He looked around the cozy cottage, his slight grimace leaving no doubt that he considered their close quarters stifling, at best. "I am sure you must be bored, sitting idle for so long."

David and Meg shot one another a careful look.

"Maybe we are. Maybe we aren't. You still haven't told us what the mission is," Meg reminded him.

"Indeed. It is quite simple, really. Mrs. Hutton, your new American president is about to do something that will cause great harm. Our aim is to stop him."

"Who aims to stop him? And to what are you referring?" David asked suspiciously.

The man waved his hand. "Who I represent is immaterial. Our goal, however, is profound."

"Please, tell us," Meg insisted.

The stranger nodded his head in assent. "In a month, the American president plans to be in Shanghai. My employer has it on good authority that while the president is there, he plans to give Beijing the assurances it wants with respect to Taiwan."

"What exactly will he be saying?" David asked, not wanting to believe what he was hearing.

"He plans to commit to the Three No's policy."

Meg froze, the twitching of her nervous hands halting as she heard the president's intent. "He can't. He wouldn't."

"But he will. He intends to repudiate the freedom of Taiwan, declaring that the United States will not support the creation of two Chinas, the independence of Taiwan, nor Taiwan's re-entry into the United Nations. For the PRC it will be its biggest diplomatic win since Nixon's visit in 1972."

"If he does so, it will embolden the Chinese," Meg protested. "It will give them the clearance they want to try to take over the island."

"It's not even a year since we abandoned Hong Kong to them!" David sprang from his chair and began pacing. "How can we let this happen? Surely the prime minister and the foreign secretary don't agree?"

"Alas, it is not clear that the Americans have consulted with the British. If they have, any British protest has fallen on deaf ears. The Americans seem intent on their goal of warming relations with the PRC. So it falls to us to stop the president before he can bring this plan to fruition."

"How?" Meg questioned, her heart sinking, for she suspected she knew the answer.

"We will assassinate him," the man said simply, snubbing out his cigarette on the edge of the jar. "And if that doesn't work, it doesn't really matter, so long as we take out a portion of his diplomatic mission. That, by itself, would freeze relations and stop this recognition. And that is where you come into the picture."

Meg felt the air go out of her as if she had been punched in the stomach.

"Impossible," David stated flatly. "An American president? There is no way we will ever get close enough to touch him. And if we do, there is no way we will make it out alive. His security detail will mow us down before we're even three feet away from him."

"We have a plan, and a backup," the man insisted. "I assure you, you will both survive and be able to return to your children. Your new life will await you when you do. But you must do this one thing. We insist."

"Who is this 'we'?"

"Again, it is no concern of yours. Your handler believes you are up to the task, Mrs. Hutton. Are you? Mr. Hutton—how about you? It's up to you, of course. Although from what I understand, you have few options if you decline to join our merry party."

Meg could see the vein throbbing in David's forehead, even from across the room.

"We need some time to think about it," Meg offered coolly. "We've never done a job together. Our children will be vulnerable if it goes badly. We can't count on my uncle being around to protect them."

"Your handler thought you might say that. She authorized me to give you this." He passed a sealed envelope across the table to Meg. She stared at the creamy paper but did not pick it up.

The man shrugged. "I will leave you to contemplate your decision."

"How will we contact you once we've made up our minds?" Meg asked.

"No need. I know how to find you." The man stood up, neatly pushing his chair into the table. "Enjoy the rest of your evening. I will see myself out."

Meg and David sat in silence, staring at the envelope.

Meg reached for it, but David stopped her. "Don't bother. There's nothing your handler could tell us that could make this any better."

Meg shrugged. "When's the last time you were in the field, David?"

He rubbed his face. "You can't be seriously considering this?"

"What choice do we have?"

"Anything but this, Meg. The risks are too great—"

He picked up the envelope and tucked it into his jacket pocket. "We'll discuss it later. Right now, we should relieve Brian of the children. It's not fair to drag him into this."

He left the table, not bothering to wait for her response.

She smarted at the reprimand. It didn't escape her notice that he hadn't answered her question.

She resented the way he shifted the debate in order to avoid confronting his own lack of readiness to go into the field—the way he reshaped the debate to take control. She resented how he couldn't acknowledge that she actually had an informed point of view on what they were being asked to undertake.

She could cut him some slack for not giving her proper credit—after all, he was still adjusting to his newfound knowledge that she was an active player in this business of spying. But it was hard for her to swallow how easily he overlooked the fact that Brian had been dragged into their business the instant David had found himself outed as an IRA traitor.

They wouldn't be in this mess at all if it weren't for David.

But she could wait him out. More than once, she'd been patient and proved herself able to bend his will to hers, without him even realizing it.

She would have to do it again.

Their lives depended on it.

She bolted upright, startling wide awake.

David's side of the bed was empty. Again.

She pulled the plaid woolen blanket about her shoulders and crept out to the tiny living area of the cottage. Her husband was hunched over her handler's letter, the torn envelope and an empty bottle of whiskey lying carelessly at his feet.

"I've spent the better part of a week looking for that envelope," Meg gently rebuked him.

"They say they will kill my parents," David said, his voice flat. "That's what your vaunted handler says."

She ran to his side, kneeling next to him to extract the letter from his fist.

Her eyes raced over the crumpled paper. "We can't let that happen. David, we can't. I need to speak to her. I'm going to Derry." She stood up and headed for their bedroom.

"What, now? At this hour?"

"Yes. I'll force her to speak to me."

He laughed, a cold, cynical sound that followed her into the room and broke her heart. "You can't force these people to do anything, Meg. They've got us trapped."

She came out, clothes trailing behind her. "We're not trapped. They need us—don't you see? As long as they need us, we can bargain."

She scrambled into a pair of jeans and looked about for a sweater, the words tumbling out of her, pleading. "Doesn't it feel good, David, to be needed? To be on the side of good? It's so clear-cut."

"Is it?"

"Yes!" she shouted, stamping her foot impatiently.

"Shh," he warned. "You'll wake the girls."

"Yes," she whispered, grabbing his hands, her eyes bright, almost feverish. "Don't you see? This Irish thing—if we don't move beyond it, you'll never trust me again. I see it in your eyes. How many nights in a row can you avoid our bed and think I won't notice? This mission, though—we view it the same way. We're on the same side. Unambiguously."

"Are we?"

She wanted to shake him. "We have our different reasons. You feel the guilt of the Empire abandoning its colonialized subjects. I feel hatred for oppression, particularly of the Communist variety—I was practically suckled on it from the time I was a babe. But it leads us to the same place—we don't want the Chinese Communist government to ride roughshod over Taiwan—or any other nation. We have a real reason for doing this, David. An idealistic one. Not just desperation."

"But assassination?"

She threw aside his hands and his question. She was moving fast now, tying her bootlace. "We need to do what it takes. If it gets us out of the spying business for good, it will be doubly worth it."

"I think you've gone mad."

"I'm not crazy. I'm motivated. I know we can do this. Please, trust me."

She stood before the front door, searching his eyes.

"Your handler is that good?"

Meg laughed, giddy on hope. "She got me in and out of the most secure facility in Ireland with barely a hair on my head being harmed. If she says she has a plan, she has a plan."

He stared at his feet. Subtly, his body sagged. "Go on, then. But Meg—"

She paused with the door half open. "Yes?"

"Be careful. I cannot . . . I could not . . ."

His voice trailed off, rough.

"You won't," she said, pausing. "I'm coming back. I promise."

———

She'd borrowed Brian's ancient hatchback to drive into the city, stowing it away in a forgotten IRA storage unit Brian had once told her about. She'd then walked a five-hour route in Derry, doubling back and circling, ducking into alleyways, checking constantly to be sure she wasn't being followed. When she was sure of it, she'd snuck into their old apartment building and taped the small X—their signal calling for a meeting in the graveyard—in the front window.

Meg then lay low the entire day, moving quietly between safe houses on an unpredictable schedule, until the sun went down and the city was enrobed in darkness.

When the time came, Judy was waiting on the gravestone, just as Meg had known she would be.

"This is very dangerous, Margaret. You shouldn't have contacted me."

"I need to speak with you."

"I see that. Get on with it, then."

"We'll do the mission. But with some conditions."

Judy's brow arched. "You're not really in a position to make demands."

Meg crossed her arms. "For whatever reason, the Agency needs us. I don't know why, and honestly, I don't care. But I will use it to my—and my family's—advantage."

"You can try." Judy lit a cigarette. She drew it to her lips and paused with it hovering there. "Don't make me wait, Meg. You're on thin ice."

"We meet the full team and vet them in advance."

Judy uncrossed her legs and stood. "That's not possible. Meeting over."

"No—wait!" Meg scrambled to stop Judy. "I can give on that one. But I want David to be on comms or surveillance. Not on the actual hit. If you put either one of us in, it will be me."

"That one is easy to agree to," Judy snorted. "Is that all?"

"One more." Meg gulped. "I want the girls to be extracted with us to a safe location upon our departure for China. Not left behind."

Judy's eyes narrowed. "You can't take children on a mission."

"I want them taken to a base. I want them waiting for us, under Agency protection, until we return. And I want your promise that if anything happens, you will make sure our girls are safe. Your personal promise, Judy."

"Motherhood makes you tiresome."

"Promise me, Judy. That's the only way I will do this."

Meg's handler tilted her head to the side, pretending to watch the smoke trailing off her cigarette. "Your husband has assented, then?"

Meg shrugged. "He'll do it. If you can promise you'll watch over the girls, he'll swallow his other objections. I will handle it."

"Fine." Judy stood and stubbed the cigarette out under her pump. "I'm glad you see it my way."

"That's not good enough. You need to say it, Judy. You need to promise."

Judy sighed. "You have my word. Now, go home and ready yourselves. You'll be contacted shortly for your briefing. Don't come back to Derry. Don't use the old dead drops or signals. None of it is safe anymore. Whatever you do, don't trust anyone. Under no circumstances can you attempt to contact me. Is that clear? And for God's sake, make sure your husband has cut off all of his contacts, as well. This must be walled off from even MI6. Understood?"

Meg shuddered and nodded once. Judy left her standing alone among the headstones, wondering just what she'd agreed to do.

Chapter Eleven

BREE

Present Day, Alabama

Bree leaned into the back of the bench seat and rubbed her neck, carefully avoiding the bandage.

Dash had worked his intelligence network to find them a way out of the country. He'd talked their way on to an American military flight out of Menwith Hill—the communications surveillance base that sat behind barbed wire in North Yorkshire—somehow managing to produce fake papers to validate the top-secret nature of their supposed mission.

When they'd gone into their IT system to validate the paperwork, he'd already created a back door for Ruby to confirm, directly, that the mission was approved.

No further questions. As a member of the mysterious global ECHELON network, Norwood status was never questioned.

Access granted.

Now, she and Dash were flying over the Atlantic, almost the only passengers in a cavernous C-130 headed to an air base in the United States.

She looked over at Dash, who sagged in his seatbelt straps, asleep.

She smiled, wistful. He'd planned ahead for the spartan conditions, carrying a flask in his boot. The whiskey had worked his magic. She, however, was wide awake and couldn't stop thinking.

Questions about Rodney plagued her. She'd never told Dash what Rodney had shared with her that afternoon on the porch—that Beatrice, his dead wife, had been a neuroscientist at the University of Bath. It had all sounded so innocent, then, but what if she was the one who had engineered the devices that tracked them, or the neuro-inhibitor drug that would wipe their memories if they stepped out of line?

Dash always said there was no such thing as coincidence. What if he was right?

She nibbled on her lip and turned her attention to the other question that plagued her: Could she trust Dash? She hated that she was even asking it. But her last conversation with Ruby had planted it. She had to take it seriously.

Ruby had been leaning over Bree's neck, diligently suturing the tiny incision she'd made to extract the tracking device. Dash was already in his room, making sure his things were in order, leaving the two of them alone under the fluorescent kitchen light.

"I put a few things in your pack, Bree," Ruby had stated in a low voice.

"What?" Bree had asked.

"Shh. Keep your voice down. I said, I stashed some things in your pack. Just in case." Ruby had taped a bandage in place. The spot was tender. Bree had winced.

"What things?"

"You can get up."

Ruby had walked away from the table then, and had thrown her instruments into the sink. Bree had picked herself up off the table and stretched. Ruby stood at the sink, watching the water rinse the blood down the drain. "You'll want to put the device someplace safe near your bed," Ruby had reminded her.

"Ruby, what things? What are you talking about?"

Ruby had turned off the faucet and turned around to face Bree. "I left you an extra passport—really, the makings of a whole new identity. I left you information for an offshore bank account. And I tucked in an extra burner phone."

Bree had tilted her head, confused. "Did you do that for Dash, too?"

Ruby had shook her head. "No."

"Ruby," Bree had demanded, voice rising. "Why would you do such a thing and not do it for Dash, too?"

"Shh. Come away from the kitchen. Let's go to the bedroom. Bring that thing with you. You don't want to lose it."

Bree had followed Ruby and carefully placed the device—as tiny as a grain of rice—in a small dish on her nightstand, next to the photo of Rodney. She'd turned the photo over and faced Ruby, who was perched on the edge of her bed. Ruby hadn't waited for Bree's questions.

"Do you trust me, Bree?"

"What are you talking about, Ruby?" Bree had countered. "You're acting like . . ."

"Like a handler. That's how I'm acting. Cynical. Suspicious. Prepared." She counted off the prime virtues of handling on her fingers.

"Ready to play her agents off one another?" Bree snapped.

Ruby had snorted. "That's not it at all."

"Then what is it? I know you blame Dash and me for what happened to Susmita. Is this some attempt to turn us against one another, to punish us for her death?"

Ruby's face hardened. "I have a bad feeling. That's all I'm going to say. You need to be careful, Bree."

Ruby's eyes had settled on the overturned photo of Rodney. After an awkward silence, she'd turned to look out the window. The sky had been a lonely gray.

"It'll be dark soon. Be ready to go within the hour."

When they'd later slipped out of Jaguar House, Ruby had been gruff with Dash, reminding him again of the tight schedule they'd be running.

When it was Bree's turn to say goodbye, however, Ruby had hugged her fiercely.

"The burner is in a hidden compartment in the bottom of your sack," Ruby had whispered. "Don't forget."

———

They landed at an air base in Alabama. There was no customs, no anything. They simply walked off the plane and up to an SUV that Dash had somehow managed to procure. The placard in the window read "Battle Axe," Dash's nickname for Dean Albourn.

"Subtle. Announcing our presence isn't exactly helpful."

Dash shrugged. "Nobody else will know what it means. You wouldn't let me give the mission a code name. I felt compelled," he explained as he threw his bag in the back of the vehicle. "You can imagine we have a driver, and are being whisked away to somewhere exotic, where a nice martini or mai tai awaits."

"A pickup truck would have blended in better," Bree muttered as she tossed her rucksack in beside his.

"Ah, yes, with a gun rack, no doubt. But then one would miss out on the armor plating and shatterproof windows." He rapped his knuckles on the hood of the SUV in appreciation as he headed for the driver's side.

"I'm driving," Bree said tersely. "We can't afford you getting pulled over for driving on the wrong side of the road."

He made a face. "You know, Briana, you're quite cute when you are angry. Your accent comes back quite strongly. And you get very prickly. Like a cuddly porcupine."

"I'm not angry. I'm nervous," she snapped. "There's a difference. Check under the vehicle," she commanded as she climbed into the driver's seat.

When he got in on the passenger side and gave the all clear with an exaggerated American thumbs-up, she rolled her eyes and pressed the push-button ignition.

They were mere hours from the orphanage. They were loaded with materiel and guns. Bree was acutely aware of the passage of time, knowing their hopes rested on Ruby's ability to stall the Norwood staff's discovery of their absence.

It was time to roll. They pulled off the base, faceless and nameless behind their moving wall of black glass and steel, and took to the road.

The miles ticked by, the silence in the vehicle punctuated only by Dash's commentary on the Alabama road signs. "What, exactly, is a pecan log and why would one pull off a major roadway to purchase one?" he pondered aloud. "And why does there appear to be a one-to-one ratio of pecan log purveyors to establishments featuring topless girls on this stretch of freeway? In the UK, the most provocative thing one can get roadside is very expensive diesel gasoline—Americans put their freedom from regulation to very strange uses."

"Live and let live," Bree said between gritted teeth.

"That's a very high-minded philosophy to apply to such mundane—one could even say, uncouth—preoccupations."

"Pecan logs are not uncouth. They are delicious."

"I wouldn't know. We didn't sample one last time we visited Thornton. Nor did you bring me to try boiled peanuts, which seems to be the other vaunted roadside food of the South."

"Dashiell Heyward," Bree warned. "If you're trying to distract me . . ."

"Is it working, then?"

Out of the corner of her eye, she could see him grinning and she smiled despite herself. "Yes, it's working."

"Oh, good. It never pays to go into an operation on edge. One must be as calm and loose as possible. At least, that's what they always said in class."

She snorted. "I think, under the circumstances, it might be okay to be a little preoccupied."

"Let's run through the plan, then. It will help your nerves if you reassure yourself with the details."

"Only *my* nerves? You're not worried at all?"

"Briana, I was sent away to British boarding school at the age of seven. And I've had to 'meet my new mother' three times. I think my nerves are quite up to whatever challenge we will face at Thornton. Shall we?"

She sighed, refraining from trying to outdo him with tales from her stint at the orphanage. "Fine."

"Very well. Let's begin with the perimeter. Do you care to refresh us?" Dash prompted.

"The north and west sides are forested, the property line adjacent to farms. The farmers are old and their farms are only minimally cultivated. The east borders a sheer cliff that drops down to a creek. South side fronts the road, with a clear view."

"So our approach?"

"We have to assume we're dealing with professionals. So, there will be some combination of booby traps, surveillance, or guards set up along the vulnerable points. Layers of defense. My guess is they would assume the cliffs aren't breachable and focus their efforts on the adjacent farms."

"Are they right? Are the cliffs impassable?"

Bree frowned. "They are technically scalable. You can reach the creek a couple miles upriver and follow the banks to their base. It would be a tough hike, especially carrying equipment—very rocky. But from there you could climb. I'm guessing most people wouldn't try it. If we did, it would add hours to our plan."

"The other property lines, then. How would you protect them, if you were the kidnappers?"

Bree sucked in her breath. "You'd have to think about the farmers. You wouldn't be able to put in too much hardware—you couldn't provoke questions. And the kids sometimes wander out into the woods. You couldn't risk hurting them. Unless you've literally taken the entire orphanage prisoner, you'd need a nonviolent way to simply watch those two sides of the property and dispatch some agents to take care of any intruders. You'd need to install video—maybe infrared, so you'd be protected at night. That kind of equipment takes time to install, especially with such long property lines. You'd take no chances with anyone discovering you."

Dash interjected. "They probably started by removing the threat posed by the farmers."

She thought of Mr. Gregory, who'd made a point of bringing the orphanage children over to see each new litter of kittens in his barn, and his wife, Mrs. Gregory, who would always be waiting with chocolate chip cookies—so fresh from the oven they would still scorch your fingers and tongue. She thought of Mr. Giffin, who'd bend your ear to read a bit from the Farmer's Almanac if you gave him enough time, sneaking a lollipop into your pocket when he thought Rodney wasn't looking.

She felt her heart hardening. She hated thinking about this part.

"It's too small a town for that. They'd be missed." She shook her head, shaking away the images of her neighbors, dead. "No. And they couldn't put up much by way of physical barriers, either. It would raise eyebrows, seem unneighborly after all these years. It's electronic surveillance, for sure. Infrared, maybe, or microwave. Maybe even LiDAR. They probably have a data center somewhere on the orphanage." Bree paused to catch her breath. "We'll disable their surveillance and come up the side of the property," she said, definitively, blinking away her tears. "It will be nightfall early—I'd say dark by five p.m. at the latest. The only question is how?"

"If they put up cameras on the perimeter, there'd have to be a cable. We cut the cable or any connection between it and the power station. Easy."

Bree frowned. "*Too* easy. And if we cut the power lines, the entire neighborhood will go dark."

"Wouldn't that be better? Give us cover?"

"It would send all the repair trucks out our way. We definitely don't want that. And I don't think they would take that risk, either. They've probably got their own generator or substation on the property. If they need power at all."

"Wouldn't that have drawn attention, though? All those trucks?"

She slapped the steering wheel. "The renovated barn! They could have snuck in practically anything under the cover of that construction. Especially if they put in a computer lab like Ollie and Rodney were talking about. I bet any data center or generator is there. If that's the power source, a direct attack will be too difficult. Looks like we'll have to take the cliffs after all."

"Can we? How will we get the children away? Surely they can't rappel down the cliffs?"

"You don't know these kids," she said drily, thinking of how well they'd done in their frantic descent from the shipping containers when she was helping them escape from Turkey. "We'll take the orphanage vans if we have to," she said, dismissing his concern. "I'm more worried about getting into the grounds than getting anybody off of them."

"You said you thought the Asker children are being kept in the renovated barn," Dash continued, prompting her through the rest of the plan.

She nodded. "It's my best guess. Especially if they have been positioned as the so-called refugees Rodney was talking about—remember? The barn was to be used for them—a strategic way to isolate them, as surely they will be distressed and possibly even disruptive to the other kids. The other kids will be in the dormitories. Rodney will be in the main house." She paused, considering Rodney and all the unknowns he presented.

"Dash," she said, keeping her voice steady. "This vehicle has wifi and Internet capabilities, right?"

"Yes," he answered. "What do you need, Bree?"

"Can you get into the European Patent Register? Or the University of Bath's research funding databases?"

Out of the corner of her eye she saw him shrug. "I suppose it shouldn't be so difficult."

Bree sighed. "Search for anything related to Beatrice Andrews. Concentrate on the mid-to-late-nineties."

"Beatrice Andrews?"

"Rodney's wife. She was a scientist. At Bath."

Dash turned in his seat, staring at Bree. "Bree! Why didn't you—"

"Don't. Just, don't, Dash."

He slumped back in his seat, shaking his head. "Anything? You want me to look for anything?" he asked quietly.

She kept her face neutral, her voice steady. "You're looking for patents and research on neurotransmitter blockers or anything related to memory. Defense contracts underwriting her research would be particularly promising."

"Just how long have you been sitting on this juicy piece of news?" he spat.

"I'm sorry," Bree said evasively. "Can you just see what you can find?"

"You know as well as I do that none of that would be public record," he said, his jaw set. But he dragged his laptop out of his rucksack with an exaggerated sigh. Bree could see him tapping the information into the search engine even while he was protesting under his breath.

"I'm counting on your skills to go beyond the public record," she said. She left him to it while she returned her full attention to the road.

They went past one exit, then another, where the boiled peanut signs competed with advertisements for fast food. Her stomach protested with a growl as she wistfully left the off-ramp and her last hopes for food in her rearview mirror.

An hour passed with only the sounds of Dash grunting and typing to interrupt her concentration. In her head, she rehearsed the wiring of her makeshift bombs, imagining how she could use different configurations to take out whatever surveillance they'd put in place.

They.

It was a safe word. A generic word that refused to name names. A word that kept her from having to deal with the realities of Judy and maybe, just maybe, of Rodney.

"Bingo," Dash stated triumphantly.

"Did you say 'bingo'?"

"Isn't that the proper colloquial usage? I'd always heard that on American television programs."

"You found something?"

"I found her doctoral thesis in the digital stacks at Bath," he said, a note of quiet satisfaction, mixed with concern, in his voice. "And some other papers. She was quite prolific. How'd Rodney meet her again?"

"Forget about that. What was she researching?"

"Rodney told you her field of study was what?"

"Neuroscience. He said she was dabbling in child psychology, stuff about foster care's impact on kids' mental well-being."

He whistled low. "That's not what this looks like. This looks like some real science fiction to me. Supplanting memories by suppressing the hippocampus. Implanting false memories. Or get this—this one was a study for DARPA."

"DARPA?" Bree frowned.

"The Defense Advanced Research Projects Agency. It's part of the US Department of Defense. They're the ones who invented the Internet, remember? Anyway, her research for them was a post-doc entitled 'Restoring Active Memory.' The abstract describes a wireless, implantable neural interface to replicate the way neurons code memories so that soldiers with traumatic brain injuries can go back into battle. Ooh, and then there's this one: 'Prosthetic Persistent Memory.' It looks like it's about a database into which one could dump memories so they would never be lost, no matter what head trauma one suffered. And get this, right in the introduction— theoretically, if the computer sensed an improper formation or recall of a memory, it could send a corrective signal back. It could prevent you from retrieving your own memory by interfering at the neural level."

"That was DARPA too?"

"Seems like it. Though the grant filing is a little hard to untangle and is, of course, redacted. Let me see what I can do to untangle that."

"Do we do work with DARPA?" Bree wondered as Dash continued to hack his way deeper into the system.

"I've never heard anyone at the Agency reference it. Not the way they casually throw about ECHELON and the like. But who knows? Ah, hullo now, what's this? This is a new one to me." He began typing furiously, picking up on this new clue.

"What?" Bree tried peering into his laptop.

"Stay in your lane, Bree," he said sharply as a semitruck screamed by them, bearing down on its horn.

She righted the SUV and waited until he was ready to explain.

"IARPA. Intelligence Advanced Research Projects Activity. Apparently like DARPA, but for spying, with no intention of ever commercializing anything. All its research goes toward collection of intelligence, plus detection and infiltration. I'm surprised we were never briefed on it. Perhaps because it's an American thing and the Americans have no intention of sharing, it was considered irrelevant? Anyway, it says here, right on its public website, that there's a whole program office—MICrONS— focused on 'reverse engineering the algorithms of the brain.' Beatrice's post-doc research was funded by a precursor to IARPA, Bree."

"That doesn't prove anything . . ." Bree's voice trailed off.

"Remember what I said about coincidences, Bree," Dash said softly. He began the complicated process of deleting his digital trail before shutting down his laptop for good. "A scientist, in Bath, doing research for US intelligence and military agencies on memory suppression and retrieval? With a direct connection to you?"

"Whose husband's orphanage is largely funded by a woman we know was a handler for the Agency," Bree added, her voice toneless. "A woman still running covert operations to this day."

They drove for three exits without saying anything more. Bree didn't let herself cry. Instead, she focused on the growing, cold pit of fury in her stomach and wondered just what—and for how long—Rodney, the man she'd considered her father, had known about Norwood . . . how long he and Judy had conspired to manipulate her into its clutches.

"We need a new plan," she said roughly. "After we get in, we'll need to split up. One of us will need to get the Askers. One will need to go for Rodney."

"You're being emotional, Bree."

"I'm not being emotional!" she shouted, slamming her fist on the console. "I'm being realistic. If he's deep in this, we can't let him have a chance to disrupt things. We can't let him get away, either."

"If?"

She scoffed. "Fine. No 'if.' You don't need to rub it in. Either way, you know I'm right. We need to neutralize him."

"I don't like us splitting up. It's not safe. You have no idea how many people we'll be dealing with. And there's still a chance we're wrong."

"You're right. We'll check it out when we get there and then decide," she conceded grudgingly. She checked the gas gauge. With double tanks, they had no risk of running out at an inopportune time. Still, she needed to pick up a few extra supplies and would feel better if she topped it off before turning on to the back roads.

She wasn't really sure how they'd get the children out of Alabama, but she knew they wouldn't have a lot of time.

—

The sun was low by the time they breached the top of the cliff.

Bree threw one leg up over the edge, making sure she had purchase on the rocks before hauling herself over. Even in the autumn chill, her cheeks were burning, her breath heavy with the effort of carrying herself and her bag, laden with equipment, up the sheer rock face.

She rolled over onto her side, gasping for air.

Below her, she heard a skitter of falling rocks.

"Dash?" she whispered, crawling to peer over the edge.

"Almost there," he said in a gust of labored breath. "Though I appreciate the concern. Get back so I don't inadvertently pull you over on top of me."

She scrambled away from the cliff edge and sat on her haunches, scanning the trees, waiting.

With a groan, Dash heaved himself over the edge. "I must say, I haven't been this exhausted since the first week of *Wonder Woman*," he grunted as he scrambled on his stomach away from the cliff edge. "A well-placed kick to incapacitate me and a few mocking words from Professor Shadduck is all that it would take to whisk me right back into the fetal position on a mat in that airless, fetid gym."

Bree allowed herself just enough time for a grim smile before standing. "Maybe it's all the whiskey. Anyway, get up. No time for reminiscing. We've got work to do."

Dash grumbled. "You are a tough task master, Mistress Bellona."

Her smile broke open wide, the use of her nickname putting her at ease. "You think I'm tough now? Give me thirty minutes. Whoever those goons guarding the Askers are, they won't know what hit them."

He looked at her appreciatively as she began unpacking her equipment. "That will be a thing of beauty. Just as long as your fury is directed at them, not me."

She shook her head. What a silly thing to say.

"Enough banter," she told him. "Help me get this sorted."

Dash obediently popped into a squat. "At your service. I await your instruction."

She peered over the pile at her feet. "Stay right where you are. And while you're at it, put these on. Night goggles," she clarified, deftly separating a pair from the mess and kicking it up to his waiting hands.

"The latest from Savile Row, I see. Very well," he muttered, plopping the system on his head. "And you? What will you be sporting from this year's autumn collections?"

She modeled for him, touching each item clipped to her belt as she did. "Top-of-the-line axe, cable cutters, and guns. But most important, we have the makings of a big distraction." She touched the pile of equipment on the ground with one toe.

Dash flinched as she did. "Please don't do that."

She laughed. "This? It's safe, for now. It's just detonating cord with a little PETN in it. And that black powder is the explosive charge. What we're building is more flash and bang than actual explosive. The material for that is on your back. I got it when we filled up the gas tanks at our last stop."

He blanched.

"Don't worry. It's not Semtex or anything that damaging. It's a mix of gasoline, diesel, and kerosene, more or less. It will make a big cloudburst of fuel when the detonator goes off, and then the cloud itself will ignite," she explained. "See? A lot of smoke, flame, and noise—very dramatic, but pretty tame in the scheme of things."

"Why bother?" he asked. Bree could see him nervously checking the security of his pack, not quite trusting her reassurances that its contents were harmless.

"Whoever is physically guarding the children will get drawn away to investigate the explosion and put out the fire. That will give us the time we need to get in." She nodded at the trees. "See those boxes? The ones set at knee height?"

Dash followed her gaze until he, too, spied them. They were nondescript, blending into the drab grays and browns of the autumn woods.

"Now, follow the tree trunk up," Bree instructed, pointing. "You'll see the same box every six feet or so. It's a microwave security system. Perfect for covering massive areas. It basically notes any displacement of space by our body mass, or anything else, like a drone. It's continuous, not intermittent. So, more secure than an infrared system. The wiring for the system is too high. I don't think I can disable the power without setting off the alarm. Not until I find the source, which means getting in closer.

"We're going to have to sneak under the surveillance area on our backs." She eyed the detonator cord. "This is long enough to get us in really close. We'll arm the explosion up here, on their defensive perimeter, and set it off once we've closed the distance. It will go fast—about six kilometers a second. They move in to check out the disruption, we cut off their power source."

"They'll be blind, unable to see what's going on in the dark, and distracted, searching the woods," Dash concluded, impressed.

She kicked over the rest of the kit to him. He looked it over, approving. A knife, two guns, and an ultralight bulletproof vest.

"Suit up," she commanded. "Let's just hope they don't have that many boots on the ground, because this is all we've got."

———

It had seemed like hours of scooting along the floor of the woods, as Bree compulsively checked the detonator box to make sure the switch was still safely in place. She'd been right, she noted with satisfaction—a chain of massive generators had bloomed behind the barn, their hum cutting through the dark, the cables twisting in the Alabama dirt, feeding power to the security system behind them and, she supposed, to whatever was along the other property lines.

"Ready?" she asked Dash. "On my count."

The explosion was deafening. The shuddering air and smell of smoke was only a moment behind it. A ball of flame and dark smoke burst over the tree line.

A handful of men dressed in bulky bulletproof vests, machine guns in hand, emerged from the barn, pointing and barking orders to one another as they ran toward the fire. Dash and Bree pressed themselves into the ground, hoping they'd be unseen in the shadows as the men ran into the woods.

Satisfied the coast was clear, Bree ran to the generators. The cable cutter was sharp. It only took a minute to sever the connection and, presumably, shut down all surveillance.

She pointed to the windows on the barn. Dash cleared the distance in a moment and peered in.

"You did it," he said quietly. "Cameras are down. It looks like the entire place was covered in them, but they're all just static now. And I don't see anyone inside. Looks like they didn't expect us."

She nodded, taking a moment to collect her thoughts.

"Check the dormitories to make sure everyone is safe. Then go to the house," she instructed him. "We need eyes on Rodney. If you find him, bring him to me."

"You're sure, Bree?"

"I'm not assuming anything. But until we know exactly what is going on, we can't take chances. Not with him. Not with anyone. Keep your comms line open in case I need you here."

He nodded once, then rolled off the side of the barn and ran into the night. She watched him until he was swallowed up in the darkness. Squaring her shoulders, she took her gun out of its holster and stalked through the door—it was time to find the Asker children.

The barn itself was unrecognizable on the inside. She followed a long, Sheetrocked hallway that cut through the main floor, opening doors along the way. A huge amount of space had been given over to the complex security system. A quick glance confirmed it was, indeed, completely disabled with the disruption of power.

Cocky, she thought. No backup had kicked in. She wondered how long the men would search the woods, looking for intruders, before circling back to the barn.

Gun ready, she continued through the main floor. She saw how smartly they'd disguised their intentions, the promised computer lab having materialized in the front of the building. A cache of laptops and digital pads were stored in cubbies along the walls. The front of the classroom, completely windowless, was covered in digital wipe boards. She pushed a button and videoconferencing equipment descended from the ceiling, promising virtual visits and lectures that would whisk the children away from Alabama, connecting them with people all over the world. She smiled to herself as she noticed a doodle of the Wonder Dog in Ollie's scrawly hand on a white board. Fancy digital printing equipment was set up in stations that dotted the room. Nothing that sophisticated, she noted, as she glanced at the children's abandoned projects—mock-ups of race cars and trains, a cat with a movable tail. She held her breath, though, when she saw a model of an intricate bridge.

It was a model of the Galata Bridge—the one that spanned the Bosphorus, which cut through Istanbul. Right next to it was a replica of a ship, the giant kind that carried containers around the world.

The lettering on the side of the ship carried the same name as the container ship on which she and the Askers had fled Turkey.

They were here.

Throwing the models down, she headed back down the hallway toward the staircase she'd spied. She began to climb toward what had been the loft, taking the steps in twos and threes, going faster and faster until she reached the landing at the top.

A guard lay disabled and unconscious on the floor. His wrists and ankles had been bound in duct tape. She knelt on the floor to check his breath—shallow, but definitely there. Still alive, and by the looks of it, not long in this state.

She looked around, confused. There was no way out of the landing, other than the stairs she had just climbed, or the door that was hanging open ahead of her.

"We're in here, Bree," a voice called out to her. "We've been waiting for you."

Cautiously, she stood up. She removed her safety and cocked her gun.

"Miss Bree," a younger voice continued. "Miss Bree, it's Arslan! It's just us in here. Nothing to be afraid of."

Bree's heart lurched with joy.

She threw herself against the wall and edged through the doorway, diving into the room, gun at the ready, as she scanned for threats.

Arslan. Gamze. Isa. Eda. All there. All whole—bigger than she'd remembered. Alive. Healthy. Standing in the center of the room, jumping and wiggling with excitement, barely able to contain themselves from rushing into her arms.

Behind them, waiting, was Agent Gul Avci.

"My God," Bree whispered, a floodgate of tears bursting from her eyes. She clicked on her safety and tucked the pistol in her waistband. "Come here!"

They ran to her, squealing with delight to be reunited with their beloved nanny. She buried her face in their hair, gulping in their familiar smells, squeezing their little limbs to satisfy herself that they were, indeed, real.

She had found them.

"I kept them safe, Miss Bree. I kept them safe for you, and for Anne and Baba," Arslan said, referring to their parents.

Gul cleared her throat, her authority emanating like waves. The children fell silent. "We don't have much time."

"Gul," Bree choked out. She stood up and closed the distance between them with a few strides. "I knew you couldn't be dead."

Gul looked at her, eyes blazing with curiosity. She gripped Bree's shoulder, a soldier's salute. "And I, you. Too bad we don't know who has been manipulating who, though I'd bet we both have our ideas. We'll have time to figure that out after we get out of here. What's the exit plan?"

Bree checked her watch. "Norwood doesn't know we're here. If all has gone according to plan, they won't have detected our absence yet."

"Our?"

"Dash is with me."

Gul frowned, but did not comment.

"I saw four guards run to the explosion, and the fifth you incapacitated outside the door. Is that all of them?"

Gul nodded. "Whoever's in charge didn't want to spook anyone more than they had to. Very light security."

"Good. We can't go back the way we came, over the cliffs. It will be crawling with those guards, and regardless, I don't want to climb with the kids. We had enough of that the last time I saw them. We'll have to charge out the front door, as it were. Weapons?"

Gul nodded toward a bag in the corner. "That's everything I could muster on my own. Between it and what we can steal from the guard station downstairs, it should be enough to get us out. Where are we headed?" she asked, as she went to fetch the bag.

"Back to the air base Dash and I flew into. We can contact whomever we need to from there. It will be secure, at least. Whomever we're dealing with, they won't take a chance shooting up a US government facility."

She looked at the children. They were huddled together, a mixture of hope, confusion, and apprehension on their faces.

"It's okay, kids," she said, tousling Arslan's hair. "We'll get you out of here. Everything will be fine."

"Mermaids again, Miss Bree?" Gamze's eyes were plaintive as she remembered the elaborate game of make-believe the nannies had used to keep the children calm during their attempted escape, so many months ago.

"No more mermaids. No witches. Just us." She looked at Gul, hoping she was right. "Sound good?"

"You weren't leaving without me, were you?"

Bree jumped, shoving the children behind her at the interruption.

Gul swung, pistol aimed at the intruder's head. "Who are you?"

Dash loomed in the doorway, looking pained. Bree felt a wave of relief wash over her.

"It's okay," Bree said, waving at Gul to holster her gun. "He's with me. You might remember him—he ran all the comms during the Turkey op: Dashiell Heyward."

"Oh. Great job getting us separated during the mission, Heywood," Gul said drily, clearly not impressed and, Bree suspected, deliberately butchering Dash's last name to make sure he knew it. "Hopefully, you've learned a few things since then. Since you're here, make yourself useful. Hot-wire one of those vehicles out front. It's time for us to get moving."

Dash paused, working his mouth like a fish. When he didn't move, Gul shrugged.

"No? Suit yourself. We can leave you behind for cleanup, if you prefer."

Bree looked at him sharply. "What is it, Dash? And where's Rodney? Did you find him?"

"I found more than Rodney." Dash sagged and walked through the door, Rodney on his heels. Behind them both, wielding two Sig Sauers, came Judy.

"Look at this, one big happy family, together again," she smiled, no warmth reaching her eyes. "Sit down, everyone. We've a lot to discuss."

"Judy? What . . .?" her voice trailed off as she watched Gul dart a stealthy glance at Judy. "Gul?"

"I knew it," Dash swore under his breath.

"You knew what?" Bree could feel the breath going out of her, the panic seeping through her veins. She wheeled around, drawing her own weapon out to sweep the room, unsure of where to point it. "What's going on?"

When nobody answered she cursed. "Somebody. Tell me what's going on. Now."

"Me, too, please," Rodney piped up. "I gather Dash thinks I'm involved in whatever this is, but I'm not, and I'm getting more confused by the minute. Not to mention uncomfortable with the guns being wielded about."

Judy tilted her head, deciding how to proceed. "You're perfectly safe, Rodney. There's no need for drama, either one of you. Gul, dear, bring me a chair. I think we have time for one cigarette."

Gul, cautious but accommodating, dragged over a folding chair from a corner and set it up for Judy.

"Gul? Your name is 'Gul'? What the hell!" Rodney erupted, watching her. "If you're not with Homeland Security's refugee program, then who are you?"

Gul's mouth twisted as she held back a retort. Judy drew a lighter and a single cigarette out of what looked like a Chanel fanny pack.

"Why don't you take the children out front?" Judy prompted Gul. "We won't be long."

The kids looked at Bree, then at Gul, confused.

Bree gulped and forced herself to smile. "You go on, now," she said brightly to the children. "Practice your American nursery rhymes. I expect you to sing them all to me once we get in the car."

Eda whined softly. Bree enveloped her in a hug, kissing her hairline. Eda wrapped her arms around Bree's neck, her grubby fingers sticking on Bree's skin.

"Don't worry, little one. I'll be down before you know it. Stick with Miss Gul."

Gul pried Eda's fingers off and swept her out of Bree's arms, giving Bree a quick squeeze on the shoulder before shooing the children out the door. They sounded like a herd of elephants, heading down the stairs. Bree waited for the door below to slam behind them.

Satisfied they were gone, she grabbed a chair and sat down. She crossed her legs, expectantly, and turned a cool gaze to Dash, then Judy.

"Talk."

Dash rubbed his face, his long, elegant fingers shaking. He took a deep breath. "I may not have been entirely honest with you, Bree," he began.

Bree cocked an eyebrow and held her breath, waiting for an explanation.

"But it was all with the utmost of good intentions, I promise you."

"Intentions and promises are meaningless," Judy interrupted. "Your word is good, until it isn't. Remember, Bree? I told you that a long time ago," Judy prompted, taking a heavy drag on her cigarette.

Bree nodded. She remembered exactly where she was when Judy had dropped that bit of wisdom on her—at Poppins's feet, back on campus.

"Did you know Gul was alive this whole time? Even before I spotted her in the interrogation?" Bree pressed Dash.

"I suspected it," he acknowledged, not avoiding her gaze—in fact, lifting his chin, defiant. "I suspected it from the beginning. And then, I knew. I knew it before we even came to visit Rodney at the end of the summer."

"But how?"

Dash was sweating. He ran a nervous hand along his collar.

"We've been running you—*and* Gul—as assets on this op this whole time, trying to flush *her* out." He tilted his chin at Judy. "Albourn, Shadduck, and me."

Bree sucked in her breath. "What are you talking about?"

Dash pointed at Judy. "She's been on the run for years. We knew if we got you out into the open, if she thought you were at risk . . . then maybe, just maybe, we'd be able to make her surface. And we were right."

"You were running me? Without me knowing it? None of this makes sense, Dash."

"You need to listen to me, Bree. Remember when those operatives in the woods outside of John's place were looking for someone they kept calling Roberta? That's her. Roberta Jude. Judy Roberts. She just flipped the names to hide in plain sight."

"Just like my parents on their marriage certificate . . ." Bree thought back to the records in the little parish outside of Derry. All they'd done was swap their surnames—McCarthy and Hutton—and they disappeared into the records. It was a simple thing, an easy thing, she knew.

"That doesn't explain what you were doing, though. Or why you thought you could use me to get her to come out after more than a decade on the run."

He looked pointedly at Judy.

"You're doing such a wonderful job on your own. Continue," Judy said, amusement curling the corners of her lips. She let the ash from her cigarette fall on the fresh industrial carpet, burning holes in the plastic fibers, before crushing the sparks under the heel of her boot.

Dash came to squat in front of Bree and took her hands in his. She flinched, causing him to wince in turn. He swallowed the insult and squeezed her hands, hard.

"You know this, Bree. Deep down, I know you do."

She looked at him, bewildered. "You're not making any sense, Dash. Whatever it is, just come out with it. You were using me, and I want to know why."

"Judy's not who you think she is."

"Yes, yes, we've established that. She was a handler for the Agency. She was David Hutton's first wife. She has at least one alias, probably dozens. Maybe she was even the one diverting arms from Turkey to China—trying to undermine the government, I'd bet. Susmita said as much." Bree shot a wary glance at Judy, knowing Judy had warned her to bury that particular piece of information.

"What I can't figure out is why she is *here.*" She stood up and confronted Judy. "Why *are* you here, Judy? You couldn't have been working with Susmita. She was trying to stop the arms shipments. Even though it was primarily out of spite, she wanted the PRC to win. If anyone threw the mission and planned the kidnapping of the Asker children, it was her. What's your angle?"

Judy looked at her coolly. "You're right. The kidnapping of the Askers was not my doing. I already told you that."

Bree was frustrated. She wheeled on Rodney. "And you? Did you know about this all along?"

Rodney shook his head sorrowfully. "I swear to you, Bree. But I take it that Judy is not the businesswoman she has always presented herself to be. Nor is that young woman who just left with the children with the government refugee program. Nor, it would seem, are either of you simple students."

"But what about Beatrice?" Bree demanded, her eyes narrowing. "She had to have been involved in all of this—which would mean it goes back for years. And that you were in the middle of it."

Rodney looked shocked at the mention of his dead wife. "What does Beatrice have to do with any of this?" He held out his hands, helpless. "Judy, help me out here. You've known me—knew both of us—from the very beginning."

"Yes, I knew you from the start. And you were perfect for each other. You and she both were brilliant," Judy added. "Brilliant and passionate to make a difference, each in your own way. You were—are—very smart, Rodney, but you're book smart. You're too trusting. That's what made it so perfect, so *easy*. You never suspected anything. Beatrice made sure of it. But when I needed you, you were ready. It didn't even matter when Beatrice died. All the groundwork had been laid, well in advance. This entire orphanage was ready."

Rodney came over to stand next to Bree, wrapping a guarded arm around her shoulder. "Ready for what?"

"It was ready when I needed to disappear into the guise of a kind benefactor," Judy answered calmly. She stood up and joined Rodney and Bree, her eyes watchful, gauging their reaction to what she was saying. "It was ready when I needed to hide my only daughter, until the time I could reclaim her. It was ready, Bree, for you."

Chapter Twelve

MEG

1998, Northern Ireland

"Mummy, sheep!"

Meg peered into the back. The girls were buckled and strapped into their car seats on separate sides of the car. Rennie was occupied with a toy. Briana had forgotten hers, her attention taken up by something in the landscape to which she pointed.

Meg forced a smile. "Yes, Briana. That's a sheep. Just like Uncle Brian's."

To the girls, it was a family outing. They were oblivious to the suit-cases in the boot of the car, to the carefully crafted new identities that were now documented in official papers, and to the meticulously planned passages to a network of safe houses that would help them escape.

They had smothered their dog with kisses and flung their arms around Brian, not realizing it might be the last time they ever saw either of them. If she and David were successful, their entire family would melt into nothingness and reinvent themselves somewhere new—somewhere where the IRA, MI5, and the Agency could never touch them.

David steered the car through the roundabout, taking the exit toward a more remote part of the countryside. They were headed toward what Judy had described as an abandoned air base, one that had been "requisitioned" by the Agency for its own purposes. There would be a dormitory for the girls, and minders to keep them safe while she and David went on to China.

"One hundred forty-four hours," Meg murmured to herself. One hundred forty-four hours and they would be free.

"Mummy, sheep! And cow!" Briana shrieked, kicking her heels against the car seat.

"Yes, Briana. Yes, I know, sweetheart. There are lots of animals in the country."

Rennie took up the refrain, kicking her heels into the car seat. "Sheep! Sheep! Sheep!"

David sighed at the noise. "It's a shame the girls have gotten so big that they have front-facing seats now, isn't it? I'm sorry, but the route we planned is all back ways. It will take a bit longer. Maybe you can distract the girls?"

"With what?" Meg snapped back, immediately regretting her sharp tone. She was on edge, she knew. It wouldn't do to take it out on David.

"It can't last much longer," she said more gently. "The sun has gone below the horizon. It will be dark soon and they won't be able to see a cow or anything else. They'll be asleep before you know it." She settled into her seat, determined to ignore them.

"Cow!"

"Cow!"

"Cow!"

"Cow!"

The girls were alternating the chant between them, now, punctuating their cries with their kicking and the wild laughter of children who had missed their naptimes.

Meg fiddled with the radio knob. If she couldn't distract them, perhaps she could distract herself.

"Cow!"

"Cow!"

"Cow!"

"There can't be that many cows in all of Ireland," David muttered under his breath. "Can you do something to quiet them?"

"Girls," Meg began, trying to be gentle with them. She peered back over her shoulder, preparing to reason with them—or bribe them—as best as she could.

"Cow!"

"Cow!"

"Car!" Rennie shrieked, pointing a finger out the window.

Startled, Meg followed her finger. She was just in time to see a large black sedan bear down on them, speeding through the country intersection, taking dead aim for their vehicle.

The impact sent them airborne. After the initial boom and screech of metal grinding upon metal, there was the tinkle of glass as their windows shattered. Then a cold silence as they flew through the air.

Their flight was stopped by a tree, the branches thrusting through the windshield.

It was over in an instant.

She was alive. At least, she assumed the pain—and the fact that she was still coherent—meant she was alive. She could not move, though. Whether it was due to injury or being pinned by the tree, she couldn't tell.

"David!"

She looked to her left. David was slumped over the steering wheel, unconscious.

The girls were wailing now.

Good, she said to herself. Crying means they are alive.

She sagged into the seat, accepting, waiting for someone to approach and rescue them. She strained to hear the sounds of the other car, or people, or an ambulance.

Instead, she heard a third car screeching to a halt, then gunshots.

More silence.

"Mummy! Mummy!" Briana screamed from the back.

"Shh, baby. Mummy's here. Rennie—Rennie, can you hear me? Are you there, Rennie?"

Rennie's sobbing voice answered, "Yes, Mummy."

Meg forced herself to think despite Briana's shrieking. She had to get them out of the wreckage.

"Rennie, listen to me. Are either of you hurt? Do you see blood or cuts or broken bones?"

"Nnn-no."

"Can you reach the buckle of your car seat, sweetheart? Mummy needs you to unbuckle it and let yourself out of the seat. Can you do that, Rowena?"

"I don't know how," Rennie sobbed.

Another round of gunfire snapped Meg back into focus.

Meg strained against her own bonds. She was trapped. Maybe David could get them out? She glanced at him, still pitched forward against the steering wheel.

A trickle of blood had escaped his mouth.

Oh, God, she thought. *He's dead.*

Despair began to snake around her as she caught an unmistakable whiff of smoke.

"Help! Help!" she screamed, her thrashing sending jolts of pain through her body.

"Meg?"

David had lifted his head and was looking at her, confused.

"David! Oh, David, you're alive. There was an accident. We need to get out. I need you to get up and get the girls out. The car is going to blow."

A bubble of blood bloomed from David's mouth. He coughed, and spat. Still disoriented, his gaze fell to his chest. Meg's eyes followed his. A large branch had pierced his side, pinning him in the seat.

"No . . . accident . . ." he muttered, wincing with every breath. "I don't know if I can move, Meg." He lowered his head onto the steering wheel and closed his eyes.

"No! No! NO! You cannot go to sleep. You cannot die on me. Wake up, David! Wake UP! There are people here, David. People shooting guns. We need to get out—the girls . . ."

He grimaced and forced his eyes open. "Okay."

He clenched his jaw and somehow managed to push himself upright, an anguished roar of pain escaping from him.

"Okay," he repeated, closing his eyes and leaning back in the seat— whether he was gathering his strength or had passed out from the pain, Meg couldn't tell. The girls had fallen into a state of shock, their shrieking giving way to quiet sniffling.

Meg's mind raced.

The gunfire had ended. It was too quiet. Eerie, even.

A plume of black smoke drifted into her line of vision. She took a deep breath and winced, tears bursting forth at the sudden pain that wracked her body.

They were running out of time.

She heard a crunch of gravel, and the passenger-side door next to her swung open.

She turned her head, and a wave of relief swept over her. It was Judy.

"Thank God," she muttered through clenched teeth. "Thank God you're here."

"Shh," Judy whispered, peering into the car to assess the situation. "Don't try to talk. There's not much time."

"What happened?" Meg pressed, still struggling to make sense of it all.

"You were set up. Luckily, you were close enough to our rendezvous point that I was in time to take them out. Too bad for our operation, but at least they won't bother us again."

"Who?" Meg gasped through her pain. "Who? Americans?"

Judy didn't answer.

David stirred in the seat next to Meg. Meg reached out to grip his shoulder.

"David! David, wake up! Help is here. My handler is here. She stopped the attack on us. She'll get us out of here."

David's eyes fluttered open. "Oh. That's good," he whispered.

He turned his head and looked across the front seat to where Judy stood. His mouth dropped.

"*She's* your handler?"

Meg nodded impatiently. "Yes. She's going to get us out of here now, David, but I need you to be alert. Can you stay awake for me?"

David let his head fall back against the seat and laughed. The sound of it made Meg's skin crawl—it was a desperate, disbelieving sound, out of control and inexpressibly sad, the wild hysterical laughter mixing with the choking sound of blood in his throat.

He closed his eyes and let his head sink to the steering wheel. "Oh, Meg. My dear, sweet Meg. You don't know, do you?"

Meg looked at him, baffled, and then looked at Judy. Judy's face bore a smug look of satisfaction.

David opened his eyes a crack and returned Meg's gaze. "You don't know what you've done." A spurt of blood gushed from his mouth, and he choked on it a little, but he pushed on. "Your handler . . . Your *Judy* is my Roberta. My ex-wife. Rennie's mum."

Meg's mind recoiled.

"No. That can't be. You're hallucinating," she whispered.

"Tell me, Meg," he continued, wincing as he spoke. "Was Judy always your handler? Or did your handler get swapped out at some stage during your surveillance of me?"

When Meg didn't answer, David continued.

"Did you get official word from your agency, have a formal debrief with your first handler, meet the new handler on the up and up? Or did all communication come through *her*? Have you heard anything directly from someone else at your agency at all?"

Meg remembered the unceremonious replacement of her original handler, with barely any explanation—all handled through Judy. She thought of all the dead drops she'd exchanged with Judy, never having seen her, until she'd been spirited away with David to Ireland. How she'd never faced any repercussions for marrying David, nor for having a child, despite Norwood's rules. How they'd never called her in for a debrief after Castlereagh—indeed, Judy'd discouraged it.

She thought of the casual but constant questions about Rennie Judy had always thrown into their conversations, and as she counted them out, she felt a mounting sense of dread.

"Surprise, David," Judy whispered softly. "So refreshing now that we'll be able to get all this nastiness out in the open—it will be so much more efficient this way.

"Meg, shall I fill you in? Where shall I begin? I was removed from my Norwood handler posting after a string of failed operations. The nastiness of the divorce—after I'd already broken the rules to marry David—just made it easy for them to push my dismissal through their stupid bureaucracy. What the Agency didn't count on, though—what frankly even I had underestimated—is how easy it is to go rogue," Judy said philosophically.

"It's easy to disappear yourself, until you're ready to be found. It's easy to take out another handler and slip into her place when everything is happening in the shadows—especially when she's been encouraged to be a loner, to have no ties. It's easy to file reports about her agents and their cases, finding reasons to avoid coming in from the field. And so, so easy, when you find that right, special agent, so eager to prove herself, so arrogant in her belief in her own skills, so eager to double-cross, that she's blind to her own manipulation. You, Margaret McCarthy, made this so much easier for me than it could have been."

"Fool me once . . ." David whispered, a sputtering cough ending his statement. "I have to give it to you, Roberta," he gasped through the pain. "You played the long con." Another trickle of blood escaped his mouth as he flopped back in the seat, exhausted. "Meg, if only you'd trusted me enough, I could have helped you. But now? I don't know who you—either of you—work for, but if Roberta's involved, this plan was a rogue op. A setup."

The effort of speaking was too much for him. He vomited a stream of blood and passed out in the seat.

"No," Meg protested, watching the life seep out of him. "No, David, no . . ." A convulsive cry escaped her lips. But she couldn't mourn David. She needed to talk her way out of this.

"David's wrong. Tell me he was wrong," she repeated, a twinge of guilt as she slipped easily into the past tense to describe him. "It *was* an Agency job, wasn't it, Judy?" Meg demanded through gritted teeth, straining against the bonds of the jammed seat belt and errant tree branches. "It had to be. You said—"

Judy cut her off. "I said no such thing. That was the beauty of running you. You filled in the blanks yourself. I didn't even have to lie to you to get you to do what I wanted. You went, willingly, wherever I pointed."

Meg hung her head, angry tears streaming down her face. "All of that talk about Britain and what it owes its former colonies. That's you, then. The Agency didn't want to assassinate President Clinton at all. You did."

"Ah, now you're beginning to catch on," Judy said quietly. "Yes, this was a private endeavor, formed with a few of my friends from the old days. This attack was the Agency's attempt to intercept us. Which, we might as well acknowledge, has succeeded, though it has left two of their agents dead. So, I won't get my way on this one, but there is a silver lining. For me at least."

Judy's cold eyes gleamed. She looked in the back seat.

"No!" Meg screamed. "No, you cannot take our girls."

"*Your* girls? David took Rowena away from me and in the process undermined my career. You've warped my daughter into loving you. I've had to sit and watch you do it, for years, biding my time. It ends today. She's coming with me. Boys?"

She backed away from the car. Meg heard the crunch of footsteps on gravel as someone else approached their car.

The rear door next to Rennie swung open. Rennie began to scream as she was roughly ripped from the car seat and carried away. A poof of flame exploded in the front of the car.

"You promised! You said you'd get us out!" Meg cried, the heat evaporating her tears before they had the chance to finish running down her cheeks.

Briana's cries of agony swelled as the flames began working their way up the driver's side of the vehicle.

"You promised! You promised! You promised!"

Meg repeated it like she was saying the Rosary, on her knees in the little chapel in Chicago, safe, before any of this happened; saying it over and over again as if repetition would make it true.

Judy looked doubtful as she eyed the encroaching flames. "David's gone, Meg. And we're running out of time. I don't think I can get you both out. You'll have to choose."

Briana was sobbing now, the cries unlike anything Meg had ever heard. Meg could barely see her, in the back seat, from the corner of her eye. She was flailing helplessly at the plastic buckles on her car seat strap, which were starting to melt.

"Please, Judy. Please," Meg sobbed, hanging in her seat. "You promised me that if anything happened to us, you would take care of the girls! Both of them! You promised me, Judy! Please don't let Briana die."

Meg could barely hear Judy's response over the whoosh of the flames.

"That's your choice?"

"Yes! Save Briana. For the love of God, save my daughter."

"David wronged me, Meg. But for you, I will keep my promise. After all, I'm a mother too. Pull her out," Judy commanded one of the unseen men who'd accompanied her. "Grab that nappy bag, too. We may need something out of it later."

Meg heard the groaning of metal as they pulled the door—already morphing from the fire—open. She heard the men swearing in the sweltering heat of the fire, heard their struggle to pull her daughter out. She relaxed, just a bit, as Briana's crying slowly faded away to a low hum in the distance.

Her girls were safe. For now.

"Goodbye, Meg." Judy's voice interrupted her thoughts. Meg watched as Judy retreated a bit farther up a slight embankment, Rennie writhing in her arms. Rennie strained away from Judy, reaching for Meg, her tiny voice calling for Mummy.

Meg threw herself against the window, hand splayed against the glass, and said goodbye.

Then she pushed the voice away. She drew herself inside her head, making her body an idea, something far, far away, something untouchable that could feel no pain—just like they'd taught her in interrogations class. She was drifting, further and further from the stench and the heat and the sorrow, so far away she barely heard Judy's parting words.

"Douse it, boys. Use up all the gas. Nothing left, understand? Nothing that enables them to be identified, nothing to suggest there were any survivors. Not so much as a fragment of tooth."

Chapter Thirteen

BREE

Present Day, Alabama

"No way. You"—Bree pointed across the room to where Judy was standing, waiting—"you are not my mother. My mother was Margaret McCarthy. My mother is dead."

"Bree, think," Dash insisted. "It's locked in your memory, but I know it must be in there. You and Gul are the only surviving witnesses, and Gul was too young to remember. You, though—you just might know enough for us to finally do them justice."

"Do who justice? And what does Gul have to do with it?"

"You're wasting your time," Judy sighed, impatient. "Even though it was a prototype, it worked. There's not a chance you will crack her now."

"What in God's name are you talking about?" Dash huffed, allowing himself to look away from Bree just long enough to skewer Judy with a very patrician look of disapproval.

"She was the first clinical recipient of Beatrice's neurotransmitter blockers." Judy shrugged. "Everything that Norwood can do now to turn off its agents' memories stemmed from her." She nodded as if to give Bree credit. "That's one of the reasons why they never let Bree alone. I could never figure out how they knew—maybe Beatrice let it slip, inadvertently."

Rodney sputtered in the corner. "You experimented on tiny children? On whose authority? And someone was tracking her, like a lab rat, to see what happened? My God, what lack of moral . . . and, Beatrice—you say Beatrice was a part of this?"

"Don't work yourself up, Rodney," Judy said coolly. "Beatrice didn't have a choice. I made her do it, on the threat of outing her to you. She protested all the way, even though I thought it a kindness, after everything that child had seen. As it turns out, your wife had a streak of do-gooder in her, just like you. Unfortunate, really. She was so talented. What a waste."

Rodney was pacing angrily, fists clenched. "We always have a choice. *Always*. I don't know what is going on, I don't even know who the hell is in charge here, but I don't like any of it."

Bree smiled weakly at him. "Me either, Rodney."

"Bree—listen to me," Dash tried again. "Maybe it will jog your memory. Agent Roberts, or Judy, as you know her, *was* running the operation on which Hutton and McCarthy were killed—but not as an agent of Norwood. She had been removed from the agency for cause years earlier."

"'Professional misjudgment' and 'operating outside regulation' was what they termed it," Judy sniffed. She resumed her seat and started a second cigarette. "It was a trumped-up charge. There was nothing illogical or crazed in any of my actions. Naturally, I resented the accusation."

Dash shot her a look over his shoulder before returning his gaze to Bree. "Yes, well, having been subjected to the whimsical proliferation of rules at Norwood myself, I can imagine how you felt. Though direct disobedience resulting in the loss of successive agents in the field over multiple failed ops, combined with a physical attack on the brass, probably made your removal seem more than a tad warranted. You could have been arrested."

"But I wasn't. I went underground." Over Dash's head, Bree saw Judy sneer at the idiocy of the Agency. "Norwood's version of events, as always, read like something from the imagination of a trashy novelist. I've no intention of re-litigating it now. What's important is that it was the Agency's fault that Hutton and McCarthy died. They died when Norwood sent agents to intercept the vehicle in an effort to stop our plans, which were of vital international importance. If the Agency hadn't interfered, we would be living with a very different geopolitical balance right now, one in which the prospect of an armed China is a fantasy. And I would add that, if it weren't for me," Judy said, pounding her chest, "Bree and her stepsister would have died in that crash, as well."

Rodney was struggling to follow. "Hutton and McCarthy were your parents, Bree?"

Bree nodded. Judy pushed her lips together in a tight line and crossed her arms. "Hutton was her father. McCarthy was simply a spy who weaseled her way into the household as my replacement."

Dash swung to confront Judy.

"They were raising both girls together, with you out of the picture. And you've conveniently forgotten one little part of the story, Agent Roberts. After you killed the attackers, you left the girls' parents to die in the car. You doused it with an accelerant to make sure they perished."

"That's a lie," Judy said calmly, ashing her cigarette.

"I have a signed statement from one of your men," Dash countered. "One of the men who was there who claims he did it on your orders."

Rodney was watching their exchange, his head swiveling between them as if it were a tennis match. At this latest statement, his mouth dropped open.

Bree's heart stopped.

"But why?" she whispered, forcing herself to listen to the truth of her past.

Dash came back to squat on his heels in front of her chair. Up close, she could see the new lines around his eyes and on his forehead, marks of worry she swore hadn't been there last week. He leaned his forehead against hers and squeezed her hands tight.

"I can only think of one explanation, Briana. Agent Roberts's feelings regarding being 'replaced' as your mother were complicated, even though she wasn't really the maternal type. From what the man's testimony covered, it appears your father couldn't be saved, and the decision to murder Agent McCarthy was improvised on the spot. The opportunity presented itself, and she took advantage. Though, to be honest, I question how they had that much gasoline on hand if it was a spontaneous decision. It was revenge, pure and simple. What happened after that fatal choice is why you're here."

"I couldn't take you with me. I needed to disappear again," Judy interrupted him.

"A reasonable conclusion," Dash acknowledged. "But you didn't have to switch them, did you?" He watched Bree carefully as he continued. "She was afraid of what could happen when the Agency hunted her down. You were always small for your age, so the swap—with no paperwork to challenge an assertion of age—was easy enough, especially with friendly doctors handling your intake. She hid you in plain sight, leaving you with the nappy bag that belonged to your stepsister so that everyone would assume you were her. She left you alone in a car seat, looking like you'd been thrown from the car in the explosion, knowing whoever recovered you would be none the wiser. Everyone would think you were Briana. But you're not. You're not Margaret McCarthy's daughter at all. You're Rowena Hutton. Judy's daughter. Did I get that right, Agent Roberts?"

Bree jerked her hands away from Dash's as if burned.

The words poured out of her, all denial and adrenaline. "That's not possible. You did the DNA test. You saw the results—I'm a McCarthy.

You know I am, Dash. I'm a McCarthy and a Donnelly. We saw the connections—all the Derry people, Brian, too . . ."

Dash shook his head. "Remember the day I took your sample, Bree? Gul was here, setting up the arrangements for the Asker children. She was the one who had lemonade and cookies with Rodney in the kitchen—am I right, Rodney?"

Bree glanced over at Rodney. Through her tears, she saw him nod. Yes, Gul had been here after all.

With Rodney's confirmation, Dash continued. "Gul was too little to remember, but she had flashes of things, mere windows into her memories, that made us suspect that you'd been switched. So I grabbed some of her DNA when I cleaned up the dishes, while you and Rodney talked. We compared it to yours. The sample that came back as related to Margaret McCarthy was Gul's sample. And you and Gul shared sufficient genetic material to confirm what we'd suspected all along—you are half-sisters."

"*Tell me about your mother,*" Albourn had demanded during that interview in her office. All along, she'd been talking about Judy.

"But why?" Bree cried. "Why did you do this to me? Why make me go through all of this when you already knew the truth? Why?"

"They didn't think they could trust you, Bree. It's as simple as that," Judy said quietly. "They didn't know for sure what you knew. They couldn't tell if you were faking the gaps in your memory. They couldn't be certain if, once you knew the truth, they could count on you to be on their side. It would be a natural thing, don't you think, to want to be with your own mother?" Judy concluded softly.

Bree swung wildly at Dash's head. When he dodged her left hook, she pummeled his chest, her fingers numb, her mind a blank of rage and pain. He sat impassively, letting her take her anger out on him, until she collapsed against him.

"Why now? Why tell me now, after all this?" she said, barely able to spit out the words between ragged, sobbing breaths.

He kissed her hair, right about the ear, and whispered, "Because *I* know. And I love you, Bree." He held her until her crying stopped and her great gasping breaths quieted into shaky ones.

"Leave me," she said to him.

His eyes widened, but he nodded, standing and taking up a spot several feet away, against the wall.

"Why are you even here, Judy?" Bree asked. "You have nothing to gain from showing up here. Nothing at all."

"That's not true, Briana. Once I return the Asker children to their father, the relentless logic of my operation will kick in. The asset—their father, the Colonel—will be stable. The asset will be secure. He will cooperate, as if his children had never been taken. The arms will start flowing again. They will flow to Turkey, and I can divert them to the Uyghur rebels. This is my life's work of nearly twenty years—stopping the PRC's persecution of the people within its borders, people who yearn to be free."

Bree recalled the interview she'd had with Albourn. The dean's parting words had been about the terrorist group demands, which seemed completely in line with Judy's story.

Judy threw a disparaging look at Dash before launching into a tirade.

"The Agency doesn't care about democracy—not really. It's just a ruse for its own blatant power grabs. I should be flattered that you took advantage of this blip to smoke me out, but really, I must insist that we bring an end to this nonsense so my operation can continue on course. And you"—she was bearing down on Bree now, a needy look on her face—"you and I can really be together, as we were meant to be: mother and daughter. We can work together and accomplish things beyond your wildest dreams! Think of it, Bree. Nobody will be able to stop us. I brought all the files—the old plans from when you were a child, and the new ones. All the documentation about the concentration camps in Xinjiang—all of it. Your life can have a purpose, just like mine."

"Did I mention that the psychiatric evaluation that clinched her dismissal included notations of delusions of grandeur?" Dash snorted.

"Shut up, Dashiell. And you, you stop right there," Bree ordered Judy, whose outstretched arms were dangerously close. "Don't come any closer."

Bree wanted—no, needed—some space. More than anything, she did not want to be touched.

"I want all of you out. Rodney, Dashiell—go wait outside. I need to be alone with Judy."

"Are you sure that's a good idea, Bree?" Rodney asked. But even as he did, he was honoring Bree's request, dragging Dash behind to hover with him at the doorway. "I don't know how I can help, but I don't like leaving you here. Not like this. I know Dash feels the same as me."

"I just found out that nothing I believed was true in my life has been true. I want you all out of here. I need to think. I need to ask about some questions, and I don't want an audience."

Dash looked hurt, opening his mouth to argue. Rodney cut him off. "It seems to me you've lost your right to comment, son," Rodney said sharply. "You came into our home and lied. In fact, it sounds like you've been doing it all along. Don't try to stuff her mind with more of your lies. Not now."

Dash made one last attempt. "I was only trying to do what's right. To help . . ."

Rodney snorted. "That dog won't hunt, son. Whatever motives you had, I'm pretty sure they were never about Bree's interests." Dash flushed, chastened into silence. Bree knew the look on Rodney's face—it was a look of satisfaction that his point had been made and he would brook no further challenges to his authority. "All right, then. You know where to find us. If you need anything at all . . ."

"I won't," Bree promised.

She waited for them to close the door behind them. Then, she turned to Judy.

She searched Judy's face. It was hard for her to be objective, but she forced herself to try. She remembered the words of the man who attacked her on the container ship— *"You look just like your mother."*

Did she?

Judy's glossy, dark hair had an undertone of auburn. Her eyes were a shocking bright blue. She was pale—Bree knew her to keep herself out of the sun—so there was no telltale smattering of freckles, but the tilt of the nose and the high cheekbones were familiar. Grudgingly, with fresh eyes, she could see her own face reflected in Judy's, and was shocked that she hadn't noticed it before. Thinking of the old yearbook photo Dash had shown her months ago, she could imagine how a young Judy Roberts and Margaret McCarthy resembled one another.

And now, as she recalled the red roots of Gul's shorn hair as they sat at the café in Istanbul and the burn scars that bloomed across Gul's chest and neck, she realized that what Dash had said must be true. It all made sense. The burn marks would have come from the fiery car crash. If Gul was really the youngest of the Hutton children, it made sense that she would have been one of the youngest graduates of Norwood. How the Agency cultivated her, how she ended up a spy, and just how deeply implicated she was in this whole plot was unclear. But it was evident Gul was her younger half-sister.

"You believe us, then?" Judy prompted, jerking Bree's thoughts back into the present.

"What was the name of my dog?" Bree asked abruptly.

"What?" Judy responded, confused.

"My dog. I think I had a dog when I was little. What was its name?"

Judy sighed. "Rascal."

Rascal the Wonder Dog. He wasn't a creation of her imagination, dreamed up to entertain Ollie, then. He was a memory. A memory that, whether through grief or drugs, had been buried deep. She realized with a start that the nightmares that had haunted her for years were memories too—memories of Meg McCarthy's last moments.

Bree took a shaky breath. "I believe you. Does Gul know?"

"I don't know," Judy conceded. "I'm not sure what the Agency has told her. When I spirited her away, my intention was to throw their focus on to her, away from you. What they told her, and when, remains a mystery to me."

"How did you know to come here?"

"I've been monitoring this place for a while. I know MI6 sent those men looking for me last summer. You and Dashiell did a nice job covering that up when it went pear-shaped, by the way. It wasn't hard to monitor the construction and determine the Askers were here."

"Then why now? How did you know we would be coming?"

"Your young man is not as good with technology as he would like to think." Bree bit back her practiced protest—*he's not my young man*—to learn how Judy had done it. "The reason the Meterpreter he uploaded last year into Norwood's system never found anything is that I corrupted it and have been using it to monitor his own comms. I've known every move you were planning to make from the very beginning. And I knew he was misrepresenting himself to you, as well."

"Why drag us into it? What do you want, Judy?" Bree asked tersely.

"You know what I want. I want to take down the Chinese. And I want you to do it with me."

Are you insane? Bree thought. But she kept her reaction to herself.

"What's the situation outside?" Bree prompted. "I know there were four guards. I'm assuming now they are Agency personnel, not yours. Anyone else? What's your team?"

"I have the entire perimeter surrounded. No one gets off this farm unless I let them through."

What about the Gregorys and Mr. Giffin? Bree wanted to scream at the idea of her peaceful, sweet neighbors lying dead.

"How many?" she asked coolly, instead.

"Enough." Judy smiled.

She needs to trust me, Bree acknowledged. *She won't let me in on her plan until she does.* Swallowing down the sick feeling in her stomach, she reached for Judy's hand.

"I used to daydream about you being my mother. That you would adopt me and we could be a real family," Bree said softly.

It was easy for her to say, because it was true.

Judy softened just a bit. "I know."

"I don't want Rodney to be hurt. Or any of the Thornton children."

"We don't need them," Judy agreed. "And for all his bluster about choices, Rodney ultimately is a practical man. He will stay quiet. I am sure of it. Our priority needs to be returning the Asker children to the Colonel. Then the machine starts churning."

"That's where Gul can come in. She seems to have been working at cross-purposes to the Agency," Bree said.

"I may have influenced that with a bit of well-placed misinformation," Judy acknowledged. "To nudge her in the right direction."

She doesn't know about Gul's nanny cam video, Bree realized. She scanned her memories of the Morse-coded message she'd picked up when she'd found the hidden camera in Eda's teddy bear, the only thing left behind when the Asker children had been snatched. The message had warned of a secret purpose to their Turkish operation. Gul hadn't named Judy, but she'd seemed to have known exactly what Judy was doing with the arms diversion.

She doesn't know that Gul had figured it out and warned me.

Bree nodded, pretending to absorb the information.

Trust no one, Judy had said.

I have a bad feeling. That's all I'm going to say. You need to be careful, Bree, Ruby had said.

Bree had one more question. "Will your men have taken out the guards by now?"

Judy nodded.

"Then we only really need to worry about Dash," she said, her face hardening.

"His father was MI6, you know. He is, too. He was a plant inside Norwood all along."

Bree stared in disbelief. *Damn him*, she thought.

"I'm not the only one who can play the long game," Judy shrugged. "Though I give them credit—that 'manny' business was a brilliant cover-up." She checked her Sig Sauers. "How well armed are you?"

"Well enough," Bree answered grimly. No need to give away more than that.

"Fair. My men will be waiting at their posts. We can take out Heyward and move from there. I'm not worried about Gul—are you?"

Bree gulped, and shook her head. She didn't trust her voice to answer any further than that. She grabbed her bag, patting the hidden compartment as if to reassure herself, before pulling out her semiautomatic. She threw the backpack over her shoulders and tightened the straps.

"Very well. Let's go." Judy strode to the doorway and just before opening it, paused. She looked over her shoulder at Bree, eyes twinkling. "This is almost fun, now, isn't it? Just as I always imagined it."

Bree smiled weakly and pulled back the slide on her gun with a satisfying *click*.

"After you," Judy indicated with a gesture. Her enthusiasm for conducting a mother-daughter operation apparently did not extend far enough to expose her back to Bree, Bree noted drily. She brushed by Judy, being careful not to touch her. She didn't want the warmth of any human connection, even inadvertently.

When they emerged from the barn, Dash, Rodney, and Gul were waiting for them.

"Where are the children?" Bree demanded.

"Relax, Bree. They are in the van, waiting, safe," Gul assured her. "We're all set to return them to their parents once we're all wrapped up."

"Parents? You mean Handan is safe, too?" Bree's heart leapt in her chest.

"Yes—she's been in hiding, but she's fine. She can't wait to be reunited with them all."

A shudder of relief rippled through Bree, but it was short-lived. Her nerves were all aflame. The amount of information—joyous news and tragic realizations alike—that she'd had to absorb in the last hour was overwhelming.

She had to keep her focus, she reminded herself. She couldn't slip now.

"Yes," she said, working to keep her face impassive, but squaring off to face Dash. "Time to wrap up. To *clean* up," she added, ominously.

Dash's chin jerked up, as if dodging a punch. "What's that supposed to mean?"

Bree ignored his question but did not break his gaze. "Rodney, this doesn't concern you any longer. I want you to go back to the house."

"That's not a good idea, Bree," Rodney stated. "You're probably feeling a little emotional right now. God knows I am. You may want to have—"

"What? A witness? Better for you not to see this." She couldn't bring herself to look at Rodney at that moment. She knew her face was burning with shame. "I love you, Rodney. And I'm really, really relieved that you didn't know about all of this," she said vaguely, waving her gun. "But this is not the place for you. It's time for you to go. See to the children." She added, gruffly, "Give Ollie a hug for me."

"Bree—"

"It's not a debate, Rodney. If you don't go willingly, we'll have to make you. Please don't make me hurt you."

She heard his sharp intake of breath. "I raised you better than this, Bree."

"This isn't about you. It isn't even about me. It's about something greater. Just go. Now."

Out of the corner of her eye, she saw him turn, defeated, to shuffle down the trail toward the house. It didn't take long for the night to swallow him up.

"You can't mean to do this, Bree," Dash said calmly. "Not after what we've been through together."

"It was all lies. I can see it now. Every little bread crumb you dropped for me—stringing me along, testing me, hoping that I would slip up and divulge something that would prove I was conniving with Judy all along. You thought you were so clever, toying with my emotions that way?"

"It wasn't like that."

"And that poor little rich boy act? How gullible of me to fall for it, when all along you were following in Daddy's footsteps, weren't you?" Bree spoke over him, building up a head of steam as she let her anger take sway. "I bet you knew not only that he had cheated my father out of Ullabreagh, but that he had done it as a plant at that game, on Judy's behest. Just whose side are the Heywards on, anyway? Or do I even need to ask? It will be your own side, of course. You're in this for nobody but yourself and your damn privilege."

He blanched and then colored a mottled red at that last remark, as if he'd been slapped in the face. "I beg your pardon," he said, retreating into formality. "You must know that is not true."

"Don't make me laugh. Bunting and fireworks are not your brand of patriotism, remember? Or did you already forget what you told Susmita? It must be hard to keep track of so many lies."

"I'm not a liar," he protested.

"You are. And I'm tired of it. I'm tired of being manipulated by you and everyone else at Norwood. Time for this to be over. The only question is . . ."

She paused, just for a second, and looked at Gul.

Gul returned her gaze. Quietly, with an almost imperceptible nod, Gul completed her statement for her. "The only question is, What are you prepared to do?"

She nodded back at Gul, then inclined her head toward Dash.

"He has a knife in his boot and two pistols—one holstered sidearm and one in his waistband. Strip him. I can't afford any funny business— not with my mother here. I'll cover you while you do it."

"I'm more than capable of defending myself, Bree," Judy clucked, amused.

"I know," Bree said gruffly. "But I'm not giving him the chance. Not when I've just found you."

Gul took out her own piece, a shiny Glock, armed it, and pointed it at Dash's head. "You heard her, pretty boy. You can hand it all over to me yourself, or you can suffer the indignity of a search. Not that I would mind the excuse to strip you down a bit," she smirked, letting her eyes rove over his tall, fit form.

"That won't be necessary," Dash responded stiffly. "I know when I've been bested."

Gul strode over and took a threatening stance in front of him, her eyes hard. He turned out all his weapons, handing them over to Gul like a child forced to part with his favorite toys. She tucked each one neatly into the pack at her hip.

"Thank you," Gul said solemnly. "You're sure that's it, Bree?"

"Positive. I armed him myself," she answered with a smug smile.

Gul acknowledged his sacrifices with a smart bow and walked backward, gun still trained on his head.

"Judy? Or should I be calling you 'Mom' now? It seems awkward, doesn't it?" Bree asked. She felt the bile rising as she thought about calling Judy anything remotely mother-like, but forced it down with a smile.

"I'm sure we'll figure out something that will be acceptable to the both of us."

"Time enough for that in the future, right?" Bree responded. "Reasonable. So, your men have taken out all the guards?"

"That is correct. I received confirmation five minutes ago via secure text channels."

"So, he . . ."—she couldn't even bring herself to acknowledge Dash with so much as a name, at this point—"he is all that stands between us and escape?"

"Indeed."

"May I have the honors, then? Consider it sort of a parting gift to the Agency, if you will?"

"Or the true start of our own partnership. Independent and, finally, united. You may proceed, Briana. Do with him what you wish."

Bree smiled. In the darkness, she knew it would be hard for Dash to see her face. That knowledge made it easier for her to do what she had to do. She clung to it as she walked purposefully over to him where he stood—helpless, defenseless.

She raised the pistol and pointed it at his head.

"This is for the pain you caused me with your lies," she muttered through gritted teeth. Before he could react, she swiftly lowered the gun, aiming for his kneecap, and pulled the trigger.

The shot rang out in the night and she watched, impassively, as Dash's beautiful, patrician face crumpled in agony and he collapsed into the cold Alabama mud.

He didn't give her the satisfaction of a scream.

She hardened her heart and strode over him.

"And this is for my mother," she said, defiantly, clearly—loud enough for Judy to hear it. She aimed for his heart and squeezed again, then stood over him, watching the life drain away, his unconsciousness instantaneous.

The night was quiet. Down the long driveway, she could hear the sounds of a lone car traversing the country highway.

"You should have aimed for his head," Judy helpfully critiqued. "You're always more certain of a kill that way."

Bree turned on her heel, tears streaming down her face.

Gul's voice rang out in the cold night air. "And you should have checked your ego at the door, madam."

Judy swung her guns around to confront Gul.

Bree didn't wait to see what would happen. She remembered what Judy had said to her the night Susmita had died: *"You have to be prepared to use your weapon, Bree . . . you could have died because you were too slow."* She remembered Susmita, David Hutton, and Margaret McCarthy.

Then she pumped the remaining four bullets in her chamber through Judy's head.

———

They'd swept the property, riding on Rodney's ATV to make time. Judy had either completely fabricated her numbered agents or they'd already fled. There was no sign of the four remaining that Gul *had* seen. That left Rodney, Gul, and Bree to take care of Dash's injuries . . . and the bodies.

"One of you can ride along in the ambulance," the paramedic offered.

Gul, Rodney, and Bree looked at one another.

Gul shrugged. "I barely know him."

Rodney held up his hands. "I can't really leave the orphanage unattended. After all the ruckus tonight, there will be a lot of restless children. If I'm lucky, we can keep the worst of it away from them. You moving the Askers out as soon as you can would be helpful," he added. "I'm not sure what I'm supposed to do about Judy." He gestured over to her body, draped in a blanket he'd stolen from the house. "Or the other bodies."

Gul knitted her eyebrows together, her face betraying no emotion as she kicked into cleanup mode, all efficiency. "Norwood will dispose of them. I already contacted headquarters. They've intercepted any comms and complaints from the neighboring vicinity and stand ready to smooth things over with law enforcement and the FBI, if it comes to that. The ambulance is clean—their plates, their medics, no trace. It will be as if nothing even happened here. No need for you to worry about any of it, Rodney.

"I've arranged it, but I do need to stay here to direct it. So that leaves you, Bree, to take Dash to the emergency room," Gul pointed out.

Riding the long route to the regional trauma center was the last thing Bree wanted to do.

"I don't think that's a good idea," Rodney said. "Since the medics are with your agency, can't *they* take care of it?"

Gul argued with him. "They'll need to disappear. He deserves to have someone familiar—someone who cares—there when he wakes up. And he won't understand the US health-care system. He may need a hand navigating it, don't you think? Bree is the natural choice—as a local, she can keep up the cover. Besides, she is the one who shot him."

"I shot him for a reason," Bree shot back. "Not vengeance. For believability. So I could take out . . ."

She crossed her arms. She couldn't say the name.

She wanted to scream. It was as if no one was acknowledging what had actually happened. She had only just learned the truth about her past, and then, with it having barely sunk in, she had snuffed out her own mother's life. An evil, divisive mother, perhaps, but her mother nonetheless, and someone with whom Bree had a long, complicated relationship. The sense of purpose and spirit of momentum were draining from her—she felt tired, and numb.

"He was there for you after Turkey, right?" Gul nudged her in the ribs when she said nothing. "Go on. You don't have to forgive him. Just help the guy out."

The focus was clearly on Dash and not on what had just transpired only moments ago.

Bree spoke through gritted teeth. "He was on *assigned* guard duty when he sat in my hospital room—he wasn't there out of the goodness of his heart. You do realize that, don't you?"

Rodney shot Gul a worried glance. Gul simply shrugged and turned away. "Your choice," she said, making it clear she was done with the discussion.

Rodney stood between them, unsure what to do.

"I'll call from the hospital with news," Bree muttered through clenched teeth, as she climbed into the back of the ambulance.

"Wait," Gul called at the last minute. She poked her head inside the ambulance. "You'll want some reading material. Hospital waiting rooms can be boring." She passed a file up to Bree. Bree looked down at it, confused.

"The papers Judy mentioned. What happened at the time of your parents' deaths. What she was planning now. The truth about Xinjiang. Should be scintillating," she said, rolling her eyes. "Do you want it?"

"Sure. Thanks," Bree said, accepting the papers and tucking them into her backpack.

They pulled away from the farm, driving down the long country lane. The sirens were off, but the strobing red light would give them clearance to break the speed limit as they cut through the night, headed toward the hospital.

It had all happened so fast. Now, reliving each second, her hands shook, the unchecked tremors of excess adrenaline and outright fear coming to the surface.

What are you prepared to do?

That question—the very question Gul had posed to her the first time they met—was her signal, her sign.

With that question, Bree had known Gul was on their side, and she had known in an instant what she must do. She needed an unambiguous demonstration of loyalty to get Judy to let down her guard, and only one thing would do: She needed to take out Dashiell.

Now, in the quiet of the ambulance, she could barely admit to herself that, for a fraction of a second before she'd pulled the trigger, she'd forgotten about his bulletproof vest. Or how lucky she'd been that Judy had not spotted its bulk.

She heard a cough and a sputter of mumbling. She peered at Dashiell, laid out on the litter they'd strapped into the ambulance. He was awake and trying to speak.

She lifted the oxygen mask from his face and waited.

"What is it, Dashiell?"

"Did you have to kneecap me?" Dash sputtered, rolling his eyes—a mixture of exasperation and pain, she wagered.

"I needed it to be realistic," she said tersely, beating back any feeling of guilt. "I aimed for more soft tissue than not. You should recover."

"It seemed unnecessarily punitive," he countered. A spasm of pain wracked his body, and he collapsed into a fit of coughing. "And sadistic."

He didn't question her fake kill shot. Would she have taken it even if he hadn't been wearing a vest? She pushed the gnawing sense of horror at what she might have been ready to do aside and focused, instead, on how angry she'd been—was—at all his manipulation.

"I was trying to sell it. She's got a keen nose for subterfuge, you know. If it seemed like I was drawing on real emotions, well . . ."

He frowned and ignored the jab. "Had. *Had* a keen nose. Am I right?" His face looked anxious as he waited for her answer.

"Yes, you're right. It worked. She's gone . . . for good." She felt strangely empty as she said it out loud. In the dark of the night, under the flashing red light, the entire episode felt surreal.

"You don't have to feel guilty, you know. She would have destroyed your life if you hadn't."

She looked at him keenly. "I know. Look at what she *did* destroy. Too much, for way too long of a time," Bree acknowledged. "I'll need some time to process what it all means."

A pang went through her. She felt the shadow of a cloud of concern pass over her face.

"What is it?" Dash managed to choke out.

"My name."

"What?"

"I'm not really Briana Parrish. But I don't feel like a Rowena, that's for sure. What am I supposed to do? What am I supposed to call myself now?"

Dash smiled and said, "It doesn't matter." He pulled the oxygen mask over his face and inhaled deeply.

She managed a grim chuckle. "That's what Judy used to say."

From underneath the mask, Dash mumbled, "You'll always be Mistress Bellona to me."

She smiled wistfully at him. "I appreciate the sentiment. Now, you need to rest. No more talking."

He closed his eyes in assent and fell back into a fitful sleep.

Once she was certain he wasn't going to wake up, she unzipped the bottom of her backpack and reviewed its contents.

Her face stared out at her from the new passport and other paperwork. She had birth records, graduation diplomas, driver's licenses—even a fake medical history, one that could plausibly account for the injuries she'd sustained on her operation, should any doctor care enough to notice.

She checked the bank accounts—all offshore. She whistled, impressed. How Ruby had managed such tidy sums, she didn't know.

She held the burner phone in her hands, feeling its heft. Bree tucked it, and the papers, back into the backpack. The other papers—Judy's files—she ignored.

She looked out the ambulance window. They were getting close to the point where the dirt road ended and they would turn onto a paved road, and the ambulance was beginning to slow for the blinking traffic light at the crossroads. She gathered her things, checked the security of the gurney, and stared at Dashiell in his tangle of tubes and wires. In the aftermath of this night, she would mourn him, too, and wonder if everything that had transpired between them had been faked—if it had all been a lie.

She was too exhausted to figure that out now. She squatted next to his ear and whispered, knowing her words were lost on him in his drug-induced haze.

"You may be a great agent, but you are a shitty friend. Kneecapping was better than you deserved."

As the ambulance took the turn, she tumbled out the back door and rolled into the ditch. She popped up to see the taillights disappearing into the night. Then she climbed out from the side of the road and started walking in the opposite direction.

⸻

The long walk in the brisk night air cleared her mind and helped her focus. She'd had plenty of time as she made her way to the next town, its Waffle House standing as a beacon in the night—it was the best place in the world to settle in for a cup of coffee and a long night of reading.

The restaurant was empty when she got there. She huddled in the corner booth, nursing the watery coffee to keep herself awake, staring at the file she'd laid on top of the sticky table as if it were toxic. Finally, when she couldn't ignore it any longer, she began.

The file was a hodgepodge. She pored through it all, trying to piece together Judy's psyche and map the truth of her past.

It began with a nearly twenty-year-old newspaper clipping from a London paper about a hysterical mother who'd left her toddler for "just a minute," she'd claimed, in a grocery trolley, stepping away to go to the ladies' room, only to return to find the infant had vanished. A stack of columns an inch thick documented the unfolding case, the infant and woman never being named, the child eventually being found in a children's home, listed as "Anonymous," after having been picked up a few blocks away on the street.

In a second clipping, the conclusion to the case claimed that the woman's husband had her declared unfit and somehow managed to have the case dismissed, after which he was granted full custody of the little girl.

In a note attached to the last article, Judy's neat handwriting had clarified, *David paid off the papers. You hadn't been taken, you'd climbed out of the trolley (always such a little daredevil!) and wandered off while I was doing a dead drop. David used it to take you away from me.*

The details in her divorce papers, the next thing Bree found in the file, were brutal. No alimony. No custody. No visitation rights. Threats of forced institutionalization if she so much as set foot near her daughter. An internal memo from MI5 censuring Hutton for misappropriation of government resources during the divorce proceedings. A copy of a wire transfer in a staggering amount—Bree wondered if she would find it had been directed to the account of a newspaper editor, or a judge.

For the first time, Bree felt something like sympathy. No, it was more than sympathy—it was regret, and a longing for something that would never be had.

Deeper in the file, Judy had included the plan she'd drawn up for what would have been Bree's parents' last mission—how they'd kill the target, how she planned to get them out. Bree found the details of the identities they were to assume in Australia, where David was to become a banker and Meg a schoolteacher. There was even a photo of the house they were to live in. Bree trailed her fingers across the faded picture, imagining what her life might have been like, had it all gone according to plan.

Maybe it wasn't a ruse. Bree felt a flare of rage at the Agency, but checked herself. Even from beyond the grave, Judy could be manipulating her. But if she wasn't . . .

My God, Bree thought. It was like the air had been sucked out of the room. *What have I done?*

Frantically she dug deeper into the file. She found the documentation for what was to be their own—Bree and Judy's—next mission. Judy had carefully collated page after page of satellite images of concentration camps in China, testimonials of Uyghurs who'd escaped torture and digital surveillance, and smuggled intelligence showing what more the Chinese had planned.

Genocide? she'd scrawled across the last page, leaving the question lingering in Bree's mind like an accusation.

The arms-smuggling route. The code name for the leader of the insurgency who sat on the other end of the route, waiting for the life-saving weapons flow to resume. Profiles of senior Chinese military officials, party officials, dissidents—too many for Bree to absorb. But nothing at all about the Agency and what role, if any, it did or should play in this planned attempt to make things right.

In the years and years of documentation and careful planning, Bree found a testimony to the single-mindedness—even obsession—that apparently had gripped Judy. Had it been a distraction? An attempt to build meaning after everything that had been taken from her? Now Bree would never know.

She wiped a frustrated tear and kept reading, losing track of time until she reached the very back of the file. There she found a letter addressed to herself. It consisted of one line.

It was something Judy had told her one other time, the night they sat at the foot of the Poppins statue, when Judy had explained the Agency to Bree—the night Bree had been implanted with the tracker that had changed her into a spy.

"Everything I did, Bree, I did for you."

Money, ideology, coercion, ego. The entire sordid entanglement of the three people who'd been her parents before her life literally went up in flames was a Gordian knot of every motivation she'd been taught to entrap a spy. And yet it seemed that they had entrapped themselves.

⁓

In the morning, bleary eyed, Bree took out her burner phone. The restaurant regulars were streaming in, and the sounds of the sizzling grill brought some warmth to her spirit.

She stuffed the file back into her bag, shoved some cash under her plate, and stepped outside, staking out a place behind the dumpsters. There, she finally succumbed to the shock, letting waves of grief flow through her exhausted body. One of the servers came out on a break, leaning against the brick wall and eying her warily as the last spasms wracked Bree's body.

Bree dragged her sleeve across her snotty face, self-conscious.

"Smoke?" the server offered sympathetically, sticking out her pack to offer a cigarette to Bree.

"No thanks," Bree said, gulping in the fresh air.

The server shrugged, finished her own cigarette in silence, and then went inside.

When Bree was sure the woman had gone for good, she pushed the button for the only number in her burner phone and waited, the odd tone of the ring giving her confidence the international connection was going through.

"Hallo," Ruby answered, breathless. "You okay, then?"

"I'm alive. The Askers are fine. We got them out with minimal collateral damage." She paused, the clinical term helping her paper over the feelings of shame and regret coursing through her. "Rodney and the Thornton kids are all safe. Gul was there, on the right side, so to speak. She's got mop-up and comms back to the Agency.

"Dash is in the hospital. Long story," she said, waving off the opportunity for explanation before Ruby could dive in. "And Judy . . ." Her voice wavered. "Judy's dead, Ruby. I can't . . ." She stopped at the sharp intake of Ruby's breath, not trusting herself to continue.

"Bree," Ruby breathed into the phone. "I'm sorry. What happened?"

"I can't explain right now. But I may have made a mistake. A big one. Listen, I'm going dark for a bit—thanks for all you did to make that possible, by the way. You should know that Norwood was in on this the whole time—they probably are just sitting on their hands, counting the minutes before they can storm Jaguar House and haul you in for questioning. If that happens, throw as much suspicion on Dashiell as you want—he's not one of us. He was undercover MI6."

The sound of Ruby angrily sucking her teeth was enough for Bree to know she'd hit her mark.

"You were right, Ruby, not to trust him—you were right about so many things. I can't talk much now, but when they take you in, I know they'll work to make you distrust me. Tell you horrible things about me. So I need you to know now, I did not shoot Susmita." She heard Ruby gasp into the phone at the mention of their murdered roommate, but Bree didn't pause. She was rushing to get the words out now, laying the groundwork for what was to come. "I wanted to tell you then, but I couldn't. Judy did it, to protect me. But Judy was a rogue agent, and I couldn't tell you until I could figure out what was going on. I know you always blamed me for Susmita's death, and maybe I am responsible, given Judy's motivations. But I never would have hurt her. I hope you can believe me one day."

She waited. She so desperately wanted Ruby's forgiveness. All she heard was her roommate's steady breathing, coming across the line from thousands of miles away.

Crestfallen, she continued. "Judy. She was behind so many things, Ruby. And you know why? Because she was my *real* mother and had been abandoned by the Agency. All this time, all these years, she was right there and never told me. Norwood and Dashiell—they knew. They were all playing me to trap her. And now . . . now she's dead."

The most important words got stuck in Bree's throat: *I'm the one who killed her. How truly I am my mother's daughter.*

If it was her fault Judy was dead, there was only one thing left to do. She squared her shoulders and delivered the most critical part of her message to Ruby.

"I need some time to clear my head and work out everything that has happened. You tell them I'll come back in when I'm ready. It may be a month, it may be a year, but I *will* come back. And then I will have one condition. Once I'm cleared for operations, I want to control my next placement. I have something very specific in mind. Something that will finish this business that has been dogging me my whole life—once and for all. The Agency owes me—owes *us*—that."

"That's it?" Ruby asked skeptically.

"No, I guess there is one more thing. If they let me do it, I want you to be my handler. I need someone I can trust, and I need the best, and that means you."

"Pffft, it's nothing," Ruby stammered, but Bree could tell she was pleased.

"You've got that, Ruby? Tell them that you can't reach me. I'm going to get rid of the burner, anyway. I'll find you when I'm ready. Okay?"

"Understood, Bree. Be careful. I need you back in one piece. Who else will be able keep the Lord Marquess in line?"

Bree smiled grimly. She was pretty sure Dashiell would never talk to her again, once he was out of surgery and the drugs had worn off. *She* certainly had no intention of speaking to *him*. Besides, he'd not be back to Norwood. He'd return to MI6, she assumed—if he managed to recover. A bad limp could render him a mediocre field asset. He might be stuck behind a desk for the rest of his career, a despised Bookworm.

"We'll talk soon." She ended the call and tossed the phone into a dumpster.

The sun was coming up, its rays lighting up the frosty weeds in the ditch next to the parking lot.

She knew she should be grateful—grateful for the sacrifices Meg McCarthy and David Hutton had made to keep her alive. Grateful that Brian had embraced her so readily as his own, giving her the tiniest of glimpses into what her brief time as part of that family had been like. Grateful that, in the end, she had found her sister and, together, they had begun to make it right.

She papered over the mother-shaped hole in her heart, packing away her regret, her guilt, and her longing. She would take her feelings out and consider them, later, when the wounds were not so fresh. She shook her head, painfully aware that, in this strategic retreat, she was walking Judy's path yet again.

Squaring her shoulders, she started walking down the road.

Last night had finally ended her parents' stories.

Her next move might be in their memory, but the fight would be all hers.

Chapter Fourteen

ROBERTA

Early 1990s, London

Rennie's whine was a freight train whistling through Roberta's head.

"Hush, Rowena," she chided, peering into the rearview mirror for a glimpse of her toddler strapped into the car seat. "Mummy has just one little errand, darling. One job to do and then I will be all yours. I promise."

Rennie's response was to kick her little heels even harder into the seat, raising the volume another decibel. The car seat strained a little, shaking loose with each kick. It was a good thing the grocery store was so close. Otherwise, Roberta would have to pull over to fix the straps more tightly.

She half smiled, despite her headache. Her daughter might be small, but she was *strong*. At least they had that in common.

Her desperate attempts to form a bond with her daughter had not amounted to much. When she had carried Rennie, she only felt revulsion at her swollen body, not the nirvana-like glow all the other pregnant women gushed about. When the nurse had placed her in her arms after twenty-seven hours of pushing, she'd felt like she was holding a mewling cat, arch and threatening to scratch. She'd waited for instincts to kick in, for motherhood to feel as intuitive as it felt to her to shoot a circle in the center of the target at the shooting range.

They never came.

Her daughter was a mystery, an enigma, an alien plopped in her arms. But despite all that, Roberta wanted her. She wanted Rennie to love her back. But she was David's through and through. Roberta had never gotten over the way Rennie, at birth, had wailed and wailed, unending protests at the top of her lungs, until David had taken her in his arms. For Rennie, no one could hold a candle to David. Anyone who tried— or tried to exert any parental authority—learned the hard way. And so another nanny had packed up in a huff, leaving Roberta in the lurch this morning, forcing her to take the child out on a small bit of spy business while David was out of town. Thank God it was a simple thing—no risk of danger. Nothing that the child couldn't see.

She pulled into the grocery lot and put the car into park. With a sigh, she blew a loose strand of hair off her forehead and adjusted her pearls. Another glance at the mirror told her she looked the part—a pulled-together if slightly harried young mother of the upper class, dashing out to pick up a few supplies for the evening dinner, child in tow.

It was the perfect excuse to be here. The perfect cover for the brush drop she needed to make.

"Darling, here we are!" she exclaimed brightly. "Be good for Mummy and we'll get a sweet after our shop."

"Want it now!" Rennie shrieked, kicking forgotten.

"After, Rowena. After. If you're good. Mummy needs you to be very, very good when we go into the store." She checked her watch. She was a little late, but she didn't think it would matter that much. She turned off the ignition and stepped out of the car. Quickly, she swung open the rear door and stooped down to extract Rennie.

"Myself!" Rennie insisted, pushing away Roberta's hands. "Not Mummy! Rennie do by self!"

"I know, I know," Roberta muttered, tamping down her impatience. *You will be happy of her independent spirit when she is grown,* she reminded herself. "Mummy will just unbuckle you, and then you can climb down. Will that be all right?"

Rennie slumped back in the car seat, acquiescing. Roberta undid the snaps, being careful with her nails, and stepped back from the car, tapping her well-turned heel, and watched as her daughter slid down from the seat, landing like a cat on the floor of the car and then sticking first her ruffly, bloomered bottom, then one leg and two out, scrambling onto the asphalt.

"Rennie did it," the toddler declared proudly.

"Yes, you did," Roberta concurred, clapping her hands. "Well done, you. Now, we're a bit tardy, sweetheart, so Mummy needs you to hurry along." She snatched Rennie's hand before she could protest and began dragging her through the lot. She didn't have time to do a normal zig-zag and perimeter check to confirm she hadn't been tailed—nor did she dare, given Rennie's mood. She made a beeline for the lineup of shopping trolleys right outside the door and plopped Rennie in hastily, ignoring the straps. She pushed the cart swiftly through the electric sliding doors, feeling the rush of cold, stale air as she maneuvered inside.

"No crying, Rowena," she insisted, a false smile plastered across her face, as Rennie began screwing up her face to howl. "Here," she said, grabbing a bag of sugary biscuits off the display as she breezed past the specials just inside the doors. She shoved it into Rennie's hands. "Have a snack while Mummy shops."

She had memorized the aisle, as well as the description of the agent she was to meet, but she couldn't go directly, in case she was being surveilled. Her contact had promised to take out the CCTV, but she couldn't afford any slipups. She'd walked the shop ahead of time, identifying the best routes to avoid being caught on the grocery store's cameras, so she meandered this way and that, pretending to check her list, acutely aware of the envelope burning a hole inside the tote bag that she clutched to her side, wary.

She had to time it perfectly, and she had to get back to the house before David, who was growing colder, combative, and more suspicious of her by the day—asking more pointed questions about her business trips, her work hours—all with one end in mind: getting her to stop. The marital counseling she'd badgered him into attending had only made things worse. The therapist's methods were colored by his advanced age and personal views, she suspected. Rather than encourage David to reflect on his actions and feelings, he offered him a stage about which to preen and complain—how Roberta had had her fun, but a woman's place was in the home. How it was her fault the nannies kept quitting because she, herself, couldn't guide them in how to relate to Rennie. How it wasn't normal how Rennie reacted to her; if she were simply more *present*, more *available* to her daughter, surely, things would get better. How a man needed to stretch his legs, spend time with his friends—he wasn't going to report on his every move as if she were his mother. How, in fact, he needed her home. To pack away her aspirations, like tidy boxes in an attic, and make babies.

"What about my career, my intellect?" she'd questioned him. "You used to find that exciting. You said you loved how we could debate into the wee hours of the night, that you adored how challenging my mind was. My ambition. Did you forget, David?"

He'd shrugged. "It's one thing when one is on the chase, my dear. There was a novelty to it then, to be sure. And I admit, our sparring was fun. But our courtship is over. Surely you didn't think you could continue on that way after we'd married and had a child? Gallivanting all over the world without a care? I've humored you long enough, and frankly, it's getting old. You need to start behaving like my wife. As someone in our class should behave. You don't need to work. It's embarrassing to me. Besides, you know as well as I do that it won't go anywhere. There's only so much a woman can do in your line of work. Even though, I grant you, you're a ballbuster."

The therapist had simply blinked behind the thick lenses of his glasses as if everything David had said was perfectly reasonable.

Roberta had bit back her retort, swallowing her anger. *Sexist pigs*, she'd thought to herself.

She didn't want to quit. It wasn't fair of him to demand it. Besides, she *couldn't*. She was stuck in the spy game for life. The only saving grace, Roberta knew, was that because she'd been put into deep cover—posing as a corporate flunky, traveling the world for deals which she could not discuss for reasons of confidentiality—she was far from the world of nannying, with nothing to link her to Norwood.

And with nothing to tie her to Norwood, she could be cut loose in an instant.

She had to be very, very careful. For herself, and for Rennie.

She shook away the thought, bringing her focus back to the mission at hand, and swerved her cart, loose wheel rattling, into the cereal aisle, preparing herself to make the drop.

She stopped still. Nobody was there.

She pushed ahead, slowly, stopping now and again to take a box from the shelf, staring blindly at the back panels full of games, the side panels of ingredients, as if the cereal was more engrossing than the Sunday *Times*.

Now what?

She forced herself to think beyond the *thump, thump, thump* of her heart in her ears.

A man came by with a pallet full of sugary children's cereals. Rennie, face smeared with chocolate, leaned over the side of the cart, arms outstretched, reaching for the cartoon characters on the boxes. Faster than Roberta could react, the man jumped, grabbing Rennie before she could fall and righting her in her seat.

"You'll want to buckle her in, ma'am. She could take quite a tumble, you know."

"I know how to care for my own child!" Roberta snapped, fighting off the criticism and her rising sense of panic.

He raised his hands in gentle protest. "Of course, ma'am. Just trying to help. No harm done now, is there, little girl?" He awkwardly patted Rennie on the head. When Roberta didn't answer he cleared his throat. "Can I help you find something, ma'am?"

"No. I'm quite fine, thank you."

"Very well. I'll just be needing to get into those shelves to restock them." He hesitated, waiting for her to move. "Now's my normal time. Not much footfall this time of day, you see."

"Yes. I'm very sorry. Let me get out of your way."

She shoved Rennie down in her seat and pushed the cart very fast, down the aisle and around the corner, to wait. She cursed her stupidity. Snapping at the stockboy could only draw notice and embed her in his memory, if anyone came around asking questions later. And now he was in the aisle, leisurely squaring off and tidying the boxes as he filled the holes in the shelves, blocking her access.

She took Rennie around the perimeter, clenching her jaw in annoyance with the listing cart, peeking up the aisles to see if her contact had wandered to the wrong spot. He was still nowhere to be found.

She parked her cart in the feminine care aisle, knowing it was not a place where men, in particular, were likely to linger, and gathered her thoughts.

Clearly, something had gone wrong. She had to move to her backup plan of a dead drop and alert her handler to extract the information as soon as possible. Rennie was beginning to whine again, banging her heels against the wire cart. She couldn't risk another scene in the aisle. And she had to make it fast. She glanced at her watch—she was running out of time.

"Here, Rowena." She thrust a sweet she'd picked off an end cap into Rennie's hands. "Stay in the cart. Mummy will be right back."

She moved back through the store, being careful to take an indirect route, until she was back in the cereal aisle, now empty. She knew what she wanted—the shelf with bran flakes, the boxes covered with a slight layer of dust. She pulled one from the back and sliced open the bottom seal with her knife. Quickly, she slid the envelope inside, securing it between the bag and the box, and refolded the bottom. Then she replaced it on the shelf at the very back.

They would have days, if not weeks, to extract it.

She turned her coat inside out and placed the hat she'd carried in her tote onto her head, before strolling out of the aisle. She walked as directly as she could back to the feminine hygiene aisle, checking her watch. Six and a half minutes total. She breathed a sigh, grateful she'd be able to make it home before David got home from the airport, relieved that she'd managed to navigate the drop without more of a dust-up from Rennie.

She turned into the aisle and stopped short.

Her cart sat, abandoned, the smattering of random would-be purchases still at the bottom. The only sign of Rennie was the crumpled-up, empty biscuit bag that sat, forlorn under the fluorescent lights, on the linoleum floor. The unused safety strap dangled through the wire, mocking her.

Her breath caught. Instinctively, she looked up, certain she would see her naughty little girl climbing the shelves, seeking adventure, as she was wont to do.

Nothing.

She walked quickly to the next aisle, and the next, and the next.

Then she began to run.

She twisted her ankle but kept running, throwing herself against the end caps and into each aisle, searching the carts for her daughter, barreling through the dirty restroom and the loading dock, touching the displays, knocking them down in her haste, her eyes nearly blind with fear and fury.

Rennie was nowhere to be found.

Had she wandered outside? That had to be it—she'd returned to the car. She was always so brave, so beyond her years, really—she knew no limits. Roberta convinced herself of this truth. Drawing a breath, she forced herself outside on shaking legs, imagining how tightly she'd squeeze her daughter in her arms, how she'd chide her for her disobedience but also praise her for finding the car amongst all the others in the lot. Her fingers fumbled, drawing the keys out of her tote, preparing herself to whisk the child away to safety.

She dropped the keys, blinking away tears as she swept down to retrieve them, before hurrying toward her automobile. It was now sitting alone in an empty part of the lot.

She walked around the entire car. Rennie was not there.

She threw herself against the glass windows, peering in, willing herself to find the child in the back seat, somehow.

It was empty.

She got down on hands and knees and looked under the car, in case the girl was playing hide-and-seek.

Nothing.

No, that was not quite true. A slip of paper had been tucked under the front tire. She pulled it out and pored over it, flipping it over, hands shaking.

It was a typed note on a piece of David's stationery. Just two words.

I know.

The *n* was off kilter, misaligned in a way she had seen countless times as she'd done up her formal reports to Norwood on the typewriter she'd hidden away—along with her other equipment, in a place she thought David would never, ever look—just for that purpose.

In a flash she knew: his business trip had been a ruse. His relentless badgering about her job was not merely to get her to quit—it was because he'd caught her out as a spy. He'd assumed, of course, that she was there to spy on *him*, to plumb the depths of MI5 . . . that their marriage was all pretense. And now he'd tailed her, seen with his own eyes her attempts at juggling her worlds, and would punish her for daring to challenge him— for daring to spy on him in his own home.

He had changed the rules of the game.

If she fought back, if she tried to use the note as evidence that he, himself, had snatched Rennie away from her, he would somehow fortuitously "find" her typewriter and say she'd done it herself, all along, the errant *n* the smoking gun to prove her guilt.

"My baby!" she cried out, collapsing back onto the dirty asphalt. Her voice broke. "Somebody help me!" But she knew no one could help her now.

She crumpled the note in her hand. David had her trapped.

Rennie was gone. And she knew without a doubt that, no matter what she did, she would never get her back.

AUTHOR'S NOTE

In setting much of *The Handler* in the period toward the end of the Troubles, I tried as much as possible to hew to historic timelines.

The dates of the pub bombing, modeled after the McGurk's Bar bombing, the collapse of the IRA cease-fire in 1996, the negotiation of the Good Friday Agreement in 1998, and President Clinton's historic overt endorsement of the "Three No's" policy during his trip to Shanghai in 1998 as depicted in this novel are consistent with the actual historical record. I also made sure that Rennie's beloved Coco Pops were, indeed, available in Ireland at the time depicted for her "breakfast for dinner."

Ullabreagh is modeled after Drenagh in Limavady, County Londonderry, located on a thousand acres of fields, woodlands, and gardens; it is indeed operated as a special-events venue and would have been so during the period depicted in this novel, though to my knowledge, it was never lost in a card game.

The one significant alteration I have made to the timing of events is the raiding of the Special Branch office in Castlereagh, which I have pulled forward from its actual occurrence in March of 2002 to 1998 in order to accommodate Agent Margaret McCarthy's spectacular release of her husband. The attribution of the release of agent records as one of the proximate causes of the Good Friday Agreement being signed is my own invention.

KEEP READING FOR A SNEAK PEEK OF

THE NORWOOD NANNY CHRONICLES BOOK THREE

With a low creaking noise, the chapel door swung open.

Bree didn't react. Not even the barest twitch of her shoulders or flutter of an eyelash to betray how fast her heart was beating.

There were no echoes of footsteps on the stone floor, but still, she knew they were coming.

She felt someone settle in the pew behind her. Soft breathing.

More waiting.

"You're going to rise and come with me," a female voice told her.

Bree's lips twisted into a bitter smile, recognizing the lilt and cadence straightaway. "Hello, Anya."

There was a pause. She felt Anya's massive hand squeeze her shoulder. Bree bowed her head at this simple gesture. Who could have predicted that it would be this particular Norwood classmate who would be assigned to bring her in? Bree had wanted it to be her former roommate, Ruby, but Ruby had disabused her of this hope, telling her in no uncertain terms that while she had managed to avoid punishment for her role in Bree's escape, she was still on thin ice, relegated to the most bookwormy of administrative work conceivable as her post-graduation penance.

Did Anya view herself as captor and victor now, Bree wondered. What had she been told about Bree and her years underground? What did any of them know, really?

Anya continued. "It's quiet here. Nobody really about. But since this is a public place, we will have to avoid making a scene. You came willingly . . . or so I've been told."

The sequence of events leading to this meeting flashed through Bree's mind. Her time on the run after closing the Asker mission—time she'd needed to sort through the confusion of the betrayal she'd been dealt by the Agency and one of her closest friends, and time to work through her complicated feelings of guilt and loss. She'd taken the life of the woman she now knew was her birth mother, after all. And then there was the news she'd gotten of her uncle, Brian's, illness . . . the cirrhosis turning into a cancer that was swiftly eating him alive. The favors Brian had called in to smuggle her back into Northern Ireland on a fishing boat so she could see him one last time.

It was he who had convinced her it was time to stop hiding.

"The past will be with you no matter where you go, *macushla*. I've learned the hard way, there is no bottle deep enough to drown the memories, and no land far enough away to escape them. Better you confront your demons than end up like me," he'd whispered, patting her hand. "Alone and in pain."

"You're not alone," she'd protested. "You have me."

"Aye, and for that I am grateful. I'd lost you for too long." He'd winced, gripping her hand as a wave of pain took him. "Go to them, Briana. You can't change what's already done. And you are too like your mother to sit idly, stewing in resentment. You need to fulfil your purpose. Go back and put this all behind you," he'd insisted before he lapsed back into a fitful, drug-induced sleep.

Those were the last words he'd spoken before his death.

No, "willingly" was not the way she would describe her decision to come in from the cold, Bree mused. But she was tired. And she had nowhere else to go. So she'd called in and arranged this rendezvous, the pickup point a country chapel one village over from Brian's cottage—the place her parents had married.

Anya interrupted her thoughts. "When you stand up, I will cuff you. Discreetly, of course. I'll pat you down and remove any weapons."

"I didn't bring anything with me. I told them when I called in. I came unarmed. I've got nothing, not even a nail clipper."

"Nonetheless. I'll pat you down. And then we'll then walk outside. The others will join us there."

Bree's heart started racing again. "Where will you be taking me?"

"Why, home, of course. Home, to Norwood."

——

She'd been surrounded by a phalanx of agents and hustled into a black SUV. Other black vehicles fell in, surrounding her as they'd pulled out of the tiny churchyard. The last time she'd driven these roads she'd been with Dashiell—her other former Norwood College roommate—an undercover MI6 agent posing as a Norwood trainee. The one who'd betrayed her. They'd been going to meet her uncle Brian for the first time, hoping to disentangle the truth about her parents and her past.

She thrust the memory aside, just as she pushed away the image of Dashiell collapsing in agony when she'd put a bullet in his knee.

She mustn't think of him, or anything, now. She quieted her mind, steeling herself for the interrogation Ruby had warned her was to come.

All that mattered now, she reminded herself, was that she get her wish. Her demand was to assign herself to a case in China so she could complete the work of her parents, honoring their sacrifices by disrupting what looked like severe human-rights abuses. Maybe then she would be able to untangle the truth—whatever remained of it. She needed to swallow her anger at the way her agency, Norwood, had manipulated her. Anything to achieve her goal.

But first she would need to convince them all that she was not a threat.

She noticed the black cars falling away, their precise pattern indicating that her own vehicle was approaching the designated drop point. Her heart gave a twang of recognition as the spire of the Memorial Chapel on Norwood's campus green rose ahead of her.

"Almost there," Anya said from the third-row seat. "We'll be going through the underground access point. Privacy, you know."

Bree nodded. There could be no witnesses, she knew, just in case anything went wrong.

They let her sit alone in one of the small interrogation rooms under the gymnasium for an ungodly amount of time. She smiled grimly. Her *Jeopardy!* class had taught her all the tricks of interrogation, so she was ready for it.

When the door opened, she was startled to see Dean Albourn. Bree didn't think she involved herself directly in operations these days, and certainly she wouldn't direct a messy interrogation herself. The thought both calmed Bree and put her on edge. Why would Albourn care about her?

Albourn's nose wrinkled slightly at the cruddy finish of the interrogation table. She pulled out the single chair opposite Bree and sat. The chair wobbled, one leg short.

"Honestly," she snapped at the camera in the corner behind Bree. "We are not Interpol nor the FSB. Get me a decent chair." She looked at Bree, who felt somewhat withered in her own chair. "And get her a glass of water."

The dean wiped her hand across the offending surface as if she could whisk away the years of accumulated gunk and began drumming her fingertips, perfectly manicured as ever, on the tabletop. She looked exactly the same to Bree. Perfectly coiffed, in a smart tweed suit, her neck strung with pearls so large you could play marbles with them.

There was a look to the women of Norwood who made it all the way to the top. Effortless, expensive, and just a little bit bland—designed to convey authority but not make you look too closely at what lay underneath the surface. Judy had had it too, Bree thought to herself.

Albourn stopped the thrumming of her fingers and looked Bree up and down.

"No worse for wear, it would seem," she began unceremoniously. "You led us a merry chase. It's a credit to you. Which means it is a credit to us," she smirked.

Bree let the ghost of a smile cross her face. Albourn was mean with her compliments; eking out any, even if she used it to congratulate herself on the Norwood training that enabled Bree to stay on the run for so long, was a minor victory.

An austere young woman slipped in the door bearing a new cushioned chair for Albourn. The dean stood, allowing the underling to adroitly make the swap. The young woman left, then came back in with a pitcher and a full glass of water for Bree, silently disappearing after she had set it down.

Bree greedily drank down the first glass while Albourn resettled herself. No ice, she noticed. Ice was something to which she'd reaccustomed herself while she was away. She poured another glass and kept drinking.

"Why did you do it?" Albourn demanded.

Bree choked on her water, spraying it everywhere. She dragged her sleeve across her mouth, wiping up the dripping mess before answering. "You can't be serious."

"Dead serious. You had no reason to go underground."

"I had every reason to go underground!" Bree exclaimed. "My entire life has been a lie. And you—Norwood—all of you have been in on it from . . . from . . ." She gave up in an exasperated sigh. "I don't even know how long you've known about it."

"It?" Albourn questioned, eyebrow in a high arch. "You must be more precise, Parrish. What is this 'it' of which you speak?"

"Please. Don't. You of all people know what I'm talking about." Bree's voice rose in anger. She laughed. "You probably orchestrated the entire thing. You and your cronies in British intelligence. Or were they telling you what to do? Is that it? Trying to get revenge for one of their fallen?"

"You're forgetting yourself, Parrish. As long as you are a part of the Norwood community, you must respect the rules and the chain of command. Which means you must respect me." She let the reprimand hang in the air.

Albourn sniffed and continued. "As for the idea that this was all some sort of reprisal for your father, the late Agent Hutton—you know that I don't take orders from MI6. We may collaborate, but we are not handmaidens. Norwood stands alone."

Bree clamped her mouth shut. She was at risk of losing it, even angering Albourn, which was a rookie mistake. She needed to calm down. Once she got going, she didn't know if she would be able to stop. She didn't want to give Albourn the satisfaction of sharing her scarred heart, nor her confusion.

Albourn sighed. "I can see I'm going to have to lead the horse to water, as it were. Very well, then. Let me fill in some of the blanks for you, as I presume that is why you are here."

Bree nodded.

"What do you want to know?"

Bree didn't hesitate. "At what point did you know who I was?"

Albourn sat back in her chair, thoughtful. "That's an interesting question. You first came to our notice when Bea was running the trials for the neuro-blocker." Bree nodded at the mention of Beatrice, the wife of the man running the orphanage at which she'd been raised—and, she'd discovered, a vaunted neuroscientist secretly working for Norwood. "We needed to have a full medical rundown and background check on any of the human subjects. Bea was entirely dismissive of it—you were an orphan, after all—but we thought better to be certain. We kept close tabs on you from that time on, watching unintended consequences."

"On that—why is it that I don't have any side effects? Why am I not incapacitated the way Alice Clark was?" Bree pointed out the after-effects she'd seen in the nanny a class ahead of her—a nanny whom they'd all been told had died in the line of duty but whom had apparently wanted out of the Norwood Agency and its undercover spy ring and suffered having her memory wiped by the neuro-blocking drug as a result.

Albourn looked surprised. "You know about Clark?"

"I saw her huddled in a doorway on a side street in Bath. It was near the end of first year. I recognized her from the photos—she was singing the alma mater. That's when I figured it out."

Albourn nodded. "Sharp of you to do so. For some reason, she seemed drawn to return to Bath, despite our best efforts. She became a wanderer of sorts. Ended up needing long-term care. Unfortunate, really. We took care of it, of course—it wouldn't do for the family to be poking around, asking questions. But, to your question, we don't rightly know why you experienced virtually no side effects. We suspect it has something to do with the age at which it was administered to you."

Bree shuddered. She was lucky, in one sense. How strange to consider her predicament a stroke of good fortune.

"We were watching you, but even then we didn't realize the truth of who you might be," Albourn continued. "Then a sequence of things conspired to make us reconsider your identity. We regularly rotated agents into Florence to keep tabs on you. The schools were an easy place to obtain regular access to you and your medical records. The woman we placed in your high school alerted us when she received an unusual visitor with a very strange request—a request to complete an application to Norwood College on your behalf."

"Judy," Bree whispered, stunned. "She went to the guidance counselor."

"Yes, it was your Judy, or as we knew her, Agent Jude. As you've surmised, the guidance counselor was one of ours. Suddenly, out of nowhere, our nameless orphan had British citizenship and, as we saw from the school video surveillance footage, a concrete link to a woman we'd been hunting for years. Around the same time, we coincidentally managed to capture the men who'd assisted Agent Jude at the scene of your parents' deaths. They told us a very disturbing tale—they knew where one of the children had ended up—in Turkey—but as for the other, it was a mystery . . . just a smattering of clues that pointed in one direction. It was a tantalizing discovery that you might, indeed, be the other surviving child. If the men we'd detained were telling the truth, you would be Agent Jude's daughter. But we couldn't be sure. And then there was the issue that, if you were in fact her daughter, you might be implicated. That became more of a concern once we'd admitted you to Norwood and our agent— your counselor—was murdered.

So, you see, we found the possibilities were endless—the most concrete of which was the reality that you might actually lead us to her, unwittingly or not."

Bree thought through all that Albourn had shared. "If it was justice you were seeking, I don't understand why you didn't just capture her. She was here, visiting me—Dashiell met her. Surely, he alerted you to that fact. You could have sprung a trap and been done with it—why bother to drag it all out the way you did? Why involve me?"

"It wasn't mere revenge we sought. We needed to take down her network. She'd managed to do quite some damage in fifteen years of going rogue. Her contacts in Asia had proven particularly troublesome. We needed to smoke her out and take the whole damn thing down with her. As for you . . . we needed to be sure of who you were, and whether you could be trusted."

"And Gul?" Bree pointedly asked about the agent whom she'd come to learn was her half-sister, from whom she'd been separated at the time of their parents' deaths.

Albourn smiled. "Agent Avci fell into our hands quite easily. Another one of Bea's subjects, you see. Seems she did have side effects from the neuro-blocker—horrible nightmares. Her nightmares were memories, locked up tight as a drum until the drum started leaking. Her psych assessments underscored what we'd known all along—that she was, indeed, one of the long-lost Hutton sisters. She just didn't know it. With both of you in hand, we took a series of gambles. The first was placing you with her on the Asker mission—an attempt to jar both of your memories and see what would fall out. The other was the gamble that, with the supposed kidnapping of the Asker children and the subsequent danger and suspicion you'd fallen into, we had enough to lure Agent Jude into the sunlight. And we were right."

"It was you all along. And MI6? Where did they come in?" Bree prompted.

Albourn waved her hand dismissively. "Oh, they wanted theirs. Petty little bureaucrats. It felt good to make them grovel and place one of their agents into our system for a change. It proved useful for us to have a tight link for this op, since we had no idea where it would lead. Luckily, Agent Heyward was game. You must admit, it was useful PR to finally admit a male student. We planted the 'manny' nickname ourselves. The front office were quite proud of it—it got the government off our backs for a bit. Though now I suppose we'll be stuck with men here for the duration. They're a mostly useless lot. Not much of a market for male nannies, it turns out."

Bree blew out a long breath. "Everything you're telling me is consistent with Dashiell's account."

"You sound surprised."

"Given my entire life was founded on lies—including this operation—I would be naïve to be anything but skeptical."

"We have no reason to lie to you anymore, Parrish. We're your family now." There was an awkward pause. "You do have our condolences about your uncle. Pity that. I'm glad you got to see him before he passed."

Bree didn't acknowledge the comment, so Albourn pressed on. "Well, then. We do need to know why you went dark. Your hasty departure caused us no end of trouble with MI6. They took it as a sign you were in league with her, you see."

"I'm sure Agent Heyward raised quite a stink."

"No, actually. He defended you to the last. He was quite smitten with you, wasn't he? He denied it in his debrief, but to anyone who'd seen you together, it was plain as the nose on your face. No, it wasn't him. It was the higher ups. Wanted your head on a silver platter for injuring their boy. We dealt with that handily, of course. Occupational hazard and what not. Agent Avci's testimony was also instrumental in establishing your motives and state of mind at the time. But the question remains: Why did you run? Hadn't you gotten everything you'd wanted, including your precious truth?"

The truth had been ashes in her mouth. Her father had sabotaged her birth mother, sundering their family apart and ruining her mother's nascent career as a spy. Her mother had in turn sabotaged him and her stepmother. All of them caught up in a tidy circle of spying that had ended with a fiery car crash, two orphaned little girls, and all their lives ruined.

"Was Judy right? Did Norwood cause the crash that killed my parents?"

"To be accurate, eyewitness accounts indicate your parents were killed by the fire, not the crash. The fire was actively encouraged by the woman you know as Judy—your birth mother. I would think the fact that she arrived upon the scene bearing extra tanks of petrol in the trunk of her own vehicle the best indicator of blame, considering the circumstances."

"You don't know for sure."

"True. We will never know if the couple then raising you—the Huttons—would have survived their injuries. Your Judy made sure of that. Did our agents stop your parents before they could head out on the foolhardy assassination mission set for them by Judy? Of course. It was our duty. It would have been an international incident of monumental proportions had they been allowed to continue on. We had no way of knowing there were children in the car. No way at all."

"How can I believe you?"

Albourn shrugged. "You either do, or you don't. It isn't up to me. You have a choice. You always have a choice. Just as you made the choice to come in from the cold. Why now?"

"I wanted to see Brian, and I didn't want to put him at risk by doing so."

"Noble of you. But I'm sure that's not the only reason."

Bree blew out a breath. "You're right. I've had a lot of time to think, and I'm ready now."

"For what?"

"I want Norwood to place me in China."

The dean rolled her eyes. "When you put it that way, it seems like you *want* to end up in the basement of MI5. Of course, you cannot go to China. That is out of the question."

"I need to."

"So you can disrupt things the way your mother did?"

"I can hardly think of her as my mother."

"Yet she was. And you have proven to be her daughter in many respects. Why should we let you go to China and risk that you were more in league with her than we thought?"

"She was set up, you know."

"When? At the time of her dismissal from Norwood? No. She harbored that fantasy, but when you wandered away from that grocery store, she managed to lose you all on her own. Horrible nanny, that one. Didn't take to children, couldn't mind them properly. Should have never been let into the field. That's where you are different—you take after your stepmother, Meg, in that respect. She could charm the birds out of the sky. Did Hutton take advantage of his wife, Agent Jude, in court? Yes. Did he abuse the resources of MI6 to do so? I wouldn't doubt it, though he had plenty of family money to do that all on his own if he wanted to corrupt a judge or bribe a newsman. Did we find ourselves with the perfect excuse to sever her? Yes, and so we did. If we'd had the neuro-blocker available to us then, we'd have used it and all of this might have been avoided." She spread her fingers wide, almost apologetic. "But it hadn't been developed yet. So she harbored a grudge and never forgot. Her obsession with China was, perhaps, a way to make up for her losses and keep herself distracted. You should not follow down that path. It's a path to self-destruction."

Disappointment seared through Bree. Albourn's eyes were on her, narrowing, as she assessed Bree's reaction.

"We cannot afford the risk that you might choose to go rogue in China right now. We are currently following the arms diverted from Turkey to the rebels and need to learn more. There's a chance that when we do, there's a role you can play. Meanwhile, we have a new assignment for you. If you're willing to take it."

"If I'm not?"

"You will effectively be resigning if you decline it," Albourn said quietly, letting the implication—the administration of the neuro-blockers that would risk Bree's cognitive destruction—remain unspoken.

"What is it?" Bree asked grudgingly.

"We are in possession of some rather odd intel from a plant inside the US government—in the Congressional Budget Office, of all places. Apparently, there's a hot start-up, privately held and shrouded in mystery, that has turned into everyone's darling. It purports to be a floating paradise for retirees. The business model seems sound enough on the surface, but the maths don't quite make sense when one digs into it—hundreds of billions of capital upfront to build massive cruise ships that will serve as floating cities for the elderly. They advertise themselves as cheaper than a typical retirement, in some cases under one hundred dollars per day, all meals and healthcare included. Just sign away your savings and divert the payments you would have received from the government—what the Americans refer to as Social Security and Medicare—and away you go. It supposedly saves the government a lot of money. A win-win, as they say."

"What's the problem?" Bree found the idea of cruising boring and was struggling to see where a nanny could figure into all of it.

"Like I said, the amount of money it would take to build out the cruise line, given the numbers the executive team are throwing about, is staggering. Nobody can figure out the source of funds, which of course makes us nervous. Especially when our source told us that the company inked a secret deal with Sinoam Industries."

"What's that?"

"That, Parrish, is the largest ship maker in all of China. This would be its first venture into cruise lines after decades focused on freight. On the surface, it makes sense—cruising is underpenetrated in China, so this could be what they call a 'synergistic investment.'"

"You don't buy it?"

"Sinoam happens to be held in the same conglomerate as one of the biggest surveillance tech and AI companies in the world, Kan-shan Jishu. The same one responsible for the technology used in the camps holding the Uyghur dissidents in Xinxiang."

Bree held her breath.

"How did our source learn of the deal?"

Albourn smiled slightly, and Bree kicked herself—she'd used "our." Albourn knew she'd reeled her in.

"The CBO apparently has some backdoor access to the books, due to the flow of Medicare and Social Security funds. Normally, they wouldn't see the capitalization tables—the records documenting investors—nor supply deals, but somehow he stumbled into this. He's afraid of what it may mean, and given the Americans seem so vested in it, he is uncertain he will receive a fair hearing if he raises it internally.

"It may prove to be nothing, but our source is concerned. His parents want to sign up for the cruise line themselves, so he has a personal interest, of course. We thought the China connection might be of interest to you?"

Bree nodded.

"And the fact that you're an American makes it easy. Very well. Luckily, one of the members of the cruise line's executive team—the CIO—is in the market for a nanny. It is fortuitous for us, as he'll be most likely to have the direct connections with Sinoam, and maybe Kan-shan."

"How'd we get so lucky?" Bree asked.

Albourn smiled again. "It seems his nanny suffered an unfortunate accident and found herself unable to fulfill her duties. Her misfortune is our chance," she asserted, moving on briskly before Bree could pull this particular thread to what she was sure would be another dismaying conclusion. "This won't be like the Askers," Albourn warned, mentioning the family in which Bree had been placed for her last operation. "They won't know your true purpose. To them, you will simply be an exceptionally well-trained nanny. You'll have to be on your guard at all times."

"What is the goal?"

"To find out whether this company is legitimate. And if not, what it is up to."

"When do I start?" Bree asked.

"We'll brief you further in due time. Before you'll be allowed anywhere, you will have to pass some basic fitness and weapons tests. And there is the matter of your psychological screening."

Bree crossed her arms, balking.

"You used your weapon on two different people, Parrish—injuring a colleague and killing a rogue operative who happened to be a blood relative. I suspect you will have a lot to talk about. You won't be going anywhere until the psychologist has cleared you. This is normal Norwood protocol, as you are well aware. We will brook no exceptions."

"What about—"

"There are no exceptions to this policy, Parrish. And there is no time like the present." Albourn stood abruptly and looked directly at the camera. "Let her wash and change. Then take her to Pressle."

⌒

"I've been expecting you, Miss Parrish."

The deceptively gentle voice of Dr. Pressle, the Agency-appointed psychologist, called out from her office. Bree squared her shoulders and walked through the door.

Pressle was seated in a rocking chair next to her bookshelf. The office seemed different to Bree. Of course, it had been two years since she'd last been cleared by Pressle to return to duty, so it shouldn't have surprised her. But what had been merely cozy before felt constricting and oppressive now. Bree felt herself too big for the room and too small, both all at once.

"Sit down."

Bree folded herself into the sofa and waited, wary.

"I was right," Pressle mused, fiddling with the nested *matryoshka* dolls she'd set in the center of the coffee table.

"About what?" Bree muttered through clenched teeth.

Pressle pulled apart the dolls, lining them up meticulously across the table. Bree's brain seized upon the memory of how Pressle had labeled them the last time she'd been here.

Grief.

Shame.

Longing.

Hurt.

Anger.

All the feelings psychologists claimed could consume a little child who'd felt abandoned by their mother, regardless of how the loss had occurred. The feelings were ones that could consume and direct one's destiny—if the psychologists were to be believed—because the original wound, unhealing, would fester and torment, no matter how one tried to move on.

Back then, Pressle hadn't told her how you were supposed to feel if it was at your own hand that your mother had perished—how you were supposed to feel if your loss was just another wound you'd accumulated and slunk off like a dog to lick, alone.

"Bree?"

Bree startled, realizing that Pressle had said something and was waiting for her to respond.

"I'm sorry, what?"

"I said, I was right. Last time I saw you. You didn't have a problem using your gun. Quite the opposite, it would seem."

Bree's face burned red.

"But I'm not sure I was right to clear you, regardless. That was a long time ago, to be sure, but it feels relevant to pick up where we left off. Are you ready to talk about your mother now?"

Bree grimaced.

Pressle barely paused, skewering Bree with a sharp look over her horn rimmed glasses. "Or would you prefer to begin with the incident with your roommate? What was his name again?" She riffled through a file. "Ah, yes. Agent Heyward. The roommate whom you kneecapped." She shrugged. "Your choice."

Bree felt a single tear trickle down her cheek.

"It's time for you to stop feeling sorry for yourself, my dear. As I said, it is your choice."

"I've never had any choices," Bree whispered.

"You always have a choice. If not to the circumstances in which you find yourself, then in how you react to them. Victimhood is not becoming in a nanny nor a spy, Miss Parrish. Now, shall we begin?"

Bree slowly counted to ten and then reviewed the motivations of an asset—the motivations that had been drilled into her in classes, so many years ago. Money. Ideology. Coercion. Ego. None of them seemed to quite capture her reason for being in this room at this moment. But she did have a reason, she reminded herself.

"Are you ready, Miss Parrish?" Pressle prompted.

"Let's do it," Bree assented, settling into the sofa and willing her pulse to slow. It was shaping up to be a long night.

ACKNOWLEDGMENTS

There are too many people to thank, but I will do my best and beg forgiveness of anyone I have inadvertently overlooked.

Thank you to my beta readers: specifically, Dr. Shami Feinglass—you have now done five books with me, and I love how you will randomly text me with outfits and other inspirations for the characters! My sons, Thomas McGurk and John McGurk—that you invested so much of your time in a book that centers around women was especially meaningful to me. You are great young men, and I am lucky to be your mom. Thank you also to Kelly Rafferty, for her close reading and advice on Irish localisms, terminology, and history. Any errors which remain are wholly my own. All of you—your feedback was exceptionally helpful in honing multiple versions of the manuscript which ultimately became *The Handler*.

Thank you to my fine team from Greenleaf: Adrianna, Ava, Chelsea, Karen, Lindsey, and Mimi—it was as much a pleasure this time around as ever! I appreciate your equal ownership of the story and its characters and your championing of the details that matter. Ava, in particular, I couldn't have done it without you. A big shout out to my publicist Kellie Rendina,

Olivia McCoy, and Andrea Kiliany Thatcher, and the team at Smith Publicity—your advocacy of *The Handler* and my work as well as your creativity in making a place for it in the world makes me smile. Special thanks to Ashley Hunter, social media guru extraordinaire, for making my life and my connection with readers so much easier and loads better.

To all the readers who took the time to read and review *The Agency*—thank you! Your desire to have closure for the Asker children and the nannies provided the tailwinds I needed to complete this sequel.

I benefited from the excellent nonfiction work of several writers and reporters covering the history of spycraft and the Troubles. I would be remiss to not particularly mention and thank Patrick Radden Keefe, who oddly enough penned both *Say Nothing: A True Story of Murder and Memory in Northern Ireland* and *Chatter: Dispatches from the Secret World of Global Eavesdropping*, two highly relevant works from which I learned a lot. I would similarly acknowledge Martin Ingram's *Stakeknife: Britain's Secret Agents in Ireland* and Richard English's *Armed Struggle: The History of the IRA*. None of these books are without their own controversy, but each provided me with a better understanding of the many sides to international conflicts, the actions governments take in their attempts to resolve them, and the particular role of espionage and intelligence-gathering in so doing. The history of the Troubles is extremely complex; the version portrayed here is one attempt to unpack those nuances and contradictions in service of what is, ultimately, a story of motherhood. If the idea that the conflict had victims and tragedies on both sides resonates with you when you are finished reading, then this story has done its job.

To the authors whose works of espionage provide inspiration—you have my undying respect and gratitude. So do all the nannies who have gifted me their wonderfully poignant and hilarious stories. You are seen, and I appreciate you so much. In that vein, a shout out to Jake, Kim, Kira,

Lana, Natalie, Kara, Kelli, and Petra—the nannies who have graced our family with their care and friendship over the years.

I appreciate the many family members, colleagues, and friends whose inquiries and support have kept me going through the multiple iterations of this book. Special thanks to Becky, Beth, Dana, Donna, Gale, Jake, Kathy, Kim, my parents—Lorraine and Ray—Nadine, my daughter Reagan, and some really lovely Tri Delts and Phi Taus who keep going to bat for me and my work.

Finally, to Tom—as always, LOML—thank you.

QUESTIONS FOR DISCUSSION

1. Besides *The Handler*, what other books or movies can you think of in which mistaken or deliberately misleading identities are so central to the plot? How about in any real-life stories you may have seen covered in the news media? What do you think would be most difficult about assuming a false identity if you were put in that position?

2. The world of genetics is changing quite rapidly, and several elements of the story center around genetic identification and ideas of inherited traits and tendencies. How did you react to learning that Brian's criminal genetic records had been illegally retained by the government? Do you find the idea of discovering unknown relations—possibly even unearthing family secrets—thrilling or daunting? Why?

3. Similarly, do you believe personality traits, interests, and even trauma responses can be inherited genetically? If so, how could that have played a part in shaping Bree into the woman she has become? Do you see Bree's behavior as a repetition of her parents' stories or a divergence from their paths? Why? What role was played by destiny vs. circumstance?

4. The group of four roommates we came to know in *The Agency* has been whittled down to three. How has the dynamic between the roommates changed as a result? Did you find Ruby's reactions to Susmita's death—her lingering suspicion—reasonable? What about Dash's seeming ability to move on?

5. The population of male characters in this novel expands somewhat—Dash's father; Rodney's friend, John; Bree's uncle, Brian; and Bree's father, David. We also see more minor male characters coming into play, such as the IRA members and the mysterious Chinese spy Bree's parents encounter. Did the greater presence of these men change your experience of the Norwood world? How and why?

6. A hallmark of this series is the author's amusing and sometimes preposterous classroom scenes. Why do you think she chooses to inject humor in this way? In what ways does it affect your reading of the book?

7. The historical references which began in *The Agency* come more to the forefront in *The Handler*, with conflicts over Chinese sovereignty and the Troubles as critical factors propelling the plot during flashbacks. How did you find these references to political conflicts? Do you think the author has a point of view about which side in these conflicts was "right"? Is the concept of government intervention—illicit or otherwise—to protect national interests and human rights one that resonates with you? Could you imagine yourself being idealistic—or cynically mercenary—enough to volunteer for such a mission? What did you think of Judy, David, and Meg's motivations?

8. How sympathetic did you find the character of Brian? How did the suggestion that he may have engaged in violent activities during the Troubles impact your reaction to him?

9. The question of identity continues to run strong through this story. The author confronts us with examples of the ways people

grapple with their own self-perception, the way they present themselves to the world, and how the world, on its own, may see them or classify them based on stereotypes. What are some of the ways this came to the forefront for you? Why do you think the author finds this so important?

10. When Bree is being cleared for action by the school psychologist, the psychologist hits a sore spot as she explains the trauma of growing up motherless. How would growing up motherless (or parentless) have impacted you? How did Bree's reaction to this and other losses at various points in the story resonate with you?

11. What elements of Bree's interest in her family's history stood out to you? What do you think motivated her search?

12. Themes of trust run deep in *The Handler.* Whom did you distrust as you read? Whom did you want to trust, even against your better judgment? Were you surprised by any of the "reveals"? Was Bree naïve in whom she placed her trust, or were there factors that made her choices understandable?

13. Motherhood proves central to this story. How are traditional views of motherhood upheld or undermined by the author's depiction of Fiona, Meg, and Judy? How did it impact your reading of the book? How did you react to David's views of his wife's work outside the home? How do views like this impact women today?

14. What did you make of marriages featured in this story? What was similar about the marriages of Meg's parents, Roberta and David, that of Meg and David, and those made by Dash's father? What was different? What do you think of Norwood's prohibition against marriage and children after reading about these marriages?

15. Did you find Meg's flirtation and seduction of David—using her femininity and gender stereotypes in ways Norwood had taught

her—to be empowering or not? Do you think she really loved David at any point? Why or why not?

16. What elements of David's character and behavior did you find most problematic? Most endearing? Did he bear any similarity to the way Meg remembered her dead father and if so, in what sense?

17. Ruby is often derided for her ambition and "bossiness." What did you think of her character's development in *The Handler*? Is she a victim of gender stereotyping or does she deserve the derision? What does it mean that even in an environment dominated by women, this criticism is made of her?

18. What was your reaction to Bree and Dash's "not quite" romance? Did your view change by the end of the book? Does Dash deserve what he gets?

19. Who do you think really was responsible for Meg and David's deaths? Do you think Judy intended for it to happen all along, or not? What makes you think so?

20. At the end of the book, how sympathetic did you find Judy? Why?

21. At the end of the book, Bree struggles with the choices she has made. How disturbing did you find her behavior in the final chapters of the book, if at all? What questions did her actions raise about her emotional state? Is she justified in worrying about or questioning her actions? Is Bree right to be angry with Dash? With Norwood? To be conflicted in her feelings toward Judy? Do you think she was wise to go underground? Why or why not?

22. As you look ahead to the next book in the series, what do you envision unfolding? Are there any open issues you feel require resolution, or are you ready to move on to Bree's next adventure?

AUTHOR Q & A

Q: **Readers may be curious to learn a little about your educational background and personal interest in world events, as the novel is packed with interesting political and historical material—which may be unexpected for some readers, given the title of the book. Can you tell us anything about your background there and how you go about researching and fact-finding?**

I was a government major as an undergrad, with a significant focus in international affairs, and have retained a personal interest in international relations ever since. I also love to travel and am especially drawn to the history of any place I am lucky enough to visit. I am very fact-based in my approach to most things. Writing is no exception! I tend to do a lot of research to make sure the details of a location, or of a timeline, make sense, even to those who may be personally familiar with the topic. As I began writing *The Norwood Nannies* series, my research has included time on the round in Bath (including scouting for the building on which to base Jaguar House!); deep dives into the politics of Turkey and China (both of which I have previously visited); reading up on the history of the British Raj; lots of listening to the music of Muscle Shoals; and, of course, delving into the wonderful story of Norland College, on which Norwood is loosely modeled. For *The Handler*, I went much deeper into the history of the Troubles, particularly the intelligence aspects of the conflict. As I research, I document things on Pinterest boards to serve as ongoing inspiration. Readers can always check them out for themselves to get a sneak peek!

Q: Were any characters based, even if very loosely, on real-life friends or colleagues, or are they entirely fictional? Similarly, did you draw from your own school experiences when writing the book?

I always warn my friends and acquaintances to be careful or I may put them in a book! In seriousness, they are largely fictional, with a few sparks of inspiration. Judy (before she turned into such an **ambiguous** character) was inspired by a fellow church member who was a supporter of a local orphanage and had, herself, been in M&A. I found her to be such a trailblazer and wanted to capture that in a character. Susie/Susmita (the roommate who figured prominently in *The Agency*) was initially crafted upon a colleague who was particularly adept at using faux naivete to get her way, but then evolved into more of an amalgam. Susmita's act of claiming her real name and deeper identity was inspired by two friends—one actually named Susmita!—who went through an experience of embracing their ethnic origins after having "Americanized" themselves for convenience and assimilation. I thought their reclaiming of their true name was inspiring and wanted to bring that to readers. In today's environment, that level of authenticity and self-awareness is so important to celebrate.

Q: What inspired you to write the series, more generally? And were there any personal nanny stories that contributed to that inspiration?

Honestly, I was driving in a car with my children, brainstorming ideas, and the concept of the real Norland College being a spy school popped up. I was immediately taken with it. As for personal nanny stories . . . let's just say that some of Rennie's toddler pranks may have been drawn from my own, and my daughter's, childhood.

Q: Can you share any of your own feelings on why you chose the setting you did, as well as the political climate you chose to anchor the book in?

Since the original idea was inspired by a real college in Bath, it just made sense to keep the location in England. It also gave me a great way to show the innocence of the main character and how she grows in a strange environment. As for the global instability—I felt it was critical to link the spying to something "bigger than" the characters themselves. I wasn't interested in corporate espionage, which would seem self-serving. I wanted to find a way to explain why these characters could ultimately become vested in what they were learning and doing—even if it involved a fair amount of coercion. The world climate is very volatile right now, which made it very easy to identify places where human and civil rights are at risk; places where spying might feel justified as serving the greater good.

Q: Was the theme of global instability and Bree's own instability an intentional pairing?

The parallels to Bree's own situation were almost coincidental. What was a bit more intentional was the exploration of the personal and geopolitical threat of imperialism, colonialism, and its aftermath. Three of the original roommates—Bree, Ruby, and Susmita—all have cultural or even personal histories imprinted by British colonialism in some way. Their identities and ways of interacting with the world are very much influenced by these factors. In parallel, in the background, is the political environment of instability created by these types of movements and histories. There are a few references to the unraveling of the British Empire and its after-math, including the possibility of Chinese encroachment in parts of the Pacific from which the British withdrew. A large part of *The Agency* was set against the backdrop of Turkey, which has moved between various empires for centuries and was occupied in some parts following WWI by the Allies, prompting the emergence of its own nationalist movement and eventual independence. And of course *The Handler*'s flashbacks are set squarely in the contest over Northern Ireland. This sort of historical reckoning moved to the forefront in *The Handler* and will be a vein in the rest of the series.

Q: The construction of the narrative—which has a relatively complex plot in both books one and two—must involve some sort of careful planning or writer's organization. Can you tell the reader anything about the process of weaving the story, and advise any aspiring authors?

This is my fifth original novel—the Norwood series and the Archangel Prophecy series following two novel-length works of fan fiction. I tend to write out the broad outline of the entire plot and then go deeper into each book, in turn. I spend a lot of time researching to get a grasp on the details, a lot of time thinking through back story and characters, and then I jump in. I write sequentially, and once I get going, I write pretty fast. I know others do not. My only advice to aspiring authors is to get something down on the page. You can always edit! Good editing was key to *The Handler*. It was an exercise in taking away, whittling down to the essentials after learning so much about the Troubles and the other aspects of political history and current events that serve as backdrop.

Q: The reader discovers truths gradually as the narrative progresses, and much of what we believe gets deconstructed along the way as

we discover the reality around Bree's past and her parents' past. One reveal negates another, thereby keeping the reader on their toes. What challenges presented themselves to you as you crafted a plot structure containing multiple levels of reveals?

It could get quite difficult keeping track of the reveals without a good outline! I also allow myself to change things up when a better idea strikes me. When this happens, inevitably I have to go back and undo some bit of plot or characterization—or embellish it—to make sense of it. I have literally woken up in the middle of the night with the sudden realization, "Oh no! That plot point is impossible!" I keep a notebook bedside for those eventualities.

Q: One of the truths we discover is that Judy is not the generous orphanage benefactor and role model Bree has held her to be. Judy plays a major role in the book, and there is a great deal of ambiguity surrounding whether she is a "good guy" or a "bad guy." Can you describe why you chose to paint her character the way you did, or speak about the significance of her character more generally?

I personally found her to be a fascinating character. I began working professionally in business during an era when it was unusual to see women in very senior roles, so I loved having this character—supposedly with a really globe-trotting, successful track record in M&A—in the mix. There is a lot of good in Judy; you can't deny it. She has single handedly kept that orphanage open. She has nurtured—even pushed—Bree to realize her potential. In *The Agency*, she seems to genuinely want to figure out what happened to Bree's parents. Is Judy Bree's guide? Or is she using Bree? I love that we—and Bree—can't tell. I love that Bree wants to believe her—because if she can't, what does she have left? And then, in *The Handler*, your understanding of her shifts as you realize the depth and complexity of her motivations and the implications of her actions. From a writer's perspective, it's a wonderful dilemma, and it gives me a lot of options for how to further develop the characters, as well as the plot.

Q: When did you first realize you wanted to write a novel, and what motivated you to pursue this path?

I like to say that I had a midlife crisis at which point I realized that while I was "all in" in this high-power career, and "all in" as a mom and wife, I had squeezed out all the little pleasures that were just for me. I had lost my creative outlets. That is simply not sustainable. It was then that I picked up writing again, after a long break. Fan fiction eased me into it, and after some success there, my husband encouraged me to write something original. So here I am.

Q: Did any books or authors in particular inspire you within the genre of suspense and mystery?

As for inspirations from the genre of suspense and mystery, there are so many. I am such a voracious reader that it would be hard to name one. Last year I focused my pleasure reading on classics that for some reason I had not ever gotten to read. There were a fair number of psychological thrillers and mysteries on that list, among them *Rebecca* by Daphne du Maurier and *The Woman in White* by Wilkie Collins. I loved them both and was particularly gratified to read the Collins, as it had been the subject of my college roommate's thesis! I couldn't believe I'd never read it. I also read a fair number of novels in the classic spy genre. This year my reading has been a bit more diverse; most recently I finished *The School for Good Mothers* by Jessamine Chan, which devastated me with its dystopian depictions of the sacrifices and double standards facing mothers who are unfortunate to make a mistake. I keep my reading lists up to date on Goodreads if anybody is interested in learning more.

Q: Was there a favorite chapter for you? Was there one that was especially difficult to write?

I always enjoy the funny and somewhat preposterous bits, like the criticisms the professor levels at the students for their failed bomb exam! And I am a sucker for a good action scene. They are so much fun to write! That said, in this book I really loved the chapter in which Bree finally clears her psychological assessment. I appreciated its depth; the way it uncovered the many dimensions of Bree's emotional state and the way it taps into the deep reservoir of need and hurt that many may feel with respect to their own histories with a parent.

My absolute favorite may have been the chapter where Dash takes Bree home to meet the duke. The nervousness Dash showed leading up to it—the sweetness of their budding relationship, even under pretense of "the mission"—was touching. It gave me a pang thinking about all Dash has been through, seeing the fraught nature of his relationship with his father—such a motivating force for him—played out before our eyes. And of course, that is the moment when Bree pulls the thread and truly starts unraveling the truth; it's when we really start to understand how the story all fits together.

Q: Who supported you most in your Norwood Nannies journey, and how important do you feel that support was? Or was writing a solitary and individual act for you? Do you have advice for writers on how much (or how little) to rely on support (whether from family or beta readers) during the process?

I could do nothing without the support of my family—from giving me space and time, to brainstorming ideas with me, they are critical.

I also have my small circle of beta readers. I have been blessed with friends who are fellow writers and family members who are quite critical readers, and they will not spare my feelings—they tell me what they really think. I truly value that. It can be hard to let go of something you have worked so hard over, so it is a gift to have people you really trust take the time to read and reflect and discuss their reaction with you. I am truly grateful.

Q: How essential are these beta readers to the process? Can you provide an example of an instance where a beta reader was especially useful?
I would be remiss if I didn't acknowledge my wonderful "beta readers"—the guinea pigs upon whom I inflict early drafts, especially those who can offer a perspective on a location or culture that I am trying to capture. My lovely colleague, Kelly Rafferty, for example, read the entirety of *The Handler* to advise me on the Irish colloquialisms and terms I had messed up (of which there were many!). She also spot-checked my timelines and grasp of history to ensure nothing was off—she even checked dates to ensure the marriage certificate of Bree's parents was legit! This is one of the most wonderful aspects of writing—with the need to research, I have been handed an excuse to travel and spend time with many interesting people. I am awed by their generosity of time and spirit.

Q: Themes of world-crisis, global suffering, and injustice lend poignancy to the novel. Is there a humanitarian message you would like to relay to the reader?
If there is a message, it is to be aware. Pay attention. Get outside yourself. Ask questions and learn. There are bigger issues in the world out there. And they are never as black and white as you may think.

ABOUT THE AUTHOR

Award-winning author Monica McGurk likes nothing better than weaving complex, multilayered stories that bring contemporary issues and strong female characters to life through different genres of popular fiction. Her previous work includes three volumes of paranormal YA romance—*The Archangel Prophecies: Dark Hope, Dark Rising,* and *Dark Before Dawn*—along with numerous works of fan fiction under the name Consultant by Day. *The Handler* is the follow-up to her critically acclaimed *The Agency,* the first novel in *The Norwood Nanny Chronicles.*

A corporate executive, she now lives in Chicagoland with her husband, Tom, their youngest son, and their dog, Ellie. You can find her on Facebook, Instagram, Goodreads, and LinkedIn, or on her website: monicamcgurk.com.